BY MAGIC BEGUILED

BY MAGIC

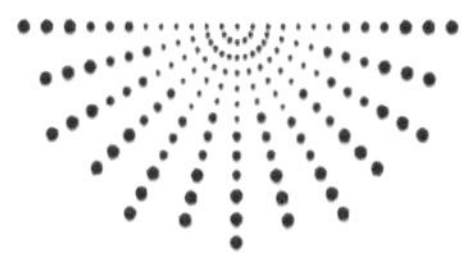

MAGGIE SHAYNE

OHB

PART I
ONCE UPON A TIME

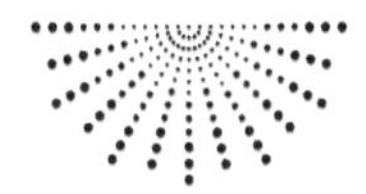

CHAPTER 1

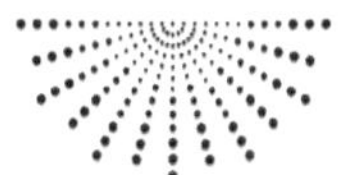

Adam
Long ago, but not too far away...

Seven-year-old Adam Reid raced through the forest, zigging and zagging like a mad bumblebee, his arms spread out at his sides. The summer breeze turned into a wind that whooshed past his ears and tangled his hair. He pretended he was flying. He liked pretending. Even though his father was always telling him how bad it was, how foolish. He got the strap for it sometimes, when his tall tales got a little too tall.

But only if his father had been drinking.

He buzzed around the base of a giant maple tree three times, then came to a halt when his keen eyes picked out a barely visible path beneath its broad, leafy limbs. No longer interested in playing bumblebee, Adam lowered his arms. He hunkered down and squinted at the almost invisible trail in the mossy ground. No matter how many times he came out here, he never failed to find a new adventure to pursue.

Adam loved the woods. He wasn't supposed to be there. The forest was not on his father's property, but on the state land that bordered it. And he'd been warned repeatedly to stay away. But that hadn't stopped Adam,

Now he began following that trail, wondering what it might be. Deer trail, he decided, his seven years of wisdom assuring him it was so. Maybe he'd see a big whitetail if he went really slow and quiet.

The path meandered for a ways, wriggling this way and that in S-patterns and loops and figure eights. Then it vanished into a patch of mean-looking blackberry briars with deceptively pretty white blossoms that smelled so good he wished he could taste them. But when he squatted on his haunches, he saw that the thorny, flowering briars sort of arched over the trail. If he bent really low, he could still follow it. So he did.

Bending almost double, even crawling on all fours here and there, he continued to follow the path. It was like a tunnel. The ground beneath him slanted upward, taking him over a small hill and partway down the other side before the brambles finally thinned out. He emerged on a grassy slope that seemed to be one side of a big old hump in the ground. And about halfway down that grassy hump, he saw a dark hole, sinking back into the mound. It looked like... Adam ran closer and stopped, bracing his hands on his knees and breathing fast from excitement. It was! A cave! He'd discovered a cave. Maybe pirates had holed up here. Or a dinosaur! Or cave men, a zillion years ago. Neat!

Without hesitation, Adam crawled inside. The opening wasn't big enough to go in standing up. It was kind of dark, and a lot cooler than it was outside. But Adam wasn't afraid. Not much, anyway. He had his penlight, which he was never without. Just like his jackknife. He flicked the light on and ventured deeper. The farther he went, the wider the walls opened out, and the ceiling got higher, too. He came, at last, to what looked like the very back of the cave. A room about the size of his tree house, and big enough that he could stand up. This was the best discovery he'd ever made.

He played in there for hours. He explored, and carved his name on the stone wall, and yelled really loud to hear his voice echo, until he got tired. And then he decided to take a short nap before heading home. It was a long walk, after all.

So he sat on the ground and leaned back against the cool wall, and closed his eyes.

When he opened them again, Adam wasn't sure if he'd been asleep or not, or if he had, how much time had passed. Not wanting to be late for dinner and risk another walloping, he hurried to the cave's entrance. He had to crouch low again, of course, but he made good time. Scuttling closer to the bright yellow sunlight, he could see up ahead. He stepped out, stood up straighter, and brushed the dirt from the knees of his jeans. Then he looked up, blinking first at the brightness of the sunlight, and then in shock.

This was not the same place he'd been before. This was...this was *different*.

Everywhere he looked, there were flowers like he'd never seen before, blossoming in every color he could imagine and a few he never had. And they filled the air with their smells. Wonderful smells! There were pebbles and stones on the grassy ground. But they were no regular stones. Every rock he saw glittered. Like...jewels or something! Adam turned to look back at the cave entrance, wondering if there had been another tunnel in there, one he hadn't noticed. He sure as heck hadn't come out the same way he'd gone in.

Okay, then. He'd take a look around, really quick, and then he'd go back inside and find the right way out. If he dawdled out here much longer, he'd be in hot water with his father for sure. But gosh, this place was too much to resist. Like something out of *The Wizard of Oz*!

He ventured farther and took a closer look at the trees. Squinting, moving closer, he looked again. Heck, there were pictures in the bark! A moon. Some stars. A sun. A fairy.

What the heck?

Adam wandered among the trees, curious, amazed. This was no normal forest. This was...this was...

"This is Rush, young man. And you are most certainly *not* supposed to be here."

The voice was like music. Like bells. Adam whirled to see a woman...a beautiful red-haired woman whose belly was swelled like she'd swallowed a basketball. He guessed she must be expecting a baby. She wore the kind of glittery, gauzy dress you'd expect to see in a fairy tale, and her eyes were just about the bluest he'd ever seen in his life.

Something moved behind her and Adam narrowed his eyes. Then he thought he was going to drop dead in his tracks. He blinked, rubbed his eyes and looked again. *She had wings!* Fragile-looking, like a dragonfly's wings. You could see right through them, but they were there.

"Who *are* you?" he managed to ask her.

"Maire," she said, smiling. It sounded like "May-ruh. But he didn't have time to ponder it long. She was leaning closer, squinting at him. "Few mortals can see the doorway to this place," she told him. "It's enchanted, you know."

Adam looked around, nodding. "Yeah, I was starting to figure that."

"Maybe you *are* supposed to be here." She tapped her chin with one dainty finger. "After all, there's no such thing as coincidence. So, there must be a reason for your coming here, mustn't there?"

"Uh—I don't think so. I ought to be getting home." He took a step backward.

She sighed. "Yes, that's probably for the best."

Adam agreed. He didn't want any part of any enchanted

forest or any fairy godmothers or whatever the heck she was. Sheesh, he'd read about fairies. They could be dangerous. He turned, feeling lucky he was going to get out of here unscathed, but then he got a chill right up his spine. Because he didn't see the cave. He'd wandered too far.

"Oh, don't worry. I'll show you the way." The lady took his hand in hers, and then she stood very still, and stared down at him, her eyes sparkling, her eyebrows lifting in surprise. *"Now* I know why you're here!" She smiled, looking at him like she was seeing something awfully sweet. One of her hands rested lovingly on her swollen belly, and she ran her other hand through his hair. If she pinched his cheeks, he was outta there, he decided. Then her smile faded, and she even looked a little sad. "You must be a very strong little boy. And a brave one, too."

"Well, sure I am," he confirmed, wondering how she could tell.

"Tell me, young Adam. Would you like to see your fate before you go?"

"My...fate?"

"Your future. I can show you, if you want."

Adam swallowed hard. His heart was racing, his hands were sweaty, and he really wanted out of here. Now. But he'd be awfully dumb to pass up a chance to see his future, wouldn't he? He'd particularly like to know if he'd missed dinner, and whether he was going to get beat when he got home tonight because of it. Trying for a nonchalant shrug, he said, "Okay."

The lady smiled again. She drew him off through the trees a little ways. Then she stopped and pushed aside a tangle of branches and vines all covered in purple flowers. "Look through here," she told him.

Adam looked.

There was a lake there, with water as blue as the winged lady's eyes. This side of it was dense with dark green reeds that led right up to the woods, but the rest of it stretched out to meet the orange-yellow sky. Splashing and laughter came from just beyond the reeds. And when he squinted harder and looked, he saw a girl.

Bunches of long, black curls trailed over her back and shoulders. She and a yellow-haired girl were playing in neck-deep water near the shore. But it was the dark-haired girl he couldn't stop looking at. He didn't usually care about girls, but he liked her automatically and wondered why. He couldn't see all of her through the dark sapphire water, which was a good thing because he didn't think she was dressed. Looked like the girls were skinny dipping to him.

All of a sudden she stopped laughing and turned her head in his direction. Her eyes were darker blue than the water and sparkled like the crystal stones around his feet. They looked right into his eyes, between the gaps in the reeds. And Adam felt a shiver work its way right to his toes. He couldn't look away for the life of him.

Then Maire let the branches snap back into place, cutting off his view.

"Who is she," he asked.

"You mean, who *will* she be," the woman corrected him. He frowned hard at her. "She *will be* your future, Adam. Your fate. She'll come into your life when you least expect it, because she needs you to show her the way."

"What way?" He was more confused now than he'd been when he'd spotted her fairy wings.

"The way to her sister, and then the way back home."

"Oh," he said, as if he fully understood, though he didn't.

"Whatever you do, Adam, you mustn't fall in love with her. She'll break your heart if you do. She has to leave you in the end. And if you go with her, your life will end within a few days. You must stay in your world, and return my daughter to hers. Don't forget."

"Don't worry. I won't." He turned and yanked the branches

aside again, but when he looked now there was only more forest. No lake. No girls.

"What the heck?" He turned back to Maire again, but she was gone as well, just like the vision. And right behind the place where she'd been standing was the cave he knew would lead him home. Though Adam was sure it hadn't been there before.

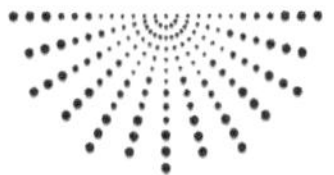

CHAPTER 2

Brigit
Long ago, and a little bit farther away...

"Read it again, Sister Mary Agnes."

Sister's gentle smile added creases to her lined face. One withered hand ruffled Brigit's curls. "All right, little one. But this is the last time."

Brigit snuggled more deeply into the small wooden bed. Her pillow was lumpy, and her blanket thin. She ran her hands lovingly over the intricate embroidery on the book's cloth cover, her fingers tracing the elegant scroll of the title, *Fairytale.* Her parents must have loved her very much, to have made such a wonderful book for her. Brigit knew that because Sister told her so often. She opened the book to the first vellum page, with its brilliantly colored, hand-painted illustration. The one showing the mystical forest, with the crystal water in the center, and way off in the distance, the castle spires. Brigit looked at the picture for a long time, before pushing the book into Sister's powdery soft hands.

"Once upon a time," Sister began, "not so very long ago, two princesses were born. No ordinary princesses, though. These babies were special. These babies were fay."

"And that means fairy, right Sister Mary Agnes?" Brigit didn't need to ask. She knew the fairy tale by heart. But her comments and questions had become a part of the ritual.

"Yes, Brigit. That means fairy." Sister Mary Agnes turned the page, and let Brigit take a good long look at the next picture. This one was of a beautiful red-headed fairy princess holding her twin daughters in her arms. One had raven's wing curls just like Brigit's, and the other had hair as yellow as spun gold.

"Their mother was Princess Maire, the only daughter of the Fay King Padraig. And their father was Jonathon, a mortal man who'd come through the invisible curtain to find her. 'Twas the hand of Fate that led him there, for the enchanted realm is invisible to most mortal eyes."

Despite the thinness of her blanket, Brigit felt warm when she thought about Maire and Jon, and the love they'd had between them. A love so strong it had crossed worlds to find fulfillment. Sister Mary Agnes said Brigit was too young to think about love the way she did. But Brigit didn't think so. She thought nine was plenty old enough to understand matters of the heart. Sister would think so too, if she knew about the dream that came to her over and over again—a lovely dream in which the fairy princess Maire appeared to her and whispered, "Would you like to see your fate, little one?" And Brigit always answered yes, and waited as Maire parted some mists with a wave of her dainty hand, and pointed.

When Brigit peered through she saw a man. A golden-haired man who looked very sad and confused, and she felt an instinctive urge to try to comfort him. He needed her, that man with the hurt in his sky blue eyes.

But she couldn't tell Sister about that dream. She'd never understand.

Sister had turned the page, and was reading again. "Their home was in the Realm of Rush, the land where magic is real, which lies right beside the mortal world, and yet remains invisible to it.

Now the princess's daughters were born at a time of peace. But alas, by the twins' first birthday there came a period of great turmoil in Rush. For even in the enchanted realm, evil exists."

A little shiver raced up Brigit's spine. The vellum made a whispery sound as a page was turned, and Sister's voice came again, as raspy and soft as the paper.

"The Prince of the Dark Side was never content to live in the part of the enchanted realm to which his family had been consigned. That part beyond the edges of Rush, where daylight never ventured. Always, those dark ones had coveted the rest of Rush, and all the hidden places and folks within it. Especially the Fay forest and kingdom. They raised up an army of trolls and goblins and all manner of dark beings, and together, they laid siege to the castle of the king."

Brigit didn't look at that picture. It was too scary. A mishmash of nightmarish creatures storming those pretty castles, wielding swords and maces and looking as fierce as death itself.

"Princess Maire was killed in the battle, her body burned with the castle. Poor Jon, who'd been out fighting with the White Knights and Heroes, who'd come to help, was beside himself with grief. Only wise King Padraig knew what must be done. He ordered Jon to take the wee princesses away from Rush. To part the invisible curtain once more, and to return with his daughters to the mortal world, where they would be safe from the Dark Prince's blade."

Brigit nodded. "And before Jonathon left..." she prompted.

Mary Agnes smiled and turned another page. "Before Jonathon left, King Paddy gave him two books, fashioned by

Princess Maire with her own hands. She'd been blessed with the second sight, Maire had. She'd been able to see the future. And she'd crafted the books for the time when her daughters would have to get by without her."

"And is this one of them, Sister?"

Sister made her eyes very big, as she always did when Brigit asked the question. "It might very well be, Brigit."

Brigit nodded. It was fun to think her mother might have been a fairy princess.

"The king told Jon to see to the children's safety. For one day, when they were grown, they would be called to return, the eldest to take her place on the throne of Rush. And the younger to assist her in regaining it. As firstborn—though only by a minute—the eldest had inherited the largest share of her mother's magic. And when the time came, she would regain some memories of the kingdom. The youngest, though, would likely remember none of it. The accepting of her fate might well be more difficult for her."

Mary Agnes flipped to the last page, the page depicting Princess Maire, with her cascades of red-orange curls and her glittering gown, and damselfly wings. Her love-filled, sea-green eyes seemed to stare at Brigit from the page.

"Trials and turmoil await you, little princesses. But when things seem hopeless, turn to the fairy tale to remind you of who you are. And remember, if you are true to your heart, happiness will greet you at the end of your journey."

As always, Sister Mary Agnes left the book open to that page and laid it in Brigit's lap.

Brigit traced Maire's beautiful face with her fingertips, blinking tiredly. "Do you think she really was my mother?"

Mary Agnes sighed. "I only know what I know, child. Father Anthony found you and another tiny girl sleeping at the altar one morning. And each of you had a book just like this one. Yours with the name Brigit inside, and the other with the name of Bridin. Tucked into a little pocket sewn within each cover, was a pendant for each of you."

Brigit fingered the necklace she never took off. A dainty pewter fairy, embracing a long, narrow crystal with points at both ends.

"The note Father Anthony found beside you said, 'My time on this earth is ending. Please, take care of my girls. Jonathon.'"

"And what happened to Bridin?" Brigit knew, but asked again anyway. Sister's tales seemed more real when Brigit made her tell them right to the end.

"Bridin was adopted right away, darling. But you'd taken ill, and were in no condition to go with her. One day, though, you'll find a fairy tale all your own. One day you'll have your happily-ever-after."

"Will I really, Sister Mary Agnes?"

For years Brigit had trusted utterly in the fairy tale. She'd had to, because she'd had nothing else. And she adored the woman who told it, knew Sister Mary Agnes would never deliberately lie. But Brigit wasn't a baby anymore. And the longer she remained here at St. Mary's, the harder it became to believe in fairies or enchanted kingdoms or...or especially happily-ever-afters. She closed her eyes as Sister's crinkled palm slipped repeatedly over her hair.

"You will, Brigit. I promise you will. No girl with a gift like yours will be alone for long."

Brigit frowned, her eyes popping open again. "I have a gift?"

Sister Mary Agnes lifted her head to stare at the picture, and Brigit followed her gaze, still unsure what was so special about it. The rectangle of construction paper hung a little crookedly above the painted white headboard of the bed. Brigit had discovered her knack with a paintbrush for the first time today, when Father Anthony had brought boxes of brushes and paints and paper for the orphans here. Sister Mary Agnes had seemed to think she'd witnessed her first miracle when she saw Brigit's painting. She'd caught Brigit balancing on a stack of pillows while trying to Scotch tape her picture to the wall, to cover a crack in the plaster.

"Yes, child. Make no mistake, you have a gift."

"Who from?"

The tears that came into Sister Mary Agnes's eyes made Brigit frown. Why did she get so choked up over a construction-paper lady? It was just a copy of a picture Brigit had found in an art book. Some lady with two first names. Mona Lucy or something like that.

"From God, Brigit."

Ah, well, there was no understanding grownups. Even Sister Mary Agnes, though the sister was better than most adults, in Brigit's estimation. She rolled over, sliding her storybook under her pillow as she did every night, and pulled the worn blanket up over her shoulder.

"You're a blessing, child. You've brought an honest to goodness miracle right here to Maybourne Row. In a shelter nearly falling down around our ears, beside a church with chipped paint and folding chairs instead of pews. A miracle, Brigit."

But Brigit was tired, and thought Sister Mary Agnes was overreacting a little. Or maybe she sensed that Brigit's belief in the fairy talewas getting shaky, and now she was trying to invent a new one, to give her something new to believe in. How could a picture be a miracle, anyway?

"Sleep, love. And tomorrow we'll show your painting to Father Anthony. He'll know what to do."

She crossed herself before leaving in a rustle of black fabric.

Only, for Sister Mary Agnes, tomorrow never came.

CHAPTER 3

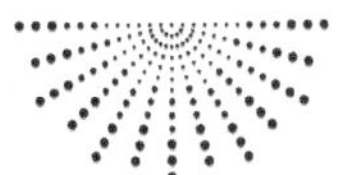

*I*n a mansion near Binghamton NY, a little girl stood back and looked at the painting she had just finished. It was perfect in every way, she thought. "It's time," she said softly.

Raze stood beside her, rubbing his white whiskers and nodding. "It's a stunner, that's for sure."

He used to sleep across the street from the orphanage, but when she'd been adopted as a baby, he'd come with her, just to keep an eye on her, he said. Her adopted family had died, and her Uncle Matthew had been too busy to care for a "troubled" little girl. That's why she was here, in this castle-like mansion now. Because they all thought she was crazy. Mr. Darque was in charge now, but he kept his distance and mostly paid others to take care of her. Her nurse, Kate, and Raze and the rest of the bodyguards. Darque said they were always around because she was such a wealthy little girl.

Bridin knew she wasn't crazy. She didn't need the medicine they made her take, and had become really good at hiding the pills under her tongue and fooling her nurse. The medicine made her groggy, made her forget who she was.

But she had her book to remind her—her fairy tale, which Raze had smuggled in when he'd been hired here as one of her watchers. He was the only one who believed in it like she did.

She knew things, too. Sometimes from dreams and sometimes in visions. She knew she had to paint this painting of the land of Rush as she imagined it to be. And she knew that Raze had to take it with him, and leave it at a gallery near Mystic Lake. She'd just told him so, and for the first time he looked at her with doubt in his faded denim eyes.

"I don't want to leave you, Bridey," he said. "I've been with you since you were a baby."

"My sister needs you more," she said. "I had a real scary dream about her, Raze. And you know how my dreams are."

He nodded slowly, not questioning her.

"You've got to go now, this morning. I'll be fine. I know who I am. And I have my pendant." As she said it, she touched the pewter fairy, hugging a quartz crystal point, on a chain around her neck. "But she doesn't. And you can't tell her either. When it's time, I'll find you both. But you have to go back Raze. You have to leave the painting where I told you, and then you have to get to St. Mary's and save Brigit. Save my sister. If you don't, she's going to die tonight. And then our story will be over."

CHAPTER 4

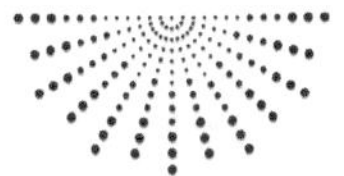

*B*rigit woke up coughing. It was very hot, and there was a dancing light coming through the open door into the hallway. Someone tugged off her blanket; Sister Ruth. "Come Brigit, wake up right now. Quick like a bunny, come on."

"What's happening?" Brigit obeyed, climbing out of her bed. The other children were doing the same, and the sisters were lining them up near the door. "Hold hands," one called. "Do not let go, no matter what."

"We have them all," Sister Mary Agnes cried, standing at the very end of the line of kids. "Go, go!" She grabbed Brigit's hand and pressed it to the hand of the little girl in front of her. "Don't let go."

The line moved quickly into the hall, and Brigit saw flames down the hall and thick tendrils of smoke. It was hot. Then she looked back at Sister Mary Agnes and said, "My book!"

Sister gave a wide-eyed look toward the flames. "I'll get it. Keep going, Brigit. Get outside." And she let go.

Brigit let go, too, and ran back into the room after her, but she couldn't see in the room. Smoke had almost filled it. Sister Mary Agnes was coughing, and she emerged like a shadow,

Brigit's book in one hand. She extended her arm, holding the fairy tale and Brigit reached to take it, and then the floor fell from beneath them. Brigit was flung backward, and Sister Mary Agnes vanished into a chasm of sparks and smoke.

Brigit scrambled backward away from what looked like the mouth of hell. Her book was somehow in her arms, clutched to her chest. She didn't know which way was which anymore. She didn't know how to get out.

And then someone was there, scooping her up in bony arms, enfolding her in the wet blanket that he wore around him. He had whiskers all over his face, and a soft soothing voice, and he said, "Don't you worry, Brigit. Ol' Raze has you now. You're gonna be okay."

CHAPTER 5

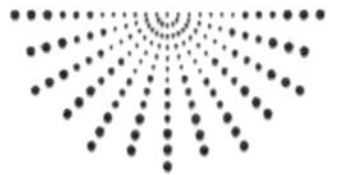

Brigit
Not so long ago, and far away...

Ten years had come and gone for Brigit since that horrible night. Ten years, and she'd been living on the streets with other homeless people like her. She was seventeen, now, but God, she felt so much older. Older than Raze. Older than Sister Mary Agnes had been.

Brigit remembered it as if it were yesterday, every word, every line in Sister Mary Agnes's face, and the sound of her aged voice rustling like dried leaves at the hand of the wind, as she read that ridiculous fairy talenight after night. Brigit still knew every word by heart. Sometimes she'd open the book, reading it in a whisper late at night when she couldn't sleep, and she'd imagine Sister Mary Agnes there beside the bed, draped in that black habit from head to toe.

So many vivid impressions, all instigated by one tiny scrap of paper. Why had she saved the thing anyway?

Against her will, Brigit scanned the clipping, reading the words again, reminding herself why she had to go through with this scheme of Mel's. Her hands trembled, and tears blurred her vision, but she blinked and made herself read.

"Fire swept through St. Mary's last night, destroying the church and leaving the children's shelter heavily damaged. So far only one death is reported, that of Sister Mary Agnes Brockway, seventy-two, formerly of Queens. One child is still listed as missing, and Father Anthony Giovanni, parish priest, theorizes the nine-year-old girl ran away in panic. He does not believe the child's body will be recovered by fire fighters as they search the premises today. 'Brigit is a special little girl,' he told reporters at the scene this morning. 'Too special to be taken like this.'"

Special?

Brigit folded the yellowed newspaper clipping exactly the way it had been folded before, and returned it to its spot in the bottom of the cardboard box where she kept her clothes. The physical act of putting it away helped her to put away the memories as well. None of them mattered. Not now. They might as well be as fictional as the fairy talethat lay in the box beside the clipping. The elaborate creation of some kind soul determined to placate a lonely little girl.

Sister Mary Agnes herself might have created the book, for all Brigit knew.

She'd called Brigit's talent a gift. A miracle.

"If she could see me now, she'd turn over in her grave."

"What's that?"

Brigit turned, looking through the sagging doorway with its peeling gray casing. The folding card table in the next room seemed to be holding Raze up as much as the stool beneath him. Even beyond the stubble, and in the shadow of his ever-present Mets cap, she could see the grayish tinge to his face. The green shirt that had once been part of someone named Bob's uniform, hung on Raze as if he were a stick figure. He coughed, and Brigit thought the rickety table would collapse.

She swallowed her doubts, lifted her chin, and went to him, running her hands over his frail back until the spasm passed. He was old. When had Raze become so old? He'd always been the strong one, he'd always been the one to take care of her, right from the start. That awful night at St. Mary's when all the other children had obeyed the sisters and joined hands and made their way out of the burning shelter. All but Brigit. She'd let go. She'd gone back, looking for Sister Mary Agnes. And she'd ended up trapped in an inferno more terrifying than anything that Dante fellow had dreamed of.

Her hands tightened on Raze's frail shoulders. He'd heard her screams that night. He'd come after her. Somehow, a man she assumed was one of the bums who slept in the park across the street, had pulled her out of that hell. And she'd been with Raze ever since. She'd been convinced that because he'd saved her from the fire, because he'd taken her from the orphanage, that somehow made her his little girl. And she'd loved the old man with all her heart from the instant he'd rescued her. He'd wanted to return her to Father Anthony. But she'd cried and pleaded and begged to stay with Raze, and he'd been too soft-hearted to send her back.

Razor-Face Malone had become the only family she'd ever had. He'd saved her life. So now she'd do what she had to do to save his.

"Come on, Brigit," Mel called from his spot in the corner. "Break's over."

She nodded in response to the slightly whiny voice. Mel sat on the bare floor, back against the naked lath wall, legs crossed. His gray chauffeur's cap was too big for his puny head, but managed to look jaunty anyway. And besides, it covered the bald spot.

"The quicker you finish up, the quicker you get a warm bed and some medicine for Raze."

"You don't have to keep reminding me of that."

"I think I do," Mel said, getting to his feet. "Hell, with your talent, you should have been into this scam years ago. You could'a been *rich* by now." He gave a sharp, slanting nod and a wink. "You stick with me, and you'll get that way soon enough. I got *connections* now."

He shrugged and paced the room. He was better off than she and Raze. But he got that way because he was a crook. Oh, she knew, she wasn't much better herself. But aside from pinching a few groceries and a wallet here and there, she'd been fairly honest, out of respect for Sister Mary Agnes, and the things the nun had taught her. *Not* for any other reason. Not because of morality or values. Hell, with the way the world treated people like her and Raze, she didn't figure she owed anyone anything. She'd do what she had to do to survive.

And when she wasn't surviving, she'd race through the alleys and vault mesh fences and cartwheel in the gutters. Because she had to. Raze said she had too much energy and she'd explode if she didn't let it out.

Not today, though. Today she was tossing Sister Mary Agnes's teachings aside, using all that pent-up energy to make her hands obey her mind. She was taking the step that would brand her as much a criminal as Mel was. And still, there were men far worse. At least Mel had never *hurt* anybody. His game was the con, though he had yet to score big, as he put it. Deep inside, Mel was good. If Brigit didn't believe that so firmly, she wouldn't be doing this.

Lately, though, he'd been keeping some bad company. These *connections* he kept talking about. One of them was a man named Zaslow, a man Brigit knew was evil just by looking at him—as if she really were half-fay and could read a man's heart by plumbing the depths of his eyes. This entire scam had been

Zaslow's idea. Fencing stolen artwork was, Mel claimed, Zaslow's specialty. So when Mel had offhandedly mentioned Brigit's "gift" in one of his endless efforts to impress the man, a plot had been born.

Raze coughed again, and Brigit caught her breath. He was getting worse.

"I know, I know," Mel said, a touch of mockery in his voice. "You're only doing it this one time. You keep telling me. But you wait 'til you have that money in your hands, kid, You wait 'til you *smell* that green, and then we'll see if you're so damn noble."

Brigit closed her eyes. There was no sense talking to Mel. He'd been a small-time con all his life, and he'd convinced himself she was his ticket to wealth untold.

But she vowed, she *swore* on Sister Mary Agnes's memory, that she would only do it once. Just this one time, and only because Raze's life depended on it. She didn't like being even remotely involved with a man like Zaslow. It made her feel soiled and low.

Raze hadn't wanted her to do it, even this one time. He'd fought tooth and nail against her going along with this thing. He said it was wrong, plain and simple. He'd even suggested she give Mel the fake instead of the original, to save her from having to commit a real crime. But Mel had told her that Zaslow would know if she tried something like that. He was that good.

Brigit didn't see that she had any choice in the matter. Raze was dying.

He was dying. That talent she had for seeing things in a man's eyes had shown her that when she'd looked into Raze's. And she'd do whatever it took to save him.

She sighed and crossed the floor of the condemned apartment to the easel that seemed as out of place as a diamond in a dime store. A color print of the Matisse was taped to the crumbling wall. She clamped her jaw against the memories the sight of it evoked; memories of Mona Lisa on construction paper, hanging crookedly above a small wooden bed, and of the awed expression Sister Mary Agnes wore when she stared at it. Better not to let the thought of that horrible night enter her mind now, or her hands would start shaking. She had to finish. Now, while the afternoon sun was still slanting in through the broken windows, giving her so much light to work by.

Brigit took a breath, squared her shoulders, took one last look at the Matisse nude, and then surveyed what she'd done so far on canvas. It would be a perfect likeness. She didn't know how she knew that, she just did. And she didn't know how she could wield the brushes and match the colors the way she did, either. There was no technique to it. She'd never had an art lesson in her life. She just studied the image she wanted, kept it focused in her mind's eye, and...and painted.

Raze coughed again, a deep, racking cough that sounded painful. Brigit picked up a palette and a brush.

PART II
IF THIS BE MAGIC

CHAPTER 6

Present day...

"I'm terribly sorry, Mr. Reid. I didn't know."

Adam got to his feet, carefully lifting the painting, his hands touching nothing but the frame. He eased it back onto its hook above the antique walnut mantel. Then he nudged it a millimeter at a time until it hung perfectly straight.

Damn cleaning service. Damn strangers, sometimes a different one every week, coming in to clean the place. You could tell them a hundred times, leave them a thousand notes, and they would still forget. He missed the old days. He missed the full-time maid he'd had to let go. He missed having enough money to pay for her even more.

Hell, he was only hanging on to the house by a thread. But to lose it, too, would be to admit defeat...defeat to a man he despised. And that was something he couldn't do.

He didn't care to analyze his other reasons for clinging to the oversized money pit. Like the woods out back, it was something he didn't care to explore further.

He turned to the woman who was still trembling a little in

reaction to his bellow when he'd walked into the study to see his prized possession on the floor. "No one," he said slowly, resisting the urge to snatch the brass-handled poker from the rack of implements near his side, and shake it in her face. *"No one* touches this painting. Tell your boss that if one of her people forgets that again, I'll..."

He gave his head a shake. He sounded like an obsessed idiot. Then again, that was exactly what he was, wasn't it? "Never mind. Just get the hell out of here."

"Yes, Mr. Reid. I'm sorry. I wasn't told."

She backed through the tall double doors, pulling them closed, probably in a huge rush to get out of his sight. He didn't blame her.

He swallowed the panic he'd felt when he'd first come into the room to see the bare spot on the stucco wall above the fireplace. Everything else had been in place. The brass candle holders and the antique Navajo pottery on the mantel didn't seem to have been moved. He bit his lip, and stared up at the painting. He ought to get rid of the damned thing before it drove him completely nuts. Short trip, he knew, but there was no sense rushing it. Getting this thing out of his sight might slow the deterioration of his mental health considerably. But he couldn't sell the painting. He wouldn't.

It wasn't the quality of the work that had so captured him the first time he'd seen it hanging in the Capricorn Gallery on the Commons a year ago. It was the subject that enchanted him.

A forest where flowers unlike anything real bloomed in riots of color. Where every boulder and every pebble were gemstones, every swirl of tree bark, a work of art. Hidden among the twisting foliage, timid creatures of no known species peered at the spectacle in the central clearing. They only appeared when one looked at the painting from just the right angle. He'd owned it for weeks before he'd spotted all of them, and he wondered even now if there were more to be discovered.

In the distance one could see towering castle spires, gleaming like silver beneath a jewel-blue sky. And in the clearing, just beyond some dark green reeds in the very center, a pool of crystalline water with dense green reeds concealing the woman who bathed there. She was stunning, her hair a tangle of black satin ribbons, her eyes so stunningly sapphire they almost gleamed from the canvas.

And when you looked at her, she seemed to be looking back.

When he'd first laid eyes on the painting, he'd wondered if he was finally having the breakdown he'd been expecting. But that concern hadn't stopped him from buying it. Nor had his shortage of funds.

The woman and the mythical forest where she bathed were the ones he'd seen in that ridiculous dream he'd had when he'd been...what? Seven? Didn't matter. He'd been convinced back then that he'd stumbled upon some secret doorway to an enchanted glade. That he'd talked to a fairy. That he'd seen his own future in the eyes of a little girl with sapphire eyes and black satin curls. And the woman in the painting was her grown up edition. The eyes were identical, from the way they looked to the way they made him feel.

He'd believed it was real so strongly he'd made the mistake of telling his parents about it. His mother had suggested therapy. His father had taken the strap to him.

Smack!

You're a man, Adam. My son, do you understand that?

Smack!

A man does not believe in fairy tales!

Smack!

A man knows the difference between the truth and make-believe!

Smack!

Do you think you know the difference now, Adam?

Yes!

I don't. But you will, Adam, you will if I have to take every bit of hide off your ass. You will.

Smack! Smack! Smack!

He blinked twice, and shrugged off the memory as easily as he always did. It was no big deal. It didn't bother him anymore. Not in the least. His father's brutality had made Adam tough, and had taught him the difference between fantasy and reality. His dad hadn't hung around long enough to see the results of his brand of parenting. He'd sold everything he owned, including the house and property while his wife and son were still living there, and he'd walked away.

But Adam'd had his revenge, sort of. He'd made his own money, bought the place back. Brought his mother there to live out her days in peace, without a hard-drinking, hard-hitting husband to worry about. She'd died there, and Adam liked to think she'd died content. But he knew deep down, she'd never gotten over her husband's betrayal.

He knew exactly how she'd felt. Because the fact was, he was on the verge of losing it all over again, due to a remarkably similar kind of betrayal.

But he wasn't going to think about his ex-wife or her uncanny similarities to his old man right now, either. Right now he was thinking about that damned dream. It must have had a basis in something he'd read or heard somewhere. His obsession with finding the source of his childhood delusion had made him one of the country's top experts on fantasy and myth. He'd made a career out of his mental lapse. He'd published books on the subject of fairy tales and their origins.

But even so, he'd never found the story that must have inspired his dream.

Or the woman that little girl had grown up to be.

The painting was his first real proof that someone else knew about the mythical land. At the bottom of the painting, cleverly woven into the lush greenery so it was all but hidden, was a single word. *Rush.*

No myths or legends he'd studied had come close to describing the land he'd believed he'd visited back then. None mentioned this land of Rush by name.

He looked at the painting again, and again a small chill raced up his spine at the powerful similarities to his childhood illusion. The artist had captured Adam's dream right down to the tiniest detail. Right down to the pictures in the tree bark. Right down to the hypnotic power of that little girl's eyes.

Somewhere, there was an explanation for all of that. And if it took the rest of his life, Adam would find it.

No time to dwell on it now though. He had a class in twenty minutes.

"So, according to this ancient Celtic manuscript, what characteristics would you expect to find in your average fay-female? If you read the assigned chapters, you'll know this stuff. Come on."

Adam sat on the edge of his desk, watching hands pop up all over the room. This group was nothing if not enthusiastic. Even if they were a bit too imaginative for his tastes.

"Miss Monroe, let's hear your opinion."

The twenty-year-old aspiring swimsuit model beamed at him, shifted in her seat, her skirt sliding a little higher on her thighs. Nice thighs, too. She was taking this class for easy cred-its. He let her get away with it mainly for the view. Carla Monroe bending over was a rewarding experience.

She ran a finger along the scooped neckline of her blouse, tracing her cleavage, drawing his eye.

He wondered if she was more interested in screwing him for

the challenge or for the grade. Had to be something. It was always something where women were concerned, wasn't it?

"They're brimming with energy," she said slowly, drawing the words out. "Particularly *sexual* energy."

Too bad she was a pink slip waiting to happen, or he might oblige her. Too bad he needed his tenure here so damned badly. A year ago, it wouldn't have mattered. A year ago, he'd had money to burn. Or he'd thought he had. He'd been blissfully unaware of the ways his young wife had of moving money around. By the time Sandra and Adam's pal Rob had sailed for parts unknown, they'd taken him for damn near every penny.

The only thing in this world worse than a thief, he mused, was a female thief. A beautiful female thief. A beautiful, ruthless female thief who didn't bat an eye at the prospect of ripping out your guts along with your money.

He swallowed hard, but the bitterness remained like bile in his mouth. "True, Miss Monroe. This work suggests that. What else?" He glanced around the room. "Michael?"

"Their power over mortal men is the most interesting thing," Michael said. He took his wire rims off as he spoke, twirled them between his fingers, then slipped them back on. "That one passage was...almost scary."

A murmur of laughter rose from the students. Adam flipped open the book and read aloud. "Many a man has died of longing for one such as her. For her skin has the flavor of honey which contains a magic all its own. Once a man's lips taste her nectar, he is bound to her for all his days. Be fore-warned, then, for her spell cannot be broken. Look for the sign...the sign of the cradle moon above the mound of Venus. Be it pale, you might yet escape with your heart and mind intact. But be it crimson, she is of royal blood, and too strong for a mortal man's resistance. Even a glimpse into the eyes of such a one may spell your ruin. For if she looks upon you with longing, your days are numbered. Run while you can, 'ere she captures your soul and leaves your body vacant, to waste away unto death with longing for a love you can never have."

The laughter died as he read, and when Adam looked up, it was to see rapt interest on the faces of his students. And someone whispered, "Maybe it's not a myth."

"Yeah," said another student. "Hell, you said this Celtic text is, what? Nine hundred years old? Maybe it's... you know... *non*fiction."

The murmur of agreement that rose in the room made Adam clench his jaw. His response was delayed by the ping of the little timer bell he kept on his desk. He sighed, lowering his head, drawing a new, calming breath, reminding himself they were just kids.

He'd been a kid once. He'd had some pretty farfetched notions himself.

Not gonna think about that. Not now.

"Okay, time's up. What do you say tomorrow you come in here with some *intelligent* theories, hmm? Like maybe, what sources the author might have drawn on to come up with his version of fairy lore."

He closed the book, turned his back, dismissing them with the gesture. But the exodus was quieter than usual, and he peered over his shoulder to see intense expressions on many young faces. They weren't actually considering the possibility that the text was anything but fiction, were they?

Imagination could be taken too far. It could be dangerous.

It can leave bruises, right Adam?

Shut the hell up.

Not to mention obsessions. Like your obsession.

He ignored the voice in his mind. The one that sounded like his father's voice. It didn't bother him again, as he dropped the heavy book into his briefcase, followed by a file folder full of essays and the wind-up timer. Which left the desktop as barren as the surface of the moon. Clean. Orderly. The way he liked it. He locked the drawers, pocketed the key.

His own theory was that the newly translated discourse on the qualities of fay folk was a collage of other myths and legends. Some imaginative soul had picked bits and pieces from stories he'd heard, and put them together to make his own version. It had the flavor of classical Greek tales of sirens, luring sailors to their deaths with the beauty of their songs. He detected a little Arthurian inspiration, as well. The Lady of the Lake with her ethereal beauty, nearly human in appearance, but too beautiful to be mortal.

Adam grinned a little as he thought there might be a bit of succubus lore tossed in for good measure. Drawing a man's soul from his body into her own, leaving him to wither and die of longing for her. Sounded like a new spin on a succubus to him. Hell of a way to go, too.

He set the case on the shiny surface of the desk, deciding to list his possible sources on the board for discussion in tomorrow's class. No doubt once he got the ball rolling, the kids would come up with several more. He turned around, picked up a new piece of chalk, and began writing in bold, noisy strokes across the spotless blackboard. Siren, he wrote. And beneath it, succubus, and beneath that, lady of the la—

He paused with the chalk a hairsbreadth away from the board. A tiny chill crossed his nape, cold fingers spreading down into his spine, and he knew he was no longer alone. He turned his head, then his body. A woman stood in front of his desk. And there was something...familiar about her. Something he couldn't quite put his finger on.

His gaze dropped slowly to the spot about hip level where pale denim crawled tightly into the juncture of her thighs. Then it rose, over the barest glimpse of smooth-skinned belly where the blouse didn't quite reach the jeans. He saw her navel, and he thought of honey.

Man, he'd been too long without sex.

He told himself to look up faster, but his stubborn eyes continued the slow scrutiny and he realized he was secretly savoring it. He wasn't normally such a hound. She must be emitting some kind of musk that spoke directly to his libido. She could be a troll for all he knew. He hadn't taken more than a brief glance at her face yet. Because, hell, why rush it? The black t-shirt fit her as if it were made of spandex. It molded and hugged her high, round breasts. And Adam figured if she didn't want to be looked at, she wouldn't be wearing it. So he looked. And then he moved up a notch, to see the pendant around her neck. A pewter fairy, wrapped seductively around a long, slender, double terminated quartz crystal.

He lifted his brows, wondering if she was a new-age yuppie or a potential student. If she was a student, he probably shouldn't be eating her alive with his eyes right now.

He brought his gaze up where it belonged, to her face.

A fist seemed to drive itself into his gut, forcing all the air from his lungs in a harsh, noisy exhale. She was incredible, and her eyes sucked him in like quicksand, and he had the oddest feeling that he knew her. Or should know her. Or...or *something.*

She wore small eyeglasses that did nothing to conceal the almond shape or invisible power of those eyes. Sapphire. A fringe of paintbrush-thick lashes surrounded them.

He blinked and shook himself, feeling awkward and even a little dizzy, as if he'd had a few too many drinks. Which made no sense at all, since he'd had nothing stronger than coffee.

What the hell was the matter with him, anyway?

"Mr. Reid?"

He cleared his throat and told himself to get his act together. "Yes. What can I do for you?"

"I'd like to enroll in your class."

Several answers sprang to mind, the first and most obvious being that she ought to be in the admissions office and not in his classroom. The second being that she ought to be anywhere in the damn universe other than his classroom.

But what he said was, "Sorry. This class is full. Check back next semester." If he didn't know better, he'd think he was afraid of her. All five feet and possibly 100-pounds-soaking-wet of her.

When her gaze fell in apparent disappointment, he was finally able to look away from the eyes that had seemed to envelop him and hold him captive. To distance himself, take in the full picture of her face. Like stepping back for a better view of that painting he'd found at the Capricorn. Exactly like that. So much like that, he shivered involuntarily.

Her face was heart-shaped. Her hair, endless cascades of riotous, gleaming black curls. She could have been any age, nineteen to thirty-nine. Impossible to tell. One delicate hand rose, and she fingered the pendant she wore, moving it back and forth on its chain.

She was nervous.

"It's very important that I take this class," she said, and her voice reminded him of water chuckling over stones. Deep and smooth and refreshing. But he wasn't too entranced by it not to notice the silt of desperation stirring beneath the surface.

"Why?"

"I'm..." She lifted her chin, met his eyes again. "I'm...it doesn't matter..."

Her words trailed off, and she averted her eyes almost guiltily.

"This is going to sound like a line," he said slowly, ignoring every warning bell going off in his head, though they were damn near deafening. "But I have the feeling I know you. Have we met?"

"No."

When she wasn't looking at him, his equilibrium seemed to

function just fine. "How can you be so sure? You haven't even told me your name."

She shook her head slowly, her raven hair falling over her face. "What does it matter? The class is full." She started to turn away.

He felt an inexplicable urgency not to let her go. "Wait a minute," he said, and she stopped. "Look, you never know when someone will drop out. Give me your name. Your phone number..."

She lifted her gaze to his, and he went tongue-tied all over again, and was forced to let his words trail off.

"I know I've seen you before...somewhere," he whispered.

She narrowed those gleaming blue eyes on him, and this time he got the feeling it was she who couldn't look away. He felt her try, then surrender. She stared into his eyes, and then a tiny frown appeared between her dark brows, and she stared harder.

Adam experienced the most peculiar sensation of...*invasion.*

And then her eyes widened.

He snapped his fingers and pointed at her. "Aha! You recognize me, too, don't you?"

She shook her head, taking a single backward step. "No."

"You do so. I can see it in your eyes. So come on, tell me, where did we meet?"

She closed her eyes, lowered her head. "It can't be..."

"Gee, was it that bad?" He dipped his head in an effort to see her downturned face, and tried to inject a little lightness, because frankly the woman looked as if she'd seen a ghost. "It *was* that bad? Hmm, maybe I'm better off not remembering."

"I have to go."

"Oh, come on. Give me another chance, huh? Isn't there a rule somewhere that says you can't blame a guy for stuff he doesn't even remember?"

She shook her head, turned toward the door. .

"Okay, what if I can find a way to make room for you in the class?" Damn, what made him say that?

She stilled, her back to him. Adam had no idea why he felt such an incredible longing to go to her, to touch her. It was powerful stuff. Made him think of that damned text he'd just been reading to the students.

"I've... I've changed my mind," she said softly, her voice a little hoarse.

And it hit him then, clear as day, that she was lying to him. She wanted *something,* all right, but taking his class wasn't it. No doubt in his mind. Though how he knew that, he still wasn't sure. What he did know was that nothing was more dangerous than a beautiful, dishonest woman. Especially one who looked the way she did. She was probably ruthless to the bone. Deadly to him. He felt her subtle threat right to his soul. But he felt this sudden, inexplicable allure, too.

Sirens and rocks, he reminded himself.

And even as he was nodding in agreement with his mind's silent warnings, his body was moving toward her. "Tell me how you know me," he said softly. "It's gonna drive me nuts if I can't remember."

"I can't," she said as her chin fell to her chest.

It was a whisper, so low he barely caught it. Something wasn't right here, and his curiosity rose up to challenge his wariness. It didn't put a dent in his attraction to this strange, familiar woman, though. "Maybe if you'd just tell me who you are..."

She turned to look up at him once more, shook her head from side to side, sparkling moisture adding a sheen to her eyes.

"Are those tears?" he asked her, resisting the stupid urge to run the tip of his thumb over her dampened cheek. "Look, if there's something wrong, maybe I can—"

She lifted her hand, laid it gently upon his cheek and stared so deeply into his eyes, he felt his world begin to tilt on its axis.

His hand floated up on its own, touched her cheek the way she was touching his. Very slowly, he trailed his fingertips down the side of her face, tracing the curve of her cheekbone, and the hollow beneath it, and the line of her jaw. And she closed her eyes, and he felt her tremble.

And then she jerked away, eyes flying wide. "No," she whispered, and backed away as if his touch burned her. Then even more softly she said it again. "No. You'll be far better off if you stay away from me, Adam Reid." She turned and ran out of the room. And though she seemed agitated, desperate to escape, Adam later couldn't recall hearing her footfalls when she raced down the hall. Which was odd, because footsteps in that hallway tended to echo nonstop.

CHAPTER 7

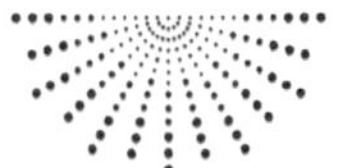

im! My God, it was him!

Brigit ran all the way to her car, but when she tried to fit her keys to the lock, she dropped them. And then she just stood there, fighting to control her suddenly rapid breathing. Her hands vibrated, and she braced them on the warm metal of the car, arms rigid, head lowering between them. She tried for a deep, steady breath but it became an open-mouthed gasp. Her heart hammered. Her pulse thundered in her ears.

This wasn't possible!

But it had happened. Only moments ago, she'd looked into the eyes of the man she'd dreamed about, on and off, for as long as she could remember. Always the same dream. It never changed, only grew longer, more intense. Her feelings about it had changed, though. They'd matured into something completely different. She used to look through the mists and see a troubled little boy, and she'd wanted to comfort him. But as the years unwound, she'd seen so much more. Her dreams of him now revealed a tortured man. One in more pain than any human should have to bear. And more. A virile man, with

"

enough passion in his eyes to burn her alive. A man in need...of her. In every way a man could need a woman.

All of that was visible in his eyes in those dreams. Dreams where the fictional Maire from the fairy tale had whispered that he was her fate.

God, what did it all mean?

Those same things had been in his eyes again, just now, when they'd met hers up there in that classroom.

He needed her. And he didn't even know it.

Worse yet, she hadn't come to him to help him. She'd come to hurt him even more than he'd already been hurt.

God, what was happening? Had that lifelong dream of hers been some kind of premonition? Was there any such thing?

The very idea terrified her, so she put it out of her mind and tried to focus on simple things. Immediate things. Crouching down to recover the dropped keys. The dirt and gravel she scraped up along with them. Getting the car door open. Adjusting the visor against the brilliant, late summer sunlight and slipping on her dark glasses. Starting the motor.

She drove down the steep inclines of the university area's streets, then turned and headed for the Commons. By the time she'd parked and left the car, she was telling herself that there had to be a way out of this mess. There had to be. She and Raze hadn't come this far to have it all ruined for them now.

This was maddening! She wanted to stand in the middle of the sidewalk and scream at the top of her lungs. She wanted to smash something.

What was she going to do?

She couldn't go through with it. Not now that she'd seen the man. Adam. His name was Adam Reid. His eyes were the deep, glittering blue of a midnight sea on a moonless night, the dark, bottomless blue-black of deepest ocean, and when she'd looked into them, she'd seen his soul.

No. She wouldn't do it to him. She told herself that again and again as she stifled her frustration and walked the last couple of blocks to the Commons. Then she paused and stood still for a moment, eyes closed, head tilted slightly back. She listened and she sniffed the air, waiting for the magic of this small strip to get to her, to calm her.

A hundred feet away, a jazz band played, and the saxophone solo wafted straight to heaven. When summer sighed, its warm breath brought the scents of fresh-baked doughnuts, because she was standing near the bakery, and more subtly, the scents of flowers. Violets and hyacinth.

That was better. Brigit opened her eyes, a little calmer now, a little less likely to smash the first breakable object she got her hands on out of sheer frustration. It wouldn't do. She had a reputation in this small college town. Among the merchants, she was liked and respected for her innovative ideas and determination to succeed.

Among the students, she was admired and sought after for long heart-to-hearts and sage advice. The town's residents saw her as a success story. A young single woman caring for her aging father, running a successful business, and doing both with ease. They called her a good example. An inspiration.

She'd fooled them all, hadn't she? No one who looked at her would see an orphan, much less a wild thing of the streets. No one would see an accomplished criminal, a master art forger who'd sold her soul to get where she was today. No one would see the wanton that lived inside. The feelings that burned in her sometimes late at night. The ones she doused and drowned and suffocated, only to have them return to haunt her over and over. The ones she'd never confessed to anyone. Not even Raze.

The ones instigated by those dreams of the man with the pain and the passion in his eyes. But she saw them. Her dreams of that man had grown up over the years. Now, when she dreamed of him, she went to him. And he looked up into her eyes and he knew her. She knew he did. He'd slowly get to his feet, and he'd reach for her, and she'd go slowly, willingly into his arms, tilting her head up for his kiss. Never a timid kiss. His mouth would cover hers, and his tongue would plunder, and his body would send silent messages to hers. He'd set fire to her blood as he kissed her. And in the blink of an eye, she'd see them naked, clinging to one another in a frenzy of lovemaking so intense it left her weak. She'd wake from those dreams breathless, shivering and damp with sweat. And because the dreams kept coming, more often and more potent all the time, she knew the wanton inside her must be growing stronger and more restless.

Sister Mary Agnes would be appalled if she knew about those dreams. It was times like these that made Brigit glad her twin sister was only part of the fairy tale, and not a real woman. Certainly not the fair angel she'd become in Brigit's mind. The living, breathing image of feminine perfection. Of goodness.

But she tamped that thought down, too, and moved forward, and thought about how stupid it had been to dress in faded jeans and a crop top in order to try to fit in at the university. To pass as a student. The scents of flowers grew stronger and more varied as she approached her place—*her place,* the little flower shop called Akasha which she had bought, which she *owned.* She smelled daffodils and narcissus.

To Brigit the mingled aromas were the smell of peace, of security, of happiness. She even managed a small smile and picked up the pace. Sun glinted from the glass walls of the little greenhouse, which projected from the rear of the narrow brick building.

The spell shattered to bits, though, when she reached the front door and saw the man sitting on the step. He wore a suit and a tie, but he was filth in human form. He was a nightmare from the past. He was the embodiment of her many sins, finally come to demand their wages.

"Out to lunch, Brigit? Well, I'm glad you're back. I've been waiting."

"Zaslow. You said you'd give me until tomorrow." She glanced up and down the walk at passersby, feeling as guilty as if they could tell at a glance why this man was here, what he wanted, what she'd done. Who she really was underneath the civilized facade. A wild child of the concrete jungle. A criminal.

That girl was a part of herself Brigit had buried a long time ago. She was the one who'd lived on the streets with Raze, who'd learned to pick pockets with the stealth of a cat when the need arose, or to spend fifty cents in a grocery store, and leave with fifty dollars' worth of food. She'd done it without compunction. It was what it took to stay alive. She could steal from the cleverest, and fight with the dirtiest. That was the other Brigit. The one she tried to pretend no longer existed. She was a business owner now.

"I changed my mind," Zaslow said, bringing her back to the present as he got to his feet. Stepping aside, he nodded toward the door. Zaslow was a big man. Barrel-chested and broad, but not flabby. Intimidating.

Brigit fished her key from her pocket and unlocked the shop. As she stepped inside the chimes above the door tinkled a magical welcome, and the countless other sets that dangled from every possible appendage followed their example. The smells of hundreds of plants welcomed her as always. But the usual, soothing effects were nowhere within reach. She felt the filth of Zaslow's presence soiling the sunlit air around her, and the smell of her own fear overpowered the calming aromas of the plants.

She fought for calm as she walked behind the counter, instinctively wanting something solid between them. She nudged her glasses up higher on her nose. Placing her palms flat on the cool marble surface, she met his interested gaze on the other side.

"I'm not going through with it. You can't change my mind."

"I can and I will."

She'd always known he was evil. Men like him were a breed apart from most inhabitants of the planet. They were hollow inside. Empty. Without a soul. It was all right there in his eyes. She couldn't look into those eyes for more than a few seconds. So much evil there, and more than that. There was certainty. He was sure she would do what he'd ordered her to do. But she couldn't. Not to Adam Reid.

"I'm not a thief," she whispered, though she knew in her heart that wasn't quite true.

A little anger sparked in his pale gray eyes, but he banked it immediately. He kept his voice level and chilling. "You think just because Mel made the switches, you're innocent? You think those art collectors you and he stole from would agree with you? Do you, Brigit?"

She closed her eyes, sought the peace she could find if she concentrated hard enough. It didn't work, though. Right then, nothing could soothe her.

"I didn't mean for it to go as far as it did," she whispered. And she was explaining it more to the violets than to Zaslow.

"You only wanted to do it once. The Matisse. I know, Brigit. Mel told me everything."

She jerked her gaze up to Zaslow's big chest. No higher. His eyes made her go cold inside. And that close-cropped salt and pepper hair reminded her of porcupine quills. "Mel's the one who told you how to find me?" She couldn't believe it was true. Crook or not, Mel was a friend. The only one from her past she still kept in contact with.

"Before I was done with him, he was begging to tell me what

I wanted to know." Zaslow rubbed the knuckles of one hand with the palm of the other.

A sick feeling welled in Brigit's stomach. Mel. Yes, he'd been a criminal, and yes he'd convinced her to help him with the scheme, and ended up leading her by the hand down a path that was barren of morality. But she'd always had a choice. It had been her decision, not Mel's. And when she'd had enough, Mel hadn't even argued with her. She'd written to him, called him once or twice. But she hadn't seen him in almost five years, not since she and Raze had left the city and come to this place she'd known was a haven from her first glimpse of it. Her salvation. Her new life. She'd thought she'd left the past behind. Until Zaslow showed up.

She saw the cruelty in his eyes, shivered, averting hers again. "What did you do to him? Did you hurt him? Is Mel all right?"

Zaslow only shrugged and turned away from her. He slowly paced the length of the shop, his fingers idly stroking fragile leaves. Bending now and then to sniff a blossom. "You didn't expect it to be so lucrative, did you, Brigit? But how could you know, at the tender age of nineteen. You didn't have a clue how much money an original Matisse would bring on the black market. And the owner not even realizing it was stolen—man, that was the beauty of it. That was the beauty. Best scam I was ever into."

"But I didn't—"

"You made enough that first time to get you and the old man some decent clothes, get you cleaned up, so you didn't look like bums when you took him to see the doc. Made enough to get old Razor Face into a good hospital, and pay for all those tests. But bills have a way of reproducing, don't they Brigit?" He came back to the counter and stood there, searching her face as if looking for an answer. When she didn't give one, he went on. "Yeah, they do. Just like rabbits. I know how it is. And then there were the treatments, and the specialists and the medicine. And hell, Raze had to have a place to come home to when they let him out, didn't he? He had to have a bed, and some heat, and regular meals, right? Hey, I'm not saying you got greedy. You did what you had to do to survive." He absently fingered the geranium that thrived in its basket on the counter. Lifting one snowy white blossom to inspect it, he nodded once, and snapped it from its stem without so much as blinking.

His figure blurred, and Brigit had to close her eyes because of the red-hot burn in them.

"I'm sorry, Sister Mary Agnes," she whispered.

"So you forged a few more masterpieces." Zaslow kept talking, ignoring her pain. He popped the little cluster of blossoms into a buttonhole on his lapel, fussing with it until it hung just the way he wanted. "So what? It's not like you went out and killed someone or robbed a bank. The owners never knew the difference. No one got hurt. It isn't as if you wanted a free ride, after all. You just made enough money off your little forgery enterprise to run away to this yuppie college town. Enough to buy this pretty little flower shop, here. Made yourself into a respectable business owner, didn't you Brigit? Member of the small business association and everything. You go to community meetings and talk to troubled kids. Donate money to the homeless. Volunteer at the soup kitchen on weekends. What is all that, your penance or something?"

She lifted her fingers to her temples, rubbing brutal circles there, lowering her chin to her chest. "Will you please just leave me alone? Please?"

His hand was suddenly clasping her chin, thumb and forefinger digging into her cheeks, forcing her head up. He leaned over the counter so his face was near hers. "You're no better than I am, Brigit, so drop the act. You're a thief. And you're gonna do this for me. I promise you that."

"No." She tried to pull away from him.

He released her abruptly, and she stumbled backward,

knocked her head against the shelf behind her. A coleus plummeted, exploding on impact at her feet. Purple and green leaves, broken stems, black soil, and bits of pottery covered the floor and dusted her feet. Fragile roots lay exposed.

"I got enough dirt on you to put you in prison for thirty years." He wasn't yelling. Just speaking calmly as he straightened, adjusted, and gave his cuffs a gentlemanly tug.

"If you turned me in, you'd go to prison, too, Zaslow."

"Wrong, little lady. I've *been* to prison. That last painting you forged for me...the buyer turned out to be an undercover cop. I did my time, and I did it with my mouth shut. They tried everything to get me to tell them the name of my forger, but I wouldn't do it."

Brigit remained where she was, back to the wall literally as well as figuratively. "Not out of loyalty," she whispered. "You only kept my name out of it so you could use me again."

"Why doesn't matter. You owe me, Brigit Malone."

"I can't—"

"Then I'll turn you in. And what do you think will happen to the old man then? Huh, Brigit? What do you think Raze will do? You think he can get by on the streets now like he used to? Hell, he can barely feed himself."

"Don't do this."

"It's done. You get close to Reid. You get inside his house, get a look at that painting, and then you make me a perfect copy. Since Mel's...unavailable, you'll make the switch for me, too. Bring me the original. You do everything I say, exactly as I say. Otherwise, I'll see to it the cops find out everything I know."

She thought of Adam Reid, though she tried to blot his image from her mind. She thought of the pain in his eyes. Passion and pain, all entwined together in eyes that glistened like gemstones. He'd frightened her and drawn her all at once. She'd never looked into anyone's eyes and felt the things she'd felt in his. She'd glimpsed goodness. Yes, she'd been sure it was there. But buried beneath so much bitter pain and anger that it might never surface again. There was danger in Adam Reid's eyes.

It would have been easier to give in, easier to save herself from Zaslow's threats, if Adam Reid had been a stranger. But he wasn't. He was the man she'd been making love to in her dreams her whole life. He was the little boy she'd dreamed of as a child, who would one day need her like no one else ever had.

Squaring her shoulders, she met Zaslow's evil gaze. "I tried," she breathed, though she was sure he wouldn't give in. "I went there today, just like you told me to, and he wouldn't even let me in his class. How am I supposed to get into his house if I can't get into his classroom?"

Zaslow shrugged. "That's your problem, not mine."

Brigit's throat felt like sandpaper. He wasn't going to back down. "Why does it have to be *that* painting?" It was a desperate attempt to divert him. "Why not pick another one, any one you want? A Rembrandt. A Picasso. Anything else. Why do you want an unknown painting by an anonymous artist anyway?"

"Because that's what my...my *client*...is paying me five hundred grand to get. Look, this guy hired me to steal *that* painting. He didn't say how, he only said do it. Making a substitute is my idea. Best way to handle the job. This way, Reid never even knows he's been ripped off, my client gets what he wants, and I get paid. Now I'm done talking to you. You gonna do this or am I gonna bring you down hard?"

She sought for excuses, and clung to the one that was the most genuine. "I can't do it without a print, Zaslow. If you don't believe me, ask Mel. He always got me a print to work from. I need something in front of me as I work."

"There are no prints of this piece," he growled. "Don't you think I checked?"

"Then how do you expect me to—"

"Like I said, you get *close* to him." His filthy eyes traveled to her toes and back again, and she felt dirtied by their touch. "Shouldn't be a problem for you, Brigit. You're a hot little number."

Her stomach churned, and she thought she'd vomit.

"Reid is healthy, male, and straight, honey. So why don't you just make him an offer he can't refuse?"

She shook her head, banking her revulsion. She wouldn't do it. Not in a hundred years. She couldn't even think of it, seeing Adam Reid's tortured blue eyes in her mind again. Yes, she'd forged paintings before, but she'd never had to look her victims in the eye. She'd never had to see their pain and know she'd be adding to it. She'd never had to get close to them, much less do what Zaslow was suggesting, only to betray them. Like slipping a blade between the ribs of a friend.

"Or, you can use this." He pulled a folded newspaper from inside his jacket, and shoved it in her face. The classifieds. With an ad circled in red.

"Boarder wanted. Estate on Cayuga Lake. Reasonable rates." There was more, but she didn't bother. She threw the paper down and stared up at Zaslow. He could send her to prison maybe, or at least ruin her business, destroy the entire life she'd built here by shouting her secrets from the rooftops.

But even if he did, Raze would be all right. She'd set aside money in his name. No one could touch that. Not even if she was caught. And it would be enough to see him through.

So let Zaslow do his worst. She met his gray eyes, not flinching from their cold emptiness this time. She wasn't a lonely, frightened little girl anymore.

Very calmly she said, "I can't. I *won't.*"

He leaned across the counter, his vile breath fanning her face. And the menace in his eyes sent ice-cold terror right to the pit of her stomach. "We'll just see about that, won't we, Brigit?"

Then he turned and walked away. The chimes jangled as he slammed out of the shop. Brigit didn't relax until he'd walked so far she could no longer see his retreating form through the windows. And then she sagged to the floor behind the counter, and just sat amid the spilled, dark soil feeling stunned, drained.

The soothing smells of Akasha wafted slowly into her psyche, like a balm to her soul. The wind chimes she'd hung all over the place tinkled magically. And she knew, no matter what consequences she might face, she had done the right thing.

CHAPTER 8

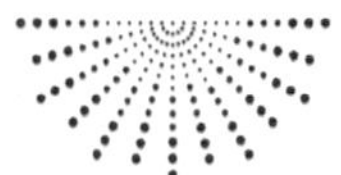

The house wasn't theirs. Not yet. They were still renting, while they waited for the mortgage to be approved. With her sterling reputation, thriving business, and healthy financial state, Brigit had been looking forward to a quick approval.

But it wouldn't happen now, would it?

No, Brigit realized as her bare feet sank into the grass at the edge of the driveway. Her shoes dangled from the two fingers of her left hand. No, the mortgage wouldn't go through, not if Zaslow was as good as his threats. Not if he exposed her as an art forger, a criminal.

She bit her lip as the wind stirred the dead leaves at her feet, and carried their scent up to twirl it around her face. The porch swing swayed, emitting a lonely creak. It was a small porch, little white railing all the way around. She'd always wanted a porch swing. And a neat white house with black shutters. It was the kind of place she'd dreamed about when she'd been a lonely little girl at St. Mary's. The kind of place she'd imagined she might live in one day, when she had a real family. The family she'd fantasized about had never come to adopt her. But she had the house now. And she had Raze. He was her family.

She liked to think that if her sister was real, she'd have found a place like this, and a dream world family to go along with it. *If* she was real. Seemed less likely all the time, though.

Brigit had tried once, a few years ago, to check into the records in Albany, to find out for sure if she'd had a twin. But she'd been told the records were sealed and that was that. She would probably never know.

There were window boxes on the front of her little house. She'd grown riots of pansies in them every summer since she and Raze had moved in.

She tried to swallow and couldn't, so she settled on blinking her eyes dry and mounting the steps. The screen door squeaked when she opened it, banged closed again when she let it go. The stairs right in front of her led up to the bedrooms. The living room lay on her left, the dining room on her right. Raze wasn't in either of them.

"Raze? Are you here?"

No answer. She dropped her shoes to the floor, and walked the full circle, through the living room, into the kitchen that took up the entire rear third of the house, around into the dining room and back to the front door. Growing more worried by the second, she called out again. Raze was getting old. Worried, she headed upstairs.

"Raze?"

Brigit's heart jumped into her throat when there was still no answer. She checked both bedrooms and the bathroom, panic taking a firm hold.

There was a thud below. Seconds later, a motor roared and revved like a frustrated bull. Brigit raced through the hallway and down the stairs. The front door stood wide open, and she launched herself through it. "Raze! Where are you? What's—"

The car's tires spun on the dry pavement, sending the stench of hot rubber into the air. She glimpsed two forms in the front seat, and the one on the passenger side was stooped. The dear face silhouetted, the whiskers familiar. The car sped away, red taillights shrinking rapidly.

"Raze!" Brigit screamed, racing down the steps, across the front lawn and into the street, running for all she was worth. As if she stood a chance of overtaking a speeding car. "No! Nooo!"

Only when the vehicle was no longer visible did she stop. Her entire body trembled, and her knees were shaking with the effort of remaining locked. Tears burned twin trails down her face. God, she had to do something!

She turned, making her way back to the house, though it was an effort with the dizziness of shock and the way her body seemed to want to turn to liquid. Looking up from the bottom of the front steps, she stopped in her tracks.

There, on the door, was Raze's Mets cap, pinned to the wood by the blade of a knife. A small square of white paper fluttered there, too, like a butterfly trying to escape the pin. It was held over the cap by the same blade. Sinking slowly to her knees, shaking all over, Brigit realized what was happening. She didn't even need to see the words scrawled carelessly across that slip of paper. But she leaned closer and read them anyway.

Do it or he dies.

Nothing more. But what more was needed?

Adam paced the admissions office like a prisoner awaiting a parole board decision. Maxine, at the desk, was in no such nervous state. She seemed to derive incredible amounts of pleasure from the slow dipping of her doughnut into her coffee, getting it just soggy enough, then snatching it up to her mouth to catch the moist end before it fell into a blob on her desk.

So far, she was two for three.

And in between bites, she glanced at her computer screen, where everything that went on in this office was recorded.

"Well?"

"No record of a new student signing up for your class yesterday, Adam. Sorry." She moved the doughnut to the cup again.

"She *didn't* sign up," he snapped, then regretted it when her hand froze in mid-dunk, and a large portion of doughnut dissolved and disappeared into the murky black depths of her coffee. "Sorry. But I told you that once. She came to ask about signing up and I told her I was out of room."

Maxine lifted the doughnut from the cup, shaking her head and clucking her tongue as she surveyed the damage. She peered into the cup, brows furrowing. "Well, what did you tell her that for? You're not, are you?" One finger plumbed the coffee sea, in search of survivors, he figured.

"I thought I was, but then I checked my roster last night and realized I have room after all." Bald-faced lie, yes, but he was desperate.

Desperate, and damned if he knew why, to see that woman again. He hadn't slept. Instead he'd tossed and turned in his bed all night, alternately sweating and shivering, seeing her face every time he closed his eyes.

Something about her had grabbed him by the throat and wouldn't let go. And if he didn't get to the bottom of this, he was going to go insane!

"Adam?"

He cleared his throat, straightened his tie. "I was hoping she left her name or an address or something. She must have had to sign in somewhere. All visitors do, don't they?"

Maxine's forefinger emerged from her coffee cup at last, with a globule of doughnut mush coating it. She popped it into her mouth. And when she pulled her now clean finger out again, it was with a loud smacking sound.

"Well, there's nothing in my notes. What did you say she looked like?"

What did she look like? Adam lowered his head, picturing her again in his mind. It was easy. Because her face wasn't strange to him. It was eerily familiar, and that was part of what was driving him nuts about this. He knew her. He just couldn't place her. "Small," he said, and his voice was a little softer than it had been before. "Delicate." The word slipped out before he gave it much thought. "And she has these *eyes* that just..."

Maxine had lost interest in the doughnut. Her attention was all his now. Brown eyebrows which had never been dyed to match her copper-red hair rose in twin arches. "Well, now. Isn't that interesting? She had eyes, you say?"

Her voice was full of speculation, and her double chin damn near quivered with amusement. "Sapphire eyes," he said, careful to keep his voice cool and detached. "Raven hair, long and curly. When she left, she seemed a little...distraught."

She'd been distraught all right. Almost as if looking at him—*touching him*—had shaken her as much as looking at and touching *her* had shaken *him*. Why, though? Why?

What did she really want with him?

A little voice inside whispered a warning, once again. But it was quieter now. This need to see her again had all but drowned it out. Still, he heard it, recognized it. A woman with this kind of power over him—one he sensed was lying—was the last thing Adam needed in his life right now.

But despite the very real, icy fear that writhed in the pit of his stomach at the thought of seeing her, Adam was convinced he could handle this thing. He could keep his feelings in check, talk to her as if she was just a stranger. Hell, he only wanted to see her long enough to make her tell him where they'd met before.

Liar!

As much as he detested dishonest women, he figured he

could stand her that long. Unless she decided to lie about that, too.

Maxine puckered her brows and sighed. "I just don't remember seeing anyone like that in here yesterday. Sounds...pretty, though." Reaching for her doughnut with one hand, she scrolled with the other. Then stopped abruptly. "Well, what do you know? Here she is. Hmm. She must have stopped in while I was out to lunch. You were right, someone added her name on the visitors list."

"Well?"

She turned the screen around and Adam leaned down. Brigit Malone. Akasha, The Commons. That was all it said. "What the hell is Akasha?"

"Akasha?" The male voice from behind Adam made him turn around to see his best student, Michael Sullivan, lounging in the doorway. "Oh, come on, Mr. Reid. Akasha. You know, the fifth element. The omnipresent spiritual power that permeates the universe and all that."

Adam frowned. "I was talking real life, kid, not religious myth."

"Skeptic," Michael accused. Then he shrugged. "Well, in real life it doubles as a flower shop on the Commons. Great place. You ought to check it out."

Adam nodded slowly. "I think I will."

"Uh, can you do us a favor and wait 'til after class? Everyone's waiting on you, Mr. Reid. I got elected to come looking."

Jerking his smart watch up to eye level, Adam blinked in surprise. He was never late for anything. He was the most notoriously prompt, organized man on campus. He never got distracted like this.

"Anything wrong, Mr. Reid?"

"No." He looked at his watch again, confirming he was ten minutes late for his own class. Distractedly, he started for the door.

"You're forgetting your briefcase, Adam."

He turned to Maxine, saw her plump finger pointing to the floor where he'd set it down. Shaking his head, he bent to pick it up.

"You're not yourself," Maxine whispered at him. She sent him a wink. "Must be those *eyes.*"

Maybe it was. More likely, though, it was this niggling feeling, half-anticipation, half-dread, when he thought about seeing her again.

He managed to get through class, but he was thinking about seeing her, getting the answers to his questions, the whole time. He couldn't seem to carry a thought to completion before he lost the thread. Couldn't seem to concentrate, wasn't focused. The kids tossed their theories at him as to the origin of the Celtic text, and he listened. Didn't argue, didn't question. Just listened.

It seemed to take forever, but the class finally ended. His timer bell pinged and he walked out, just like that. Papers strewn over the desktop. Drawers unlocked. And ten minutes later, he was at the front door of Akasha.

The sign said closed. But as he peered through the glass, he saw movement, so he tried the doorknob and found it unlocked.

He stepped through and into what seemed like another world. The place sparkled. It actually sparkled. And it wasn't just the crystal prisms turning slowly in the windows, and reflecting rainbows of color that danced with a life of their own, touching everything. It wasn't just the many windows that seemed not only to admit golden sunlight, but to enhance it somehow, or the plants that lined every available bit of space. The place smelled magical. A mingling of incredible perfumes, plants and flowers, and some sort of incense, too, he thought, permeated it. And the sound of it sparkled, too. Mystical music floating softly on fragrant air, touching him, caressing him. Those wind chimes that came alive with the slightest change in the air currents, whispering, tinkling whenever he moved.

He stood still, just inside the door, lost in sensations for several moments, before he gave his head a shake and reminded himself why he'd come here. To see her and figure out why he felt he knew her. It was important, somehow. He'd sensed that from his first glimpse of her.

No one stood behind the counter. He heard something. A sniffle. A sob. Adam was still holding the door in one hand, and he let it go now, stepping farther inside, scanning the aisles in search of her. The door swung closed, tinkling the chimes overhead as it passed.

"I'm sorry, but I'm not really open today."

It was her voice, but not deep and resonant as it had been yesterday. It was tear-choked and hoarse. It came from somewhere beyond the slightly opened door in the back. And he moved toward it, an odd sensation snaking around in his stomach.

"I just came in to take care of a few things," she went on, guiding him in, drawing him nearer. He thought of sirens, and wondered if he was about to crash on the rocks. "And then I'm going..."

He nudged the door open and stepped through into the warmth, light and humidity of a small room made completely of glass. Her greenhouse.

She stopped speaking as if she sensed him there. Lowering the watering pot to a bare spot between several ferns, she lifted her head, met his gaze. And behind the glasses, those blue eyes were as mysterious as ever, more so even, because they glimmered beneath an ocean of tears. She wore a pretty green blouse and a modest black skirt that skimmed the tops of her knees. Her wild dark hair was caught up in a tight French braid that hung down to the middle of her back. This was her costume. He knew it instinctively. Yesterday she'd taken it off, and tried to look like one of his students. And he thought maybe she didn't even realize that she'd been more herself in jeans and a crop top with her hair wild and free, than she was now in her uniform of propriety.

And why the hell was he thinking as if he knew her better than she knew herself? He hadn't even met her, yet, technically speaking,

"And then you're going...?" he asked.

She blinked, averting her face and removing her glasses long enough to swipe the back of one hand over her wet eyes and tear-stained cheeks. "Never mind. It's...not important."

"Looks pretty damned important to me."

He moved closer, because he couldn't stop himself. And she stood still, watching him, quickly slipping the glasses back on as if to hide behind them. Fear and—God, was that longing?—mixed in her eyes, and he almost believed she couldn't have moved away if she'd wanted to. He reached out, unable to control the impulse to brush at a tear she'd missed—or was it just because he had to touch her again? He ran his thumb across her cheek, his other fingers spreading gently over her face. And there was something. Something that sent his heart slamming against his ribs and made his throat close up. Something potent and startling and unexpected. Though it shouldn't have been. He'd reacted much the same yesterday, hadn't he? It was as if he fell under some kind of spell every time he looked into her eyes. And yet he couldn't seem to resist looking into them anyway.

The way her eyes widened, the way she sucked in a sharp gasp and pulled away from his touch, he was well on the way to convincing himself she'd felt it too, whatever the hell *it* was.

His hand hovered in the air for a moment longer. Then he lowered it, feeling like a fool. And he searched for something to say. What did you say to a beautiful, weeping stranger?

"Is there anything I can do to help?" She held his gaze with those moist, mesmerizing, soul-searching eyes of hers...and very slowly, she nodded.

CHAPTER 9

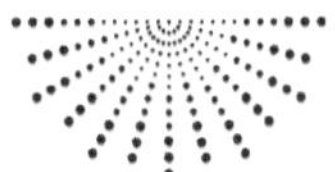

She tried not to look into his eyes. She couldn't afford to feel his pain, or to see the other things coming to life in those deep dark wells. Other things. Like the way he looked at her. As if he was seeing the epitome of his fondest dream. As if she was something precious, rare, something he'd never thought he'd see.

She was nothing. Less than nothing. A criminal unworthy of even a passing glance from this beautiful, tormented man.

Brigit strained, for once, to find the girl she'd been years ago. The one who'd been willing to do whatever it took to survive. The one who'd felt that as lousy as the world had treated her, it had no right to expect anything better in return. The one who'd lived in a condemned building, and who'd sold her soul without batting an eye, to save the life of the old man who'd once saved hers. Right then, instead of denying the existence of that wild child inside her, she longed to hide behind it. To once again become ruthless and clever and devious, the way she'd been back then.

She had no choice but to do it again. And it was going to be the hardest thing she'd ever done. She told herself it shouldn't be. All she had to do was think of Raze in the hands of that monster Zaslow, think of the things Zaslow might do to him if she failed. It would give her the strength to go through with this. She'd do whatever she had to. She'd forge the damned painting.

How, though? How the hell was she going to lie her way into Adam Reid's house? Into his life?

She dared a glance at him. He stood there, waiting for her to speak. Okay, then. There was no more putting this off. She knuckled her eyes dry again, and replaced her glasses with careful deliberation. She straightened her spine.

"Sorry," she said. "I don't usually greet my customers with tears."

He tried for a smile, but it was unconvincing. He wore the confused expression he'd sometimes worn in her dreams of him. "Maybe I should come back another time."

"No. I'm fine now, really."

He looked at her, one brow arched in disbelief.

"Really," she told him. And he nodded, though she didn't think he believed her. "So what are you doing here? Is it about the class?"

"Yes." His lips thinned, and he tipped his head back, looked at the clear sky beyond the glass ceiling, then lowered it again, shoving one hand backward through his honey-colored hair. "No."

Brigit tilted her head. "Which is it?"

"It doesn't matter. You didn't want to take the class anyway. Did you?"

She lowered her head to hide the jolt those words caused. He was too perceptive. How could she ever deceive him? She wondered what had brought him here, and wished she had the powers Sister Mary Agnes had woven into the fairy tale. She'd wave a wand and whisper a mystical chant, and she'd be given instant access to his mind, his home, his life.

His painting.

He was a volatile man. Such conflicting emotions passing through his eyes. From near reverence when he looked at her, to wariness. And always that old, well-worn anger simmering just below the surface. Crossing him would not be pleasant. And fooling him would not be easy.

She fingered the pendant she wore and ordered herself to calm down.

He was looking around the greenhouse now, turning slowly, so she could better appreciate the lines of his face. Harsh and angular. A straight Roman nose and wide-set almond eyes. He had the eyes of a wizard, she thought. Hypnotic, mesmerizing. Eyes like an oracle. They seemed capable of seeing everything, right to the soiled hubs of her soul. His lips were thick and sensual. She'd tasted them in her dreams.

He turned, caught her staring at his mouth, and one corner of it twitched. His eyes registered sensual awareness, followed by a flare of alarm. He concealed both immediately. "This is quite a place."

She thought of her mission, thought of the classified ad Zaslow had shown her, and tried *not* to think about Adam's lips, or look at his eyes.

"Thanks. It better be, I guess. I'm stuck here for a few weeks. That's why I wasn't opening today, in fact. I need time to pack up some things . . ." She let her voice trail off as his sharp eyes narrowed, probing hers. She couldn't help it when she looked away.

"Why's that?" he asked, his voice soft and wary. As if he was fully expecting—even awaiting—the lie she was about to tell.

She'd always been better at thievery and forgery than outright, face-to-face deception. She'd never been able to tell a lie without seeing Sister Mary Agnes, arms crossed over the front of her black habit, one foot tapping the floor, staring her down until she squirmed. For a while, she'd seen that vision face to face. Now she only saw it in her mind, but it was no less effective. She writhed inside.

"Radon," she blurted.

Oh, yes. She'd nearly forgotten the other reason she never lied. Because she was so terrible at it.

He crooked that one brow again, his eyes still piercing her. "Radon?"

She nodded, turning away from his knowing stare, absently straightening the amaryllis at her right, letting her eyes drink in the perfection of its large white trumpets rather than face this man as she lied to him. "My house is built over an old shale bed, and it turns out there's radon seeping into the basement. It causes cancer, you know."

"I remember hearing that somewhere."

Of course he did, she thought. It was last week's lead topic on the local news. "I have to move out until it's safe again."

"That shouldn't take long, should it? A couple of days, maybe?"

She paused, biting her lip, her back still to him. "Well, there's all that construction. The whole basement needs to be... um... radon-proofed."

"Of course it does," he said, and the sarcasm was so subtle, she couldn't be sure it was there.

She set her jaw, and tried to read his eyes, but he'd put up some kind of invisible shield. One she thought was as effective as the glasses she wore. She was shocked that his eyes told her nothing. That had never happened to her before.

"I don't suppose you've considered staying in a hotel?"

She shook her head quickly. "Can't afford it. All that construction and all..." He probed again, silencing her, but this time she held his gaze. She was determined to see whether he believed a word she'd said, or was just letting her finish her performance for his personal amusement. And still his eyes revealed nothing.

Except that, bathed in the sunlight streaming down from above, their flecks of turquoise showed here and there.

"Your shop is nice," he put in. "But it's small. Where are you going to sleep?"

She shrugged. "I'll just spread a sleeping bag on the floor."

He took a breath, shook his head. He looked into her eyes, probed, then looked away again. "Are you going to tell me it's a coincidence, Brigit?"

She heard a ripple of anger in the words, but oddly enough, it sounded more like a plea. "What's a coincidence?"

"Just yesterday I ran an ad in the *Times*. Room and board, cheap, or in exchange for light housework. I don't suppose you saw it?"

He wouldn't release her gaze. She tried to look away and couldn't. He knew she'd seen that ad. He knew she was fishing for an invitation. God, he saw right through her!

"Yes," she admitted. She faced him squarely, waiting for the disdain to appear in his eyes. It didn't. There was relief instead. Silent gratitude for something as simple as the truth. Impulsively, she added more. "To be honest, that's why I came to the university. Not for the class. Just to..."

"Check me out."

Lips thinning, she nodded. He knew she'd lied to him. She'd never get into his house. God, how could she save Raze now?

"And what's the verdict?"

Her head came up fast, and she bit her lip. "What?"

"Do I pass inspection, Brigit? Am I the kind of man you think you could...live with?" There was a slight tilt of his lips, as if he was trying to lighten things up. But it didn't reach his eyes. They were more intense than ever, and she had a feeling the question meant a lot to him.

"You mean...you'd let me?"

"Assuming you have time for a little light housework. With the shop to run and all, maybe you'd rather not—"

"No! I mean... yes." Her voice softened. "Yes, I'll have time. I'll make time. I have to..."

If she wasn't careful, he'd see how vital this was to her. She cleared her throat, met his eyes, shivered at the potency of the impact whenever she held his gaze for more than an instant. It was electric, and revived her forbidden dreams of him, and made her shiver with awareness of him. Their gazes held for far too long. She was reading things in his eyes, and showing him things in hers...things that shouldn't pass between strangers. Unspoken longings and erotic promises. All slipping from somewhere inside her before her conscious mind regained control. She blinked rapidly, embarrassed at the intensity of that long glance. From the corner of her eye, she saw him give his head a fast shake, as if trying to wake himself up.

"Akasha's hours are a little unorthodox," she said, to cover the awkwardness. "We open in the afternoon and close at eleven p.m. It seems to fit the schedules of the students much better than nine to five would. I have free time in the mornings."

He nodded, seemingly lost in confusion. Chaos. Determinedly keeping his gaze on the floor he said, "So would you like to see the place?"

She didn't answer because she was busy studying the way the sunlight illuminated the swirls of paler blond and darker gold in his hair. He looked up again, met her eyes. For a second, she thought he knew damned well she wasn't telling the truth.

A ripple of fear raced up her spine and she shivered involuntarily. How could he melt her soul with the heat and wanting in his eyes one minute, and chill her with suspicion and mistrust the next?

He didn't hold her gaze this time. It was a brief, chilly clash before he focused on the plants, feigning interest in them. "Well?" he went on. "Are you still interested?"

She paced slowly away from him, pushing one hand through her hair as if deep in thought. And then she turned to pace toward him again, stopping halfway, gnawing her lower lip, making him want to do the same. A lush begonia hung between them, its leafy, twisting strands interfering with his view of her, and for a second he resented it, because he enjoyed looking at her so much.

And then he went still, and he felt his blood slowly freeze over in his veins, because he suddenly knew why she seemed so familiar. She was the woman in the painting. The woman he'd seen in his childhood delusion all those years ago. She was...

No! No, she couldn't be. She was not the woman he'd obsessed about for the past twenty-five years. The resemblance was coincidental. It had to be, because the thing that had instigated his obsession had never really happened. It was just a story he'd heard somewhere and incorporated into his dreams. He hadn't *really* seen this woman as a child, bathing in a pond in an enchanted forest. He hadn't *really* been told that she was his fate. That she would come into his life so he could show her the way home, and that if he fell in love with her, she would break his heart.

But then again, he'd never *really* believed it had only been a dream, had he? Not deep down inside, where it counted. And right now, there wasn't a kernel of doubt in his soul or body that this was her. It was only his practical mind that rebelled.

She turned to look at him from beyond the plant's twisting vines. Just the way she had before, in the dream or vision or hallucination or whatever the hell it had been. And just the way she looked between the reeds in the painting. His knees tried to buckle and he couldn't breathe. In a second he'd be gasping. Chilled beads of sweat broke out on his forehead, and his damned hands were shaking.

He suddenly remembered the question he'd asked her just then. Whether she would come with him, to his home. Whether she'd stay for a while. And he was terrified she'd say yes, and just as terrified she wouldn't.

His mind all but begged her to come with him. Into his home. It scared him, the amount of tension that coiled in his stomach as he awaited her answer. She'd lied to him, for God's sake. And he had a feeling she still was, despite her uncanny resemblance to his lifelong fantasy. She wasn't even a very *good* liar. Radon. Right.

But he'd taken the bait. Not because he'd believed her, but because he'd wanted to. And he supposed it was a good thing he did. Because when she looked into his eyes, he didn't think there was a way in hell he could say no to her.

She hit him on so many levels she left his head spinning. She was his obsession. As if someone had breathed life into his childhood dream. As if a magic wand had been waved and she'd just walked right out of his head, and into his life. He'd searched for her for so long...

No. Not for her. For the source of that fantasy, the myth that had to have inspired it. You never searched for her!

Was that true? Because it certainly *felt* as if he'd been searching for her. He'd thought the painting was as close as he'd ever get to finding her. But now she'd stepped off the canvas. And he wasn't capable of letting her just walk away. Not without knowing her, trying to find out what all of this meant.

On an entirely separate level, he resented her. Because she had this incredible power over him, and because she was lying. She was up to something. His need to know everything there was to know about her was something he understood. Her desire to entangle herself in his life, though, was baffling. Every defense mechanism he'd developed through the betrayals he'd been dealt had jumped to full alert. Alarm bells were going off in his head, warning him that he was walking right into yet another heartache.

And yet he was powerless to resist. When he wasn't looking at her, he could convince himself that he was going in with his eyes wide open this time. But when he looked into her eyes, he felt as if he'd tumbled headlong into a trance state, and that he'd be her willing slave for the rest of his life if she asked.

The effect she had on him reminded Adam sharply of the descriptions of fairies in that newly translated Celtic text, and countless others. The enchantments they could place on the man of their choice. The way he'd waste away from sheer unfulfilled longing. A passage of John Keats came to mind. Adam tried to shake it away.

Ridiculous!

And yet he heard the words echoing in his mind.

> *I met a Lady in the Meads*
> *Full beautiful, a faery's child,*
> *Her hair was long, her foot was light*
> *And her eyes were wild.*
> *I set her on my pacing steed*
> *And nothing else saw all day long,*
> *For sidelong would she bend and sing*
> *A faery's song.*
> *She found me roots of relish sweet,*
> *And honey wild, and manna dew,*
> *And sure in language strange she said*
> *"I love thee true."*
> *And there I shut her wild wild eyes,*
> *With kisses four.*
> *"La belle dame sans merci*
> *Thee hath in thrall!"*

She came toward him, touched his shoulder, and he jerked at

the heat that hissed through him, shaking the verse from his mind. He'd never thought of his shoulder as an erogenous zone before.

"Adam?"

"Yes?"

Stop looking into her eyes. It's that simple, just don't look at her and you'll be fine.

"Did you hear me?" she asked in a voice like silk. "I said I'd like to come with you."

His vision blurred as he deliberately misinterpreted her words, and let himself fantasize, just for a second.

"To the house," she added quickly, almost as if she could read the pictures in his mind. "To see the room."

"I'll take you," he told her, and then he turned away, leaving her to interpret that whatever way she wanted. He headed for the door, his neck damp and prickly, and his heart doing things that might be described as palpitations.

"All right."

She was with him, right beside him, and he hadn't even heard her footsteps.

Her hair was long, her foot was light...

Shut up, he thought. Just shut the hell up, Keats.

Adam Reid didn't live in a house. He lived in a fantasy. From the steep, curving drive to the majestic pines that lined it, to the electric-blue sky above. Beautiful. And when she caught sight of the house, she lost her breath. It reminded her of a medieval monastery, tall and square, and made entirely of huge blocks of reddish-brown stone. The house wore an ivy coat, Brigit noticed, and she thought it must need it to ward off the chill of all that stone. And then she frowned, because for just a second, looking at the rows of arched windows had felt a lot like looking into someone's eyes. And what she read there was sadness. An old hurt. Just like the one that she sensed lived in Adam Reid's soul. A hurt he kept hidden beneath layer upon layer of bitterness, wariness, and anger.

"Here we are," he said, pulling his little red Porsche to a halt and killing the motor. It was the first time he'd spoken since they'd left the Commons. There had been something in the car besides the two of them, an invisible, pulsing tension so tangible she thought it might be a living thing.

"It's beautiful," she told him. She opened her door and got out. And as soon as the wind hit her, she knew there was something very special about this place.

Beyond the house, she could see Mystic Lake, its swirling waters stirred by the wind's fingers. And to her left, a pine covered mountain made love to the deep blue sky.

The girl she'd been so long ago seemed to yawn and stretch from her enforced slumber, summoned awake by the magic of this place, perhaps. Brigit had managed to lock that wild child away, to make her a prisoner of the controlled, responsible woman she'd become. But now the girl sniffed the scent of the lake and of the pines on the wind. And she suggested, in a mischievous whisper only Brigit could hear, that it would be wonderful to run barefoot through those tall grasses and wildflowers, to cartwheel and somersault all the way down the hill, to frolic naked in the lake as its vigorous waves tossed her to and fro. Or to stand fully clothed in a rainstorm, right there on the cliffs that jutted out over the water.

For a moment, she envisioned herself doing just that. Standing on the cliffs, soaking wet, her hair whipped by the wind, arms outspread as she welcomed the storm, taunted the lightning. It wasn't the respectable owner of Akasha standing there in Brigit's vision. It was an untamed hellion. And there was a glint in her eyes, and she was laughing aloud as she dared

Adam Reid to take her in his arms and kiss her the way he really wanted to.

Brigit slammed her eyes shut, mentally thrusting the wild thing back into her cell and locking the door. There was no room in her life for that wanton anymore.

"Are you all right?"

Blinking him into focus, she managed a firm nod. She wasn't all right. She was falling apart. God, where was her hard-won control now? Everything had been taken out of her hands. Raze's well-being. Her own decision to become a mature, responsible, socially acceptable woman. Maybe even her ability to remain that way.

And her deeply rooted feelings for this man. Her dream man.

"You looked...odd."

"It's this place," she said, and turned to look out over the water again. "It's magical."

"I used to think so."

When she looked at him, one corner of his mouth pulled into a sad, perhaps nostalgic smile.

"Come on. You're going to have to see the inside before you decide."

But she'd already decided. She'd stay here. Under any other circumstances, she'd have run from this place as fast as she could and vowed never to return. It would be difficult to keep her facade in place here. Nature knew the wild thing inside her. Nature seemed to be calling to her, rousing her, and beckoning her to take over.

Brigit would just have to deal with it, though. If she did manage to get through this and save Raze, she would have a life to go back to. A business to run. A place in the community to fill.

Adam took hold of her elbow and propelled her away from the stunning view, back along the path she didn't even remember walking, to the front of the house. Wide stone steps and an arched wooden door with stained glass. His keys jangled, and then he opened the door and ushered her inside.

A huge room spread out before her, white stucco, big windows. A wide mahogany staircase split into opposite directions halfway up, and ran into hallways on either side. At the bottom of the stairs, on a pedestal stand, a sparse fern with yellowing leaves made her grimace. She instinctively went to it, touched one withering strand, rubbed it between her fingertips.

He led her through the cathedral foyer, from which she could see rows of bedroom doors upstairs. He never slowed down. And she should have wondered why he was making a beeline to the double doors at the far end of the room. He flung the doors open with a flourish. "This is my favorite room. Technically, it's the study, but to me it's more like a haven. Come in."

Brigit stepped into Adam's haven.

And then she froze in utter shock. Her gaze riveted to the painting that hung above the mantel. She couldn't look away. She couldn't move. She couldn't even draw a breath.

"Beautiful, isn't it," he asked in a soft voice. He stood close beside her, and she assumed he, too, was staring at the piece. But she couldn't look at him to be sure.

"It's...it's not possible..."

She felt Adam's eyes on her. "Brigit?"

She shook her head, trying to remind herself not to speak her thoughts aloud, when what she felt like doing was screaming at the top of her voice. The painting was the perfect image of the first page of her precious *Fairytale.* The one Sister Mary Agnes had read to her every night. The one she'd clutched to her heart, even when she'd expected to burn to death in the fire. The one she'd clung to as Raze carried her to safety, and that she'd cherished ever since. The one bright spot in an otherwise heartbreaking childhood.

And here was its opening page on Adam Reid's wall. The

picture of the forest and that magical lake, with the castle spires visible if you squinted at the silvery clouds, and the images hidden in the swirls of tree bark, and the furry creatures like nothing real, peeking out of the foliage here and there.

Only in the book, there had been no woman bathing in the waters.

"I think she looks like you," Adam whispered. He sounded almost reverent.

"No. Not me." Brigit wanted to close her eyes, because the woman in the painting was staring straight into her soul. Oh, she looked like Brigit all right, what you could see of her, at least, between the tall grasses and fronds between her and the shore. But she wasn't. Brigit knew her, knew exactly who she was. She was the image of the wild thing Brigit kept locked inside.

And all of a sudden it occurred to her that *this* was the painting she was supposed to steal and replace with a perfect forgery.

She actually staggered backward. The blood drained from her face and her eyes widened. She parted her lips on a silent exhalation.

"Brigit?" He caught her shoulders, steadying her when she wobbled on her feet, and she realized how close she was to collapsing in shock. Gently, he pulled her a little closer, cradling her to his chest for all too short a time. And she couldn't stop her arms from linking around him and burying her face in the crook between his shoulder and his neck. He'd held her this way so many times before, in her dreams.

She felt him shiver, heard him draw a harsh breath. A moment later, he led her to a sofa and she sat down. He went away and returned in seconds with a glass of water, which he pressed into her hands. His hands covered hers, and warmth suffused her right to the core. He didn't remove them right away, and she saw him blinking down at his hands on hers, as if trying to solve a puzzle.

He finally sighed and took his hands away. Brigit sipped the water. Adam studied her.

"I've shown that painting to a lot of people," he said at last, taking the water from her hands and setting it on the glass-topped coffee table beside yet another dying houseplant, this one a geranium. "None of them have ever reacted like that."

"It...it wasn't the painting," she told him, though she knew it was.

"No?"

"No. I've just had a few rough nights. No sleep. And I skipped a couple of meals, and I guess it's probably catching up with me."

He nodded, but skepticism darkened his lake blue eyes. She'd better get used to the idea that lying to him was to be used only as a last resort. She got the feeling he could see through every fib she concocted.

He sat down beside her. His gaze went back to the painting on the wall. "Have you ever seen it before, Brigit?"

Her throat went dry at his question. That insight again. But it couldn't possibly be *that* sharp. "I don't think so."

God, why would he ask that? And what was he doing with this piece of her childhood?

"It's incredible, though," she said, trying to keep the emotions out of her voice. "Who is the artist?"

He shrugged. "It's anonymous. See, way down near the base, where the water ripples? There's a word there. The dealer at the Capricorn thought it was the artist's signature. But I disagree."

Brigit tilted her head and looked for the word. When she saw it, her heart tripped over itself.

Rush.

"What..." Her voice emerged as a croak. She reached for the

water for another sip to clear her throat, then tried again. "What do you think it means?"

"I think it's the title of the piece," he said slowly, softly, not taking his eyes from the work. "I think it's the name of that place. Rush."

"How do you—" She blurted half the question, jerking her head around to face him. Then she bit her lip, stopping herself from asking how he could know the name of that place. The answer was simple enough. He must have heard or read the fairy tale, too. And so had this anonymous artist.

She felt an acute sense of disappointment. All this time, she'd honestly believed that story was hers and hers alone. Or that if it hadn't been created by a fairy princess for her twin daughters, maybe Sister Mary Agnes had made it up for one lonely orphan. It took away the magic, knowing it had been an ordinary fairy tale that hundreds or thousands of others had shared.

She closed her eyes to prevent him from seeing the way the revelation hurt her.

"It touches me," he told her. "Did from the first time I saw it hanging in the gallery downtown. I wouldn't trade it for anything."

That brought her gaze back to him. And if there was guilt in her eyes before she lowered them again, it was no wonder. A tidal wave of the stuff had risen up to engulf her at those words. He wouldn't trade it for the world. But he was going to trade it. For a fake.

"You feel better now? Strong enough to continue the tour?"

She met his eyes again. "I don't need the tour," she told him. "The place is wonderful, Adam. If you'll have me, I'd like to move in."

He smiled, and she thought it was genuine. "When?"
"Tonight."

CHAPTER 10

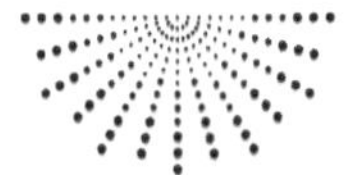

"I'm in," Brigit said into the landline phone to the criminal on the other end.

"Well, now, that *was* fast," Zaslow replied. "You're better at this than I thought you'd be."

"I'm not sure I can succeed at this." She kept her tone firm and calm. Men like Zaslow preyed on weakness, so she must not show any. "It's more complex than anything I've tried before."

"You'll do it, Brigit. You don't have a choice."

There was a pause, tension, as her breath rushed in and out a little faster than before. "I need to know more," she said at last. "Who is this client? Why does he want—"

"No sense asking, Brigit. I don't have the answers either. You just do your part and don't worry about the rest."

"Adam Reid is an intelligent man. He's going to catch on."

"You'll just have to see to it he doesn't. *Distract* him, Brigit. Come on. Use your imagination."

"You're a pig!"

His reply was low, vile laughter.

"I want to talk to Raze." Her voice emerged choked and raspy, no longer assertive or sure.

"Then I suggest you get the job done."

There was a click and then silence. Brigit swore and slammed the receiver home.

Adam didn't hang up until the other two had. He drew his brows together in a frown, and wondered just what on earth he'd got himself into. This woman who looked like his fondest fantasy was conspiring against him. Plotting with someone else...to do what? He couldn't even begin to guess. Hell, if they were planning to con him out of his fortune, they were almost a year too late. Sandra had seen to it that there wasn't anything left worth stealing. And it was a sign of his own hardened heart, he supposed, that he missed his wealth more than he missed her. Hell, no wonder she'd left him.

Brigit was up to something, though, and he had an instinctive feeling in his gut that she posed far greater danger to him than his wife ever had. And it was too late to back out now, whatever it was. Brigit had arrived later that same night with three large suitcases and a bulky garment bag. He wondered why she was in such a damned hurry to get under his roof, and what the hell she was planning to try to pull on him. He'd find out. He'd find out if it was the last thing he ever did.

Easy to say, now, he thought. With her in his ex-wife's bedroom, out of his sight. But when he *was* near her and she started working him over with those eyes of hers, his common sense seemed to go on vacation. It was because of her likeness to the woman in the painting, who'd become the center of his obsession, he realized. He had to find a way to get past that. He had to get a handle on his rampant interest in her. Distance himself. Find out who she really was and why she'd nearly fainted when she'd seen the painting. She must know something about it. She had to. It was the only rational explanation. If it killed him, he would find out what. And while he was at it, he'd find out what she was after.

To do that, he realized, he'd have to spend time with her, and do so without falling under her spell. Away from her, he was sharp and objective and insightful. Near her, he became a helpless puppet, incapable of thinking beyond the moment. The beauty in her eyes. The shape of her mouth. The satin curls of her raven hair.

Adam closed his eyes and banished the apparition from his mind. God, he'd conjured her image with no more than a thought. And there he'd been again, hit by what felt like a mortal blow from the sheer force of her presence.

This kind of attraction just wasn't natural. But it was understandable. He rationalized that it was only because of this long-time obsession. Only because he saw her as its center, its essence. If she were a green-eyed blonde, he told himself, he'd feel nothing.

He stared for a long moment at the telephone on his nightstand. And finally, with a sigh, he gave up trying to untangle the reality of the conspirator in the next bedroom, and the fantasy woman who'd haunted his soul for nearly all his life. He needed to stop thinking about all of this, just let it go. His head throbbed and his nerves stood on their quivering ends. He wasn't thinking about newly translated texts, or tomorrow's class, or his tenure, or his finances. He wasn't thinking about the approaching winter and the need to have the heating system replaced, or the ominous clunk in the aging Boxster's transmission. He was only thinking about Brigit Malone.

Impulsively, he turned to the French doors. With the darkness outside and the lights on within, their smooth glass became a mirror. He could see nothing outside. Only the perfect reflection of his own, gloomy bedroom. And the image of a man in abject—if inexplicable—misery.

As if in an act of defiance, he cranked both handles and threw the doors open wide. Autumn's chill had taken a respite today. Tonight, even the breeze had died away. The night air lay oppressive and silent over the world, heavy as a woolen blanket. Humidity smothered him as he stepped out onto the wrought-iron deck he'd built along the entire length of the house's back side. From there, he could look out over the lake. Usually there would be a refreshing breeze waiting to greet him.

Tonight there was only a humid, sweaty hand. Invisible. Holding him in its fist until he could barely draw a breath. Enfolding him the way his obsession did.

Adam stared out at the dark water, seeing no movement. Only able to make out the crooked-finger shape of Mystic Lake by the darker shade of the water compared to the land around it. He turned toward the south, so he faced the forested hillside. Its shape swelled toward the sky, and he remembered playing there as a child. He remembered what he'd seen there, where he'd gone.

Someplace that had shaken his world to its fragile core. Someplace that had twisted his insides up so much he hadn't dared go back. Not in almost thirty years. And part of him, way down deep, knew that he hadn't stayed away out of fear of his father's brutal reprisals. He could have explored those woods again after the bastard had abandoned them. There had been time before the new owners had tossed Adam and his mother out of their home. And more time after Adam had bought the place back again. But he hadn't. Because he knew, somewhere inside him, that he was terrified of what he might find out there. He'd never been sure whether his mind could handle going into that forest again, and seeing the magical doorway that led to another world, an enchanted realm. And he was equally unsure he could handle not seeing it, as little sense as that made. That, perhaps, was the basis for his obsession to find the source of his fantasy. The fact that he'd never been able to fully convince himself it hadn't been real. Oh, he pretended to believe that. But the doubt still lingered.

Blinking, bringing his focus back, he looked at where he stood. He'd stopped walking right outside Brigit's bedroom. The French doors that matched the ones in his own, stood right in front of him. Closed, but bare. Sandra had kept all her bedroom windows uncovered. No need for drapes or blinds, she'd insisted. This was the second floor, after all, and only the lake lay beyond the glass, and far below. There was no way anyone, even if they were on a boat, could see inside.

He wished now that he'd had the windows covered after Sandra had taken off. It had never seemed important, somehow. At least, not until this very moment.

He closed his eyes, opened them again. It didn't work. Brigit was still there. Pacing the bedroom like a caged lioness, tear tracks scalded into her cheeks, lashes still damp. She hugged herself, as if to ward off a chill, though Adam belatedly remembered he'd forgotten to turn the central air back on in her room. It must be stifling in there.

She wore the clothes she'd been wearing earlier. Convervative black skirt almost to her knees. A shimmery green blouse, tucked into it, and a narrow black belt around her tiny waist. The belt buckle was a golden sun with wavy rays sticking out all the way around. Her earrings matched. And her hair was pulled into a knot at the back of her head, though the heat and humidity had coaxed several curls loose. Even her glasses were still firmly in place.

The only other difference was that she'd taken off her shoes. She paced, in black-stockinged feet.

The double doors, bare as they were, gave him a wide-angle view of the entire bedroom. He saw open suitcases on the darkly stained four-poster bed. Draped across one of them was a length of vanilla satin with two spaghetti straps, her nightgown.

She paced in a repetitive pattern, then broke it, and walked through the open door into the bathroom. He heard the water splashing into the bathtub. And in spite of himself, he took a few more steps. Steps that brought him to the arched bathroom window. He could see the water spewing full force from the faucets, foaming as it hit the shell-shaped tub. He wondered briefly why the window wasn't coated in steam. Then she stepped into his line of vision, and he only wondered how the hell he was going to make himself turn around and walk away.

Hot. The place was hot and humid. Heavy, thick air. Didn't the man have air conditioning in a house this size? She hadn't noticed this sticky heat downstairs. Then again she hadn't remained down there long. Unable to look him in the eye, because of the guilt she knew he would see in hers.

Besides, she'd been in a hurry to get the big garment bag out of his sight. With his piercing eyes, she could almost believe he could see right through it to the canvases that were hidden inside. The ones that were the exact size and shape of the painting downstairs in his study. The painting he'd said he wouldn't trade for the world, of an image that was sacred to her. The one she was going to steal from him.

She felt sick to her stomach, and lowered her head until her chin touched her chest.

If I survive this, I'll kill that bastard Zaslow!

Brigit blinked in shock at the potent anger in that voice from within. The voice of her other self. The wild one. She quelled it quickly, because the anger she heard in it frightened her. No. She wouldn't kill him. She was a sensible, civilized woman. She wouldn't *kill* anyone. She'd just do what she had to do, and find some way to go on.

God, she was so worried about Raze. She'd wanted to talk to him, to hear his voice. Zaslow could have allowed it. He was being deliberately cruel, and enjoying it. Either that, or...or he'd done something to Raze. Hurt him so badly he was unable to talk...or killed him.

Tears spilled from her eyes again at that thought, but she pressed the back of one hand to her lips to keep from sobbing, and rapidly blinked the tears away. She couldn't afford to think that way. Not now, not here, with Adam Reid's sharp gaze always probing for secrets and lies. And finding them.

Now...now she needed a cool bath...and rest. She needed rest. Her wits were already dulled from lack of sleep. She'd need to be sharp if she hoped to fool Adam.

She wondered if now that she'd met him, he'd still appear in her dreams at night. Those erotic dreams woven by the wanton inside her. Brigit lost control of the wild child when she was sleeping. And her control during the hours of wakefulness would be sorely tested, she thought, now that she was living under Adam's roof. Even now, she felt a ripple of desire for him flitting up and down her nerve endings. She hoped the spell of those dreams would be broken now that she'd met the real man. But somehow, she doubted it. If she had those kinds of dreams about Adam Reid tonight, she wasn't sure she could get up and look him in the eye tomorrow morning.

Brigit brushed her fingertips across her damp forehead, pushed sweat-soaked tendrils of hair off her skin. She lifted one hand to begin unbuttoning her blouse as she walked into the bathroom to check on the cool bath she was running. The tub was like an ivory seashell, with little steps cut into one side. No curtain around it. No frosted glass doors. It was open, and she squirmed a little at the idea of feeling so exposed as she bathed. The one inside disagreed. *She* found the idea tantalizing.

Brigit wished *she* would go back to sleep and stay there.

Still, she supposed it would be all right. There was only one arched, floor-to-ceiling window in there, and nothing but the lake beyond it. She could see nothing outside now, of course, but by daylight, or if she turned off the lights, she'd be able to see the incredible view from the comfort of the tub. She could almost envision some purely sexual creature soaking in that shell of a tub, like a pearl. Sipping champagne and staring out at the lake and the hills and the greenery. The blue sky above. From way up here on high. Queen of all she surveys, Brigit thought.

And oddly, she thought of the painting again. Of the woman bathing in the midst of all that natural beauty.

Brigit glanced at the tub, and thought she should have settled for a quick shower.

Oh, go on! Who's going to know?

That one inside her was yearning to try a little decadence on for size. And Brigit was tempted to let her. She'd never lived in a place like this...never had the chance to feel such luxury. She went back to the bedroom for a vial of essential vanilla oil. And while she was there, she removed her glasses, and placed them carefully on the bedside stand. A little more of the wild one's impishness possessed her as she hurried back to the bathroom and poured a generous amount of oil into the cool water. Impulsively, she leaned over the tub to inhale its fragrance.

This was not what he'd had in mind when he'd decided to come out onto the balcony. Nor when he'd decided he ought to keep a close eye on her. She was doing nothing more suspicious than running a bath, and he ought to leave.

Right now. He ought to leave.

He didn't, because there seemed to be some kind of magic at

work. He watched her as she shook her hair loose. The first time he'd seen it down, wild and untamed, since that day in the classroom. Her glasses were gone now, too. And—and she'd somehow lost the appearance of the staid plant shop owner. He realized with a little jolt of surprise that his instincts about her had been right on target. The primness had been an illusion. He saw that now, in the simple way she ran her fingers through that mane of hair, arching her back and tipping her chin up. She was a creature of pure sensuality. She was desire in a physical form. Venus. And the transformation seemed to come from within her.

Her back was toward him as she slid the green silk blouse from her shoulders and let it fall to the floor. And why had he somehow known her skin would look luminous? Satiny? That the curve of her spine would be perfect and enticing, beckoning him closer?

Her hands moved around to the front, and a second later, she was pushing the skirt away. Stripping away the vestiges of civilized woman she'd been wearing. Pushing the skirt down over her hips, letting it pool around her feet. Standing there in a forest-green slip with black lace trim. Further evidence of the woman she was pretending so hard not to be. And the black stockings she wore only came to mid-thigh.

She lifted one leg, propping her foot on the edge of the tub, and she pressed her hands to her thigh. Adam shuddered with a primal twinge. Those small, efficient hands rolled the stocking down all the way to her ankle, then worked it off her petite foot and dropped it carelessly on the floor.

Sweat broke out on Adam's forehead. His breathing was deep, ragged. He told himself to look away, to leave this deck right now, before it was too late. But he couldn't do it. It was almost as if some spell was keeping him there, as if she'd truly mesmerized him, cementing his feet to the spot, refusing to release the hold her body had on his eyes. His physical self refused to obey his mind's commands. In fact, his body refused to do anything at all, except respond to the slow revelation of hers.

By the time she'd removed the other stocking, he was aching.

But it wasn't over yet. Not yet. Because her hand came up, and pushed the thin strap down from her shoulder.

She bent over to shut off the water, then lower, swishing one hand through it.

He choked out a hoarse, involuntary curse and she lifted her face toward the window, startled as if maybe she'd heard him or sensed him out there. Her silver necklace winked and glimmered from between her breasts, and the pewter fairy that embraced the diamond-like quartz crystal took on a new degree of sensuality. One he would remember whenever he saw it from now on.

He stood motionless on the other side of the glass. And though he knew she couldn't see him with the light on inside and the pitch darkness without, he got the feeling that she knew he was there. Sensed his presence somehow.

Or did she?

She quickly peeled the slip over her head, and he turned away immediately, but not before he'd glimpsed a small red mark on her lower abdomen.

The spell broken along with his line of sight, Adam finally convinced himself to walk away.

At breakfast, she was once again the reserved woman he'd first known. She wore a loose-fitting crinkle dress of deep blue, with yellow stars dotting it. She'd belted it at the waist with a braided yellow belt, and there were tiny golden suns and cradle moons hanging from the belt, moving when she did. And, of course, that necklace hung around her neck. He'd come to the conclusion that she never took it off, and he wondered why.

Her hair was in a tight French braid all the way down to the middle of her back, again, and her round wire rims were perched over those mystical eyes. She was hiding. This was her facade. He knew the real woman. He'd seen her last night. But he'd known her even before then. He'd met her almost thirty years ago.

Full beautiful, a faery's child.
Her hair was long, her foot was light
And her eyes were wild.

"Sleep well?" he asked, silencing the poet in his brain.

She lifted her gaze from her clean coffee cup beside her place setting to meet his. "Fine, thank you. Although...I thought I heard something on the deck outside my room."

He crooked a brow at her. "Really?"

"Probably an animal."

A barb...meant to stick him. No doubt about it, she had known he was out there last night. Why not just say so, then? Why not call him on it?

Because she had to stay here in order to pull off whatever con she was working up to. And if she admitted that she knew, then she'd have to leave, wouldn't she? No self-respecting woman would stay. It was easier to play word games, to throw missiles and see if they hit any targets.

Well, he wasn't rising to her bait. He'd turned away at the crucial moment.

"I'll take a look around out there tonight before you go to sleep, if it will make you feel better."

Her round eyes met his, wider than ever. She said nothing. He almost got lost in her eyes, but caught himself in time, and averted his gaze. Distance, he reminded himself. Objectivity.

"Coffee?"

"Just hot water." She pulled a tea bag from a deep pocket and dropped it into her cup. He went to the kitchen, returned with the pot he'd heated just in case, and poured steaming water into her cup for her. Then he sat back down.

The space between them wasn't empty. There was something there, something alive and crackling and hot. He could feel it, and he was sure she could as well.

"I have classes most of the day," he said. "I won't be back until tonight."

"Oh. Well, I won't see you, then. I don't close Akasha until eleven."

He nodded, wondering what she'd do while he was gone today. Wondering if he should even leave.

"What...do you want done? You know...to the house."

He shrugged. "If you can manage to keep the rooms I use every day in something close to livable conditions, I'll be happy. I don't expect you to do the whole house. The service sends someone once a month to do the major cleaning."

She didn't seem satisfied with the answer. She sat there, dipping her tea bag in synchronized movements that started to work on him as surely as a hypnotist's pocket watch.

He cleared his throat, jerked his eyes away from her hand, stopped fantasizing about how it would feel running softly over his skin. "You can clean up the breakfast mess, I suppose. You remember where the kitchen is?"

"Yes."

"And if you get a chance, you can straighten my bedroom."

Again her head snapped up and her eyes sparked. "Where—"

"Right next to yours, Brigit." He enjoyed her surprise, and allowed himself a smile of triumph. "The room you're sleeping in belonged to my wife. She made sure it was the nicest one in the house. I thought you'd like it."

"I do." She lowered her gaze, sipped her tea. Then she frowned and met his eyes again. "What happened to her?"

The words that formed in his mind were *none of your damned business*. But the ones that fell from his lips were different ones. "Last I heard, she was in Saint Tropez."

Her gaze flickered, but held his by sheer force. An invisible force. One that made him answer questions he had no intention of answering.

"She left you?"

He only nodded, telling himself to finish his coffee, to break eye contact so he could regain some control.

"I'm sorry," she said so softly he almost believed her. "That must have hurt."

It had hurt. It had torn him apart. Not that Sandra would have had any way of telling. He was an expert at keeping his feelings to himself. And it wasn't so much losing *her* that had given him all that pain. It was the loss itself. The feeling of being stabbed in the back by someone he'd been foolish enough to care for, to trust, yet again.

Hell, he should have known better. Wouldn't happen again, though. He'd finally got the point.

"Adam?"

He looked up, having lost the thread of the conversation.

"Are you all right?" she asked him, as if she gave a damn.

Those eyes worked their magic, sucked him in. Damn, he wanted her. Maybe this whole thing wasn't such a great idea after all. The way she was looking at him, he could almost believe this mind-blowing desire might be mutual, and that made it even more potent. He stood abruptly. "I have to go."

Glancing through the glass that lined three walls of the breakfast nook to judge the weather, he yanked his suit jacket from the chair where he'd tossed it.

"It's going to be a beautiful day," she told him, reading his thoughts it seemed.

"Dark clouds on the horizon."

She shook her head. "The rain will hold off until tonight."

He frowned at her. "Amateur meteorologist?"

Her smile was quick and blinding. "Good guesser," she replied.

He shook his head, not returning her smile.

"Have a good day, Adam."

He stopped at the doorway that led out to the foyer, wondering at the odd tingle that had raced down the back of his neck at her words. The feeling of warmth, of... optimism... that seemed to sink through his pores. As if it was more than a wish.

Damn. He'd better try getting some more sleep tonight. "You, too," he muttered, and then he hurried away from the woman and her mysterious vibes. In the foyer, he took a moment to snatch his raincoat from the rack near the door, his way of thumbing his nose at her predictions, he figured. But before he left, he turned, looking back toward the room where he'd left her.

She was humming, her voice angelic, her tune, haunting and strange. His throat went dry. He reached for the doorknob, and just before he turned away again, his gaze fell on that fern at the base of the stairs.

He frowned hard. It was green this morning. Last night it had been brown and withered, but this morning it was green. Now what the hell was up with that?

CHAPTER 11

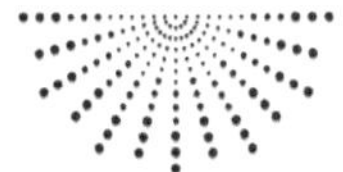

$\mathcal{I}$t was not pleasant, what she had to do. But she had no choice. She waited until she was sure Adam had left, until she heard the sound of his car driving away, and then she went up to the bedroom, lugging her equipment downstairs and through the double doors into the study. She spread a drop cloth on the floor, and set the tripod atop it. Then she stood the canvas up. She'd donned a smock for the occasion, and she pushed her sleeves back automatically. And then she stood poised, and still, and silent. She focused on the painting above the mantel. Not just with her eyes, but with her very soul. And she waited.

As always, it happened. Her hands chose a color, and squeezed a daub of it onto the palette. She didn't look at the tube of paint. Her gaze never wavered from the painting as she sought to cling to that state of soul-deep concentration she had to achieve in order to work. Without looking away, she grabbed another color, and squeezed it beside the first. She dipped her brush in one, and then the other, and then back again, and she rolled the bristles against the wood until she felt the mixture was just right. Her eyes still on the painting, she lifted her brush.

With the first stroke, she heard Sister Mary Agnes's voice, rustling like dried leaves in a wind, reading the fairy tale aloud as she had so often.

Once upon a time, not so very long ago, two princesses were born. No ordinary princesses, though. These babies were special. These babies were fay.

Brigit's lips automatically mouthed, "And that means fairy..." She tried to tune the memories out, to tune everything out. She needed to focus. But her hands continued wielding the brushes as if operating without her control, and the voice in her mind went on, skipping ahead.

Father Anthony found you and another tiny girl sleeping at the altar one morning. And each of you had a book just like this one.

It wasn't real, Brigit told herself. It was a fairy tale.

One with the name Brigit inside, and the other with the name of Bridin.

"And what happened to Bridin," Brigit allowed herself to whisper. "What happened to my sister?"

Ridiculous. It was a fairy tale, and there was no more to it than that. A story Sister Mary Agnes had used to give her comfort. Why was she thinking about the nonexistent Bridin so much just then, anyway? While thoughts and questions about the mysterious twin popped into her mind every once in a while, and always had, lately she'd been besieged with them. It seemed Bridin, real or make-believe, was a constant presence in Brigit's mind these days. Why?

The painting. Something about the painting. God, it was all tangled up with her disjointed memories and that stupid fairy tale she was beginning to wish she'd never heard! Sister Mary Agnes should have known better than to fill a child's head with fantasy and tell her it was real. Didn't she realize how confusing it could be?

Her hands moved faster, brushstroke upon brushstroke

coating the canvas. Her arms worked furiously, and a thin sheen of sweat coated her forehead.

Confusing? No, it was maddening! Brigit had never known exactly where to draw the line between the story and the facts of her own life. Had her mother really died, for example? And had her father only given her up when he, too, was about to lose his life? Had there ever really *been* a twin sister? Or was all of that just part of the fairy tale Sister Mary Agnes had passed on to her?

She hadn't let those questions surface with this much insistence in years, because they only brought frustration. Her files were sealed by the state. She would never know. Short of going to court over it, she didn't think there was much of a chance she'd ever know.

She blinked then, and her flying hands slowed a bit.

Maybe there *was* a way. Why hadn't she considered it before? Adam would know. He was an expert in fairy tales, wasn't he? He'd published books on the subject, taught classes at the university. He probably knew every fairy tale ever told. And she already knew he'd heard of hers. If he hadn't, he wouldn't have likened this painting to the Land of Rush. Where else would he have got the notion that Rush was the name of a place and not a person? The fact was, he'd probably read accounts of the fairy tale she'd always thought of as hers alone. And he would *know.* He could probably even tell her its origins and point out hidden symbolism in the words. But most importantly, he would know whether the twin sister was, indeed, just a part of the story.

But how could she ask him? She certainly couldn't tell him the truth. That *she,* orphaned Brigit Malone, who'd taken the last name of a homeless old man because she hadn't had one of her own, had once believed herself to be the daughter of a fairy princess. He would laugh her right out of the house. And she couldn't show him the book. Not now. She'd already told him she'd never seen this painting before. If he saw the book, he'd know that was a lie. Though the illustration in her book and the painting on his wall held a few differences that she was only noticing now, they were also, obviously, the same.

She could ask him about the story, though. And since she was so bad at lying, she'd keep her version of things as close to the truth as possible. Without making him think she was totally insane, anyway.

She lowered her gaze from the painting on the wall to the canvas in front of her.

Perfect. She'd captured the background. The stunning blue of the sky and the silvery shapes of castle towers in the distance, hazy and unfocused. So a viewer might wonder if they were real, or just shapes in the clouds.

The world in the painting was a magical place. A place that couldn't exist, except in the vivid world of imagination. The artist's. And Sister Mary Agnes's. And even her own.

A shame...such a shame...a place like that couldn't be real.

"'And when she looks into your eyes, sir, you're helpless to disagree. A man will grant her every wish, answer her every query, for his will melts under the power of her stare.'"

Adam closed the book and sat at his desk, staring down at the leather binding. If he didn't know better, he'd swear the author was describing Brigit Malone. The woman who'd taken up residence in his house... and more importantly, in his mind.

He shouldn't be thinking about her. Okay, he should be, but he should be thinking about what she was up to, rather than the astonishing allure of her petite limbs and the lightness and grace of her every movement. The spirals of hair curling against petal-soft skin. Those eyes. Those breasts. That glittering pendant dangling in between.

Adam groaned under his breath. What he ought to be

thinking about was the little detour he'd taken on his way in to work this morning. The one that went past her house out on Sycamore. It had been a simple thing to look up her address on the net. Simpler yet, to punch it into his GPS and take a drive by the place.

There was no sign of any construction going on in the neat white cottage. No sign at all. But that shouldn't have surprised him. He'd known she was lying about that from the second the words had left her succulent lips.

He pulled his car onto the roadside, and went to the front door. Breaking and entering would have been the last thing Adam Reid would consider doing under normal circumstances. However, things were far from normal between him and his houseguest. He had to know about her. He couldn't help himself.

First he knocked, just to be sure no one was home. And then he peered through the window, cupping his hands on either side of his face to block the morning sun.

Guilt twisted in his belly. He spotted ordinary things, modest furniture and a small television. But then he saw the other things. The telltale signs. The brown leather work shoes on the mat beside the door. Size eleven or so, he figured. The flannel shirt, big enough to fit two her. The man's CPO jacket on the coat rack.

He didn't walk off the porch, he staggered from it. And only when he'd stood braced against the Porsche, gasping for air, had he noticed the damned mailbox. "R & B Malone"

A man. She lived with a freaking man. And they shared the same last name.

Dammit.

Hours later, he was still swearing as he sat at his desk. He wondered if R Malone was the same man he'd heard her talking with on the phone last night. Or the one she'd asked about. Raze. She's asked to talk to Raze. He pictured a biker type, all tattoos and piercings. Who the hell called themselves Raze anyway? How the hell had he let himself fall into this? He was tangled up with a married woman. And he was so obessed with her he couldn't think straight. She had some kind of hold over his mind. Maybe it was deliberate, all part of whatever scheme she was hatching. He didn't know. Until now, he'd thought he could let her stay until he found out.

Now though, he wasn't so sure. He had a feeling the best thing to do would be to go home, right now, and throw her out.

Home. Yeah. He'd had a plan when he'd left there this morning. He'd intended to be back by noon, but he'd lied to her, deliberately told her he'd be gone all day long when he'd had every intention of arriving early, surprising her. Catching her red-handed...

Doing what, he wondered? Somehow, lifting the silver seemed beneath her.

Anyway, his well-laid plans had gone to hell when the dean had Sneichowski called a staff meeting, and made it a priority. Adam had no choice but to attend. His job was too damned important to him to rock the boat. It and his ever shrinking quarterly royalty payments were the sum total of his income these days.

Brigit put away her paints, cleaned her brushes, and carried the canvas upstairs to hide it in the back of the huge closet again. She'd cleared a space so it could stand there freely, propped on a stand and able to dry without smudging. She'd opened the windows in his study, found the A.C. controls and turned them on full blast in both rooms, to blow away the smell of paints. She left them that way while she speed cleaned the house.

But when she came to his bedroom, she hesitated at the idea of going inside. The idea was so disturbing... Why?

She told herself that a little housekeeping was the least she could do to make up for what she was going to take from him. Then she stiffened her spine and walked down the broad hallway, past her own room, looking down over the gleaming hardwood railing on the right, into the study below. Her gaze lingered on the painting for a moment. She turned at Adam's bedroom door, put her hand on the knob, and walked in.

And then she became lost in sensations. Because his scent lingered there. Subtle. But there. Surrounding her, touching her skin.

The rumpled bed drew her gaze, and she moved toward it, unable to stop herself. She put her hands on the wrinkled sheets that bore the imprint of his body, and imagined she could still feel his warmth there. That bed, with its covers flung back, looked incredibly inviting.

She stopped herself from crawling into it. Barely. It took longer than it should have taken for Brigit to realize what was happening. That wanton inside was in the driver's seat, running the show, acting out her fantasies. Whispering how delicious it would feel to strip to the skin and slide between the sheets that had so recently been wrapped around Adam's flesh.

Brigit put an end to that at once. She pushed that other one into her cell and closed the door. And then she efficiently made Adam's bed, refusing to pay any attention to the images of him in it, of the two of them in it together, that kept whispering through her mind.

When the job was finished, she turned away, relieved. Her hands trembled. Her breaths came unsteadily. Her heart raced.

Swallowing hard, she bent to pick up his discarded robe. But as she did, she saw a fat book under his bed. And that made her pause.

Brigit stood very still, staring at the book. She knew she shouldn't look at it. She shouldn't. But something drove her, probably the irreverent imp that lived in her soul, and she folded the robe to her chest with one arm, and reached for that book with the other.

An album, she saw as she tugged it out. A photo album. She sank onto the bed, folding her legs underneath her, and she pulled the album into her lap. His terry robe ended up slung over one shoulder as she opened the cover and began studying photographs. Family photographs. And she knew instinctively that this album hadn't belonged to Adam. It had belonged to his parents. There were baby pictures, dozens of them. And she knew by the golden hair and intense purple-blue eyes—those wizard's eyes—that they were of him. And later, school pictures. Year by year, she saw Adam grow. There was his kindergarten class photo. He stood proudly in the front row, beside a little girl with lopsided pigtails, and he must have been fighting that day, because he had a hell of a shiner.

And on the next page, a similar shot, this one of a cluster of first-graders. And again, he was easy to spot, because of the big, purple bruise high on one cheekbone.

Something broke inside Brigit as she continued turning pages. Something ached and cried, and an anger was born. She flipped the pages faster, and her throat closed off. Adam's handsome young face appeared bruised in too many of these pictures. Here a shadow on his jaw. There a split lip. Here a tiny line of stitches in his forehead. In one there was a cast on his arm.

Confusion knitted her brow, as she examined every page, until she knew the faces of Adam's parents. And curiously, the bruises stopped showing up in Adam's photos at about the same time his father stopped appearing in any of them. The last half of the book was filled with photos of a teenage Adam, and then a young adult.And many of the shots were of him with his mother. At his graduation from high school. From college. No bruises. No father.

The explanation was obvious. Tears burning her eyes, she

tipped her head to one side until her cheek rubbed against the terry robe on her shoulder. She inhaled, to smell him in the fabric. This was the source of all the pain and anger she saw in his eyes. This was the wound that wouldn't heal.

She could heal it. She knew she could, if he'd let her. Only...she'd have to injure him again before she finished, wouldn't she?

"You enjoying yourself?"

She'd been looking forward to seeing him again, so she could ask about her fairy tale. Only now, that was the farthest thing from her mind. She didn't want to see him at all. Not like this. There was anger in his voice and blazing from his eyes when her head snapped up and she faced him. But she understood that anger now. She knew about his old hurt.

And there really wasn't a thing she could do about it, was there? No. Not when she'd come here to hurt him just a little bit more.

She closed the album, slid it back under the bed, and slowly stood up. "I'm sorry," she told him. And she thought he must know it didn't apply to her snooping.

She held his gaze, lifting one hand to swipe the tear from her cheek. The anger in his eyes flickered, lost power.

"You told me you were going to open up the shop today," he said. "Why didn't you?"

"I... got distracted."

"I can see that."

"That's not what I meant." She cast around for a plausible reason she didn't go in today. "The construction people called, and there were problems to be sorted out. Decisions I had to make." The lies were not flowing smoothly, and his skeptical, piercing stare wasn't making it any easier. "By the time I got everything sorted out with them, I just didn't feel up to much of anything."

~

Liar! he wanted to shout at her.

But that wasn't all. There was more than her lies happening here. He'd expected to catch her up to no good when he'd come home. What he'd found, instead, had almost put him on his knees. She'd been curled up on his bed, absently rubbing his bathrobe against her cheek, occasionally turning her nose to the fabric and inhaling, closing her eyes. She'd been crying. Staring down at something in that old album that had been under the bed since before his mother had died and crying in silence.

Why?

She was lying, dammit. Lying about everything. Married. He'd come here with every intention of telling her to leave. Go back to good old Raze, whoever the hell he was, and stay out of his life forever. So why wasn't he?

She stepped closer to him. Closer still. And he just stood there, watching, waiting. She stopped when her body was so close to his there was barely space between them. He felt her heat, and more. A sort of tingling that seemed to crackle from her flesh to his. As if she couldn't help herself, she lifted one hand. When her fingertips touched his cheekbone, he sucked in a breath. But he didn't move. Her touch traveled over his face until her fingers skimmed the tiny scar on his forehead. And then she pressed her palms to either side of his head, tilted it downward and stood on tiptoe to press her lips to the very same spot.

She released him then and hurried from his room. He heard her car start up seconds later. And then it roared away, down the drive, fading in the distance.

What in the name of God was going on with her?

Frowning, Adam wondered just what there was in that old photo album that had got to her so much. And though his family history was something he tended to avoid like the plague, he reached for the album now, flipped it open, and scanned the pages, trying to see the photos through Brigit's eyes.

And then it hit him. The bruises. The way she'd touched his face, kissed that scar on his forehead.

Ah, hell, she knew.

He heard her car pull in hours later. Hard not to, as noisy as it was. A tide of relief washed over him, that he'd chosen the perfect time to be away from the house. He was sitting on the cliffs, telling himself that he shouldn't be so mortified she'd learned about his secret. Hell, it didn't make him less of a man, did it? He'd have fought back, if he'd been older. He'd have probably killed the old bastard.

It was the thought of her sympathy he couldn't stand. He'd rather have her take him for whatever meager assets he still had, than to call her scheme on account of pity. He couldn't handle that.

Nor could he look into her eyes knowing she'd seen those photos. Not yet, anyway. So, like a coward, he'd come out here to hide from her. He sat staring down at the roiling waters of the lake, waiting for the storm she'd predicted to move in. She'd been right about that.

So in tune is she with nature, that even the weather cannot hide its face from her seeking eyes. Whatever she wishes to know is eventually revealed to her. Such is the nature of the fairies.

He shook his head at the nonsense playing through it. Passages from that Celtic text. He'd been reading it too much. Determined for some reason to get through every page of it as soon as possible.

As if it was anything but another tale to add to the collection.

"Adam?"

He didn't turn, just went stiff at the sound of her voice. "How did you know I was out here?" If she gave him some mystical answer about *just knowing* he was going to scream.

"I looked for you in the study. Saw you through the windows."

"Ah."

"I came out here to apologize for going through your album before. That was wrong. I'm sorry."

He said nothing, but a second later she was sitting beside him on the flat stone ledge that jutted out over the lake's rocky shore. "The view from here is incredible."

He turned to look at her, then. Surprisingly enough, there was no pity in her eyes. No hint of the secret she'd discovered. "On that shore, there are rental cabins. You can see them clearly in the winter, against the snow, they're almost invisible now." She looked where he was pointing. "And then over there, where it gets really steep, there's another cabin, a bigger one with no road anywhere near it."

"Wow. Talk about the ultimate privacy." The incoming wind whipped tendrils of her hair loose. He wanted to undo the braid that held those raven locks captive. He wanted to pull her glasses off and set them aside so he could really look into her eyes.

"There's a storm coming," she said, turning her face into the wind. And almost as if she'd read his thoughts, she took off her glasses and set them down.

"I know."

She nodded.

"She hated storms," he said, and it was as if the words just jumped from his tongue without permission.

"Your wife?"

He met her eyes, wondered how she saw things even he didn't see. "Yeah."

"Has it been...very long?"

Why was it, he wondered, that whenever he spent time with Brigit, he wound up answering questions he'd have been furious with anyone else for even asking? "Almost a year since she walked out. Along with my best friend, and most of my money. One big happy family." He continued staring out at the white-caps, and the foaming lake. "I was a very rich man once. Not anymore."

"This place of yours is worth more than a million fortunes."

He hadn't looked at it that way. Not in a long time.

"Still, it's no wonder you're bitter."

"Not bitter...just a little poorer. And a lot wiser."

"Wiser? In what way?"

"I know better than to trust again," he said, and he knew she would disagree. She needed him to trust again, didn't she? She needed him to trust her, if she was going to pull off whatever it was she was planning.

"That's a hard line to hold... and a lonely way to live."

"Lonely is better than used, Brigit. Besides, who the hell is there to trust? Who do you suggest I start with? You?"

She met his eyes, held them steady. "No. Not me."

He studied her face. So perfectly lovely. So open and honest. So damn deceiving. Sitting there in the purple twilight with the wind in her face, telling him not to trust her. What the hell was it about her, anyway, that drew him so much?

She tilted her head and tried to read his face. Her eyes raced over it as if over the lines of a book. "I get the feeling this cynicism of yours started long before your wife left you, though. I think it started a long time ago. In your childhood."

He lowered his chin to his chest. So she wasn't going to let it go after all. "The only thing I learned in my childhood, Brigit, was not to believe in fairy tales."

She laughed, but it was a sad sound.

"What's funny?"

She reached up to tuck a loose lock of hair back into place, and he caught his own hand lifting, reaching out, as if to stop her. Or maybe to unbraid all the rest and run his fingers through it and watch the wind shake it loose. He stopped himself in the nick of time.

"Not funny, ironic. Fairy tales were the only thing I *did* believe in." The wind blew a little more of her hair loose. "I wonder which is worse," she said softly. "Believing so strongly and having the fantasy shattered? Or never having the chance to believe at all?"

She reached up to push the hair into place again, and this time he covered her hand with his own, stopping her. She turned her head, met his eyes. So much pain there. He had to know. He had to.

"Tell me," he heard himself whisper, and the sound of the words was swallowed up by the wind, but he knew she heard them all the same. "Tell me what you believed in so strongly. I really want to know."

She lowered her head. "If you'll talk to me about what you learned not to believe in," she replied.

Watching the way her lips moved nearly did him in. But he blinked and gave his head a shake. "I don't talk about that," he told her. "Not to anyone, Brigit. Don't ask me to."

"Do you talk about your father, Adam? Do you talk about what he did to you?"

He wanted to look away, and he couldn't. "No," he said. "Because it doesn't matter anymore."

"He hurt you. He's still hurting you. That matters."

"Not to me, it doesn't."

"To me, then."

He closed his eyes to block out the sincerity in hers. He wasn't going to talk to her about this. He wasn't. He...

"You know, they say abused kids can grow up to be abusers."

"Yes," she said softly. "I've heard that."

"But not necessarily, you know?"

"Of course not. Lots of abused kids grow up to be wonderful parents."

"You know why?" Why? Good question, he thought. Why am I blurting my most secret feelings to this woman? This stranger? And yet his mouth kept right on moving. "Because they know what a little kid longs for in his heart. They know how bad it is for a kid to go without the one thing he craves. All it takes to put a kid in bliss is for his parents to love him. It's so damned simple. How is it some parents can't see that?"

Her hand covered his where it rested on the stone. It was warm and small.

"Maybe they're blind."

"When I have a son, I'm gonna love him with everything I've got." He opened his eyes, saw her staring at him, and saw her tears. "Don't pity me."

"I'm not. I'm jealous of you."

He lifted his brows.

"You'll be a wonderful father someday, Adam," she told him. "Your children will be lucky, and beautiful, and your family, deliriously happy. I envy that. I really do."

No pity. No poor baby routine. Maybe it was okay that he'd opened up to her a little bit. Even if it had felt involuntary. Just being around had him spewing his life story on command. What was wrong with him?

She'd throw his weakness right back in his face someday. She'd find a way to use his feelings against him. He'd forgotten her lies for a few minutes, hadn't he?

"I don't want to talk about me anymore," he said, looking away from her. Maybe if he didn't look into her eyes he could keep his mouth shut for five minutes.

"All right."

His relief was intense. If she'd insisted, he'd have probably gone on with the conversation and tell her every secret he had.

She was still looking at him. Involuntarily he looked back and found her searching his eyes. He looked into hers and found he couldn't stay angry over her nosiness.

Her eyes were too potent. He managed to fixate on her mouth instead, and soon couldn't stop thinking about kissing them.

She was spinning some kind of magic, damn her. And he was caught like a fly. "Tell me about the fairy tales you believed in."

She smiled very slightly, not smugly. Maybe it was more of a self-conscious smile. "I wanted to tell you anyway. So that maybe, you could tell me where the story came from. There are parts of it… parts that are important for me to understand."

"I will, if I can." Anything, he thought vaguely. Dark clouds skittered over the half moon, making shadows on her face, and the wind coming off the lake, whipped more of her hair loose. It reached for him, caressing his cheeks like loving fingers. Right then, he was afraid he'd do anything she asked of him.

She leaned back, hands flat on the ground behind her, and her legs stretched out in front, one crossed over the other at her ankle. She wore no stockings tonight. Her lean legs were bare and smooth and tempting him to touch. He realized she was barefoot. And he thought about kissing her all the way from her toes to her lips.

God, she was beautiful. Like an angel. Or something else ethereal and elusive and mysterious. Something you could glimpse and observe and long for, but too precious ever to hold.

But he wanted to hold her. He wanted it so much he couldn't look away. He was mesmerized by her eyes and the musical quality to her pure voice.

Her eyes focused on the roiling lake. But her gaze was turned inward as she began, "Once upon a time…"

CHAPTER 12

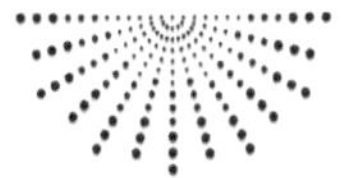

"Where the hell did you hear that story?"

The harsh tone of his voice startled her, and she snapped back to the present, out of the past that had been swamping her mind as she recited the fairy tale from memory. "I told you. It's just a story I heard when I was..."

"It's just the one story I've been searching for my entire career. My entire life." He wasn't raising his voice just to be heard over the wind. He was angry. "Just a story I've never been able to find, Brigit."

"But—"

"Once more, where did you hear it?"

His face was hard. Granite lines and angles and shadows. And the wind came in stronger than before, whipping his hair into chaos. Roiling storm clouds obliterated the moon's glow, now. But they were nothing compared to the ones raging in his eyes.

"An old nun called Sister Mary Agnes told me that story on the nights when I was too afraid or too lonely to sleep. I used to think it was true. That I was really..." She let her voice trail off, shaking her head slowly at the expression he wore. "You don't believe me."

He said nothing, just got up as the first raindrops plunked and smattered the flat stone under his feet.

"Come inside, Brigit. You'll get soaked."

"But, Adam, you've heard that story before. I know you have. You knew about the forest of Rush."

"What?"

He seemed so alarmed that she blinked in surprise. "You said you thought 'Rush' was the name of the forest in the painting. Adam, that's why I assumed you'd heard my fairy tale."

"*Your* fairy tale?"

She lowered her head. "Well, I used to think it was mine. First I thought it was about me, and then later I thought someone, probably Sister, had made it up just for me. I only now realize that can't have been true. You know the story. So does the artist who created your painting."

She looked up at him, standing above her, staring down at her with an expression that combined so many emotions she couldn't name them all. Disbelief. Confusion. Rage. Suspicion.

"Adam, I don't know what you suspect me of here. I only told you about the story because I wanted to know if the version you'd heard included the twin daughters."

His eyebrows bent into question marks. "I'm damned if I'm going to stand out here in the rain and discuss something I know is impossible. That the only person I've met who knows the story I've spent my whole career trying to find just happens to be renting a room in my home by coincidence?"

"It's not a lie. But maybe it's not coincidence either." The rain fell harder. "Adam, that fairy tale was the most important thing in my life for a long time. I clung to it when I had nothing else. I've been looking for its source my whole life, too. So maybe fate threw us together. Or maybe the story did. I don't know.

But if you know anything about it, about where it comes from, you have to tell me."

He stared at her, and she felt his eyes probing her soul. Felt his doubts. And something else...

"The only thing I know about it, Brigit, is that it doesn't exist."

She got to her feet, leaning close as the wind came in harder, off the lake. "If you heard the story, and the artist heard the story, I heard the story, and Sister Mary Agnes heard the story, then how can you say it doesn't exist?"

"I *didn't* hear the damned story! I—" He pushed a hand through his damp hair. "I'm going inside."

She closed her eyes, refusing to watch him go. Dammit, she'd been worried he would see through the lies she was being forced to tell. Instead, he was seeing lies when she told the truth. Why was he so sure her fairy tale didn't exist? What kind of cruel joke was this, anyway? He knew the story, but claimed he'd never heard of it? And what had he meant when he'd told her it was the story he'd been searching for all his life?

What did any of this matter? She'd let herself get distracted. She was here to do a job, not to find answers to the mysteries of her birth and history. Not to find out, once and for all, if she might really, truly have a sister.

She closed her eyes, released a long, slow, shuddery breath, and with it, a bit of her tension. The rain was cool and heavy and she stood still, letting it soak her clothes and hair. It didn't matter that she didn't know who she was or where she came from, or what she was supposed to be doing with her life. It didn't matter.

She shouldn't be asking anything from Adam Reid, anyway. Not when she was about to steal from him. Let him go inside. She'd stay outside. And maybe the rain would cleanse her guilty conscience. She tipped her face up to the droplets, felt them cooling her heated skin. And she couldn't stop the tears of shame from falling from her eyes, but they mingled with the rain and were hidden.

This was too far-fetched to be for real. Now, more than ever, he knew that Brigit Malone was lying. Trying to convince him she held the answer to his childhood delusions. Trying to make him believe she'd heard the tale...that he'd finally found the source for those fantasies that had nearly got him beat to death by his own...

Not nearly beat to death. It was a few broken ribs. A half-dozen stitches in the back of the head. Kids get hurt worse than that playing baseball or riding their bikes.

He hadn't been playing baseball or riding his bike, though. He'd been in second grade. He remembered thinking that if this was love, he wanted no part of it. And he'd held that lesson in his heart, ever since. Love and pain were one and the same in his scarred mind. And whether it made practical sense or not, he'd learned the lesson too well to ever forget it.

Adam stood at the bank of windows in his study, and he stared out to the stone ledge. She was still out there. Had been for hours. He'd turned out all the lights so he could see her in the darkness and the rain. The yellow stars and moons on her dress made it a little easier to spot her.

She'd remained as she'd been, standing there and letting the rain pummel her body. He'd had to come inside. God, she'd been so alluring, lying beside him on that cool rock protrusion, with her eyes closed and her dress getting wet. All he could think about was lowering his body on top of hers and kissing the rainwater from her skin...

Not about the lies she was telling or the reasons behind them. She couldn't have heard the story when she was a kid.

Why not? I apparently did.

Only he didn't remember it as a story. He thought he'd actually gone there. Seen that place called Rush, firsthand. Talked to a pregnant fairy named Maire, for God's sake. And seen a little girl—*a faery's child*—bathing in a magic lake before she'd even been born. And she'd looked into his eyes.

So what are the odds of Brigit making up a name like that? What's the likelihood she'd come up with the same name I dreamed?

But he hadn't gone there. It *had* been a dream, instigated by a tale he must have heard... but one he couldn't have heard, because he'd searched the world over for it, and he'd never found it.

Brigit must know about his dream. She must know details. How, though? He'd never told anyone. Except his old man, who'd beat the hell out of him for it.

There was no conceivable reason for Brigit to deceive him this way. And even if she somehow knew all the details of his childhood delusion, and was making up all this about having heard the story of Rush herself, there was one thing she couldn't fake. Couldn't lie about. Her likeness to the woman in his fantasy. The woman he'd been told was his fate. The woman who was supposed to break his heart, because he had to let her go in the end.

In a dream, he reminded himself. Only in a dream. He turned to stare at the painting, at those glittering sapphire eyes.

An old doubt came whispering through his mind like a cold, bracing wind. *It wasn't a dream, Adam. And it wasn't a delusion. It was real, and deep down inside, you know it. No other explanation makes sense.*

A shiver worked up his spine. The practical part of his mind dismissed that whimsical voice, ignored it, but his heart couldn't do the same. What if it was true? What if his experience hadn't been a fantasy? And what if Brigit was really...

His gaze returned to the ledge outside. She stood with her

arms stretched out to her sides, head tipped back to the rain. And she turned in an excruciatingly slow circle.

She is a faery's childe, and her joy is the rain. From it she draws comfort.

Quit thinking in terms of that damned Celtic text!

But he couldn't stop thinking of it, because she was the embodiment of all it described. Damn, could she really be...

Finally she stopped turning, let her arms fall to her sides, and turned to walk along the path, and out of his line of vision. She was coming back to the house.

Maybe, he reasoned, as he built a fire in the fireplace and tried to convince himself it was for his own benefit, not hers, maybe there really were more things in heaven and earth than were dreamt of in his philosophy. Maybe.

So either she was telling the truth, and had no more idea than he, where the story had come from. Or she was lying in a deliberate attempt to perpetrate some complex scam.

Or maybe all of this was real. Part of him wanted to play with that theory, examine it and dwell on it. But most of him rebelled. He wouldn't let himself linger in those long-forbidden areas of his mind, realms he'd deemed off-limits, like the woods where it had all begun. But it kept coming back to him, teasing his brain the same way sounds on rooftops on Christmas Eve teased children's minds the world over. The notion dared his imagination to explore it.

She'd told him a tale of Rush. And in it, a fairy princess named Maire, pronounced May-ruh, had twin daughters. Brigit and Bridin. She'd asked him about that part of the tale, whether it was included in any versions he might have heard. Why? The only logical answer was that she, Brigit, believed she might *be* the Brigit in the story. And that somewhere, she had a twin sister named Bridin.

If that were true, then the pregnant Maire he'd dreamt of

had shown him a vision of her own soon-to-be-born daughter. And told him she was to be his fate.

He blinked, recalling that fairy lady's words to him when he'd been a little boy. "She needs you to show her the way...the way to her sister, and then show her the way back home."

He gave his head a shake to silence that bell-like voice he remembered so well, but it went right on. "You mustn't let yourself fall in love with her. She'll break your heart if you do."

A cold chill crept into his nape, and he shivered. As he passed the geranium on the end table, he paused, doing a double take. The plant's leaves were vivid green.

His stomach knotted a little. Just yesterday the plant had been withered and brown. He remembered the way she'd paused beside it, rubbed her fingers over the drying leaves.

Brigit, his mind whispered. *She must be...*

"She must be the owner of a nursery on the Commons, stupid," he said aloud. "She must be applying her talents to save my pathetic house-plants. And that's all."

But overnight?

Tomorrow, he decided, dropping to his knees in front of the hearth and adding larger bits of wood, he would do some further research on Brigit Malone.

He woke to screams so harsh and so frantic they made his heart freeze in his chest. And then he smelled the smoke.

"Oh, shit!"

He dove out of bed in his shorts, and took only the briefest second to feel his bedroom door for heat before flinging it open, lunging into the hall, and leaning over the railing, automatically checking the fireplace. He immediately saw what was wrong, and his entire body sagged in relief. There was no fire. Something had plugged the flue. Smoke billowed from a smoldering log on the grate and floated upstairs. Brigit had stopped screaming, so she must realize now that there was no danger.

He took the stairs two at a time, and used the brass pail and the matching shovel to scoop the offending log out. Smoke spiraled off the charred lump. He rapidly shoveled up a few other smoke-belching embers, and added them to the pail, then carried the mess outside, into the rain, and dumped it right into the first puddle of water he came to.

He left the front door open, and opened all the windows in the study before going back upstairs again. And then he tapped on Brigit's door, wanting to check on her before going back to bed.

There was no answer.

Frowning, Adam pushed the door open and stepped inside. But she wasn't in the bed. He flicked the light on, and then crossed the floor to open the French doors, and allow fresh air in to cleanse the room's slightly smoky air. And that's when he saw her.

She sat on the floor in the corner, knees drawn to her chest, eyes wide but, he thought, unseeing. She was pale and trembling, and tears had burned tracks into her cheeks. She clutched a book to her chest with white knuckled hands. And she wore only that vanilla satin nightgown. One of the thin straps had fallen from her shoulder, and the way her knees were bent, the bottom of it was bunched up around her hips. She looked, he thought sadly, like a frightened little girl. And that was what did him in.

A shiver ran up Adam's spine at the fear in her eyes. He'd never seen anything so desolate in her before. She always seemed so vibrant, so full of life. But right now, her eyes were vacant. Dead.

He crouched in front of her, his hands automatically closing on her shoulders. "Brigit? Hey... come on, talk to me." He shook her a little. "Brigit?"

Her eyes seemed to focus on him. But her breathing was still ragged and too fast.

"It's all right," he told her. "There's no fire. Just smoke. The chimney was plugged. It's no big deal."

She closed her eyes, released a shuddering sigh. "I was so scared..."

"It's all right." He sank to the floor beside her. It was a good spot. The night breeze rapidly filled the room with rain-washed air that swept through, whisking the smoke back outside with it before blasting more fresh air in.

She pressed close to his side, her head on his shoulder. "Sister Ruth told us to hold hands," she whispered. "But I let go. I went back...for Sister Mary Agnes."

A cold chill raced up his spine as she whispered the words, and he wasn't sure she knew who she was talking to. He put his arms around her to stop her shivering, but it didn't work.

"B-but I couldn't find her," she said. "There was so much smoke...and then the flames..."

"There's no fire, Brigit. You're safe." He clasped her nape, turned her head so he could look into her eyes. They were still closed so tight it was as if she was fighting not to see something. But he had a feeling she was seeing it anyway. "Open your eyes, Brigit. Dammit, look at me. There's no fire, you understand?"

Her eyes opened, but he wasn't sure if it was in response to his command or to her own nightmares. They opened wide. Too wide.

"I couldn't get out! I couldn't breathe!"

A lump came into his throat, one so big he nearly choked on it. This was no dream. No nightmare. This was a memory.

"You're safe now," he told her. He took her hands, pressed her palms to his own face. "Look at me, will you? It's Adam. There's no fire. You're safe, Brigit."

She blinked several times. "Adam..." She sat up a little straighter, searching his eyes, then she covered her face with her palms and muttered, "Oh, God, oh, God." Her entire body shook with the force of her sobs. She drew her knees to her chest, wrapped her arms around them, and she rocked back and forth.

There was the slightest hesitation on Adam's part. Slight...as his wariness kicked in to analyze her behavior. Real trauma, or clever ploy?

No. She wasn't acting. Whatever was happening to her, or had happened to her, was real. And like it or not, it was tearing his heart out to see her like this.

He got to his feet, bent over and picked her up. He lowered her onto her bed. She rolled to one side, her back to him, and curled herself into a little ball. She reminded him of the woolly bear caterpillars he used to search for as a child. The way they'd curl themselves up when he touched them. An act of self-preservation. She trembled, and every few seconds a sob racked her body. She still clutched that book to her breast, whatever it was.

Adam swallowed hard. He looked at the door, even then knowing he couldn't leave her. Not like this. He whispered a prayer to St. Francis of Assisi, and then he laid down on the bed beside her. He snagged a handful of covers, pulled them up to cover them both.

It was right. He knew it was a second later, when a sob choked her, and she turned to him. She curled up against him, burying her face in his chest, pressing so close it was as if she'd like to crawl inside him. As if she'd like to hide there, from her memories.

And dammit, he knew that feeling all too well. He had a few memories of his own that could put him in a similar state. And he couldn't turn away from another person who'd had a childhood full of nightmares. He couldn't do it.

He wrapped her up in his arms and he held her. The rigidness left his shoulders and his spine. He stopped grinding his teeth. This was right. This was where he needed to be. There was nothing more important in the world he could be doing than comforting her right then. So he stopped fighting it and let his instincts have free rein. He stroked her hair, and rubbed her back, and squeezed her tighter. He whispered that it was all right, that she was safe, that he wasn't going anywhere.

Her trembling body relaxed in his arms. Her face lay tight to his unclothed chest. He felt her hot tears there, and her warm breath. He felt her quivering lips each time she parted them on a sob. The scent of her hair and that of her tears mingled to create a bittersweet perfume he would remember always. Her skin slid beneath his hands like silk.

He kept it up until she cried herself to sleep.

And then he wondered what demon had possessed him to end up in bed with this woman. Was he so far gone that, even knowing she lied with every breath, he was still this...this...?

Enchanted.

Yeah, that was the word for it, all right. If he didn't know better, he'd think he was under an enchantment.

And maybe that's exactly what it was. And maybe it was about time he remind himself that if all of this really *was* true, if his childhood fantasy really *had* happened, and if Brigit Malone truly *was* the little girl he'd been shown... then lying here, holding her this way, was the stupidest thing he could do. Because it made him want more, and it made his heart go soft when it had been a solid lump of granite for such a long time. And he couldn't let himself care for her. He couldn't.

Because if this fairy tale was true, he already knew the ending. And it wasn't going to be happily ever after.

He lay awake, bathed in her warmth and her nearness, telling himself to leave her alone and holding her tight in his arms, for the rest of the night.

～

"Adam...?"

Brigit lifted her head from the firm, warm, male cushion beneath it, and realized it was Adam's naked chest. Her first impulse was to return her head to that wonderful pillow, after trailing her lips over it to see how it would taste.

Fortunately, she came a little more fully awake before giving in to that impulse.

"Oh," she whispered, and then, more softly, "oh."

His eyes were open, clear, and focused on her face with a mingling of concern and awareness. "Yeah. You can say that again."

They were incredibly dark this morning, his changeable eyes. Like the needles of a blue spruce on a cloudy day.

She remembered last night. The smell of smoke, the waking nightmare. And Adam, coming to her, holding her and making it all disappear. Her eyes widened as she thought of her book. The *Fairytale*. But a quick glance confirmed she'd tucked it back under her pillow as she did every night. She sighed and sat up, then belatedly clutched the blanket to her chest. Her choice of sleeping attire hadn't been exactly modest.

"Too late, Brigit. I already have intimate knowledge of that nightie."

She lowered her eyes, feeling her cheeks burn.

"Don't be embarrassed. You look beautiful in it."

"This shouldn't have happened." She spoke quickly, softly, keeping her eyes averted.

"Nothing *happened*, Brigit."

"I slept in your arms."

"Yeah. And I was warm until you moved away. Now I'm freezing." He flung back the covers and surged to his feet, heading toward the wide-open French doors. She couldn't take her eyes from his scantily clad body...those hair-smattered thighs, hard as tree trunks, that small, compact butt covered only by a thin pair of boxers. The broad, smooth width of his shoulders. The way his golden hair touched his nape. The way it curled slightly there. The way she wanted to touch it.

He closed the French doors, and turned to face her. And the color of his eyes turned darker still. They took on a gleam she hadn't seen before. He took a step toward the bed.

"I... I'm sorry," she said softly. "About last night."

"Don't be." He took another step.

She met his gaze, held it, and very slightly, she shook her head. "I can't..."

He stopped in his tracks, blinking as if snapping out of some trance state. He lowered his chin to his chest, blew all the air from his lungs.

Then he came the rest of the way to the bed and sank onto the foot of it. No longer the predator. She wasn't afraid of him now.

"Tell me something, Brigit," he said, and he ran two hands back and forth through his hair roughly, as if it would somehow invigorate him. All it did was make the hair stick up like feathers, which made her long to smooth it down again. "How old were you when you got trapped in that fire?"

She closed her eyes. He knew it was real and not a dream. There was no use denying it. She already knew he could see right through her lies. So she opened her eyes again and met his. "Eight or nine."

"My God." He lifted his brows then, not asking, just waiting.

"It was an orphanage. St. Mary's, in New York. Sister Mary Agnes...she was the one who used to tell me the story...she died that night."

He was searching her face. For what, she wondered?

"But you got out."

She nodded. "A homeless man who spent most of his time in the park across the street came into that hell and carried me out."

"No kidding?"

"No kidding," she whispered. And as she did, she thought of Raze, and all he'd done for her. She adored him. There was nothing in this world she wouldn't do to keep him safe.

And unfortunately, that included betraying the man who sat in his underwear on the foot of her bed, staring into her eyes as if he were seeing her for the first time.

Adam had left her in the bed. He still wasn't sure how he'd worked up the will to do that, but he had. She'd been lying there looking sleepy and vulnerable, and very much like she'd rather he stayed.

Right. And she'd told him things, things she'd been holding back before. And now maybe he had a jumping-off point. He had to know everything about her. He had to find a way to determine once and for all if there was even the slightest possibility she was...what he suspected she was. God, he couldn't even complete the thought without feeling ridiculous.

But he had to know the truth. Before she destroyed him. Because if that was her goal, intentional or not, Adam was sorely afraid she was going to succeed.

Funny how a woman he was afraid would destroy him could manage to heal him while he awaited the killing blow. Because that's what she was doing. He'd realized it that morning. It was the damnedest thing. She seemed to have the same effect on his heart that she had on his houseplants.

Pure, impossible magic.

Facts. He needed facts.

He sat in a booth at Hal's Deli right now, across from the man who could get them for him.

"Don't worry about the money, Adam. Look, you paid me plenty for trying to track down that lousy wife of yours, even though I offered to do it as a favor, and even though I wasn't able to find her for you."

"Successful or not, you put a lot of time into tracing her, Mac. What kind of friend would let you do all that for nothing?"

"Yeah, well, I'm doing better now. The business is thriving. Anything you need, I'll do at no charge." He looked Adam in the eye, his expression intense. "I mean it. You offer me a dime, I'll blacken your eye. You're my best friend. Just tell me what you want."

Adam nodded, admitting defeat. "Thanks, Mac."

"So what's up?"

He sighed, feeling inexplicably guilty for what he was about to do. "She goes by the name of Brigit Malone," he said finally. "And she spent some time in an orphanage called St. Mary's, in New York. She mentioned that she might have a twin sister, but that she doesn't know for sure. There was a fire at St. Mary's while she was there. Burned the place to the ground. Now, she owns a shop on the Commons. Akasha. And that's just about every goddamn thing I know about her."

Except that she loves the rain. And that having her around seems to make dying houseplants thrive. And that her eyes...

He gave his head a shake. He also knew her address. And that she'd lied about the construction going on there. He gave Mac the former.

"But you'd like to know more?"

He nodded, and took another sip of the best coffee in the state of New York. "Yeah. Everything you can dig up, okay?"

"You got it, Adam. It would help if I could see her. Do you have a photo?"

"No." *But I have a painting.*

"Well, could you arrange for us to run into each other somewhere?"

"You could come to the house" Adam suggested, barely following the conversation. Why, when she was the one lying to him every time she opened her pretty mouth—probably—was he feeling guilty for asking a P.I. to check her out? Why?

"Oh, that'll work," Mac said. "Assuming she's brain dead."

Adam frowned, trying to get his mind on the matter at hand. "Hmm?"

"If she's plotting something, she'll have reason to be suspicious of me, Adam. And if she is, and she has something to hide, she might take measures to *keep* it hidden."

"Oh."

"So take her out somewhere. Some university function or other. There's always something going on, isn't there?"

"Yeah. There's always something."

"Adam, are you okay?"

He met the other man's eyes and nodded. "So far."

"If you're so sure she's lying to you, why the hell don't you just toss her out?"

He shook his head. "I can't. I can't explain it, Mac, but—"

"Don't put yourself through this again, pal."

He met his best friend's eyes. The concern he saw there was genuine. He wished he could tell Mac everything, but he knew he'd sound totally insane.

"Look," he said at last, changing the subject. "There's a thing tonight. Cocktail party for university alumni, to kick off a fund raiser. Starts at nine. Okay?"

Mac sighed, but shrugged in resignation. "Okay. Meanwhile, I'll see what I can find out about her."

"Thanks."

Mac slid out of the booth, apparently out of reasons to stay. He could be overprotective of his friends. It irritated some of them, but Adam saw it for what it was. Genuine caring. The guy felt things deep. Especially loyalty. His friends were lucky people.

Adam lingered after Mac had gone. He still had time left on his lunch break. Customers came and went, sat and ate, chatted and read their newspapers. But he wasn't seeing them. More and more, he saw only one face in his mind. A face far too innocent to belong to a liar. Maybe even too beautiful to belong to a mere mortal. If she'd lied her way into his life, then it was only because he'd let her. And he would let her remain, because he was so desperate to find out her true connection to the tale that seemed to have been a part of her childhood as much as his own. And *its* connection to the painting that hung over his mantel and haunted his thoughts.

He still had to know those things. But now...he had to know them before she managed to lie—or to enchant—her way right into his heart.

It scared the hell out of him to admit, she already had a pretty decent start.

The way it was going, she'd be finished within a day or two. Brigit was more careful when she carried the canvas up the stairs this time. She'd worked on it most of the day and barely given the paint any drying time at all before she'd had to move it. Dangerous, lugging a wet painting around like this. It could smudge or smear.

But it didn't. Not this time.

She heard a car out front, and looking down at her paint stained fingertips, she panicked. But then she narrowed her eyes, tilted her head, and listened closely. And she knew the sound wasn't coming from Adam's Porsche.

Wiping her hands with a soft rag, she continued down the curving staircase, hearing the doorbell now. She dropped the rag on a table as she passed and went to open the front door.

Zaslow stood there leering at her.

Brigit gasped. "What are you doing here?"

His smile was slow and deliberate. "Came to check on your

progress, Brigit. Wouldn't want to think you were pulling one over on me."

Brigit ignored him, her gaze shooting past him to where his car sat in the driveway.

"Raze isn't there. You think I'd be stupid enough to bring him along?"

"Where is he? Is he all right?"

"Relax, Brigit. He's fine. And as long as you do what you're told, he'll continue to be fine." His hands snatched hers without warning, and his grip was unnecessarily cruel as he lifted them, turned her palms up, and examined her fingers. She tried to pull free, but he was too strong. And he smiled at the paint stains still visible on her fingertips.

"Looks like you've been a good little forger, Brigit. How much longer?"

"Let go...dammit, Zaslow, you're hurting me. I said let go!" Her words were firm, and delivered as commands as she tried to twist her hands free of his grip.

He smiled fully, but the smile died a second later. A large hand came down on Zaslow's shoulder, jerking him backward, out of the doorway, so he stumbled on the stairs. He released his grip on her, more out of surprise, she thought, than anything else. She was surprised herself.

"Adam," Brigit breathed.

He didn't look at her. His eyes blazed with midnight-blue fire, and stayed riveted to Zaslow's. At some point, she wasn't certain when, he'd grabbed a handful of the other man's shirt, and held it now, bunched in his fists.

"When a lady tells you to let go," he said, his voice dangerously soft, "you let go. Got it?"

"You misunderstood, mister. Brigit and I are old friends..." Zaslow tried to wrest himself free. Adam finally let go, but did so with a little shove that sent Zaslow the rest of the way down the front steps.

Adam glanced her way, one brow lifted in question.

"Tell him, Brigit," Zaslow said, and she grimaced, ready to declare that the very sight of him made her skin crawl. But before she got a word out, he added, "Raze wouldn't want you to bad-mouth me. You know he wouldn't."

The fury that had been bubbling inside her froze, and slowly turned into fear. The bastard had her firmly in his control. She had to say and do exactly what he told her, or dear, sweet Raze would suffer for it. Damn Zaslow for using a helpless old man this way. Damn him for this!

She saw Adam watching her, saw his eyes narrow.

She lifted her chin, swallowed hard. "We're old friends," she confirmed with a slight nod. "Just had a disagreement."

"That's right. Just a little disagreement. But we've settled it now."

A muscle worked in Adam's jaw. He held her eyes captive, refusing to look away, merciless in his probing and searching. And there wasn't a doubt in her mind that he knew she was lying. For once, she was glad. She didn't want him to think she'd have anything this vile as a friend.

"Brigit doesn't need friends like you," he said, never turning to look at Zaslow, never taking his intense stare from her. "If you darken my door again, you'll have to be carried out of here."

Zaslow's icy eyes flared with anger and maybe a hint of fear. The way Adam delivered the threat left no doubt he meant every word of it, even without eye contact. And though Zaslow was the bigger of the two, Brigit found herself believing Adam could and would do exactly what he'd said.

Zaslow never answered, just turned and headed down the driveway, got into his car, and drove off, spitting gravel in his wake.

Brigit closed her eyes, her breath escaping her in a rush, her back bowing a little.

Adam came inside and closed the door. He stared down at

her. She could feel his intense gaze even before she opened her eyes.

"He's no friend, is he Brigit?"

"No."

"Lover, then? Or a former one?"

Her eyes flared wider. "No!"

Adam nodded thoughtfully, pursing his lips. "You called him...Zaslow?"

She only nodded.

"He has some kind of hold over you. That much is obvious."

She held his gaze, said nothing.

"But you don't want to tell me about it."

Drawing a long, deep breath to battle her constricting throat, she whispered, "Yes I do, Adam. I want that more than I've ever wanted anything, I think. But...I can't."

Adam frowned, searching her face, waiting.

"I'm sorry," she added, finally forced to lower her gaze from the power of his.

He was silent for a long moment, and she knew his eyes were still probing and searching her face. Finally, he sighed, and turned away. "Do you like parties, Brigit?"

Frowning, completely thrown by his change of topics, she looked up quickly, turning to stare after his retreating back. "Parties?"

"Boring faculty thing. Lots of pretentious donors and socially awkward intellectuals, sipping punch and yapping about their subjects to anyone who'll listen. A string quartet. Dancing." He turned around, sent her a wink and a sheepish smile. "Hell, it's free food, if nothing else. My attendance is pretty much required. It might be a little more bearable if you'd come with me."

She just stared at him, and she knew she must be gaping, but she couldn't move or speak,

"If you don't want to, that's—"

"No. I mean, yes, I want to." Oh, why had she said that? She should have stayed here. It would have given her more time to work on the painting. "When?"

He glanced at his watch. "Two hours."

She had a feeling she'd regret this. "I'll be ready."

"Good." He turned as if their conversation was over, resumed walking toward the study.

"Adam?"

He stopped, not turning around.

"Thanks...for not pushing me about...about Zaslow."

"Don't thank me, Brigit. That conversation isn't over yet." Then he walked into the study, closing the doors behind him.

He closed his eyes and told himself he was a hundred kinds of fool. He'd been shaking with anger. *Shaking* with it. It had taken every ounce of will he'd had in him to keep from knocking that bastard on his ass when he'd come in and seen the way he was manhandling Brigit.

Zaslow. She said his name was Zaslow.

It was ridiculous to feel so protective of her. Stupid, when she obviously knew the man, and when the man obviously knew things about her that she hadn't shared with Adam. Hell, he was a fool. For all he knew this Zaslow might be in on whatever plot Brigit was working here.

His instincts, though, balked at the notion that Brigit would willingly have anything to do with a lowlife like him. He obviously had something on her. Something powerful enough to make her lie for him. She'd been ready to spit venom when he'd claimed to be her friend. And then he'd said something cryptic. Adam bit his lip, trying to recall it exactly as Zaslow had said it. "Raze wouldn't want you to bad-mouth me."

So who was Raze? R. Malone? Her husband? What was

Zaslow's hold on Brigit? What was her true reason for being here, in Adam's house? And what did Zaslow have to do with it?

Damn, the longer he knew the woman, the more questions he had about her. No answers. Just more and more questions.

He was turning into a basket case. And in his rush to get to the house to see who the hell the stranger in the doorway was, he'd left his briefcase in the car. Yup. A basket case.

He left the study, headed through the foyer to the door. As he passed the marble-topped pedestal table at the base of the stairs, he glanced at the now-thriving houseplant there, wondering again at her green thumb—or was it fairy dust? Then he absently snatched the wadded rag from the stand's surface, thinking Brigit must have been dusting and forgot it.

He stopped, opening his hand and staring down at the soft bit of cloth on his palm. It was smeared with colors. Greens and blues and gray here and there. He lifted it to his face, sniffing.

Paint.

He frowned and sent a questioning gaze up the stairs, but Brigit was nowhere in sight.

Paint.

And a slime bag of a man holding something over her head, something deadly.

And knowledge of a forest that had existed only in his own imagination.

And the ability to make him forget all of it, just by looking into his eyes.

"Just what in the hell are you up to, Brigit Malone," Adam whispered, staring up the staircase she'd just ascended. "Just what in the hell am I going to do about you?"

CHAPTER 13

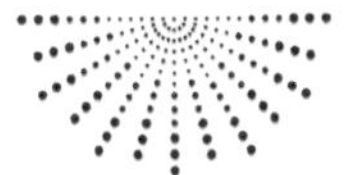

"Why did I say I'd go with him? Why, why, why?"

Brigit could have slapped herself for idiocy. She'd blurted her acceptance before giving it any thought. So here she was, going to a party, while poor Raze was God only knew where...afraid and alone...

Someone should knock her upside the head for her foolishness.

Deep down inside, she knew she couldn't have painted anymore tonight, anyway. Even if she'd stayed. She'd poured every ounce of...of...juice, for want of a better word...into the work today. She'd wielded those brushes until she was completely dry. She couldn't find another drop of whatever it was that made her able to reproduce perfect likenesses on canvas. Creative energy. Magic. She didn't really know what it was. But she'd tapped it to the bottom of her toes today, and there just wasn't any more. So she'd stopped.

There would be more *juice* tomorrow. She wasn't afraid there wouldn't be. But she still felt guilty for going to a party with Adam when Raze was in such dire straits.

Maybe because she was afraid she was going to enjoy it too much.

Too late now, though. She'd agreed, right or wrong. So she might as well make the best of it.

She wore a green skirt that was made up of countless long strips. Its tendrils reached to the middle of her shins, and rippled and swirled like leaves in the wind when she moved. And brown sandals. Her top was a forest-green with a scooped neck. And of course, her pewter fairy, caressing the glittering quartz point, hung around her neck.

She was sitting at the vanity, rebraiding her hair nice and tight, when she heard a soft tap, and then her bedroom door opened.

She met Adam's gaze in the mirror. His expression was speculative.

"Am I late?" she asked.

"Not yet. But you will be if you continue with the braid."

She turned around, but he was already coming forward. He stopped when he stood right behind her, and then he gently turned her face back to the mirror. His fingers dove into her half-done braid, and she felt them moving there, separating, smoothing. Part of her wanted to close her eyes and revel in the feeling of his hands in her hair. There was something so intimate about it. Another part wanted to pull away and rapidly bundle her hair back up.

He shook it loose, then bent to reach past her for the brush, without asking permission. He ran the brush through her hair, slowly, right from the top of her head, all the way down to the middle of her back where it ended. Over and over again. His free hand followed the path the brush took, and finally, she sighed, tipped her head forward and let her eyes fall closed.

The brushing stopped. And she felt her glasses being gently removed from her face.

Her eyes flew open. She came face to face with the wild little girl she'd been. Only she was a woman now. Sensual and impulsive.

She saw him in the mirror, standing behind her, staring at her as if he couldn't do otherwise. This man from her dreams with his honey-gold hair and wide-set, almond-shaped wizard's eyes. This man with the sadness in his cheeks giving him a haunted expression, even when he smiled. This man who moved her like no man ever had.

"Why do you hide?" he whispered.

She stiffened, her gaze shifting lower, skimming over his lips, drawn there by their movement when he spoke. She brought her eyes up to meet his again in the mirror. "I don't know what you mean."

"Yeah, you do." He held her gaze, and his was probing in search of secrets. "You're not this sophisticated, serious woman you pretend to be."

She swallowed, but her throat remained dry. "Why do you say that?"

"Because it's true. I see it right there, in those bottomless eyes of yours." He leaned a little closer, so his breath fanned her neck as he spoke, and his head was close beside hers.

Impulsively, she closed her eyes, fearing this man who could see all her secrets. "You're imagining things, Adam. There's nothing in my eyes except—"

"Fire." His voice had lowered. It was little more than a whisper now, but somehow more powerful than it had been before. "Your eyes damn near boil over with passion, some-times. Your skin...it just about simmers. I feel it when I'm close to you...like this."

He was close. Too close. And she did feel as if her skin was on fire. Her breathing quickened and her lips parted. The wild child inside grew stronger.

"I think, Brigit Malone, that deep down inside, you're a hellion."

Her eyes fell closed again. Her head tipped back of its own accord. Or maybe not. Maybe it was the hellion he'd seen so clearly controlling her movements now. Her hair slipped back, away from her shoulders, and she felt his warm breath on her neck. The fire burned hotter. His lips moved closer. She knew it without looking. And then his mouth touched her skin, and he had to feel the wild thudding of her pulse. He mouthed the skin of her neck as if tasting it, slowly parting and closing his lips again and again.

The power of her desire for him was beyond anything she'd ever known, and it left her trembling and weak with longing when he lifted his head. She lowered hers, meeting his gaze in the mirror again. Her eyes were heavy lidded, passion glazed.

His lazy smile did little to disguise the hunger in his own. "See? There's the real Brigit."

She shook her head in silent denial,

His hands came down to her shoulders, kneading gently. "It's true. I think you're just afraid of her."

"I'm not..." She blinked at the reflection of the two of them; the sight of his hands on her bare shoulders, those long fingers moving so slightly against her skin, brought the flames roaring back to life, and she couldn't suppress a small shiver. "Maybe...maybe I am, a little."

"It's okay," he said softly, as his fingers splayed over her flesh. "I am, too."

She turned a little to look up at him. "I'm not sure I believe that. It's hard to imagine you afraid of anything."

His gaze roamed her face. "Oh, I am. I'm afraid of you, Brigit." His hands rose, and his fingers moved slowly through her hair. "And I'm even more afraid that in another few seconds, I'm not going to be the least bit interested in going to this thing tonight."

She bit her lip, because she was rapidly losing interest in going out as well. "You said your attendance was required."

"It is."

She clasped his hands in hers, and pulled them gently from her hair, holding them, looking down at his long, slender fingers as they twined with hers. "Then we should go."

"If you insist." He closed his hands around hers and pulled her to her feet.

"I can't go like this." She glanced over her shoulder at the mirror once more, and ran a hand through her wild hair.

"Sure you can. In fact...I dare you."

"Y—you *dare* me?" It was difficult to speak when he was looking at her that way. The touch of those blue eyes on her skin was doing odd things to her pulse and her breathing all over again. All it took was a glance...at least, when he was looking at her the way he was looking at her then.

"Yeah. I dare you. What do you say?"

His words, his breaths, caressed her lips because they stood so close, and a brand new shiver worked through her. Only the slightest movement would bring their lips together. And God, what would *that* be like?

Forcing her gaze up, away from his mouth, she saw the mischief and the challenge in his eyes. It touched something inside her. Her own well of mischief, she supposed. And she smiled. "Let's go."

Adam was bored. His eyes had a glazed-over look about them as he stood, the obligatory glass in his hand, discussing admissions policies with a stuffy-looking man who was thirty pounds overweight. The place made Brigit feel inferior, to say the least. Educated, sophisticated types lingered everywhere. The very rich and the very literate. They sipped champagne from fluted glasses and spoke about politics and travel.

On a raised platform, a string quartet played classical music, and she couldn't begin to imagine anyone dancing to it. Dainty round tables stood at strategic points, laden with tiny and nearly inedible lumps that claimed to be hors d'oeuvres. Very nice to look at, but worthless as sustenance. There were bowls of nonalcoholic punch scattered here and there. Neon-colored stuff. Green, yellow, and blood red. Yum, she thought.

The women in the room represented the woman she'd always wanted to be. Sleek and polished. Not a hair out of place. Beautiful, smart, successful women who always knew what to say and what to do. How to act. Which fork to use. They were respected. They were admired.

Brigit felt more like the homeless, dirty-faced street kid she'd been than she had in a very long time. She stood rigid, back ramrod stiff, chin high, and she tried to pretend. Maybe, she thought, she could fool them. Maybe they wouldn't see the street brat beneath the facade. Maybe. If she was very careful and very quiet.

"Anything wrong?"

She glanced up at Adam, startled by his voice coming so close to her ear. The man he'd been talking with had wandered off, leaving them alone together in this crowd of glitter and wealth and intelligence.

She shook her head, looking down. "I don't fit in here, Adam. I shouldn't have come."

He smiled. It surprised and then shook her. He was so handsome when he smiled, and he looked incredible in his dark suit. It made his shoulders seem even broader, his waist narrower than before. He fit in here. He was born for this kind of gathering.

His hand closed around hers. "You're right. You don't fit in here. Everyone here is a phony, Brigit. Hiding behind a mask. Using either their money or their degrees to make up for their lack of character. Or even soul. Look around."

She did. He nodded toward a couple who stood near the ghoulish green punch. "Those two like their cocaine more than their money. They're probably high right now."

Her eyes widened, but he was already steering her gaze elsewhere. "And there's Jack. Alone tonight. Probably gave his wife a few bruises she couldn't hide with makeup."

"No."

"Yes. And the fat guy over in the corner?" He nodded in that direction. "He's only been out of prison for six months. Embezzling. And see that incredibly intelligent-looking woman by the stage? The one with the slicked-back hair and the glasses? She likes sleeping with her freshmen students."

Brigit gave her head a shake.

"And the guy who just went—"

"No. I don't want to hear any more."

"Okay. Point is, Brigit, they're just people. Good and bad in all of them. Brains and money don't make them any better than you."

He wouldn't think that if he knew the truth. That she was a thief. A forger. A woman out to steal, even from him. She lowered her chin to her chest in abject shame.

His forefinger caught it, lifted it, and his eyes probed hers in that way that made her tingle all over. "You're the most beautiful woman here tonight, Brigit. That's why they're all staring."

She shook her head in denial, felt her cheeks burn.

"You are."

"Adam? Aren't you going to introduce me?" The deep voice came from just behind her, and Brigit turned too fast, as if caught doing something she shouldn't, when in fact, all she'd been doing was drowning in Adam's eyes.

"Hello, Mac," Adam said, pumping the man's hand, and turning to Brigit. "Brigit Malone, meet Mackenzie Cordair. Mac, for short. He's an old friend of mine."

Brigit offered her hand and Mac took it. He smiled at her, but there was something in his eyes. Some questioning, searching kind of interest that made her uncomfortable. He wanted something. She could feel it.

"Good to meet you, Brigit," he said.

"Likewise." She narrowed her eyes, peering into his, seeing goodness and honor there. A strong sense of loyalty. No menace or evil. Then why this feeling? She felt he was a threat to her.

"I've heard a bit about you," Mac said, snatching a drink from a passing tray. "You're Adam's new boarder."

"Yes." She took a sip of her own drink, and its sweetness made her grimace. "And what do you do, Mr. Cordair?"

His brows went up as if the question had taken him by surprise. Adam cleared his throat, and Mac seemed to hesitate before he answered. "I'm a teacher, like Adam. Only, I teach over at the elementary school, instead of here at the university."

"How nice." He was not being honest with her. She didn't know what he was hiding, but there was something, and the knowledge scared her.

So find out what he's up to, the wild one inside whispered. *You know you can. Pick his pocket.*

She shouldn't, even though she knew she could. She'd mastered the art of lifting wallets before she'd turned eleven. Still, he was Adam's friend.

A friend who's lying through his teeth. Check him out, for heaven's sake. You're not going to steal, you're just going to look. Don't be such a wimp.

Her fingers inched nearer to his pocket, while she distracted the men by gesturing with her other hand and commenting on the music and the food. Inside, she felt the old excitement welling up. It had always been a challenge to try and a thrill to succeed. And damn, but that wild thing inside was getting a charge out of this.

The wallet practically fell into her hand, and she couldn't restrain her satisfied smile. She'd just check his ID, and then she'd know...

Adam was staring down into her eyes when she looked his way. Staring at her with a hunger that frightened her, and something else that looked a little like trust.

God, he couldn't let himself trust her. Not when she was about to steal from him.

Guilt swelled like a tidal wave, and overwhelmed her wariness of Mac Cordair and his motives. She bent over, straightened up again, and held out the wallet. "I think you dropped this."

Mac's eyes widened in shock, then narrowed on her. As if he knew full well he hadn't dropped the wallet.

The place was stifling all of a sudden, and that knowing look in Mac Cordair's eyes frightened her. She had to get out. "You two go ahead and catch up," she managed. "I'm going to find the powder room."

And before either of them could say another word, she turned and lost herself in the crowd. She didn't go to any powder room though. Instead she made her way to the nearest exit and slipped outside, into the parking lot. The fresh, night air on her face revitalized her, gave her a little more sanity and strength.

She leaned back against the cool wall of the building, staring up at the star-speckled sky and trying to shake the feeling of impending doom that had settled over her in there.

She heard the door open and swing slowly closed, and she knew it was Adam who'd come to join her.

"Will you promise not to laugh if I tell you something?" She said it without turning to look at him.

He came closer, stood beside her, one arm sliding around

her waist to draw her tight to his side. "I can't imagine I'd laugh at anything you had to tell me, Brigit. But yeah, I promise."

Biting her lower lip, she worked up her nerve. "I hate crowds. Mainly because... because I *know* things about people. When I look into their eyes, I can see..." She closed her eyes and simply blurted it. "I can see inside them. What they're feeling. Who they really are."

"You see inside them?"

She expected ridicule, but there was only confusion.

"Your friend, Mac, he wasn't being honest. I don't know why, because he seems like an honest man. But he was keeping something from us... or at least, from me."

She dared a peek up into Adam's eyes. He was looking at her as if she'd told him that pigs could fly. She lowered her face. "It's always been that way. I'm weird, Adam. I'm not like normal people. Never have been. I don't—"

"What do you see when you look into my eyes?"

Her head snapped up sharply. The question startled her.

"Tell me."

Oh, God, why had she confided in him like that? He couldn't possibly believe her. He was playing along now, because it amused him.

"Tell me," he said again, and she made the mistake of looking at him. Right into those dark sapphire eyes, with the occasional fleck of turquoise. So changeable.

Mesmerizing and so very sharp.

"I see goodness," she heard herself whisper, as if she couldn't help but answer him. "Under a mountain of anger and rage. A mountain built on pain. That's what I see most of in your eyes, Adam. A pain that never dies."

He blinked as if she'd slapped him.

"I want to make it better," she whispered. Her hand drifted upward, and her fingertips stroked his corded neck. And then she realized she'd spoken her thoughts aloud, and her eyes widened. She started to turn away, mortified, but he caught her shoulder, stopping her.

"I have a feeling," he whispered, "that you're only going to make it worse."

She closed her eyes, shook her head in denial, but knew he was right. And how on earth could he know that she'd hurt him in the end?

"Problem is, I don't have brains enough to let that bother me."

She noticed the change in the music, the way it suddenly grew louder as someone opened a window. Adam's arm crept around her waist and he drew her close to him. His fingers twined with hers, and he turned in a circle.

She put her hand on his shoulder and looked up at him in surprise. He just sighed and shook his head. "What the hell am I gonna do with you, Brigit Malone?"

She didn't answer. She couldn't, because being in his arms this way was too potent an experience not to rob her of her powers of speech. She clung to him, and they danced. And it seemed to Brigit that he held her a little closer, and then a little closer still.

The music wove a spell around her as magic as anything Akasha had to offer. By the time the song ended, her head was resting against Adam's chest. She could feel the pounding of his heart beating in perfect time. Her arms had curled around his neck, and he clasped her waist tightly, so their bodies were pressed together from hip to head. She felt him bend a little, felt his face pressing into her hair. She was in a dream, floating amid an ocean of stars. And no one existed, no crowd filled the room on the other side of the nearby door. She was alone in a glittering galaxy, wrapped in Adam's arms, and she'd be content to stay right there forever.

Someone cleared a throat, very loudly, and she felt Adam

stiffen. He stopped moving but she clung tighter, keeping her eyes closed and having no desire to leave his arms.

"The song's over, Brigit." He spoke near her ear, one hand stroking her hair. "From the way everyone seems to be emerging from the building and staring, I'd say the party is, too."

"Mmm." Then his words sank in, and her eyes flew open. She stepped away, looking around to see several pairs of eyes glued to the two of them. People made their way to their cars, gawking at the couple who'd still been dancing to music only they could hear.

"Can we leave now, Adam?" she whispered, head lowering.

"Damn right we can." His voice was coarse and a little choked.

He didn't know what the hell was happening. It was almost like magic. While he'd been dancing with Brigit, he'd lost track of where he was... of *who* he was, for God's sake. The music had died away. The ground beneath his feet had dissolved. He'd closed his eyes, but he'd still been able to see. He and Brigit had been floating, dancing and floating, in a midnight-blue sky that sparkled with diamond-like stars.

Not a feeling. Not a daydream. No way. It had felt as freaking real as...

As his trip to the forest of Rush when he'd been seven years old.

He didn't know what kind of spell she was weaving around him. He didn't know much of anything right then. Except that he wanted Brigit. He wanted her so much he was shaking with it. And it didn't matter that he had no idea who, or for that matter *what,* she really was or what she was up to or why she'd wormed her way into his life. He wanted her. She could be an ax murderer and he'd still want her.

And he'd tell her so, too. The second he got her home.

~

He was silent in the car, and that was okay. She was, too. And she supposed he might be lost in the impossible task of making sense of their momentary lapse back there at the university. Or maybe he hadn't lapsed at all. Maybe it was only her, and maybe he'd just been humoring her.

She'd always been able to tune out the world. To lose herself in her own magical place of twinkling stars and rainbow glimmers flashing sporadically. A place without gravity or sound or thought.

Usually, though, it was up to her to make it happen, to just close her eyes and focus on tranquility and peace, and to find that place. This time it had been spontaneous. It had happened as if on its own, without warning. Like magic.

Why?

God, for those few moments she hadn't even thought about Raze.

Adam shut the car off and she realized they were back at the house. Nerves made her throat narrow to the size of a piece of straw. It made her stomach into a small, hard chunk of ice. That dance had altered things. She'd revealed her innermost fantasies, her secret desires. She was sure she had.

Without a word, she shoved her door open and got out, heading for the front door more quickly than she should, ashamed of running from him without explaining herself, but too afraid to do anything about it.

Her sandaled feet made little tapping sounds on the steps, and she gripped the latch, only to yank in vain.

She let her head fall down until her eyes focused only on her own bare toes, and didn't even turn when he came up behind her, reached past her to insert his key in the lock. He twisted the key, then hesitated. His warm breath fanning her neck was almost more than she could bear.

She nearly collapsed in relief when he finally opened the door and stepped back. But instead she managed to remain standing. Even to walk into the house. And he stepped in behind her, closed the door, and said, "Are you really magic, Brigit? Is that what it is?"

His hands closed on her shoulders from behind, turning her slightly, and then he pointed. She looked up. The chandelier's crystal prisms were on fire, bathed in moonlight that slanted In through the wall of windows. They sparkled, throwing beams of gem-colored light like the storm god hurling lightning bolts. Flashes of red and green and gold bounced from the walls, danced on the floors, caught and blazed in the mirrors.

"It's never looked like this before," Adam whispered. And the tone of his voice was like a child's...filled with wonder. So she turned to see him, and a blaze of green painted his eyes. Both eyes, making them flash unnaturally. "A lot of things are like they've never been, since you came through that door."

She shook her head.

"It's true." His hands came up to cup her head, fingers spreading tingles of awareness over her nape and down her spine. "What is it about you that has my dying plants looking as if they could grow into an entire rain forest?" He searched her face, iris eyes still glowing, sparkling, catching and holding hers until she couldn't look away. "What is it about you Brigit...that makes me feel..."

She caught her breath as he drew her, gently, inexorably closer. Until he held her the way he'd been holding her when they'd danced.

"...makes me feel I'll wither and die unless I kiss you...right now."

He kept his eyes opened, kept her captive in their depths. One hand continued to cradle her head, but the other slid down, curled around her waist, and pulled her tighter. So tight she felt every ripple of muscle in his chest. And then his head came down and he kissed her.

His lips touched her mouth, tasted, testing, she thought. And she surrendered with a small sigh. Her entire body melted in his arms as she opened her mouth in gentle invitation. Sweet surrender.

And she knew she'd never be the same.

CHAPTER 14

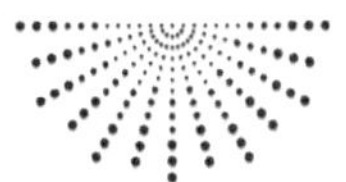

$\mathcal{H}$e was drowning. And the same sensation overcame him as before, when they'd danced. That almost out-of-body experience that she seemed to insti-gate. He wasn't here. There was no floor beneath his feet, no ceiling. The glimmering lights from the chandelier's prisms became palpable. Warm, pulsing as they painted his face. The focal point of his entire existence became Brigit. Her lips beneath his, her body in his arms. The soft sounds of surrender she made.

Every whisper-soft touch of her fingers in his hair was as powerful as a 220-volt shock. Every breath passing from her parted lips into his, carried the very essence of the woman he held. Every touch of his tongue as it pressed through the moist barrier brought a taste so sweet it was beyond description. Drugging. Addictive. So that he pressed deeper, seeking more. The very heat of her body was a song...music he could hear only in his soul. Blending and mingling with his own. He wanted to devour her!

When her knees seemed no longer able to support her, Adam bent and scooped her into his arms, never taking his mouth from hers. And somehow he moved through the glittering night that surrounded them, swimming through space thick with rainbow flashes that he could now hear as well as touch. And then he was lowering her to the floor he couldn't feel. Like a cloud under her back, and he was lying there with her, on top of her, kissing her because he couldn't seem to stop.

And she was kissing him back just as eagerly. Her arms twined around his neck and her hands threaded in his hair, and her body moved beneath his, rubbing against him, pressing closer. But still not close enough.

His hands slid beneath her hips, pulling her tighter to him, and he pressed his hips against her softness.

And all at once she twisted her face to the side, and their lips came apart. She was gasping for air, and her words came out desperate and hoarse.

"No more, Adam. We can't..."

Like ice water, those words.

Adam blinked rapidly, and as if the spell had suddenly been broken, the room came into focus. They were in the study, on the Oriental rug near the barren hearth. There was no music. And part of him thought that was because the music had been her...or the two of them, together. But that was foolishness. Fantasy. The flashing prisms had lost the supernatural glow— the one they'd never really had in the first place.

And he was lying on top of Brigit with one knee wedged between her legs, holding her so tight he was surprised she could breathe.

What the hell had happened to his brain? His mind? He'd never lost himself like this. It was only sex, for God's sake. He'd always thought about it ahead of time, planned a time when he wouldn't be interrupted or rushed, made sure he had a condom or two nearby.

It had never been desperate and mindless like that. On a floor! A floor. She must think he was some kind of animal.

He rolled off her, glanced at her face, expecting to see revulsion in her eyes. Maybe even fear.

But she wasn't looking at him. She was staring up at the painting that hung above the mantel. And she was crying.

"Brigit? What's... tell me I didn't hurt you."

She brought her gaze to his, levering herself up onto her elbows. "You didn't hurt me. I was as carried away as you were," she whispered, and there was pain in her voice that belied the words. He *had* hurt her. Not physically, though.

"Then why—"

She only shook her head, and he didn't have a clue what the hell to say to her. She got to her feet, turned toward the stairs. "You don't want to get tangled up with a woman like me, Adam. You really don't."

She was right. He knew she was right. He didn't *want* to get tangled up with her. It just didn't seem to Adam that he had much of a choice in the matter. He shook his head, pushing his hands through his hair in frustration. "Why don't you let me be the judge of that?" He rolled to his feet, came up behind her, and settled his hands on her shoulders. "I don't know what this is, Brigit, but it's powerful."

"It's madness."

He lowered his head, intent on kissing the crook of her neck, but she danced away before his lips could taste her skin again.

"I'll only hurt you, Adam. Destroy you, maybe. I don't want to do that, but if you touch me... if you kiss me once more... I might not be able to help myself."

And before he could reply, she ran from him, right up the stairs, and he heard her bedroom door slam.

Damn.

What was happening to cool, calm, analytical Adam Reid? The man who'd decided he wanted nothing more to do with conniving women? This one all but *admitted* she was up to no good. Told him not to trust her, promised she'd hurt him, destroy him, maybe. And what does he do but hunger for her all the more?

And how was it that her words of warning mirrored those spoken to him by Maire, that fairy he'd encountered as a child? Or imagined he'd encountered. God, the longer he knew Brigit, the more inclined he was to believe it was all true. And if it was true, she *had to* leave him.

And there was nothing he could do to prevent it. Hell, he was supposed to *help* her to leave him.

It would kill him.

No. No, he couldn't let this go on. No way. He had to get past this obsession with Brigit Malone. He had to find a way.

She'd always known she didn't fit in... always felt there was something different about her, something lacking.

She hadn't realized what it was until tonight. But now she suspected the reason for her oddness was the lack of a single shred of decency. If she hadn't been able to tell another thing about Adam, she knew these two facts. He was good. And he was hurt. Injured... perhaps beyond repair. Betrayed again and again by people he trusted. His father, his wife, his friend.

She was about to betray him, as well. She was going to steal his most precious possession. How could she let herself make matters worse by making love with him?

If the poor man fell for her, her guilt would be compounded.

It was bad enough, wasn't it... that she'd let herself begin to fall for him? To care for him?

The phone was ringing. It woke Adam from a fitful sleep filled with dreams of having wild, delicious, irresistible sex with

Brigit. He was damp with sweat and panting like an addict in need of a fix. Trembling. Gooseflesh crawling over his arms and thighs.

He snatched up the phone and growled hello in a voice that sounded barbaric and raw. Like his yearning for her.

"Adam? It's Mac. You all right?"

He cleared his throat but his voice wasn't a hell of a lot more civilized when it emerged. "Fine."

"Sounds like you've been wrestling a bear. Well, I have a shit load of information on your lady friend. Interesting stuff, too. You want to meet me?"

Adam sat up straighter. Information. On Brigit. Yes, that was what he needed. Maybe he could figure out what she wanted from him, other than to drive him out of his mind. "Just tell me. What did you find out?"

"On the phone?"

"Yes on the freaking phone! Talk, already!"

"Okay, okay. Damn, you wake up cranky, Reid."

Adam rolled to his feet, fumbling in the night-stand for a pad and pen in case he wanted to make a note. He heard Mac shuffling papers.

"I got most of this before last night, Adam, but I couldn't very well blurt it out right there in front of her."

"Go on."

"Before I start, there's something else."

"What?" Adam's patience was down to its ragged edges.

"I did not drop that wallet last night."

Adam frowned. "What the hell are you trying to say, Mac?"

There was a thoughtful pause. And then, "Nothing. Never mind. Listen, here's the rundown on your girlfriend. There was only one child by the name of Brigit who was at St. Mary's at the time of the big fire. Brigit Doe, they called her. Last name unknown. Mother unknown. No birth certificate was ever on file for her. None that was found, anyway."

"What, she just appeared at the shelter one day with no past, no story?" Adam was beginning to think his friend was doing shoddy work. Then again, who could blame him? He was working gratis, after all. And then he gave himself a mental kick for doubting Mac's integrity. Man, what was happening to make him think this way?

"Oh, she had a story all right," Mac said, unaware, apparently, of his friend's treasonous thoughts. "But there's no verification to speak of. Whatever records existed were destroyed in the fire. All I have is word of mouth. The reminiscences of an old nun in a nursing home."

"I don't give a damn if you heard it from a talking jackass, tell me."

Mac sniggered, then stopped himself when he seemingly realized Adam was not trying at levity. "Ahem...All right. Here it is. One morning the parish priest, a Father Anthony Giovanni, walked into the church to find two babies at the altar. Twins, maybe, but not identical. The other one was blond. Anyway, there was a note, but that gave them nothing. Just said to take care of the girls, and was signed Jon. The only other clues were a pair of identical, handmade storybooks. One was tucked in beside each kid, and each book had a name on the inside cover. The names were Brigit and Bridin."

The last vestiges of doubt were rapidly disintegrating. Funny, how they felt the same way the ground would feel if it were crumbling beneath his feet.

"The old nun said there were pendants inside the books as well, though she couldn't remember exactly what they looked like."

Adam knew what they looked like. At least, he knew what *one of them* looked like. A pewter fairy twined around a quartz point. The one Brigit never took off.

"This retired nun says she knew both Sister Mary Agnes and Brigit, and that she got the story straight from Sister Mary

Agnes," Mac continued. "Anyway, the twins were taken to the children's shelter attached to the church. The nun—Sister Ruth—says Bridin was adopted right away. Brigit was sickly, though, so no one wanted her. She lived with the sisters until the night of the fire."

Adam tensed. "And after that?"

"Never seen again. Someone said she'd gone back into the flames after Sister Mary Agnes. The old nun died in the blaze, but no sign of the girl's remains were found. Two eyewitnesses reported seeing an older man rushing into the burning building. From the descriptions, the local cops identified him as a transient who went by the name of Razor-Face Malone."

"Malone?" R. Malone. My God, not her husband. But a homeless man who'd saved her life once? Was it possible?

Raze wouldn't like you bad-mouthing me. Zaslow's words rang in Adam's ears. What the hell did it mean? Had this *Raze* turned against her? Was he working with Zaslow? Did he have something to hold over her head?

"I told you it was interesting," Mac went on.

"Was it arson, Mac?"

"Nope. Faulty wiring. No question about that. Besides, old Razor-Face wasn't a firebug. Just a little delusional. According to police records, the few times he was picked up for vagrancy he'd done some talking about fairy princesses and some enchanted forest. Rush, he called it."

"Holy...." Icy chills raced up and down the back of his neck, and he rubbed it with one palm to chase the feeling away.

"That's it for now, pal. But you know, you're onto something here. Until now no one knew the woman going by the name of Brigit Malone was the same kid who disappeared in that fire. The question is, why?"

"Why," Adam repeated stupidly.

"I still have feelers out on this. Looking for anyone who knew Razor-Face Malone. And I'm still pulling in tidbits about

Brigit Malone, the businesswoman. Trying to see what came between the night of the fire and the day she turned up in town. Nothing earth shattering so far. I'm trying to track down the missing twin sister, too. You want me to keep on this, right?"

"What?"

"I said, should I keep digging? Or do you have enough?"

Adam gave his head a shake. He could no longer feel his lips, and there was a loud buzzing sound in his head that seemed to be drowning out Mac's voice. "Yeah," he managed. "Yeah, keep digging."

"Are you sure you're all right, Adam? You sound..."

"I'm fine. Listen, check out a guy named Zaslow, too." He didn't wait for an answer, just hung up the phone, vaguely aware that the pad and pen he'd been holding had fallen from his suddenly numb fingers. "I'm fine. Unless you count the fact that I'm ninety-nine percent sure I'm living with a real live fairy, that is. Other than that... I'm fine."

Brigit hadn't slept well. Couldn't. There was still a faint trace of wood smoke in the air, clinging like a ghost from the past trying to haunt her dreams. Before dawn, she rose. She needed good, clean, dawn-fresh air and dewy grassy earth under her feet.

She dressed quickly, pulling on an ancient pair of faded, frayed cutoffs and t-shirt that had been tie-dyed. She wondered for a moment why she'd brought these things. She hadn't worn them in years. Hadn't intended ever to wear them again. They clashed with her role as a normal, respectable businesswoman. They would give her away as a phony.

But she didn't really feel as if it mattered anymore. If anyone had ever bought the act, it was a miracle. She couldn't play the part anymore. Hell, for a while, she'd even fooled herself.

But she knew what she was. She was strange. A misfit wherever she went. She'd been more at ease living in that condemned, rat-infested heap of bricks with Raze and the other homeless people, than she'd ever been moving among "civilized" types. She was wild and wanton, constantly at war with desires so hot they burned her at night. She'd dreamed of Adam last night. Dreamed of him as she'd never dreamed of him before. All night, images of the wild sex she wanted to have with him had drifted through her mind, in vivid, electrifying detail.

She might as well stop fighting the wild child inside. It was a part of her she could no longer deny. And this morning, she felt more like her wild self than ever. She finally admitted that she'd be more content to feel her bare feet sinking into soft brown earth or lush grasses, than she could ever be in high-heeled shoes, clicking over shiny parquet. She was filled with nervous energy. She wanted to run like an untamed thing, like a mustang filly, kicking her heels up behind her and running until her lungs burned. She wanted to dance and jump and spin and cartwheel.

She just wasn't normal. And it was high time she stopped trying to pretend she was.

She slipped out the back way, not bothering with shoes, leaving her glasses behind and her hair flying free. She took her time. The sunrise would be incredible. She could smell it in the air. Already, out over the lake, the midnight-blue sky was paling, and there was a narrow ridge of pink lining the mountains where they made love to the sky.

Oh, and the water! Look at the water!

There was a path, a jagged path fraught with loose stones, bordered by boulders and so steep it seemed impossible to travel by. She would try it later, she decided. But for now, the cliffs were her destination. That beautiful outcropping of rock where she and Adam had sat together in the rain. She'd watch the sunrise from there.

As soon as she sat down on the cool stone, she felt stronger.

Not a bit happier about what she had to do, and certainly no clearer about her own lost identity. But physically better. The morning breeze and the waves crashing below seemed to rinse away the exhaustion of a sleepless night, taking it with them back out into the depths to leave it there. And the sun's upper lip was fiery orange as it kissed the sky...

As it rose, she remembered the way Adam had kissed her. Gently, then deeper. Parting her lips with such care and tenderness, working his way inside...just the way the sun slowly worked its way into the sky. His kiss had freed that part of herself she'd been fighting for so long. Fully formed now, it seemed. The wild girl. The wildness raged in her now, and she wondered how she'd ever cage it again.

God, why couldn't she be like other women? Cool and sleek and in control?

The sun beamed its full force down, warmth and light washing over her, through her. The headache burned away. She was strong again. But no more knowledgeable than she'd been before. "Who am I," she whispered, and choked away her tears to voice the question again, louder. "Who am I, dammit? Where do I belong? What cruel god created me, and why, for heaven's sake? What the hell am I *doing* here?"

Each question was louder than the one before, and the final one was shouted as she shook her fists at the sky. Fury and rage and confusion all exploding from her in the form of questions she already knew had no answers. Questions that had plagued her even at St. Mary's. And then she had to be rid of it. All of it. She stood up, filled to brimming with nervous energy and anger, and sick to death of worry and remorse. She didn't want to think about it anymore.

For the first time in years, Brigit only wanted to feel alive. She wanted to feel wild and free, and filled with reckless abandon the way she used to feel before she'd decided to become responsible and respectable. She wanted to do something utterly thrilling.

She looked down at the waves rolling to shore below, and slowly, she smiled. "Yes," she whispered. Then she turned around, and walked several yards. When she faced the lake again, she drew a breath, and the wild one inside her grinned. She ran as fast as she could, right to the edge, stretched her arms up over her head, bent a little at the knees... and then she dove.

God, it was wonderful! Just like flying. She pointed her body like an arrow, and watched the stone walls speeding past her in a blurred gray rush. The air whistled past her ears, whipping her hair up behind her, whooshing over her body. Then she punctured the lake, stabbed into it, torpedoed down deep. And she arched her back, and pushed with her arms, and shot up toward the surface. Her head broke through, and she flung her hair backward, tipping her chin to the sky and inhaling the fresh morning air until her lungs were filled to bursting.

It felt good to be wild again. She'd stifled herself for too long. She'd lived calmly and quietly and become staid and complacent. No more, dammit! The turmoil inside her needed release, and a little wildness was exactly the way she ought to vent it.

And since she still had a lot of venting to do, she began swimming away from shore, burning all the energy that had been pent up inside her for so long.

She swam faster, harder, and her heart pumped and her muscles burned. But it felt good. It felt good to take her anger out this way. She had every right to be angry with the way things had turned out.

Growling with effort, she paddled onward. Raze had been taken from her, was being used to force her to lie and steal one more time. And she slashed her hands through the water as if Zaslow's evil face were there on the surface. She took out her fury toward him on the lake.

When she was too tired to swim another stroke, she slowed, and floated on her back, rising and falling with the swells of the blue water. And she knew the source of her anger as well as she knew her own reflection in the mirror.

She cared deeply for Adam Reid. And she was being forced, against her will, to betray him.

"I don't want to do this," she whispered, and the waves gained strength until she couldn't float anymore. So she rolled over, still breathless, panting, and just treaded water. "I don't want to betray Adam."

A wave slapped her face, sloshing water into her mouth, and she realized that her anger and her energy were spent. Only remorse for what lay ahead of her remained. Tears fell to blend with the waters of Mystic Lake. "I just don't want to."

But you know you have to.

Another wave slapped her. She swallowed more water, and turned to look back toward the shore. And then her heart skidded to a halt in her chest, because she'd swum so far the shore was a hazy outline in the distance.

She blinked in shock. "Oh, God, what have I done?"

Closing her eyes, she called on that wild one inside, knowing instinctively *she* was the stronger one. The braver one. "Have to try," she told herself, and she began swimming shoreward.

Ten strokes...twenty. Why didn't the shore look any closer? Forty...fifty. She paused to catch her breath. The water's caress was chilling her overheated flesh, and her lungs were beginning to ache. A sob tore at her breastbone, but she battled it into submission, and launched herself shoreward once more. But she knew her progress was minuscule at best. Before she'd made it halfway, she was too exhausted even to keep her head above water. Damn, she'd been an idiot. A fool. She'd let the caged one take control, and it was going to cost her. Her longing gaze swept the shoreline once more. "It's too far... "

Try!

Slap! She spit water out of her mouth and nodded tiredly. She had to keep trying. She was a lot of things, but not a quitter. Not a coward. She began paddling again. But her muscles screamed in protest, and burned with every movement. Another wave splashed her, pushing her under. She fought to the surface, choking and spitting, and then another swept her under. Her arms ached and her legs cramped when she broke surface yet again, straining onward. A few more strokes... and that was all. She tried, but it was simply impossible to go any farther. Impossible. And she'd given it her best shot.

Numbly, she lifted her arms again, tried to kick her feet, but the merciless water pulled her into its cool embrace, and closed over her head.

Adam had almost reached her when she went down for the last time. Dammit! It was all but impossible to keep an eye on her with the morning breeze rippling the surface, and those swells out there where she was. He'd been looking for her, intent on telling her what he knew and asking her what the hell was really going on.

But she hadn't been in the house, and when he'd looked outside, he'd heard her. Her anguished cries to a deaf god had blasted the anger from Adam's mind. *Where do I belong? What the hell am I doing here?* Her voice arced through the dawn sky so clearly it hurt to hear the pain in it.

And the questions... he didn't want to analyze them then. He told himself that it was normal for a person who'd never known her parents to feel an identity crisis now and then. He didn't believe that was the case, here, but he told himself he did, and focused on getting to where she was. Talking to her.

Taking her pain away...

No. Not that. Just... just...

He followed the sound of her voice... catching sight of her just as she dove from the cliffs like an eagle swooping down on its prey.

"Holy God. Brigit!"

He ran to the ledge as well. Crying out in anguish when he saw her body pierce the lake, holding his breath while she was hidden from view by the sapphire waters, and then nearly collapsing in relief when she surfaced again.

Like a mermaid when her head emerged. Like a pagan goddess as she tipped her head skyward, eyes closed as if to receive the kiss of the sun.

And then she began swimming. Adam shook his head in disbelief. Then realized he shouldn't. He'd sensed from the beginning that the staid, reserved Brigit was only a mask she wore. That the real woman within was a hellion. Well, he'd been right. Though even then, he'd underestimated her.

He caught sight of her again, diving under the waves. She surfaced some yards out, and dove again. And again. And again, each time swimming farther from the shore.

"Brigit," he said softly, wondering if she was even aware how far out she'd gone. "Brigit! Can you hear me?" He shouted, cupping his hands around his mouth. She didn't respond, didn't look back. Damn, she hadn't looked back since she'd hit the water. Not once.

Okay... there. She was stopping, floating. Resting. Maybe she was okay. But, damn, she was a long way out. He turned his body, not his head, and started heading toward the path that led down to the shore. Keeping his eyes on her as he decided to swim out in case she needed help.

But then a wave hit her and swept her under. She came up sputtering, and he knew she'd finally seen how far away the shore was. He couldn't see the panic in her face, but he could feel it. He could feel it as surely as if it was his own. And he didn't even stop to wonder how that was possible.

She stroked toward shore and was swept under water again. Adam didn't hesitate. He turned back toward the cliff, heeled off his shoes, and ran, peeling the shirt over his head as he went, and letting the wind take it from his hands. The jeans stayed where they were. No time for those now. He hit the edge running and pushed off hard. And then his body was knifing downward at what felt like the speed of light. Cold water met him head on, engulfing him, chilling him through to the bone by the time he curved up to the surface again. And then he poured every cell into making his strokes powerful, making each movement of his body propel him forward as fast and as far as possible.

And he'd just about reached her when she vanished beneath the surface, like a rebellious mermaid struggling against her fate, only to be yanked into the depths by some overbearing sea god. And then he was diving down, deeper, stroking madly, eyes wide and straining to see her through the ever-darkening water.

And then he did.

Stroking straight down, he caught her under the arms, yanked her to him, got his legs under him again. His lungs burned. He couldn't hold his breath much longer, but he wouldn't let her go. He wouldn't. He might not find her again. His legs pumped. He moved his entire body to propel himself upward. And finally his head emerged in an explosion of droplets... and hers with it.

Holding her from behind, he maneuvered her head onto his shoulder as he dragged gulps of air into his starved lungs. His legs still working to keep them afloat, he gripped her chin with one hand, turned her head a little, stared down at her beautiful face. Satin skin. Huge eyes, closed now, thick long lashes beaded with lake water. Rivers of it running down over her throat.

He put his lips to hers, tried to breathe for her. It was awkward, all but impossible to do while trying to tread water. Three breaths. Then he struck out for shore. And in a few seconds, he paused to force his own breath into her body again. Then swam some more.

He'd nearly reached the shallows when she choked and began twisting in his arms.

He only held her tighter, and stroked onward until his feet reached bottom. They were still many yards from the shore, but he could walk now. He got his footing and picked her up, carrying her the rest of the way.

They emerged from the water like that. Adam still searching her face for the signs of life that had subsided into stillness again, and Brigit just lying in his arms, head thrown backward, long hair trailing in the water.

He laid her on the shore. No sand. Mystic's shore was grassy down here, rocky in other spots. With barely time to catch his breath he bent over her again, covered her mouth with his, pushing air into her chest until it rose.

Seconds ticked by, and then he felt her moving. Her hands came up, threaded into his hair, tugging gently until he lifted his head away. She rolled weakly to one side, choking and spewing lake water into the grass. And then she sat there, her head hanging down between her braced arms.

"Are you all right? Do you need an ambulance?"

She said nothing. Her back to him.

"What the hell were you trying to do, Brigit?"

Silence.

He gripped her shoulder, pulling her around to face him. "Talk to me, dammit! What the hell is going on with you? You could have got yourself killed out there. Or is that what you wanted?"

Her eyes seemed to recapture a bit of life then, and her chin came up a little. "I was coming back. I was coming back... I just couldn't make it."

"Why?" His grip on her shoulders tightened, and he shook her a little. "*Why,* Brigit?"

She shook her head slowly. "It was stupid... but it wasn't what you think."

"At this point, I don't even *know* what I think." He wrapped his arms around her in abject relief, held her to his chest, and ran his hands over her wet skin. "I'm just glad you're okay."

She straightened away from him, and a worried frown puckered her brows. Her palms came up to run slowly down either side of his face. "Adam," she said, and it was no more than a whisper. "Don't care about me. Whatever you do... don't care...
"

And then her back bowed with a spasm of coughing, and her shoulders shook with it. He pulled her to his chest again, and just held her there. "What the hell makes you think I care? Adam Reid doesn't care about anyone except Adam Reid. Anything else is lunacy." He only wished it was the truth.

He scooped her up in his arms and carried her back to the house, taking a longer but safer path up the steep, rocky hillside. He didn't bother trying to silence the voice inside that told him every word he'd just uttered was a lie.

Turmoil. So much of it in his eyes and his face. Even his hair showed signs of stress. It stuck up a little crazily from the many times he'd shoved his hands through it. He was sitting in a leather armchair, just staring at her, when she awoke some hours later. Those eyes seemed to be eating holes through her, intense. Burning. He sat slouched, one elbow propped on the chair's arm, and his hand buried in his hair.

He'd put on dry clothes. A pair of pleated black trousers with knife-sharp creases. A clean white t-shirt, and a black suit jacket. The jacket hung open. He had classes today, she realized. But he was waiting...

He hadn't shaved yet this morning. Soft golden bristles

coated his face. A shade or two darker than his hair. He looked tired. So tired.

Brigit blinked, realizing she'd been staring at him as intently as he was still staring at her. She looked away, tried to take stock of herself instead of him. Her lungs hurt. Her throat hurt. Her head hurt.

Her clothes were damp. He'd laid her on the sofa in the study, built up a fire in the hearth. But he hadn't undressed her. Just wrapped her in so many blankets she couldn't help but feel warm.

She looked at him again, and trembled because he was still staring at her that way. Disturbing.

"You should change."

His voice coming so suddenly amid the silence made her jump.

"I'd have done it myself, but… " His lips thinned and he shook his head. "I think we both know what would happen if I were to undress you. With my hands, I mean, instead of just with my eyes."

Her face burned. She brought her hands to it.

"Why are you here, Brigit Malone? What the hell are you trying to do to me?"

"Adam…"

"No. No more lies. Just tell me. Dammit, Brigit, just open your mouth and tell me." He closed his eyes, laughed just a little, a bitter, harsh sound. "Did you really think you could convince me you were some kind of supernatural being? *A fairy* for God's sake?"

She sat up straighter on the sofa, fear somersaulting in her chest. He wasn't making sense. "I never said I was—"

She stopped speaking when he pulled her book, her copy of *Fairytale,* from behind his back, and laid it gently on the coffee table. "Never said it. But set it up so I'd find all the clues. What did you do, Brigit, throw my old plants out and replace them with new ones when I wasn't looking?"

"Adam, I don't know what you're—"

"So I was supposed to see the suddenly thriving plants and immediately think of that Celtic text. I was supposed to remember how it said animals and plants respond to the presence of fairy folk, and I was supposed to wonder."

She frowned at him, shaking her head slowly from side to side.

"And that story someone planted with the old nun. Now that was the kicker, that really was. Brilliant. Did you think of that, too, Brigit?"

She felt her eyes narrow. "Old nun?"

"Oh, come on, you had to know I'd check up on you. You had to know... That's why you left that story with the nun, for me to find. No mother. No birth certificate."

"You checked up on me?"

"I had a P.I. do it."

She was stunned, shaken right to the core. But she knew, at once. "Mac, from the party," she whispered.

"He talked to this old nun, Sister Ruth..."

"Sister Ruth," she echoed, her voice a choked whisper.

"So old she's easily persuaded to forget about the privacy laws. She told the story of twin girls with apparently no past, left at the altar of a church. Twin girls... who just happen to have the same names as the ones in the fairy tale you told me. The motherless fay princesses whose mortal father brought them to the human world to keep them safe."

She shook her head, slowly getting to her feet and letting the blankets fall to the floor around her. Automatically, she grabbed her precious book and held it to her chest. "I told you the story, Adam. I told you myself... but what difference does any of it make? It was just a story. It wasn't real."

He shook his head, looking as if he wasn't entirely in agreement with that statement. "If it isn't real, then someone went to a lot of trouble to make me think it was. It's almost as if this thing has been planned from the day you and your sister were left at that..."

He stopped speaking at the thump her book made when it hit the floor. His gaze went from it, up to her face, and she tried to close her mouth, tried to stop her eyes from watering. She lifted her hands to him, gripping his t-shirt in trembling fists. "I have a sister?" She searched his face, trying to see, no longer caring about anything else, breathless and hurting, but desperate to know. "Bridin is *real?*"

"You didn't know... "

She blinked, choking on tears. "I... Sister Mary Agnes told me... about a sister. But I thought it was something she just made up, to make the fairy tale more real to me. She pretended to believe I was one of them. I guess she thought..." She released his shirt, lowered her head. "I believed it... for a while. Once I was old enough to realize it was only a story, I thought *all* of it was a story." Lifting her eyes to meet his once more, she went on. "I tried checking my records once, but the lawyer I spoke with said it was impossible. They're sealed—"

"Your records were destroyed in the fire. But according to a retired nun who claims she was there at the time, you had a twin sister who was adopted almost immediately."

His voice had lost its accusatory tone, and his eyes had taken on a wide, wondering expression. She sank backward, until she was sitting on the floor. "I have a sister."

"You really didn't know. You really didn't make any of this up, did you?"

She said nothing, just sat there, stunned. Adam rose and came forward. He stood close to her, towering over her, his hands on her shoulders. "Why are you here, Brigit? Why did you come to me?"

She blinked and lifted her eyes. "I can't tell you that."

"Then—"

"No. I can't leave, either. Adam... " She drew a breath, fought for strength. "You saved my life today. And now you've given me... given me a reason to go on..."

"Your sister."

She nodded. "I—" A sob interrupted her, but she fought it and began again. "God, I can't believe it. Bridin is real. She's real."

"Brigit—"

"I won't hurt you, Adam. I swear... whatever my intent was...I won't. I can't. B-but I need to be here."

"Why?"

"J-just for a few more days. Just until I figure out what to do."

"Why, Brigit?"

She gripped his lower arms and pulled herself to her feet. She stood so close to him that she could feel the warmth of his body. Feel every breath, almost every thought. She tipped her head back, staring into his eyes, wishing with everything in her that he would let her stay. She'd find a way to solve this thing without hurting him or getting Raze killed. She *would*.

Pouring her heart into her eyes, and from them, into his, she whispered, "Please don't make me go, Adam. *Please.*"

In her eyes is the power to bend a man to her will.

The words from the ancient text whispered through Adam's mind as he stared at Brigit's dark blue eyes.

"Okay."

The word slipped through his mouth without warning. He didn't think about it first, because she was so close that all he could think about was holding her, warming her, healing her. She could have died out there today. Hell, she'd stopped breathing. That had been no act, and neither was this.

My God, it was true. This woman was the child in the fairy tale. The one he'd been shown long ago. The daughter of a fay queen. No. Yes! And it was Adam's destiny to help her... and then to let her go.

He closed his eyes in misery, but quickly shook off the self-pity. Because there was more going on here. She didn't seem to realize who she really was, let alone what she was supposed to do about it. She had her own reasons for coming to him. And whatever she was up to, he had to believe she didn't want to do it. Someone was forcing her. And when he thought about that, he thought about the creep he'd found here yesterday. Zaslow, and this mysterious Raze, the mere mention of whose name had forced Brigit to lie. What the hell was he to her? What was Zaslow? What were they up to?

She was in trouble. Or she'd convinced him that she was. And instead of feeling bad for her, he felt good. For himself. Selfish bastard. All he could feel was gratitude that whatever deceptions she'd committed, she'd been forced to commit. He was sure of that, now.

He searched her face, fell into her eyes, and ended up holding her tight against him. His hands dove into her hair, stroking and untangling it. "Dammit, Brigit, why won't you open up to me? Why won't you let me help you?"

"I can't," she whispered. "This is my problem, Adam. Mine. And only I can solve it."

CHAPTER 15

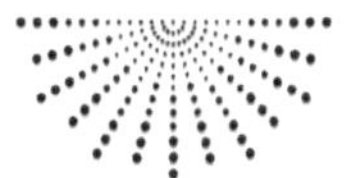

$\mathcal{A}$dam left for his class, but she could tell he wasn't happy with her answers. Or... her lack of answers. And she had a feeling he was somehow letting her stay here against his will. As if he was being blackmailed the way she was. Or... or maybe as if he was being hypnotized into doing what she wanted.

He'd wanted to throw her out. At least, part of him had. So why hadn't he?

Didn't matter. She had to get in touch with Zaslow. Since her recent communion with her "other self," the wild one, she'd found a bit more courage and strength. Enough, she thought, to try again to fight Zaslow. To take her life back again. To regain control. She had to find a way to make Zaslow give this whole idea up. She had to.

But how?

Brigit paced the study, her eyes going often to the painting on the wall above the marble hearth. Watering each time they met those dark, mysterious eyes peering at her from amid the bushes.

She had a sister. God, even with all this garbage going on,

she couldn't get past the wonder of it. The joy of it. All this time, not knowing. All this time, wondering, wishing, hoping. Dreaming of her sister.

Her perfect, golden sister. Bridin. Brigit wondered if Bridin could be as wonderful as she'd dreamed. Oh, but she had to be! She would be.

Brigit owed Adam more than she could ever repay, she realized sadly.

And that brought her back to the matter at hand. Her impending betrayal of Adam Reid, the man who'd given her a dream come true. A sister.

She had no idea what was going on with Adam. Why he would accuse her of trying to convince him she was some kind of fairy or something. His anger confused her, and his words this morning... God, she'd lost track of when he was speaking about her fairy tale and when he was speaking about her real life.

Except for the part about a sister.

Brigit closed her eyes and tried not to dwell on that aspect of this mess. Not right now. Right now, her only goal was to convince Zaslow to let her off the hook. She had to find a way. She considered giving him the copy, trying to pass it off as the original, but he'd told her he would know if she did. And she'd looked into his eyes when he'd said it, and knew he was telling the truth.

Money. The man was greedy, and he was doing this for money. He'd told her he was being paid a hundred thousand dollars for the painting. So if she could find a way to give him an equal amount...

Oh, but how? Where the hell was a formerly homeless street brat going to come up with a hundred grand?

She blinked in surprise as the answer came to her. The shop. Akasha. It had been just another condemned heap when she'd discovered it. The city had been about to tear it down to put up something new and shiny, when Brigit had come along with her plan to repair it, to make it into something special and new.

Other business owners on the Commons had jumped onto Brigit's bandwagon, and the local students had joined her in her campaign to save a building that turned out to be over 150 years old. And after that the loans had come easily. With the money she'd already saved up from her former career as an art forger, it was enough to get Akasha up and running. And when her business had thrived as she'd known it would, the loans had been repaid on time and with interest, and the entire city won.

It had been a lonely street brat's dream come true. But it wasn't half as important to Brigit as Raze was. Or as her sister was.

Or as important as Adam Reid had become to her.

It was the only way.

With trembling hands, Brigit picked up the telephone, and dialed the number Zaslow had warned her to use only in an emergency.

Zaslow was there. He answered on the third ring.

"It's me." Why was her voice shaking so much?

"Is it done?"

"N-no. Not yet."

"Then why the hell am I hearing your voice?"

Brigit licked her lips, cleared her throat. "I have a deal to offer you."

"We already have a deal, Brigit. Finish the damned painting and I won't kill your friend."

"I know, I know, but—"

"But?"

He sounded ominous. Her hand was sweaty, making the receiver slick. So much riding on her words. Raze's life. Her own future. She had to be careful.

"If I were to sell the shop, Zaslow, I could get at least a

hundred grand. Maybe more. I'll give it to you. All of it, if you'll just let Raze go."

Silence. Dead and heavy. Lengthening.

"Please," she whispered.

He sucked in a slow breath. "It's Reid, isn't it? You sleeping with him, Brigit?"

"No!"

"I had a man watching you at that little snob-fest last night, honey. I have a man watching every move you make. He's got his eyes on you right now. I heard all about your little dance with Reid. Seems the two of you were so into it, you forgot to stop when the music did."

She swallowed, but almost choked on it.

"Did you take him to bed when you got home, Brigit? Did you show him all the tricks you learned on the streets?"

Fear made her heart trip over itself. But anger set it right again. "If you have someone watching my every move, as you say, then you already know."

He laughed and it made her skin crawl. "You apparently don't understand how this works, Brigit, love. But don't worry. I'll make sure you get the point. This is life and death, honey. You cooperate, there's life. You give me bullshit like this, and there are gonna be some corpses turning up in odd places."

"What do you mean by that?"

Again, that low, evil laughter. "You need a lesson in obedience, Brigit. A little class in cause and effect."

"Don't do anything to Raze!" She shouted at the receiver as panic bubbled in her chest. "Please, don't hurt him! I'll finish—"

The phone went dead.

Frantic, Brigit dialed the number again, only to hear endless ringing. God, what was Zaslow thinking? What was he going to do?

She paced, wringing her hands until she'd made red marks all over them. And finally, she hauled her equipment down to the study, and she painted. She worked slowly, carefully, taming her trembling hands by the sheer force of her will, battling the fear and the imaginary horrors it induced... until she finally found that place where it all faded away, and her mind floated free as her hands worked.

Free. And images of a sister who radiated goodness and purity and control, and had hair as golden as the sun. She was everything Brigit had tried to be, everything she'd failed to be. If only she knew her. Bridin. If only she had her here, to talk to, to confide in.

Maybe... maybe someday, they'd find one another.

And maybe those people who'd adopted Bridin had known what they were doing when they'd chosen not to take both babies. Maybe they'd somehow sensed that Brigit was less than worthy of a family's love and of a sister like Bridin. Maybe she didn't deserve to find her twin. It might be fate.

She came back to herself with a start when she heard vehicles out front. "Oh, God, Adam!" Whirling, she stared at the sun slanting low through the study windows. Late afternoon. He was back. And he wasn't alone.

She grabbed the painting and took the stairs two at a time, running full tilt to her bedroom, lunging to the back of that oversized closet. She only paused long enough to place her painting carefully, not smudging the paint or allowing anything to touch the sides. Then she raced downstairs again, dumping the palettes and dirty brushes and uncapped tubes of paint into a heap in the middle of the color-spattered drop cloth, and gathering the entire bundle like a peddler's pack. She slung it over her shoulder and snatched up the tripod under her arm.

Her trip up the stairs was a little slower this time. She kept tripping, and the tripod was awkward, swinging sideways and knocking against her legs every couple of steps. But she made it to the top, and flung everything into the closet. She slammed the door, panting.

Still no sound from downstairs. Adam must be busy with whoever had arrived with him. She ran into her bathroom, cranked on the faucets and scrubbed the still-wet paint from her hands. When stains remained, she used nail polish remover to lighten them.

Good. Barely noticeable.

She turned to head back downstairs, stopping in the doorway when she heard Adam come in.

"Brigit?"

"Up here," she called, and at the same moment, realized she was still wearing a paint-smattered smock over her clothes. She hauled it over her head, tossed it behind her into the bedroom, and slammed the door just as he reached the bottom of the stairway and looked up at her.

She forced a smile, and tried to remember if she'd checked her face for paint flecks.

Adam glanced at the stool that stood in the middle of the study, then up at her, then back at the stool again, frowning.

"There was a big cobweb I couldn't reach," she lied, feeling miserable. "I was on my way back to the kitchen with the stool and I got distracted. Sorry."

He only shrugged, looking up at her again. "Can you come down here? There's a package for you."

Brigit felt her brows crease. "A package?"

"Delivery men were just unloading it when I pulled in, so I signed for you. Did you order something?"

She shook her head, running her palm over the cool hardwood rail as she walked toward the stairway, then started down it. "No," she said. "I can't imagine what..."

Halfway down the stairs she stopped, recalling Zaslow's evil laughter, his cryptic threats.

"What kind of package?"

"A big one," Adam said.

She blinked, forcing herself down the remaining stairs, turning to go out through the foyer.

The front door felt heavy, the knob, hard to turn. Slow and sloppy. She forced it open and took a single step outside.

The coffin-shaped wooden crate sat on the sidewalk, daring her to step forward, daring her to look inside.

Brigit screamed.

He'd only been a few steps behind her, but when she screamed, Adam shot forward, adrenaline propelling him like rocket fuel.

She'd fallen to her knees on the front steps. Her face covered by her trembling hands, her entire body shaking, she was muttering...or maybe praying. "Please...nononono...please, please, please...no...no...pleeeease..."

Adam caught her shoulders. "Easy, Brigit. Come on, get up. Turn around. Look at me."

She tried, but her knees buckled. He had to help her. She was breathing too fast, in short, choppy little gasps. He helped her to her feet, and he turned her, nice and slow, holding her steady. She was clearly terrified. He'd never seen terror etched as clearly and plainly as he saw on her face, in her eyes. Her color had fled, leaving her skin as smooth and white as bleached linen. Her eyes were wide and unfocused.

Shaking uncontrollably, she clung to him with her hands and with her eyes, clung to him as if for her very salvation.

"Just what do you think is in that box, Brigit?"

Her lips parted, but only jerky, spasmodic breaths escaped.

Shaking his head in frustration, Adam guided her hands to the railing, and anchored them there. Then he quickly jogged across the lawn to the tool shed. He grabbed a pry bar, and hurried back to the front of the house. God knew he didn't dare leave Brigit alone out there for more than a second or two. She was where he'd left her, her eyes glued to that damned box as if she expected a dragon to jump out of it and swallow her whole.

He jammed in the bar, pried up a board, then another, and another. He tossed each one aside, letting them clatter to the ground and then moving on to the next. And then he dropped the bar, looking at the box's contents. When he could breathe again he said, "Come here, Brigit, and take a look. And then tell me what the hell this is all about."

Her frightened eyes met his. She tried to take a step forward, but that was all. "I... I can't. J-j-just t-tell me... "

He picked a brick from the top of the pile, and held it up.

She frowned, blinking.

"Bricks. A bunch of them."

Brigit moved then. She came off the step as if shot from a cannon, and a second later she was on her knees beside that crate and bricks were flying everywhere. She snatched them up, clawed them into her hands and tossed them aside, one after another, as if she were digging for something.

"That's enough!"

He grabbed her wrists when she went on digging, pulled her hands up, holding them prisoner in his. "Look at this. What the hell is the matter with you?"

He held her hands up in front of her face, so she could see what he did. Her nails were broken, fingertips bleeding from her frantic search. But her eyes were still wide, still jumping wildly from his to that box full of bricks and back again.

"There's nothing there," he told her. "Nothing. Just bricks. Nothing else."

Her breaths quickened, roughened. Her eyes squeezed tight and she clenched her jaw. "Thank God," she whispered, and then, eyes opening, calmer now, but beginning to burn with something...anger, maybe. "Damn him, damn him, damn him."

And that was all. She melted into Adam's arms, tears flash-flooding, sobs spasming hard in her chest and wrenching her small body. He held her, and he felt the sharp angles of her shoulder blades, and winced. He hadn't seen her consume enough to keep a bird alive since she'd moved in, though he hadn't given it much thought until now. And come to think of it, judging by the circles under her eyes, she hadn't slept much, either. She was an emotional cauldron, and she was damned near bubbling over. Terrified for sure. And yes, trying to pull something on him. Which, for some reason had fallen to the very bottom of his list of things to worry about.

Oh, he had questions all right. He was brimming with them. But the questions would have to wait. Right now the only thing he wanted was to make her nightmares go away.

Her sobs stopped, and it was several moments before he realized she was unconscious in his arms. She'd fainted.

Brigit woke slowly, her senses coming to life one at a time. Bit by bit. And the very first was the sense of smell. Even before she was aware of it, she smelled the violets on the air. Sweet honeysuckle. And... sandalwood? Yes. And wax. She could smell the wax. Candles, her mind whispered. And incense.

Was she dreaming? Was she at Akasha? It felt as if she was.

A touch, gentle and warm on her face, stroking a slow path down over her cheek. Fingertips, tracing the line of her jaw, so slowly, stopping at her chin, trailing down the arc of her neck, and making her tip her head back further in response. They felt good, those warm fingertips. And when they reversed their path, moving upward again to her cheek, she pressed closer to their touch. Her face found the entire palm, and she rubbed her cheek against it.

"Ah, Brigit..."

The voice was deep and very soft, barely more than a whisper. A familiar one, though. A comforting one. The hand caressed her face, fingers threading through her hair.

"You're magic, you know. Everything you do... "

And then lips—their kiss so light she was almost convinced it had only been imaginary—gently brushed her forehead.

Adam. She wanted to see him. She needed...

Her eyes opened about the fourth time she commanded them to, and things were blurry. She felt lightheaded, fuzzy, drunk.

"Just like Sleeping Beauty," he said.

His face swam into focus, and she saw that he was smiling, slightly. Just slightly.

"I..." She licked her parched lips and tried again. "I feel. . . funny." She was only gradually beginning to hear the soft strains of music, and the gentle tinkling sounds of a wind chime. They came as if from a great distance.

"It's the tranquilizer," Adam told her, and his hand was moving into her hair now, stroking up and back, the way he'd stroke a cat. She liked it.

"Tranq...?" Her mouth refused to shape the rest of the word.

"You passed out, Brigit. I called an ambulance. When they arrived and brought you around, you started shaking and hyperventilating again, so they gave you a shot."

"Oh." She didn't remember any of that.

"Just try to relax."

"Mmm." She was nothing if not relaxed. Her eyes fell closed, but popped open again. She looked past him this time, saw the foggy halos of candlelight and the fiery red tip of an incense stick. "Drugs... work harder in me than they do in most of you."

"Most of us?"

"Most of... us. Yeah." She inhaled the delicious smell of sandalwood. "What... *is* all this?"

Adam shrugged. "I thought it would make you feel better. If

you lose it again, I'm under orders to take you to the ER, and I'd prefer to stay in."

Her lips pulled up at the corners. "I'll try not to freak out again. And it does make me feel better. It reminds me... of Akasha."

He took his hand away. She caught it with her own and pressed it back to her head.

He smiled and resumed stroking her hair in a soothing, relaxing rhythm.

"Your shop is a special place. When I walk in there, I get this instant sense of... I don't know. Peace, I guess."

"Yes."

"I thought you could use a little peace right now."

Oh, he had that right.

"So I brought some of your things over to try to duplicate the atmosphere for you."

She frowned a little. "You went to my shop?"

"I borrowed your keys and sent one of my students with a list. Michael. He left payment in the register. And he's the most trustworthy guy I know. I hope you don't mind too much."

"I don't."

"I had him bring one of those CDs you still sell. I noticed them when I came there before. So old fashioned, selling CDs. I thought it so clever, you playing one in the shop and putting a "now playing" sign in front of the stack of CDs on the counter."

"Hardly anyone wants a CD anymore. I'm gonna have to start carrying cards with download codes on them or something."

I asked him to pick up some scented candles and incense, so I could get the smells right. It was easier than bringing all your plants."

She closed her eyes, again hearing the soft music. No wonder she'd felt so relaxed when she'd awakened. "Enya," she told him as she recognized the hauntingly beautiful voice, in a song called "Fairytale." She turned to him then. "My favorite."

"Good."

"You're a sweet man, Adam."

"Not a chance, Brigit."

"You did all this for me..."

"Oh, I did more. I undressed you. Or hadn't you noticed?"

She drew a short, sharp breath when he said it coming a little more fully awake than she'd been. She lifted the blankets that covered her and peered underneath. She was naked, except for the white panties she still wore. Lowering the covers, she met his eyes.

"I told myself it was just to make you comfortable," he said slowly, his eyes pinning hers, holding them prisoner in their depths.

She sat up in the bed, very slowly, because she was dizzy, and moving made it worse. The bed seemed to spin in uneven circles. Adam's hands came to her shoulders, as if he wanted her to stay down to the pillows.

"Don't, Brigit," he told her. "If you want to be away from me, I'll leave. You have to stay here. You need to rest."

"I don't want to rest." She lay back down, though, too weak to argue. "I want...to know..." His eyes narrowed, searching her face.

"To know what?"

"How," she whispered. "How you touched me."

Adam stood beside the bed, staring down at her, his face unreadable. "How?"

Lifting her trembling hands, Brigit caught the blankets at her shoulders, and slowly pushed them down, all the way to her hips, just as far as she could reach. "Show me."

Adam slammed his eyes closed. "Brigit..."

"I want you to..."

He would have turned away. But her hand shot out to

capture his wrist. She held him as tight as she could, and she drew his hand downward. He didn't resist. He let her bring it lower, let her settle his palm on her breast. She saw him clenching his jaw, and she heard the air rush out of his lungs.

She released his hand. When he drew it away she sat up again, battling the dizziness and winning. "You don't want me, then. Is that it Adam?"

He stood there, right beside the bed, looking down at her with fire in his wizard's eyes, and candlelight gleaming from his golden hair. A pagan god. His hands closed around one of hers, and he drew it closer until her palm pressed right to the zipper of his jeans. She felt the iron bulge beyond the denim.

Does it feel to you as if I don't want you?"

"Then why—"

"I don't *want to* want you, dammit. I don't want to feel anything for you."

She pressed her hand harder to him. She drew back, lifting her chin, the wanton inside having escaped and taken charge. "I don't think you have a choice in the matter."

"Witch," he breathed. But he didn't turn away.

"I don't think any of us do. We feel... what we feel." She undid his jeans, the button and then the zipper.

With a groan of surrender, he kicked free of his jeans, and climbed into the bed with her, his flesh hot, burning. His kisses, passionate and eager. He pushed at her panties. She helped him, crazy and clumsy and slowly losing her mind.

Brigit closed her eyes and clutched his shoulders as he wrapped her up against him and slid inside her. It felt so perfect, so right, that she made a little cry of surprise when it hurt just a little.

He froze, right where he was, his eyes popping open, his face stricken. "What am I doing?"

"Adam," she whispered, searching his dark blue eyes,

knowing he'd been lost in passion for a few moments. But he was back in control now.

She threaded her fingers into his hair, and drew his head downward. But he resisted.

"Brigit..." he whispered, searching her face. "Am I the first for you..."

"I've waited a long time to find you, Adam Reid." She leaned up and kissed him. One second. Two. Three, and more. And then he kissed her back. His lips moved, nuzzled, tasted, and his body rocked slowly with hers. His arms cradled her tightly and closely, and he made slow, exquisite love to her. He kissed a hot path down her jaw, over her neck, and sucked the skin between his teeth, nibbling, tasting.

"My God, Brigit," he whispered as their hips met again and again. Not roughly or hastily, the way he'd begun. But with such exquisite tenderness it brought tears to her eyes.

"You taste so sweet...so sweet..."

He was kissing her again, then. Her neck, her shoulders, her chest, her arms. Her breasts. He couldn't seem to get enough of kissing her skin. And as he kissed he moved, and she moved with him, feeling more and more as if they were melding into one beautiful sensual being riding the river of sensation. Every move, every breath, like a raft in the rapids, until ecstasy swept them both over the falls.

He gathered her into his arms, and she held on tight, and for long moments they just clung that way, floating.

He rolled her onto her back, and laid beside her, propping himself on one elbow. His eyes took their time, roaming up and down her body, and there was a look of wonder about him.

"I shouldn't have done that. Dammit, Brigit, I shouldn't have. But you... you enchant me. Why do you have this power over me? This freaking magi..." He stopped speaking, and she saw his gaze skid to a halt, focused on her abdomen. His eyes widened, and he shook his head, blinked, and stared some more. "What is that?"

Brigit sat up fast, defensive, and looked down at herself. "What?"

His hand came forward, forefinger tracing the little red mark just below her belly button. "This."

She frowned harder. "It's just a birthmark."

"In the shape of a crescent moon," he whispered. "And it's blood red."

"So?"

He lifted his gaze slowly, met her eyes, his own narrowing, searching. "Brigit?"

"What?"

He licked his lips, swallowed hard. "Brigit, you told me that when you were a child, you believed in that fairy tale of yours. That you believed it was true, and that you really were—"

She shook her head quickly. "A childhood fantasy, Adam. That's all it was. A silly dream."

"What if it wasn't?"

Brigit frowned at him, shaking her head in confusion. "What do you mean, what if it wasn't? It had to be. There are no such things as fairies. Everyone knows that."

"But what if there were? What if you really—"

She shook her head hard, and started to turn away from him. But he slipped his hands into her hair, and gently made her face him. "Have you ever really considered the possibility? Have you ever put it to the test?"

Her lips thinned. "Sure I have, Adam. I check behind me every day for wings, but so far—"

"I'm being serious here."

She didn't want him to see the tears forming in her eyes, but he wouldn't let her turn away, so see them he did. And he leaned closer, to kiss the tears away. "Why does the thought of it make you cry, if you're so sure it's all nonsense?"

"Because I believed so strongly once, Adam. And when I found out the truth, it was like someone took away my heart. It hurt to grow up, and face reality, and put fantasy away where it belongs. In a little box of childhood memories. But I did it. I don't want to have to do it all over again."

He blinked and shook his head as if trying to shake water from his hair. "Okay," he said softly, stroking her hair with his soothing hands. "Okay, I won't push it. Not now. Not if it's gonna make you cry. But..."

"But, what?"

He shook his head slowly. "Nothing. Never mind."

She didn't want to "never mind." She wanted to ask him if he actually thought it possible. And she would have...except she wasn't sure she was ready to hear his answer.

CHAPTER 16

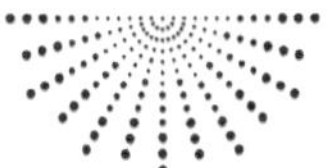

*H*er mind was clearer when she woke, sometime later. And the sensation that had drawn her out of sleep's warm embrace was one of loss, of emptiness, of coldness.

Blinking in the newborn sun's soft amber light, she struggled for memories. Her eyes shot wider when she found them. She'd fallen asleep wrapped tightly in Adam's arms, right after making incredible love to him.

"Oh, no," she whispered, scanning the room in search of him, not seeing him, feeling her face heat anyway. "God, tell me I didn't." But she did. She knew perfectly well she did. And she'd been so determined not to. Not to let him too close. Not to let him care.

She could only hope it had been no more than physical to him. She could only pray he hadn't let himself develop any feelings, not even a passing fondness for her. Because she might be forced to betray him in the end. She closed her eyes, bit her lower lip hard. Not "might be," she told herself with brutal honesty. She would be forced to betray Adam. She'd tried buying Zaslow off, and his response had been that horrible delivery last night. That coffin-shaped box. His message was loud and clear—Raze's body could've been in that box, and would be, if she resisted his plan.

What a cruel, malicious bastard to torture her that way. For a few unbearable seconds, she was sure Raze lay still and cold in that box. God, the feeling that had swamped her then—the very thought of that sweet, gentle man dying at the hand of one so evil...

She slammed her eyes closed as the desolate image crept into her mind.

Fight him, said the one inside. *Don't let that bastard do this to you.*

No, she couldn't fight Zaslow again. Not while he still had Raze. She would have to betray Adam. And he didn't deserve to be hurt like that. Not again.

She knew what lay at the heart of the pain she saw in Adam's eyes, shadowing his soul, never leaving him. She knew it was centered on betrayal. The betrayal felt by a boy whose own father turned on him like a vicious animal. The betrayal felt by a husband whose own wife takes everything he has and slips away like a thief in the night. The kind that was the most deadly. That which came from someone he loved. Trusted. Believed in.

He might seem tough and hard-nosed, but she could see through that shell to the man inside. He was fragile. It wouldn't take much to do him in.

She hoped to God the killing blow wouldn't be the one she had to deliver. And she assured herself it wouldn't be. Not as long as he hadn't let himself care.

Where was he?

Frowning at the new thought, Brigit got out of the bed. His bed. The pillow beside her was still sunken where he'd laid his head. Everywhere there were signs of Adam. His scent filled the room, and his clothes lay strewn on the floor. Golden strands of his hair clung to the brush on the dresser, glimmering like fire in the morning sunlight.

But Adam wasn't there.

She snatched his robe from the bedpost and wrapped it around her as she hurried to the French doors that matched those in her own bedroom. She pushed the latch down, stepped out onto the balcony to look up and down its wrought-iron length. But he wasn't there, either.

And then she saw him. He was standing on the outcropping of rock where they'd sat in the rain. He stood there, just staring out over the water toward the fiery ball of the rising sun. And he seemed... God, he seemed tortured. The wind came rushing off the lake to whip his pale hair into chaos. He stood, braced against it, facing it. His hands shoved into his jeans pockets, his eyes distant. He was staring out over the wind-tossed waves, but, she thought, not really seeing anything there.

Oh, Lord, what had she done?

Ducking back inside, she raced to her own bedroom, yanking a pair of black leggings on just because they were the first things she grabbed when she opened the dresser. No time for the hairbrush. She snatched an oversized gauzy white blouse from a hanger in the closet and pulled it on, fastening its big gold buttons with trembling fingers. She stuffed her feet into her favorite leather thong sandals and ran into the hallway and down the stairs.

Outside, the air still held the chill of night, but dawn's warmth was already invading. The breeze drew goosebumps to the surface of her skin, but the sun on her eyelids warmed her. She folded her arms over each other and ran along the path that skirted the house, just in time to see Adam disappearing in another direction. He hadn't taken the path that led down to the lake's grassy shore. Instead, he'd gone off into the woods nearby. A steep hillside, thick with pines, rose regally on the western side of the house. State land, she knew. Not Adam's own. He headed up the hill, and vanished as soon as he passed the first row of thick-needled sentries.

Where in the world was he going?

Brigit tilted her head to one side and debated with herself for no more than a minute. Then, her decision made, she started after him.

Adam could no longer see the old path. The one he'd followed as a small, adventurous child. It hadn't been made by man, anyway. Probably a deer trail or something. And deer changed paths all the time, to keep a step ahead of their predators. There were new paths trodden into the mossy forest floor. Mazes of them, going off in a hundred directions, and crisscrossing themselves often along the way.

Where was it? And how the hell was he supposed to fulfill his destiny—to show Brigit the way home—if he couldn't even find the trail that had once led him there?

He remembered crossing a stream. And there'd been a rise within the hillside, a hump of sorts. He'd had to climb it. He'd had to do that on hands and knees, he recalled, because the hump had been wearing a coat of blackberry briars. The cave was partway down a grassy slope on the far side of that briar-riddled hill.

If there ever had actually *been* a cave. Adam had long ago convinced himself—with a lot of help from his father—that there hadn't been. That it had all been in his imagination. But now, he'd swung the other way. He'd decided that he'd been right all along. Even as a child. He really *had* found some kind of mystical doorway to some enchanted realm. He really *had* talked to a fairy there, who'd shown him his fate.

All his life he'd been searching for proof it was real. Oh, he thought he was trying to find the source of the legend he must've heard and believed was real. But he'd never really believed that, not down deep. Down deep the little boy he'd been had always known it was real.

And Brigit was the proof he'd been seeking.

His fate, it seemed, was to have his heart broken by that beautiful half-fairy enchantress, and he'd likely waste away with longing for her the rest of his life, just the way Keats had tried to warn him he would.

Too bad he hadn't listened.

He'd got out of bed this morning, determined to get it over with. If he could find the spot in the woods, he'd show it to her, take her through to the other side, and be done with it. The longer he put it off, the more it was going to hurt. He was getting too damned used to having her around.

But now he faced another roadblock. One he hadn't even considered before. What if he could never find that place again?

It felt good, in a way, to let himself explore the possibility that his childhood fantasy had been real. That he really had crossed some invisible threshold into a fantasy world called Rush, and he really had met a fairy princess there, a pregnant one, who'd shown him his future. He hadn't realized how much he'd missed believing in fantasy until he'd started to let himself do it again. And it was all because of Brigit.

Her presence made his houseplants thrive, and she could tell a man was lying to her by looking into his eyes...

That was something, wasn't it? The way she took one look into Mac's eyes and just knew. Just like that. She knew he was lying.

Her footfalls always seemed soundless and she could predict the weather. And that birthmark... only, it was more than just a birthmark, wasn't it? It was the mark of the crescent moon that was talked about in that old Celtic text. The sign that marked her as a fairy of royal blood.

He could barely believe he'd let himself be convinced by all of this. But he had. And in doing so, he'd regained something he'd thought he'd never find again.

That's what had driven him to come out here. He hadn't trusted in his own mind enough to do so in nearly thirty years. He'd try now. Maybe, the small part of his mind that remained stubbornly skeptical told him, maybe being here again, in this forest where it had all started, would trigger something in his memory. Some logical explanation that would account for everything. All of it.

Or maybe he'd find that doorway he'd been trying for so long to believe had never existed.

Her skin was sweet.

He stopped in his tracks, frowning as the realization hit him right between the eyes. He'd kissed her, he'd kissed her all over. He'd tasted her skin. And it had truly seemed as if there was a flavor to it. A sweetness.

Honey. Just like in that Celtic text.

"My God," he muttered, and forced himself to continue walking. But after an hour trudging through the woods, he realized he wasn't going to find the place. Not now.

And for some reason, even that didn't convince him that it had never existed in the first place. It only made him worry that he'd be unable to complete his destiny, and to give Brigit the help she wasn't even aware she needed. Or maybe it simply wasn't time yet. That fairy had told him he had to show Brigit the way to her sister, and *then* the way back home. Maybe he had to do this in the proper order, if it was going to work at all.

Or maybe... maybe he really *wouldn't* be able to find it again.

Sighing in defeat, he sank down onto a damp, rotting stump and wondered what the hell his next move should be. Hell, if he couldn't find the doorway, did that mean he could keep her here, with him?

"Whatever it is, Adam, you can get past it."

He jerked his head up at the sound of her voice, squinting in disbelief when he saw her. Her sudden appearance there seemed to add even more credence to his theory. No normal woman could follow a man through the forest without making a sound, could she?

She came closer, sank down onto the forest floor, hooking her elbows on her knees, feet crossed at the ankles. "When I'm in a place like this, it reminds me how insignificant our troubles really are. I mean, what do they matter, in the scheme of things? We could disappear tomorrow, and the world would keep right on turning. The wind would still blow... " She closed her eyes, tilted her head back, and inhaled nasally. "...Mmm. And forests would still smell like no other place can smell. And the pines would still whisper their secrets to one another... "

He frowned, but found himself listening in a way he never had before. And suddenly he heard them. As the wind brushed through the needled boughs, it seemed as if the trees themselves were whispering in a million hushed voices. He'd been able to hear them once. He'd been in on those secrets, a long time ago. It had been magic.

He lowered his head, caught her staring at him.

"I'm sorry about last night, Adam. I... know you didn't want anything to happen between us. And I...kind of pushed you into it."

He was surprised at her heartfelt apology, and he couldn't stop himself from smiling at the embarrassment in her huge, dark blue eyes and the color in her cheeks. Her take on what had happened between them... What had happened between them had been incredible. It had been beyond anything he'd ever experienced with a woman.

"I don't recall begging for mercy."

She dipped her head, gnawing on her lower lip.

"I wanted it as much as you did," he said, and his voice tightened and roughened. "I still do."

Her head came up, eyes glittering. "No, you don't, Adam. It was a mistake and I—"

"Don't tell me what I want. I know. I've been wanting you since I laid eyes on you. Maybe even longer than that."

"How—"

He gave his head a firm shake. "Don't ask. Believe me, angel, you don't want to go there."

She looked alarmed, frightened for him, as she searched his face. "I didn't come out here for this. This isn't what I—"

"The point is," he said, interrupting her deliberately, "I resisted everything my body was screaming for, for one simple reason."

She tilted her head, waiting.

"I didn't trust you, Brigit."

He saw the flash of guilt in her eyes, the remorse, but the truth, too. Right there. She didn't duck it or try to hide it. She took his direct hit, and she never even flinched.

"I know you're up to something. I know you're keeping the truth from me... about a lot of things. From who you really are, to what you expected to find in that crate yesterday. But knowing all that doesn't stop me from wanting you." He shrugged, wishing she was sitting closer. Wishing he could touch her. "So there's my dilemma."

Without meeting his eyes, she whispered, "I'm sorry."

"I was afraid. See, I've trusted the people I care about before. And I've been hurt before. I was afraid it would happen again if I let myself feel anything for you."

She said nothing, only sat there looking miserable.

"Problem is, I can't stop myself from feeling something for you."

She gasped, started to argue, but he didn't give her time.

"I don't even know what it is, exactly. But there's definitely something. Something powerful. Something... " He reached across the distance between them, cupping her chin and lifting her gaze to his. "Something I've never felt before," he finished, and he felt a little sick to his stomach. "So the whole caution thing is really a moot point. The choice has been taken right out of my hands."

She shook her head. "Adam, don't—"

"It's a relief, really. I don't have to struggle against it anymore. I'm sort of left with no choice but to go with this thing."

"I don't want to hurt you."

She sure looked as if she meant every word of it. But she was going to. She didn't realize it yet, but she had no choice in the matter. Before she did, though, he was going to get to the bottom of whatever she was up to and confront her about it, and make her tell him why.

There was a powerful reason motivating her. He knew that as well as he knew everything else. A reason that had to do with the fear he'd seen in her eyes yesterday. And with that Zaslow creep. These were things he knew, beyond doubt. Not like those other things. Those fairy things that he couldn't begin to understand.

"I believe that," he told her, because he did.

"Adam, I'd tell you everything if I could. I swear it."

"I know."

Tears brimmed in her eyes, and he found himself wanting to change the subject. He could see the agony this one was causing her. She wanted to tell him the truth. He knew she meant it when she said that she did. But she couldn't, and the conflict was tearing her apart.

"Adam—"

"Shhsh." He stroked her hair, studied her face. "I want to tell you something." He saw her press her lips together, and she nodded for him to continue. Adam took a deep breath and let his hand fall away. He looked around at the pines and the myriad paths twisting through them. "I used to come out here when I was a little boy. But I haven't been back in almost thirty years."

Her brows lifted, in interest, he supposed, but mostly, in surprise that he'd changed the subject rather than grilling her.

He got off his stump and sat on the ground in front of it, leaning his back against the uneven bark. He lifted his arms toward her, waiting.

With a little sigh, she came closer, curling into the V between his open legs, and laying her side against his chest. He closed his arms around her. It felt good to hold her there. It felt right.

"Why did you stay away so long?"

"My father forbade me to ever come back here. And I knew better than to disobey the old bastard."

"He was a monster, Adam." She snuggled closer to him as she said it, and her arms tightened around his waist. "It wasn't your fault, what he did to you. You know that."

"It's taken a long time, but yeah. I know that."

She lifted her head, scanning his face with eyes that seemed to see more than they should. When he looked away, she lowered her head again. "Why didn't he want you out here?"

"Because... I thought I saw something out here. Something... that shouldn't have been real. And I guess the old man thought he was making sure I knew the difference between fantasy and reality."

"No," she whispered. "No one believes beating a child will keep him sane. No one who abuses their own child does it for the child's own good. Though I imagine they all say they do." She sat up, looked him in the eye. "He did it because he was sick, Adam."

It was as if she sensed the bolt of pain that shot through him when he remembered. And she deftly pulled that bolt out again, snapped it in two, and tossed it aside.

Brigit's hand ran over his nape, the warmth of her fingertips infusing him.

"Damn," he said softly. "You're good for me, Brigit."

"That's what friends are for," she whispered.

"Is that what you are? My friend?"

She lowered her eyes. "I care about you, Adam. No matter what else happens, don't doubt that."

She turned sideways again, as she'd been before, tucking herself against his body. And he closed his arms around her almost automatically. It was such a natural thing to embrace her, to hold her, to talk to her this way.

"So, why did you come out here this morning, after staying away for so long?"

He stiffened a little. "That gets back to what I was starting to tell you before. About what happened the last time I came up here."

"Thirty years ago," she whispered. "What did you see, Adam?"

He drew his brows together, glancing down at the top of her head, which told him nothing. "What the hell. You deserve to be warned, Brigit. Hell, you're living with me, *sleeping* with me... though you might change your mind about that soon enough. You might as well know the worst. I found a cave out here, somewhere. And I crawled through it and emerged... somewhere else."

She sat up, her eyes sharp and probing as they met his. "Where?"

"Rush." He blurted it before he could think better of it, waited for the fear or the sympathy to fill her eyes. He never saw it. He saw something more like childish excitement and wonder, instead.

"Rush?" she breathed. "The one in the painting? God, Adam, the one in my fairy tale?"

He shrugged. "Yeah. It was exactly like the one in the painting. And... " He closed his eyes, letting his voice trail off.

"That's incredible."

"In-credible. Meaning not credible. That's exactly what it was. A kid's daydream. Nothing more. At least, that's what I thought... until I saw that book of yours."

She sat up straighter. "It looked like the Rush in my book?"

"Down to the tiniest detail."

"What happened there?" She was all but bouncing up and down as she spoke. "Did you see anyone? Talk to anyone? How did you find your way back?"

"Slow down. Are you sure you want to hear this? You said before—"

She stopped speaking, eyes narrowing. "Well, just because I want to hear it doesn't mean I have to believe in it again. Please tell me the rest, Adam." Like a little girl pleading for a bedtime story. He couldn't have resisted if he'd wanted to.

"All right. I met a woman who claimed to be a fairy. I... she had... wings. And... Brigit, she said her name was Maire."

Brigit looked up at him slowly. She pressed both hands to her chest, fists clenched until her knuckles whitened. Her eyes were wider than he'd ever seen them.

"Don't," he whispered. "Don't look like that. There's a chance I heard some version of your fairytale somewhere, and just transferred it to my dream. Maybe."

She blinked, gave her head a shake, and finally nodded. "I know. I know none of it can be real. For a second, I just... let myself forget. You know, when I was a little girl, I honestly thought of Maire as... as my mother."

"Maybe I shouldn't have—"

"Go on," she whispered, and he thought she was holding her breath. "I want to hear the rest. Please, go on."

He swallowed hard. "You're sure?" She nodded, and he began again. "Maire told me she'd show me the way home, but first she wanted to know if I'd like to see my fate, because she'd seen it the second she'd looked into my eyes."

"Yes," Brigit whispered. "That's the same question she used to ask me... "

Adam looked at her sharply.

"I used to dream about her, too, Adam. But go on," she told him. "Did you say yes?"

"Yes." He wanted to ask questions, but he was compelled to get the entire story out, here and now. No more hiding from it.

Brigit blinked fast, and he thought there were tears trying to work into her eyes.

"What did she show you?"

"You," he said, and the single word slipped from between his lips without his consent, and fortunately, without a sound. She never heard it. He hoped she never saw it. He was confessing enough as it was.

"She pushed aside some bushes and told me to look through. I did, and I saw a girl, bathing in a pool, all but hidden by rushes,"

"Like the painting?"

"Not *like* the painting. It *was* the painting. Only... instead of an adult, she was a child. There was a little blond haired girl splashing nearby but I couldn't take my eyes from the one with the raven curls and sapphire eyes. Maire told me she was my fate. That my destiny was to show her the way home, and that I mustn't let myself fall in love with her, because she would break my heart. And then she let the bushes come together. When I looked up at her again, she was gone. I pushed the bushes apart again, but there was no lake, no woman. Just more trees. I turned around, and there was the cave, right in front of me, though it hadn't been there before. So I crawled inside, and, I don't know, I guess I fell asleep there. When I woke later and came out again, I was in these very ordinary woods, not far from my house." He smiled at her, seeing her confusion, and decided to give her a way out, in case she wasn't ready to swallow all of this. "It took me a while to realize I'd probably fallen asleep the first time I entered the cave, and that the rest was just a dream."

"You really believe that?"

He was surprised she would ask the question.

He thought she'd already made up her mind that none of this could be real.

"What else could it have been?"

She blinked, looking a little dazed. "I know... it had to be a dream. What else could it be? It's just that... Adam, you have a painting of what you saw, hanging in your study. Unless you painted it yourself..." She lifted her brows, waiting.

"No. I found it in a shop on the Commons. The Capricorn."

"Then how can you dismiss all of the rest so easily?"

"I don't know. Anything can be explained if you try hard enough. Say...the painting is only *similar* to that childhood fantasy, and when I saw it, I subconsciously substituted it for the image I'd seen in the dream,"

"But you don't believe that. Do you, Adam?"

He wasn't sure he should tell her what he believed. So he shrugged, drew a breath. "Lately..."

"Lately, what...?"

He wanted to tell her. He wanted to see if he could scare her into running from him, because he'd already decided he couldn't run from her. He didn't have the strength, let alone the will.

But he couldn't do it. He couldn't deliberately drive her out of his life by telling her the thoughts he'd been having about her. Not now.

Or... not yet.

Maybe it would be better to let her see that Celtic text. See if she saw the parallels that he did. See if maybe it stirred something in her.

He shook his head. "Doesn't matter."

She stepped closer, ran her fingers through his hair, searched his face. "Why did you tell me all that?"

"I'm not sure," he told her, in all honesty. He wrapped his arms around her waist to hold her close to him. Seemed he couldn't get enough of having her close to him. "Maybe so you'd know my deepest, darkest secret, Brigit. Maybe I thought it might make you feel a little safer, later, when you're ready to tell me yours."

She closed her eyes, as if afraid he might see it written right there, in neon ink. "I will tell you," she whispered, and the words carried the force of a vow. "Very, very soon. I promise, Adam."

"But not yet."

"No." She lowered her head to his chest, but not in time to hide her fresh tears. "Not yet."

CHAPTER 17

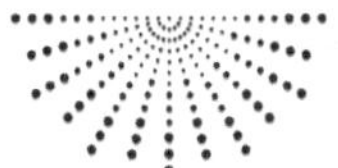

$\mathcal{H}$e was hurt that she couldn't tell him the secrets she was keeping, and that she was still holding herself at arm's length from him. She could feel his pain. And while she could strive to keep her heart set aside, she couldn't physically put a distance between them. When he slid his arm around her shoulders and drew her close to his side for the walk back to the house, she didn't resist. Didn't pull away. Couldn't.

"I don't want to worry about it anymore," he whispered, leaning close to her ear. "I don't want to think about anything bad. Not until I have to."

"But, Adam, I—"

He silenced her with a finger to her lips. And then he replaced it with his mouth. He kissed her deeply, thoroughly, pulling her tight against him.

"You're good for me, angel," he whispered against her neck, as his mouth moved there. "You make me feel like I've never felt. And I want to feel that way again."

"We shouldn't—"

"I need you, Brigit."

It was a confession that was wrung from him, she realized. And it was her undoing. The next thing she knew, she was the one kissing him. Holding him so tight her arms ached, wishing she never had to let go. He did need her. She'd always known that. She was the one who could heal his old wounds. And God, how she wanted to do that. There was nothing she wanted more.

His kisses became feverish, and hers responded in kind. They made frantic love on the forest floor, with the blue sky overhead and the music of birds playing in time with their breathing and their whispers and their kisses and the gentle sounds of their bodies sliding one against the other.

And when it was over, and he scooped her into his arms and carried her naked, back to the house, she realized it wasn't over. Not at all. It was only beginning.

The entire day, and long into the night, they spent together. Talking and laughing and making love, over and over again.

It was, Brigit thought, the most perfectly wonderful day of her entire life. And the most perfect night. She wished to God it didn't have to end.

But it did. The next morning, when Adam headed out to the university. She kissed him goodbye, and pretended to believe he'd come home that night, and the magic would begin all over again.

But the magic was make-believe. And the time for her betrayal came again. Her heart felt as if it was made of lead when she took out the canvas, and the paints, and set up the tripod in the study. And it took a lot longer to achieve the state she needed in order to work. But she did it. Because Raze's life was hanging in the balance, and because she had no choice.

She felt like the lowest, most vile being on the planet.

And even then, she let her mind wander back to the story Adam had told her out there in the woods. And his earlier questions. What if it was all true? What if she really was the little girl in the fairy tail?

Impossible.

And yet, here she stood, wielding paintbrushes without looking, letting some other force control her hands. The ability had been a part of her life for so long, she'd accepted it as natural. The way some people can do acrobatics, and some can run like the wind, and some sing like angels. But now, she wondered if maybe that thing, that *juice,* as she called it, might go by another name. Like "magic."

Silly. Ridiculous.

And what about her green thumb? Sure, lots of people were good at growing things. That was no big deal. But often, when a plant seemed to be in trouble, she'd instinctively go to it, and rub its leaves between her fingers while envisioning it healthy and strong. She'd done that automatically. Without forethought. The way one pets a dog. But every time she did, the plant would begin to thrive within a day or two. More than thrive. Those formerly ill subjects often grew better than any other plants in the shop.

And then there was the way she could read a man's heart by looking into his eyes. Another talent she'd grown accustomed to. So much so that she never questioned it.

But now she wondered if there was the slightest chance...the tiniest possibility that...

No. No, letting herself believe again would only bring disappointment.

Inside, the wild child called Brigit a fool for refusing to see what was staring her in the face. But Brigit ignored her, and she painted all the same.

~

Adam didn't actually sit down. He was knocked there, hard, right into the chair facing the desk in Mac's shoddy little office. Mac's words, his information, hit him like a fist, and Adam simply collapsed, the wind whooshing from his lungs in response to the imaginary blow.

"That's not possible. It can't be..."

Mac crooked one eyebrow. "Jeeze Adam, don't tell me this woman means something to you." When Adam didn't answer, Mac, came around the desk, staring down at him, looking scared. "Dammit, this is exactly what I was afraid of. Are you all right?"

He shook his head, but couldn't speak. Words deserted him. Pain took their place. Pain so intense there had never been its equal. His muscles went limp. He was drunk with pain.

"You *knew* she was scamming you." Mac tugged his tie loose and began pacing the office in quick, angry strides.

"You knew it right from the first day, Adam. How could you let yourself—"

"Doesn't matter." He managed to speak the words, but they were muffled, dull. "Doesn't matter at all, does it?" He flipped open the file folder he'd slammed shut only seconds earlier, looked at the police mug shot of the man who'd been at the house. The man who called himself Brigit's old friend. Ernie Zaslow was only one of his many aliases. The man was into many scams, but his favorite, it seemed, was brokering stolen art. He'd served eight years when he'd tried to sell a stolen Picasso to an undercover fed. The police had suspected him of many similar acts of fencing, but had been unable to prove many of the charges.

Most interesting of all was his m.o. Zaslow had got away with his crimes for so long, because his victims rarely knew they'd been robbed. He replaced each stolen painting with a duplicate so perfect even the owners had trouble telling the difference.

But Zaslow was no forger. He'd been working with a partner. And that partner had never been caught.

Adam recalled the paint-smeared rag he'd found on the marble pedestal stand the other day, and he felt sick all over again.

"What could she be after, Adam? Come on, you have to snap out of it. You want to catch her, don't you?"

He lifted his head, but it seemed too heavy. Did he? He wasn't sure.

"The only painting I have that's worth anything is *Rush*." He shook his head slowly. "I can't believe she'd be involved in a plot to steal it. She knows... "

"Knows what?"

Adam didn't answer aloud. Internally, though, he was kicking himself. Brigit knew how much that painting meant to him. How could she be plotting something like this?

And why?

He remembered the stains on her fingertips, and the faint aroma in the study...

...and the look in her eyes when he made love to her. And the feel of her skin under his hands, and the smell of her hair.

God!

"But *Rush* isn't valuable, is it? It wasn't done by a master..."

"It's anonymous. Unsigned. Art dealers speculate all sorts of theories about it, but none have been proven. It's the mystery that makes it so valuable. But not priceless. It's only priceless... to me."

How could she... after what they'd shared? He'd let himself believe in her, let himself care.

"What're you gonna do?"

Adam shook his head. "I don't know."

"According to the FBI files, Zaslow is only a broker. A fence, if you want to call it that. He had a forger who was never named, and he had a talented burglar by the name of Melvin

Kincaid who made the switches for him. He and Kincaid both did time. They went up for a heist they pulled fifteen years ago and either one of them could have reduced his sentence by naming the forger, but neither would do it."

God, Brigit couldn't have been much more than a teenager back then. A teenage art forger? How much sense did that make?

He looked up at Mac, who was still pacing. "So why do you think they didn't turn her over, pal? Loyalty. Honor among thieves?"

"Her?" Mac stopped walking and stared at him. "You think Brigit's the *forger?*"

Adam nodded.

Mac swore. Then he walked to the window and swore some more. "With Mel, it might have been loyalty. From what I've dug up on him, he was damn likeable, if a little light-fingered. Adam..."

Adam looked up, coming alert at Mac's tone.

"Adam I tried to check these two out. Mel Kincaid is dead."

Adam blinked. "How?"

"He was tied to a chair and beaten to death with a baseball bat. They found him in an abandoned apartment building in Brooklyn. The day he was killed was the same day Ernie Zaslow hopped a commuter flight into Lansing."

Adam's devastation was compounded now. By fear. "You think Zaslow murdered him?"

Mac shrugged. "If he did, he's one dangerous son of a bitch, Your Brigit Malone has herself mixed up in some bad company. She's either in league with a killer, or in danger from him. Either way, you have to get the hell away from her. Throw her out before she drags you down with her."

The thought that she might be in danger sent cold chills racing up his spine, and slapped a little more sense into Adam. He grimaced at his own idiocy. He'd known for days that Brigit was up to something, and suspected almost from the start that she was being forced, somehow, to do whatever it was she was doing.

So nothing had changed, had it? Except that he now knew what it was she was being forced to do.

He was angry. Yes, he was still very angry at the thought that this morning Brigit had kissed him goodbye, and then she'd gone into the study to work on her forgery. And he was furious that she hadn't trusted him enough to tell him the truth. Didn't she know that he'd have given her the damned painting if she'd asked?

He closed his eyes tight.

"Adam?"

"I know," he said softly, though he didn't know. He didn't know anything anymore.

"So what are you going to do?"

He only shook his head.

Mac sighed, impatience making him grimace. "You're not gonna toss her out, are you?"

"No. Not yet."

"Adam, come on, snap out of it. You go home, right now, and you throw her out the front door, bag and baggage. You tell her you're onto her little con game, and if she ever shows up at your door again, you'll turn her in so fast she won't know what hit her."

Adam looked up into his friend's concerned eyes and simply said, "I can't do that."

"Then what are you gonna do?"

He rose, surprised to find his legs unsteady. The pain was hardening, changing. "I don't know. But I know she's not a criminal. She might've been once, Mac, but not anymore."

"This isn't enough to convince you? Hell, I never thought of you as gullible."

Adam almost laughed out loud. If Mac had a clue the kinds

of things that had been dancing through his mind, he'd have thought the word gullible was too mild. He had to convince Brigit to trust him. Had to make her let him help her out of this mess. And then... and then he had to let her go. He knew that. Had known it from the start. He had to let her go.

Even though it would tear his heart out.

Mac sighed long and hard, but went to his desk and unlocked a drawer. He withdrew what looked like a marking pen, brought it over, and tucked it into Adam's pocket. "The ink only shows up in a black light, pal. Take my advice and mark the back of your painting. At least take that precaution."

"All right."

"Adam..."

Adam looked at Mac, and knew his friend was genuinely afraid for him. "I'll be okay," he said, but even to his own ears, it lacked conviction.

"If you need me..."

"Yeah."

~

She stopped painting earlier than usual, and put her things away. The juice just wasn't flowing today.

The manuscript Adam had been reading was still sitting on the desk in the study, and some force she didn't pretend to understand, had drawn her to it. It felt as if, from the second she'd stepped into the room, that book had been calling to her.

And she'd never been one to ignore her instincts. So she went to the desk, and she looked at the leather-bound translation of some ancient Celtic text.

And then she stood motionless, blinking in shock because the words on the pages had a magical cadence, a lilt of sincerity. They rang true, somehow, as they outlined the characteristics of fairy folk. Especially those of the feminine ilk. It told of their affinity with nature, and the way plants and animals thrive when a fairy is near. It told of how a fairy could read a man's soul by looking into his eyes, and how she could capture the soul of a mortal man, and enslave him forever.

Breathless with wonder, Brigit sank into the chair behind Adam's desk, and continued to read. When she came to the pages describing the crescent moon birthmark and what its color might signify, she started shaking all over. Goosebumps traveled up and down her arms and chills tumbled over her spine.

What in the name of God was this?

"Interesting reading, isn't it?"

Her head came up fast at the sound of Adam's voice. She stared at him, not really seeing, heard him, but wasn't really hearing.

"Where did you get this?" she asked softly.

Adam tilted his head, sniffed the air. "What's that smell?" he asked, and his face was hard. No hint of a smile touched his eyes. "Almost smells like paint. Ridiculous, isn't it, Brigit?"

She blinked, shook her head, wondered why he seemed so...so empty. So sad. Glancing down at the book on the desk, she jerked in surprise when he spoke again.

"It's a translation of a text uncovered in an archaeological dig in Ireland. They figure it's around nine hundred years old."

He spoke as if that bit of information held some particular relevance, but she didn't know what. "Adam... this is uncanny. The... the birthmark..."

He lowered his head, no longer looking her in the eye. "Yeah. It blew me away when I saw it on you. But, dammit, Brigit, that isn't important right now. What's important is that you don't trust me. After everything... everything I've told you... you still can't be honest with me."

He was angry. He'd been angry before he'd ever spoken to her, and she would have realized it if she hadn't been so shocked by what she'd read. "What's the matter? What did I do?"

He opened his mouth but snapped it closed again, apparently changing his mind. He lowered his chin, shook his head. "Nothing. Nothing at all."

She came from behind the desk, moving toward him. "Talk to me."

Shaking his head, he started to turn away.

"Adam, please. This is scaring me."

She saw his back stiffen, his head come up, though he didn't turn to face her. "You're scared?"

"Of course I'm scared. How can I not be?"

He turned then, slowly, his eyes narrow, and wary, and hurt.

"Adam, how long have you known about this," she asked, pointing at the book on the desk.

"Almost a year."

"Then you knew... about these similarities. You already knew..."

"Knew what, Brigit?"

"The... the things that book says... they're so similar to..."

He averted his eyes, nodding

"There's an explanation. There has to be. Maybe my birthmark is just a coincidence. Or maybe..."

"Or maybe what? Come on, Brigit, tell me what you're really thinking. Don't keep lying to me."

It was her turn to narrow her eyes, search his face. "Why are you so angry with me?"

He blinked twice, then turned away from her.

She ran around him, stopping in front of him, blocking his exit. "Please . . ." It was a faint whisper, a hoarse plea. "Don't walk away without telling me why."

"You know why."

She nodded slowly, understanding coming to her in waves

that nearly knocked her breathless. He'd had enough of her lies. He was tired of waiting for her to trust him with the truth.

"It's almost over. I swear, it won't be long now, and I'll be able to tell you everything. Please, don't give up on me. Not yet."

He started to walk past her, and anger surged through her more forcefully than it had ever done.

"No!"

She yelled it at the top of her voice, sending the force of her fury into the word. Adam stopped dead as if he'd slammed into a brick wall. He blinked in shock, his eyes widening.

Brigit paid little attention to that. She was too busy searching for answers, fearing the worst. God, did he know then? Had he somehow found out that she was about to steal his painting?

It didn't matter. She had no choice but to go through with her plan. She couldn't risk Raze's life. But when it was over, maybe when she explained what she'd done, and why she'd done it, maybe he'd understand. Maybe he'd find some way to forgive her. Maybe...

But she knew better, didn't she? Maybe another man would be able to forgive this kind of betrayal. But not Adam. And it would be wrong of her to even ask him to.

She tried to stifle her sobs as she turned away, and ran through the study and up the stairs to her room.

Adam stood precisely where he was, not moving, not even breathing.

Something had just happened, something that defied explanation—well, defied every explanation except one. When Brigit had shouted at him...she'd hit him. Hard. Only... she hadn't moved. A solid blast of hot anger had slammed into his chest.

He'd been heading for the door, and it had stopped him in his tracks. *Wham!*

And it had vanished just as suddenly.

He lowered his chin to his chest, shook his head. No more room for doubt. It had happened. And he was either completely insane, which he knew damned well he wasn't, or Brigit Malone was a fairy.

And she doesn't know, he thought in stunned silence. Hell, she was probably more confused by all this than he was.

Brigit Malone. Fairy or thief? Or both. Somehow, in some twisted-up way, she must be both.

He'd stick it out for a few more days. Watch her every move, and find out for himself.

~

She tossed in the bed, twisting and writhing until the sheets had tangled around her legs like boa constrictors. God, what had come over Adam?

He must have been checking up on her. It was the only answer. He must have been trying to verify the lies she'd told him, about her reasons for not being able to stay in her house, about her past. Could he have found out the truth? No one knew why she was really here. No one but Zaslow. How could Adam have found out?

He didn't trust her anymore. Not the way he had. And it was killing her. It was tearing her apart not to have him here, to hold her the way he had before. It was too lonely, now, in this bed without him. She sat up, wrenching the covers from her body, dashing the tears from her eyes with the back of one hand.

She'd go to him, right now, and tell him everything. Maybe he'd understand. Maybe he'd help her find another way out of this mess. Maybe...

She whirled, uttering a little squeak of surprise when there was a tap on the French doors. And then her eyes widened and her heart sped up.

The doors were flung open, and Zaslow stepped through them, shaking his head slowly. "Sleeping alone tonight, are you? What happened? Trouble in paradise?"

She shook her head rapidly, backing toward the door.

"Is he onto you, Brigit?"

"No." Her back pressed to the cool wood, her hand rose behind her to grasp the knob.

"You're not going anywhere. Not unless you want Raze's heart delivered to you in a candy box."

Swallowing the sandy feeling in her throat, she lowered her hand. She was shaking all over, fear making her feel as cold as if she was standing naked in a snowstorm.

"Why are you alone? Tell me, and tell me the truth, or I'll hurt your old friend. And I'll enjoy it."

She shook her head rapidly. "I don't know. I swear, Zaslow. He... he came home in a bad mood. I... I don't think it has anything to do with me." It was a lie, but one she hoped he wouldn't see through. Brigit knew damned well that Adam's mood had everything to do with her.

"Make up with him."

She blinked, not understanding, and Zaslow rolled his eyes, sighing loud and long. "Show me the painting, Brigit. I want to verify you haven't stopped working on it."

"I haven't."

"Show me," he growled. And she felt her teeth chatter.

Keeping her back to the wall, she sidled toward the closet, only edging nearer him when she had no choice but to go around the chestnut vanity beside her bed. She opened the closet door, reached inside to turn on the light. Inclining her head she said, "It's in the back. Don't smear it."

Zaslow's eyes narrowed on her face. "You leave this room, Brigit, or call out or do *anything* other than stand there, and you can kiss your friend Malone goodbye. I didn't leave him alone."

And then he ducked into the closet, and she stood there. Trembling, impotent with fear for Raze and enraged that she was so helpless.

But you're not helpless, you fool! came the all-too-familiar voice of her wild side. *Something happened downstairs tonight. When you yelled at Adam, he stopped as if he'd walked into an invisible wall. You did that.*

No. That was impossible. It made no sense.

So what in your life ever has *made sense?*

She frowned, refusing to believe, not wanting to believe. But her anger at Zaslow came bubbling up, and she had the feeling that the wild one inside was deliberately rousing it. Brigit looked into the closet where the self-assured bully stood examining the painting, and she recalled the sight of that coffin-shaped box, and the fear that had nearly paralyzed her. And she got angrier. With her eyes tightly closed, she wished with everything in her that she could hurt Zaslow. Make him pay for what he was putting Raze through. Pain, she thought. The man deserved severe pain.

"Dammit!"

A muffled thud accompanied his cry, and Brigit jerked rigid, her eyes flying open. Zaslow emerged from the closet, pressing three fingers to his forehead. Blood trickled from beneath the fingers, trailing down onto his nose, a single droplet dangling from the tip.

Wide-eyed, Brigit backed away from him... from the undeniable evidence. "What happened?"

"Nothing," he snapped. "A box fell from a shelf." With his free hand he jerked tissues from the dispenser on the vanity and swiped the blood away, then pressed the wad to the cut on his head. "The painting looks nearly finished."

She couldn't stop staring at the cut on his forehead, couldn't slow her racing heartbeat, or the new knowledge that was slowly making itself a home in her mind. "It is," she whispered. "Almost done, that is."

"How much longer?"

She shrugged, lowering her gaze to the floor, shaking her head in wonder.

"Three days," he told her. "Three days, Brigit. It will either be the length of time it takes to finish the painting, or Raze's life expectancy. Understand?"

"It's not enough—"

"It's more than enough. Meanwhile, you'd better take your pretty backside down the hall and wiggle it for Mr. Reid. You'll never finish the painting if he throws you out, will you?"

She lifted her head, glared at him. "You son of a—"

"Seduce your way back into his good graces, Brigit. You can do it. You managed it the first time around."

"It wasn't—"

"Good night." He tossed the tissues into the wastebasket, and walked back out the French doors, the same way he'd entered.

She stared after him, and thought about trying to see if she could wish him to fall on his head from the balcony. Only the fear of never knowing where Raze was, of him dying slowly because she couldn't find him, kept her from experimenting on Zaslow just then.

Brigit wondered how he'd managed to get up there in the first place, whether he had a rope ladder dangling from the deck outside or what.

She was exhausted, physically, emotionally, and mentally. This was too much. Too damned much for anyone to go through. Not just Zaslow and his threats, but this feeling that was slowly encapsulating her entire soul that maybe the reason she had never felt as if she belonged in the world was because she *didn't*. Maybe she belonged somewhere else. Like Rush.

God, it was too much to take in all at once. Especially alone.

She sank down to the floor, giving in to the turmoil, letting the tears come at last.

"God, Adam," she whispered. "I need you. I just need you to hold me so much. Can't you just hold me?" And she lifted her head, looking toward the wall that separated his room from hers, and she closed her eyes. "If there's any magic in me at all... let it bring you to me tonight. I don't want to spend the night alone."

CHAPTER 18

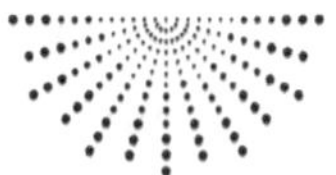

She was still lying to him. Even now.

She was a beautiful woman who smiled with her eyes whenever he looked into them. She touched him in a way no other woman ever had, in a way he sensed no other woman ever would.

After what they'd shared—the things he'd told her, things he'd never shared with anyone, and the hours of lovemaking so intense and soul-deep it had to be supernatural—she still couldn't bring herself to trust him enough to tell him the truth. Hadn't it meant a damn thing to her? Had it all been an act? If she cared in the least, wouldn't she have opened up to him by now?

And did it matter? Because he still wanted her. He wanted her all the time, day and night, asleep or awake, at home and at work. She was never far from his mind. He couldn't stop thinking about the way it felt to hold her, to kiss her. The taste of her skin. Those honeyed kisses.

She was plotting to steal his most precious possession, even knowing what it meant to him. And he didn't care. He'd rather burn the thing in the fireplace than lose her now.

That was the problem. He cared. He hadn't meant to. He'd been warned not to. And he had to resist her. He had to stop himself from getting any closer to her, because he knew she'd leave him. He knew. And knowing made every breath he drew sheer hell.

He had to stay away from her. Help her, yes, but somehow keep a distance. Keep his emotions safe. He had to...

She was in trouble. In so much trouble she couldn't find her way out. And... and she needed him.

Adam flung back the covers, sitting up in the bed. He gripped his pillow in his fists and he shook it. Damn, damn, *damn!*

He wanted her.

Slamming himself out of bed, he paced the floor, plush carpeting cushioning his bare feet, warm summer air greeting his naked flesh. He was lonely for her soft, silken body. For her sweet lips and for those little sounds she made when he...

Damn!

Five steps to the French doors. He stopped there only briefly, then turned on his heel. Twelve steps past the foot of the bed, to the closed door that led to the hallway. And he stopped there a little longer. A second longer. Long enough for his hand to touch the doorknob. Long enough for him to curse himself for being an idiot.

He turned again. Ten steps to the bathroom door, four through it, and a cold shower was within reach. It was also the last thing he wanted.

He *wanted* Brigit.

How many steps, he wondered, were there between his room and hers? Only a few, and he'd be there, with her. He could have her.

Keep your distance, you idiot! You're walking right into heartbreak!

She was longing for him, aching for him, right then, calling to him, somehow. He could feel her calling out to him, though he couldn't hear her. A psychic lure tugged at him, teased him, tempted him. Its touch was physical. Something very real, dammit, had twined around him and pulled tight, so that he felt like a fish caught in a net. And he didn't bother struggling because he thought it might kill him. The net pulled tight, so there was no chance of escape, and then it drew him across that soft carpet. It drew him right up to his bedroom door.

Through it.

He was hauled in by this mental net, and it was against his will, against everything he knew to be practical and smart and necessary. She would hurt him. Again. She would lie to him, and she would leave him. And yet he walked a little faster instead of fighting the current that carried him through the hall. He twisted the doorknob, swung her bedroom door open, and stepped inside. She was on the floor, by her bed, her legs curled underneath her, tears scalding her cheeks.

She looked up, met his eyes. "Adam..."

"I didn't want to come in here," he whispered, and his voice sounded ragged and broken. And even as he said it, he was dropping to his knees, clasping her shoulders, running his fingertips over her skin.

"I was wishing for you, Adam."

"I heard you," he said, and he covered her mouth with his. His breathing was ragged and his hands were pushing the thin straps of the camisole down from her shoulders.

Her hands came around him, and her fingers dove into his hair. She leaned back, opened her mouth wider, and he devoured her, unable to help himself. He moved his mouth sideways, over her face, and down her neck. He tugged the camisole lower, and tasted her breast, the rounded, firm flesh, and then the succulent center.

He had to know her, all of her. He had to experience every sensation, every nuance, every inch of her. It was a compulsion.

An obsession, or perhaps an addiction to that honeyed flavor. He kissed a wet trail over her thighs, down the backs of her calves, tasted the hollows behind her knees.

And still he craved more of her, more than he ever could have. He couldn't tell her that, couldn't give words to a need so fierce, so powerful.

He crawled back up her body, then sank sideways, turning so he was on his back beside her and pulling her on top of him. She settled herself over him, lowered herself slowly, closing her eyes as she did. She remained upright, and when she opened her eyes again, it was to stare straight down into his. And he saw the wildness in her eyes. The part of her he'd sensed her struggling against so often. It was loose now. And he was glad. Slowly, she moved. Her head fell backward and her eyes closed.

His hands at the small of her back pulled her forward though, and then down to him, so he could kiss her and taste her mouth as he made love to her. He didn't want it to end. Not ever. It didn't matter that she was lying to him, or that she was going to leave him in the end. Because there was something bigger than both of them, something that seemed to be pushing them together. A force neither of them could understand, let alone overcome.

She held him inside her, and she moved with him, and when she drew the release from him he felt his very soul flowing into hers, mating with it, entwining in a knot that could only be eternal.

God, she owned him now. What hope was there for him after lovemaking like this? He'd surrendered his soul. Her hold on him was greater than anyone's had ever been. Greater than Sandra's. Greater even than that of his own father when he'd been just a child. Brigit owned him, because he'd given her his heart and soul. He'd shared everything with her, unable to do otherwise. And now he was like a duck at a carnival game, waiting for her to do her worst, praying she'd have mercy, and knowing she wouldn't...*couldn't.* The choice wasn't hers.

When she left him, when she took the blade that fate had forced into her hands, and drove it straight through his heart, it was going to be the killing stroke. He'd given her too much of himself, now. There was no getting it back. She would destroy him.

And he'd let her.

He was intense, and energetic, but not rough. It wasn't in his gentle soul to be less than tender with her, though his tenderness was ablaze with passion. It thrilled something in Brigit's heart to know she was capable of stirring so much reaction in him. So much need. It seemed a miracle to her that he would come to her even though he didn't want to.

But it was no miracle. It was magic. And she felt guilty for using it on him. Moreover, she was afraid she wouldn't be able to resist the urge to do it again.

Poor Adam. So sure she was dishonest, so sure she was up to no good, and yet unable to stay away. She should leave here. That would end his misery. She should go away and just let him alone.

But she couldn't. If she did, the man she loved—the other one—would die.

She stirred. They'd been lying in silence for a long time, he on his back beneath her. She, collapsed atop him. Naked. Without covers to hide under. Slowly, though, the love languor faded, and she became aware of how still he was. Not relaxed stillness, either. She felt the tension in every bit of him. He lay stiff, and his arms were on the floor at his sides, rather than around her as they had been.

Slowly she lifted her upper body, so she could look down

into his face. But the expression he wore was one she'd rather not have seen. Self-disgust. Regret. Despondency. All so clear in his eyes. Eyes she'd always been able to read.

She shook her head slowly. What could she say? She couldn't assure him that he'd been wrong about her, that she was honest and faithful and true. She wasn't. She was exactly what he thought she was. A liar. A thief.

She lowered her chin in shame and slid off him, ending on her knees beside him. She watched as he sat up and got to his feet. He looked down at her once, closed his eyes as if in horrible pain, and then he left her to face her fears alone. Just as she'd had to face them before. Their passion had been a fire in the night. But all that remained now were ashes.

She showered quickly before crawling into the bed, pulling the covers over her head, and burying herself there. She only wished she'd never have to emerge. But she did. Eventually. And when she did, Adam was gone.

Adam didn't go to the university that morning. Instead, he made a call, early, while Brigit was still sound asleep. He'd made sure of that before calling. He'd crept along the deck outside her bedroom, and peered in through the French doors, like a burglar in his own home, and he'd seen her. She was lying naked on the bed, swathed in white linen, with her raven curls spread around her and her coal-black lashes resting gently on her cheeks. The contrast of honey-smooth skin, bright white sheets, and her jet hair, was magical. She looked more like an angel than ever. A dark angel. A passionate angel. An angel who could love a man to the brink of madness.

La belle dame sans merci.

It had been a long time before he'd been able to tear his gaze from her, there, sleeping. Spellbinding.

Interesting choice of words, he thought. He felt as if he was under a spell, caught in a magical web too sticky to allow him to get free. She'd *made* him come to her last night. He'd wanted to stay away, but she'd worked some kind of magic on him, and he had the feeling she knew it. She'd admitted it, when he'd gone to her. "I was wishing for you, Adam." Worst of all, he wasn't even sure he minded all that much.

No matter what he believed about Brigit, he couldn't stop himself from wanting her. From...from *liking* her. More than that. Caring about her. And more than *that,* too, though he refused to give a name to what else he felt. No matter how conniving he believed her to be, he couldn't help enjoying her presence in his life, couldn't help thinking about her when he wasn't with her, reveling in her company when he was. And he couldn't help worrying about her involvement with a killer like Zaslow.

Maybe there was still some part of his mind that wasn't convinced of her intentions. Maybe after today, that would change. Because once he saw what she was doing with his own two eyes, he couldn't doubt any longer. Could he?

He didn't leave. Instead, he drove his car a short distance away from the house, and walked back. Then he stationed himself just outside the bay windows in the study, and he waited.

He didn't have to wait long.

Brigit came into the room, lugging more equipment than she should've been able to manage. He watched her from outside as she dumped everything on the floor. She spread drop cloths over the carpeting and set a tripod in their center. She made a couple of trips upstairs, to bring back tubes, brushes, a palette. She brought in a stool from the kitchen. She was wearing a paint spattered white smock.

It hurt to see the proof that she was going to betray him,

though it shouldn't. He should have been prepared. He was only seeing what he'd known he was going to see.

He continued watching, unobserved.

Brigit headed upstairs one more time, and this time she returned with the canvas. She took her time with it, holding it with flattened fingers pressed to its very edges. She set it on the tripod with extreme care. And then she stood poised over it for a time, gnawing her lower lip as she eyed it critically.

Adam's moved farther to the left to get a better view, and when he finally did, his jaw dropped. It was perfect. It was freaking *perfect!* She'd captured every nuance of the original. He couldn't spot a single flaw, except for the parts that remained unfinished. And those, he saw with regret, were surprisingly few.

She was a fast worker.

He looked from the painting to her face again, and then he looked harder. She stood very still, just gazing up at the original that hung over the mantel. Minutes ticked by. She didn't move, didn't even seem to breathe. She didn't blink, just stood that way, looking at it. But her eyes were kind of soft and unfocused, as if she wasn't looking *at* the painting, but through it. Or maybe, *into* it.

It seemed to Adam as he watched her that her breathing got slower, and deeper. When she finally did begin to move, it was with the slow, almost awkward motions of a sleepwalker. Her hands rose in slow motion and worked the tubes of paint and balanced the palette. She never looked at them. And while she seemed clumsy, she didn't drop anything. It was all done with an unconscious ease. Then she lifted the brush. And the whole time, her eyes never left the painting on the wall.

Adam couldn't believe what he was seeing. She painted without looking. He couldn't take his eyes off her face and her hands as she worked. As he watched, she wielded the brush faster, and with more confidence, but still never blinking and never even peeking at the work in progress.

Watching her sent chills right down his spine, but he couldn't look away. He was as immersed in staring at her as she was in staring at *Rush*. The spell was only broken when her movements slowed, became more lethargic, and her eyelids drooped, as if the entire exercise had exhausted her. Her shoulders slumped a little. She tried to keep going, but it wasn't like before. She was looking at the canvas, frown lines between her brows. After a few seconds, she closed her eyes, nodded and set the brush down. Then, finally, she stood back and surveyed what she'd done.

So did Adam. He looked from her canvas to the one on the wall several times, astonished, not only at the sheer perfection of the work, but at the amount she'd accomplished in a single session.

As he looked on, she conducted a similar survey, looking anxiously from one painting to the other. From the original to the forgery. Eventually she nodded in apparent approval, but her face held no joy, no excitement. She looked sad.

With a heavy sigh, she started recapping the paint tubes. Then she gathered up the brushes and took them away, moving off in the direction of the kitchen. Probably to clean them.

Only then was Adam able to focus on anything besides Brigit and what had been happening inside that room. Now he noticed that he was too warm with his light jacket on. The sun burned over his back, heating him right through it. Frowning, he glanced down at his wristwatch. Three hours. Three hours he'd stood there, all but motionless, lost in watching her. Three hours, she'd waved her brush like a wand over that canvas, with her eyes focused elsewhere.

It was one more thing about Brigit Malone that defied explanation. How the hell did she do what he'd just seen her do? He wondered how she explained it to herself. Maybe she thought she was channeling the work or something. He just didn't see how she could do the things she did, and not realize it was... it was magic. There was no other word for it.

Just as obvious to him, was that he could no longer doubt her intentions. She'd been lying to him all along. She planned to steal a painting she knew meant more to him than anything else he owned. She was going to do it despite what they'd shared, or what he *thought* they'd shared.

She could take the damned painting. Hell, if the idea was to switch the forgery for the original, he'd rather have the forgery. Because it was hers. Something *she'd* done. Why couldn't she see that?

Maybe because he was the only one who felt that way. Maybe because this caring was all on his side. Maybe because he didn't mean a damn thing to her.

Brigit came back into the room, drying her hands on a rag. She carefully lifted the canvas from the tripod, and he almost winced. Moving it while it was still wet was risky.

He supposed she had to though. She had to keep what she was doing a secret, after all. It wouldn't do to have Adam waltz in one afternoon to see it sitting there, big as life.

He had to crouch down low to see her head up the stairs, and then crank his neck uncomfortably to watch her enter her bedroom. So she kept this masterpiece hidden somewhere in her room, then. Okay. Fine. He'd know that much at least. Meanwhile, he decided it would be a damned good idea to mark the original with that pen Mac had given him. Not because he wanted to prove her guilty. Not even in hopes of recovering the work. But just in case she disappeared from his life before he got his answers, he'd need to know, for his own peace of mind, whether she'd gone through with this or not. And because if all he had left of her ended up being the painting she'd created through her own, incredible magic, then he at least wanted to know which one was hers.

Finished. The painting was finished. And so was Brigit. Done for. She wanted to save Raze. She needed to find her sister. And she was in love, deeply, madly in love with Adam Reid. No matter the risk, she couldn't betray him. She couldn't.

Zaslow had given her three days. And that was good, because that would give the paint plenty of time to dry. She had no choice, the way she saw it. There was nothing else she could do.

She'd have to leave Adam, because it wasn't fair to stay. But she'd tell him the truth first. Everything. Everything. She pulled a sheet of paper from her bedside stand, and began her letter to him.

Adam waited until he was sure she was asleep. Then he crept out of bed and downstairs into the study. He carefully removed his painting from its spot above the mantle and set it on the floor. Then he wrote a single word on the back, in the lower right-hand corner. *Rush.* He watched as the letters faded before his eyes, until only a trace remained.

Then nothing.

Why, he wondered, was he still doubting Brigit's true intent? Why was there this one, stubborn, stupid part of him that was hoping against hope she would change her mind? Why did he have even a kernel of doubt she'd go through with her plan to betray him?

But he knew why he held on to that tiny shred of hope. He knew perfectly well why, didn't he? He was in love with her. He loved her with every part of him, and if she'd just reconsider, if she'd just turn to him instead of away from him, trust him enough to be honest and let him help her...

Who was he kidding? It wouldn't matter. Because in order to help her, he had to try to help her find her sister, and then he had to let her go. In the end, he'd lose her, either way.

There was nothing left for him, was there? He didn't honestly think his heart would survive a single day once she finally left him forever.

The telephone rang, and he picked it up with a weary, "Yeah?"

"I found the sister," Mac said without preamble. "And, buddy, you're not gonna believe it."

CHAPTER 19

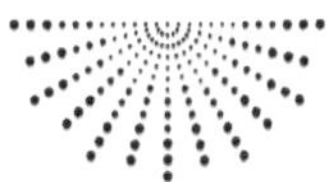

There was something on Adam's mind. Something important.

He'd changed since she'd moved into his life. He'd lost weight. His face seemed drawn and tight, and he rarely smiled. His eyes had lost their sparkle and their life. The spring had gone from his step, and Brigit knew it was because of her.

He'd gone and let himself care. The fool. The poor, beautiful, wonderful fool.

He sat in the study, staring into the dying embers that glimmered cherry red in the hearth. He'd gone off to the university that morning, just like always. And with the painting finished, Brigit had spent the day at Akasha, tending to the plants that had been neglected these last few days. She'd tried to find that old feeling of peace the shop usually gave her. She'd slipped a *Clannad* CD into the system, adjusted the music nice and low. She'd lit a few sticks of sandalwood incense and opened a window to admit the autumn breeze, just enough to set all the wind chimes tinkling.

But it hadn't worked. Nothing could ease her mind. And she knew why. For a brief space in time, she'd been allowed to touch paradise. Adam had let her in, admitted her to that secret place inside his heart. It had been blissful.

And it had been over too soon. For some reason she could only guess at, he'd changed his mind. He'd tossed her out and locked the iron door to the cell where he kept his heart prisoner. And she didn't think he was going to let her back in again.

It had been bad enough before she'd known how sweet it felt to love someone the way she loved him. Now... now it was torture.

She hadn't expected to see him waiting up for her when she'd come home from Akasha. It was almost midnight and she winced again as she noticed the marked change in him.

He sat just as tall, there in the leather chair near the fireplace. His shoulders were every bit as wide as before. But he seemed wounded, someplace so deep it didn't show. Except to her. She could see him bleeding.

"Sit down, Brigit. I have to talk to you."

She came forward. Her knees were shaking and weak. If he was going to ask her again for her reasons...

"I have something for you," he said softly, not even meeting her eyes as he took a piece of paper from his pocket. She took it from him as she passed him on her way to the sofa. But her feet stuttered to a halt when his fingertips touched hers. He closed his eyes and she felt the shaft of anguish that shot through him.

An answering bolt of guilt assaulted her. God, she was so glad this would soon be over. A few more days. Long enough for the paint to dry thoroughly. And then she'd be gone.

And that was a damned lie. She wasn't glad. Because she knew that once she left him, she could never see him again. For his sake, she had to get out of his life.

She took the paper, unfolded it. It was an address in a nearby city. Her vision blurred as she sank to the floor, her legs folded beneath her, the paper trembling in her hands.

"Bridin McAllister," she read aloud, and she felt dizzy. "Bridin..."

"Your twin sister was adopted by Rebecca and James McAllister," Adam said softly, slowly. "But they were killed in an auto accident ten years later. James's brother, Matthew, took custody of Bridin after that, but something went wrong."

Brigit looked up at him, met his eyes. She parted her lips to question him, but no words emerged. Through her tears she saw the struggle in his eyes. The indecision. And finally he sighed, and reached out a hand to stroke her face.

"I can wish I'd never set eyes on you until hell freezes over. You know that, Brigit? But even then, I can't stand to see you hurting."

She sniffled and blinked her vision clear. "You found her? You know where she is? You found my sister, Adam?" She shook her head because she couldn't believe it.

It seemed as if he had to force himself to continue. "Yeah. I know where she is. But like I said, Brigit, something went wrong." He closed his eyes and sighed. "Maybe I shouldn't be telling you any of this." He opened his eyes, stared hard into hers.

"I've been dreaming about Bridin all my life," she whispered, still unable to coax her voice to full life or any real volume through the tightness of her throat. "You have to tell me."

He nodded. "She started having dreams right after the accident that killed her adoptive parents. Only, she called them visions, and began insisting her parents had been murdered by some supernatural force. She started talking about her memories of her true home, 'on the other side.' Kept claiming she was only half-mortal. That the other half was fay."

Brigit shook her head slowly. It seemed all she was able to do as she let the information sink into her brain and felt a blade slice her heart.

"Her uncle thought she wasn't right and psychiatrists recommended commitment. Instead he put her under constant care in his home. He didn't let her attend school, had her tutored instead."

She blinked, the story stinging like a slap. "Poor Bridin."

"Brigit, she's still there..."

She felt her facial muscles contort as grief overwhelmed her. God, all these years she'd wondered, dreamed even, of having a sister, and the idealized image of her, she'd built up in her own mind. To learn this... it was worse than learning Bridin had never existed.

The book. If her poor sister was mentally ill, it was because of that stupid fairy tale. Whoever gave those books to two unsuspecting babies ought to be horsewhipped. Didn't they know the kind of confusion that would cause?

She hadn't been aware of curling up against Adam's legs, or of lowering her head to his lap, or of the way her tears were soaking through his pant legs. But then he was stroking her hair, and calming her. Helping her. She didn't deserve this. And she lifted her head to tell him so.

"How do you know all this?" was the question that came out instead. And then she answered it herself. "That private investigator you had checking me out. It was him, wasn't it?"

Adam nodded. "Mac's good, and he has low friends in high places. His methods aren't always... ethical, but he gets the information he needs." He licked his lips. "He used to date a woman who knows the nurse who cares for Bridin."

She knuckled a tear from her eye.

"When he found out that this twin of yours was probably real, I asked him to keep digging "

"Why?"

He shrugged. "Because I think I was supposed to. And because you'd told me how much it meant to you. I just... "

"And what about me? Is he still investigating me?"

Adam shook his head. "I told him to drop it."

"Why, Adam? Why would you do that, when you know…"

"Know what, Brigit?" He got to his feet, paced away, then turned to face her, accusation and a dull ache in his eyes. "That you're still lying to me?"

She flinched away from the accuracy of his words. But he held her eyes, dove into them, probing and searching. "Maybe I'm hoping it won't matter," he said "Maybe I just don't want to know anymore. Dammit, Brigit, maybe I'm hoping you'll forget about this whole thing, whatever the hell it is, and just… just start over. With me."

Her tears brimmed anew, and she had to avert her face. She knew he was waiting for her reply. But she couldn't lie to him again. She wouldn't.

He sighed, turning away from her and tugging at his hair. They stood that way, afraid to face each. Brigit could barely contain the urge to crush herself up against his chest and tell him she was sorry.

Finally, Adam cleared his throat. "Either way, I think you ought to see your sister."

She gave her head a fast, firm shake. "Not now, Adam. Not yet."

"It's a short trip. We could drive there in a couple of…"

She climbed to her feet, feeling more tired than she ever had in her life. Physical and emotional exhaustion tugged at her. "I don't want her… involved. Not until…"

"She's been locked up like a prisoner for most of her life, Brigit. If she doesn't belong there, even one more day is too long."

Brigit stopped and stood motionless in front of the fireplace, her eyes scanning the hot coals for answers. "She thinks she's a character from a fairy tale. How can she not belong there?"

He didn't answer and when she turned, she saw the way he was stroking the lush green leaves of the geranium on the end table, the way his eyes danced over the riots of ruby blossoms that had exploded to life overnight. The wonder in his face. The childlike wonder.

"I think maybe she is exactly what she thinks she is. And I think you know it. You must know it by now. Don't you? Don't you know what you are, Brigit?"

She blinked at him, unable to believe he was actually saying what she'd been thinking, afraid to voice. "She can't be," she whispered. "*I* can't be. It isn't..."

"You made me come to you last night," he said softly. "You touched this plant and made it flourish. You taste like honey. You have the mark—"

She pushed her palms at him. "It doesn't matter. I can't deal with this right now. Not yet."

"We could visit her for an hour or two. Drive right back. It would barely qualify as a trip."

Fear twisted around her heart.

"She's your *sister*," he told her. "And I think you two need to touch base. I think there's probably a lot more riding on it than you could even imagine."

She frowned at him. "What could you possibly know about this?"

"I'm a fairytale expert, remember?"

She closed her eyes and turned in a full circle. "I just—no. Not now. I'll see her, but later. After..."

"After what Brigit? After you steal my painting for Zaslow?"

She made herself face him, forced herself to look into his eyes and saw that he knew. How long, she wondered? She stood there, unable to look away until a storm of emotion just unleashed in her. She burst into tears, bending nearly double with the force of her sobs, shaking all over.

He swore, his voice loud and harsh, and then he was pulling her against him, holding her hard. He held her like he was trying to keep her from shaking apart. And when the shaking eased, he ran his strong, soothing hands over her back, and up to her nape beneath her hair. His mouth moved over her face, dropping kisses and whispers at the same time.

"It's okay. It's okay."

"I'm sorry, Adam. I never meant to hurt you. God, I'm so sorry!"

"I don't care, Brigit. Can't you get that through your head? Take the painting if you have to. It doesn't matter to me. Just let me help you. Tell me what's happening and let me help, dammit." His hold on her tightened still further. "Let me take the damned painting to Zaslow. Or be there, beside you, when you do. I'll protect you, I promise. That bastard won't ever hurt you again."

"No." She sniffed and straightened away from him, brushing at her eyes with the backs of her hands, getting her sobs under control.

"Adam, he's already threatening to kill a man I care about. I can't risk him hurting you, too."

"Raze?" Adam asked.

"How did you know?" she asked, her eyes widening.

"Doesn't matter. Is he holding the old man, is that it? And threatening to hurt him unless you get the painting?"

"Yes. Yes, Adam, but please don't get involved in this. If you care about me at all, don't get involved. If he hurts you, too, it'll kill me. Just let me handle it."

"When do you deliver the painting to him?" Adam asked, searching her face.

"Two more days," she told him, and she saw in his eyes that he wasn't going to stay out of it. He wasn't. He was going to try to be a hero, and probably get himself killed, and that was something she couldn't let him do.

So it would have to be sooner. It would have to be... tonight.

Tears welled in her eyes again. This would be the last night for them. Even if she pulled this off, and got Raze back in one piece, Zaslow would never leave her alone. Not now. She'd have to run, change her name, start again somewhere else and pray he'd never find her. But she'd always know he was only a few steps behind.

She wouldn't put Adam through that.

Before she disappeared, though, she'd do as Adam suggested, and see her sister. At least that one dream could come true. And maybe Bridin would know something more about these apparent... powers. Where they came from. What they meant.

But for now... it was her last night in Adam's arms, and she was going to make the most of it. She went to him, tipped her chin up, and stared at his lips in blatant invitation. He didn't disappoint. He kissed her and she tasted her tears on his lips.

"I don't deserve this," she told him, when she paused for a breath. And Adam's troubled eyes caressed her face. "You're so good to me, Adam. But I'm not. I'm no good at all."

"Shhsh." He pushed her hair out of her eyes, kissed her forehead. "Don't."

And he kissed her again.

Adam recognized the desperation in her kisses. He knew it well, because he felt it himself. He made love to her. Right there on the floor in front of the hearth. And it was different. Yet another facet of what he felt for her. Because this time it was healing and comfort they exchanged, a depth of sharing that he'd never experienced before.

And when she'd started to claim her unworthiness, and he'd told her "don't," he'd been silently saying so much more. *Don't ruin my fantasy by reminding me that you're going to leave me in the end. Don't destroy me, Brigit, because you can. With just a flick of your fingers, you can.*

It didn't matter. Adam's obsession was complete. He was captivated by her, and until she broke him to bits, he'd go on being her willing worshipper. He'd do anything for her, go anywhere. He'd protect her, and God forbid he got his hands on the man who was hurting her this way—this Zaslow creep— because he'd probably murder the bastard.

When Brigit walked away, as she must, she'd be leaving behind a mannequin. A body without a soul. A man without a heart. And he knew it, and there was not one damn thing he could do about it.

Two more days. For two more days, he could love her.

And then he'd personally see to it that Zaslow got his precious painting. And he'd keep the one Brigit had made, and love it all the more. He'd see to it that Raze was safe and sound, and then he'd reunite Brigit with her sister.

Somehow, he would lead the two sisters to that place in the woods he wasn't even sure he could find anymore.

Somehow, he would find the strength to let her go.

Brigit couldn't put this off. Not any longer. Not now that she knew Adam would try to intervene. To protect her. He'd get himself killed.

He would never forgive her for going ahead without him. She knew that. But the way she saw it, she had little choice. Raze's life was hanging in the balance as would Adam's if she waited.

She had to get this over with, and the sooner the better.

The thought of hurting Adam by leaving this way twisted her insides into hard knots. He'd found her sister for her. He'd given her something more precious than all the world. He deserved so much more in return.

She slipped away from him late that night.

They'd made love for hours, with the French doors open wide, so they could hear the soft, swishing sounds of the lake in the autumn breeze. He was sleeping hard as she tiptoed across the floor and out through those doors, then across the balcony to go into her own rooms.

For one fanciful moment in time, she wished that cave Adam had imagined in the woods would turn out to be a real one. She would like to go there. She'd like to crawl through it and find herself in another world, a fantasy world without such things as hurt and betrayal.

Was there such a place? Could there be? Would she ever see it?

She went to the closet to check the painting one more time. She would make sure it was perfect before she continued in this dangerous plan. She opened the closet door and brought her painting out. She held it at arm's length, her eyes running over its familiar colors and swirls.

And then they halted on something she hadn't seen before. She squinted, still unsure. It might just be a twig, or a falling, misshapen leaf.

But no, it couldn't be. She set the painting down and took her glasses from where she'd left them on the dressing table. She slipped them on, picked the painting up again, and studied it intently.

The shape rested in a spot that would be right about the breastbone of the woman who stood in the water. Though that part of her body was hidden by leaves and rushes. The pendant shone through, though, a darker shadow amid the greenery. But there, all the same.

Brigit lifted her hand, her fingertips clasping her own pewter fairy and quartz crystal.

"No," she whispered, blinking in shock. "It can't be..."

But it was. She knew, deep in her gut where you knew things despite what made sense and what didn't—she knew. That fairy in the painting, the one who looked so much like Brigit, only untamed and wild, wore the same necklace. "How?"

The telephone's shrill call made her jerk her head around. Her eyes widened at the thought of its noise waking Adam, and she laid the painting across the bed, snatching the thing up before it could jangle again.

"Brigit?"

She clenched her teeth at the sound of Zaslow's voice. "What do you want?"

"Is it done?"

"It's done." She closed her eyes, the finality of her words weighing heavy on her shoulders.

"Good. We can make the exchange—"

"Tonight," she said quickly. "I want this over with, Zaslow. The sooner the better."

"Good."

She thought about Adam, thought about how hurt he'd be when he realized what she'd done.

"Maybe... maybe tomorrow would be—"

"No. Tonight, like you said. Don't try changing your mind, now."

"But—"

"Raze is sick, Brigit."

The blood left her head in a rush that made her dizzy. Her stomach convulsed at the words. "What do you mean?"

"I mean what I said. He's sick. Feverish. Talking crazy and thrashing around in his sleep. He has the shakes."

"Get him to a hospital, Zaslow. Do it now. Call an ambulance and—"

"Not on your life, honey. Listen and listen good. Make the switch. Do it tonight. Bring the original to me in Binghamton."

Binghamton. It was where her sister was. "Why there?" she asked, trying to speak in a normal tone of voice.

"Because my client is meeting me there later. Bring the painting to the ball park, Brigit. Raze says you know where that is."

She knew, all right. She and Raze had gone there to watch the local Double-A team play baseball.

"The place will be deserted this time of night. There's a chain-link fence between the diamond and the parking lot. You know where I mean?"

She nodded and then said yes, tears scalding her cheeks as she heard a hoarse moan in the background that had to be Raze.

"Meet me there in two hours," Zaslow went on.

"Sooner if I can make it. Bring Raze, Zaslow. Bring him with you or I swear I'll slash that damned painting to ribbons."

"I'll bring him all right. And if you try to pull anything on me, Brigit, I'll be the one doing the slashing."

The phone clicked in her ear. Brigit took a shuddering breath, and replaced the receiver. Then, trembling all over, she stepped out onto the deck and crossed to Adam's doors, to peek inside.

He thought he heard the phone, but he fell back into a contented doze so fast, he was never sure. And moments later, he vaguely recognized her scent. That intoxicating, roses and honey aroma she seemed to exude, and he relaxed again. Good, he thought, in the mists of his slumber. She's coming back to bed. I just want to hold her. Forever. Two days will never be long enough.

She came close, very close. He felt her presence as surely as he felt the cool breeze rushing in through the open doors, even in his half-asleep state. And then he felt her lips on his cheek, feather-light. Still touching his skin, they moved, and her whisper was no more than a fairy's breath in his ear, barely audible. Maybe he even imagined it. It couldn't be real. She couldn't have just whispered, "I love you, Adam Reid."

And then, just like the autumn breeze, she blew away. The doors closed, and that sense of her was gone.

Adam waited, groggily expecting to feel her body rolling up against his, her arms wrapping around his waist as she came back to bed. But he didn't. And gradually, that lonely feeling woke him up. He rolled over, sat up in bed, his lips forming her name, though he didn't speak it aloud. His body shook, and his throat tried to close itself off. Where was she? What was going on?

He took a shaky breath, and tried to tell himself the feeling of foreboding that crept up his spine was imaginary and didn't mean a damned thing. Tossing the covers aside, he put his feet down on the soft carpeting. Imagination took wing, telling him he could feel the warm imprints her bare feet had made in the pile.

He half-turned, reaching for the lamp, but something glimmered there on the pillow, and he paused, frowning. And then he saw it. The necklace. The one she never took off. It lay there on his pillow. *My God, she'd left it for him.*

Adam's heart sank in a quagmire, even as he lunged from the bed. His hand closed around the dainty fairy. He lifted it, held it in front of him and stared for a split second, as it dangled from its chain. Moving automatically now, and quickly, he fastened the thin chain around his own neck. The pain constricting his heart was almost crippling. But somehow, he managed to get moving. To pull on the jeans he'd left tossed on the floor. To stuff his feet into shoes. He didn't even bother with a shirt.

He couldn't let her leave. He just couldn't. Not like this. Not until he talked to her, told her...

He yanked the bedroom door open and stepped into the hall. From where he stood he had a clear view of the study below. And he saw the stepladder under his painting of Rush—or was it hers? He heard the door slam, and then a car spitting gravel as it tore away.

Ah, hell, she was going ahead with this thing alone. He raced down the stairs, pausing at the bottom to snatch his keys off the stand where he always left them. But they weren't there. Instead, there was a note.

And he picked it up, his hands trembling.

I don't know what I am, Adam. But thanks to you, I think I might be more than I ever believed I could be. You gave me back my childhood dreams, and I'll always be grateful to you for that.

I don't know what's going to happen to me tonight. I only know that I love you too much to let you follow me, and end up getting hurt or killed because of the foolish mistakes I made in the past. You deserve so much more, and a woman far better than I've ever been. Find her. Do it for me.

I'm sorry, but I've taken both sets of your car keys. If I can, I'll mail them to you when this is over.

I'll always love you, Adam. Always. No matter what.

Brigit

Adam turned in a slow circle, frustration burning a hole through his chest as liquid heat swam in his eyes. Tears. Damn, he hadn't shed a tear since he was seven years old. Hell, Brigit had accomplished the impossible. She'd taught him how to cry again. And how to love.

CHAPTER 20

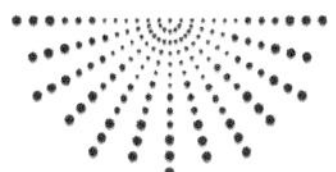

*S*he's close to you now! Closer than ever!

Bridin woke to those words ringing through her psyche. She lay still in the familiar bed; the bed she'd slept in for most of her life. But in her soul, she knew this would be the last time she'd wake there. Her battle of wills with the Darque would end today. But the war would be far from over. Just beginning, in fact.

Things would change then. No more would he look in on her when he believed her to be sleeping. No more would she be the prisoner, locked in this castle-like mansion, medicated when they could get the pills down her, and dependent on him for her every need. No more.

Once she returned to Rush, she would reclaim her kingdom. And she'd be obliged to destroy him.

She knew who Darque truly was, though she didn't even know his given name. She never had. When his family had been banished to the dark side of Rush, centuries ago, their name had been outlawed. No one could utter it in Rush ever again. His family were the dark ones, and the name he used in this realm, Darque, was only an extension of that.

Not that it mattered. Not now. Her time had come. All these years she'd awaited this day, and now it was here. She knew... it was time.

Darque must sense something was about to happen. She could feel his nervousness, hear him pacing in the room beside hers. He would not be an easy man to trick. His keen mind would spot the slightest flaw in her performance. But she suspected she held the weapon that would make her the victor in this particular battle.

He couldn't hurt her. And not just because of the pendant she wore, although that in itself was a powerful advantage and probably had kept her alive all these years. But there was more. All the time he'd held her prisoner, watched her grow and change, she'd watched him remain the same. Dark, charismatic, and evil. But he'd never been cruel to her, despite that she was his sworn enemy. And she had made sure to look deeply into his eyes whenever he approached her. She knew she possessed the allure of the fay, a power dangerous to mortal and fay males alike. And she'd focused that allure on Darque, praying he'd be susceptible as well, and that she could soften his barren, black heart toward her... just a little bit. Just enough.

She relaxed her body, muscle by muscle, and focused on a single spot on the white ceiling above her. She concentrated, waiting for the knowledge to come to her. She would know what to do. She'd know exactly what to do.

Staring at the ceiling, but not seeing it, she pictured her sister's beautiful face, put Brigit foremost in her mind, just the way she had imagined her. The way she had painted her. And she concentrated. When she'd focused every part of herself, mind and spirit on her sister, she consciously relaxed, letting her mind open like the petals of a flower in the sun. And she knew what she had to do.

She had to get sick. Very sick. Sick enough that they'd take her from this place to a hospital. She wasn't sure why she was supposed to do that, or even if she could do it, but she would certainly try.

Her focus shifted. She concentrated now on the physical rather than the spiritual. And as she willed it, so it happened. Her state altered, and her breathing slowed. Her heart rate followed suit, and her body temperature dropped.

Yes. That's it. But more. Just a bit more.

Focus. She tapped the strength of her will, used all the power she had. And consciousness began to recede. Not enough oxygen now, she supposed, to maintain it. She reached for the lace doily on her bedside stand, caught it, and tugged until the lamp that rested atop it crashed to the floor. That done, she rolled onto her side, close to the bed's edge. Teetering now. This experiment could kill her. She must be careful.

She leaned a little farther, heard the door open just as all thoughts faded away. She felt her body falling from the bed, felt the crushing impact on her right side when she hit the floor.

And now she would learn how effective her attempts to enchant her dark enemy had been. He would either get her help or watch her die.

She remained aware, watched it all unfold as if from a great distance. Darque flung the door open, surged inside. The blood drained from his face as he saw her on the floor, amid a litter of broken glass.

"By the Gods, why now?" He moved forward, bending over to pick her up, then hesitated. She knew why. The pendant. He couldn't lay his hands on her as long as she wore that pendant.

And then Kate was crouching beside him, pressing her palms to Bridin's face.

"Lord, she's cold as ice!" Kate caught Bridin's wrist in her hands, and shook her head. Her eyes widened as she looked up at Darque.

"Damn you, Bridin, your timing couldn't be worse." He stood

straight and paced away from her, rubbing his forehead with his fingertips.

Bridin was astounded that she could hear his thoughts as clearly as if he spoke them aloud. At any moment now, someone named Zaslow would be taking possession of a painting. Her painting, she wondered?

Darque thought he had to be there when it happened. He had to be sure it was destroyed before Bridin's sister ever set eyes on it, for it would bring the twins together and his goal was, and had always been, to keep them apart. For only together could they return to Rush. He intended to witness her painting burning with his own eyes.

But he couldn't leave Bridin in this condition. He couldn't just let her die.

He turned abruptly, as Kate maneuvered Bridin's limp body back into the bed and stroked her hair, muttering softly.

Darque told himself that he could not care less whether she died. It wouldn't matter to him in the least, except that he needed her. He needed her to secure his hold on the throne of Rush.

"What's wrong with her?" he demanded.

"I don't know."

Darque paced toward the bed, stood beside it, looking down at Bridin's face.

Kate pulled a stethoscope into place, pressed it to Bridin's chest for a moment, leaning slightly, listening intently. She pulled a blood pressure cuff from a deep pocket and wrapped, and pumped and listened. When she finished, she said, "Her heartbeat is irregular, and her blood pressure is dangerously low. We need to get her to a hospital, Mr. Darque."

He narrowed his eyes and moved closer. Without taking his gaze from Bridin, he said, "Call an ambulance and go downstairs to let them in. You're to ride with her, you and one of the guards. You're both to stay with her at all times, Kate. Do you understand?"

Kate nodded and started toward the door.

"I'll join you at the hospital soon. I have something I have to do first, but I'll come there directly. Do not let her out of your sight until I get there."

"I won't," Kate said. "I'll take care of her. Don't worry, Mr. Darque." And then she left the room.

Darque bent over the bed, lifted his hand as if to touch her face, but caught himself, and drew it away again. "I'm warning you, Bridin of Rush, if this is some kind of a trick..."

His words trailed off as she seemed sucked back into her weakened body. Her eyes fluttered, and then she managed to open them. He couldn't touch her while she wore her pendant, but she could touch him with no ill effects if she wanted to do so. She lifted her palm, and settled it on his cheek, and she tried to pierce his eyes with her.

"Before I... go..." she whispered. "I wish to know... your name."

"My name?" Darque blinked in shock. "You're not going to die, Bridin," he assured her. "You'll live... long enough to serve my purposes, at least. But since you asked, my name is the same as my father's before me, and his before him, and many before them. I am Tristan of Shara." He held her gaze and added, "Ruler of Rush."

Her hand fell away from his face, her eyes fell closed, and she said no more.

Tristan of Shara lifted his hand, and spoke the words that would remove the invisible barrier he'd erected around the mansion, which had kept Bridin from passing through her entire life.

And then he sat down in the chair beside the bed, and he stared at her a while longer.

CHAPTER 21

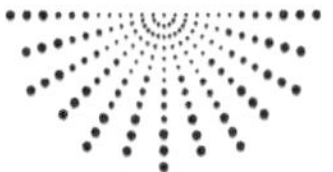

The pounding on the front door came just as Adam reread Brigit's letter for the fourth time, while racking his brain to figure out where she'd gone. How he could get to her in time to protect her when he didn't even know where she'd gone?

The interruption irritated the hell out of him.

"Dammit, Adam, open up!"

Mac wasn't the type to yell and pound on a door at this hour unless something was very wrong. Adam clasped the letter in his hand, went to the door, yanked it open.

"What the hell are you doing here?"

"Sticking my nose in where it doesn't belong." Mac shoved Adam aside and came in, heading straight for the study. "You're going to knock me right on my ass for this, buddy, but do us both a favor and save it for later, okay?"

Adam shook his head in confusion. "Look I don't know what you're talking about, and I don't have time to find out. And since I need to borrow your car, I'm not likely to knock you on your ass just now."

"Good, because I tapped your phones."

"You..."

"Tapped your phones. Illegal as hell. I could lose my license."

Adam blinked. "Why?"

Mac's face twisted into a grimace. "Because you're my friend and I was worried about you. I thought you were about to walk into another scam perpetrated by another woman. Jeeze, Adam, I was with you last time, remember? I didn't want to watch you go through all that again." He tilted his head, surveying Adam's face. "Or am I already too late? Is she gone, Adam?"

"Yeah, and I have no idea where."

Mac sighed in disgust, stomped straight through into the study, and reached for the painting. With a quickness that made Adam cringe, he jerked the painting off the wall, flipped it around, and scanned the back. "Did you do what I told you? With the marking pen?"

Adam nodded, moving forward quickly and restlessly, wishing he knew what to do to help Brigit. "Yeah. But there's no sense looking for it. She switched them, Mac. Took the original with her, and I don't even give a damn. It's her I want, not the freaking painting."

Mac's head came up sharply. "You *knew* she'd switched them?" At Adam's nod, he rushed on. "And you just let her go? Just like that? What's got into you, Adam? You lost your mind or what?"

But even as he spoke, Mac was scanning that canvas again, yanking a flashlight the size of a pen from his shirt pocket, flashing its purple glow over the back in search of the ink.

"I didn't just let her go! She told me she had two more days, and I was planning to be there with her when she delivered the damned painting. But she left early, took my keys so I couldn't follow. She's meeting the bastard alone and there's not a damned thing I can do about it."

"Yeah, well you ought to know, Adam, that I just eaves-dropped on a phone call from Zaslow. He didn't *ask* her to pull this scam. He didn't give her any choice. Sounds as if he's holding the old man, just to be sure she complies."

"I know all that. She came clean, told me everything."

"He's a sadistic bastard," Mac went on. "Told Brigit that old Raze was sick, started listing symptoms and sounded like he was enjoying it. I thought I heard a moan in the background, but—"

"No wonder she took off in such a hurry."

"Ah, hell, Adam," Mac's words held a new urgency, and Adam looked up fast. Mac stood, staring at the lower right-hand corner of the painting, and shaking his head. "She didn't do it, pal. She didn't switch them. This is the original."

"What?" Adam lunged forward. A rush of adrenaline flooded his veins, and it propelled him, pushing him.

He looked over Mac's shoulder to see the word, scrawled in Adam's own hand, illuminated by the ultraviolet glow. *Rush.*

"Brigit..." Adam breathed, almost limp with relief. She *hadn't* betrayed him. Even with all the pressure on her to do it, and even when he'd told her he didn't care about the damned painting, that he'd willingly hand it over to Zaslow himself, she'd been unable to go through with it.

"This isn't good," Mac said. "Zaslow is no slouch. He's an expert. She might've pulled it over on him if she'd waited a few days, let the paint dry. But man, he's gonna see through this so fast he won't have to look twice. And we both know this bastard has killed before."

Adam blinked, shock seeping through his bones, and the need for action making every nerve ending in his body twitch and jump. "Tell me you know where she's meeting him, Mac."

"Oh, yeah," Mac said, with a hard nod. "You bet your ass I know. Binghamton. At the Double-A ball field there. We can call the police and have them—"

"No cops." Adam headed for the front door at a run. "You leave your keys in the car?"

"Yeah, but Adam, we have to notify—"

"No cops, Mac." He stopped with his hand on the knob, his palm itching and shaking to send a glance back over his shoulder. "They'd connect her with the other forgeries...the ones in the past. She'd end up in prison."

"If she's guilty—"

"She was a kid, Mac. She couldn't have been more than a teenager when those other heists went down."

Mac's lips thinned, but he nodded. "Okay. All right. It's your call. But I'm coming with you. You can't take on a thug like Zaslow alone."

Adam shook his head. "No way, pal. This is my fight." Adam started through the door.

"Adam, aren't you even going to put a shirt on first?"

Adam didn't answer. He jumped into his friend's car and twisted the key.

She couldn't do it. She couldn't betray Adam that way, not when she knew how often he'd been hurt in the past. It didn't matter that he'd told her he didn't care. *She* cared. She'd tried to make herself switch the paintings. She'd gone so far as to take the original off the wall. But she'd never removed it from its frame. Adam had done too much for her. He'd taught her how to love. And there was no room in that love for betrayal. She ended up hanging the original back on the wall, and leaving the house with the copy, even though she knew there was a good chance Zaslow would know.

The forgery, its paint still tacky, rested face forward in the back seat of her car as she paced back and forth beside it. The moon was waning, but bright, a lopsided half circle of goodness and light, spilling down on the grassy baseball diamond. The place was abandoned tonight, the season over, the bleachers empty. The grass needed mowing, she thought, and the chalk lines had faded. She looked through the link fence that stretched around the near end of the field to the deserted dugouts. She thought about Raze, and how much he loved to come here and watch the Binghamton Rumble Ponies, who he would forever refer to by their previous name, the Binghamton Mets. He would order a hot dog with extra relish and a Cherry Coke every time, like some kind of ritual. He knew every player by name, and could predict which ones were destined to get called up to the major leagues.

She loved that old man. She'd never loved anyone as much as she loved Raze. Until now.

A black van rolled in and Brigit stiffened. The vehicle pulled up beside hers. Its headlights went out and its motor died.

A door opened and Zaslow stepped out, came around to stand near the van's nose. She remained where she was, in front of her own car. Both vehicles were aimed at the fence and the field. As if they were sitting there awaiting the first pitch.

"Well? Where is it?"

She lifted her chin, felt the wind whipping tendrils of hair around her face. "I want to see Raze first."

Zaslow tilted his head, shrugged. "Fair enough. Let's just get on with this, Brigit. My client was in touch right after I talked to you, and he's running out of patience." He stepped between her car and his to open the van's passenger door. Brigit moved to stand beside him, and when the interior light came on, she saw Raze, slouched in the seat. His careworn face was relaxed, his head tilted to one side. He slumped there, so still she jerked in shock at first, thinking he was dead. But then she saw his chest rise and fall, slightly, but enough, and she took a steadying breath. She'd take care of Raze. Right now, nothing mattered but that.

She was about to lean into the van, but Zaslow stepped right in front of her, blocking her path. "Not so fast, Brigit." He closed the van door. "The painting."

She glanced past him, through the window. In the pale moonlight, she could see a set of keys dangling from the switch. Hope surged in her chest.

"It's in the back seat of my car," she said, inclining her head toward her car, three feet behind her. "Go ahead, take a look."

She stayed where she was as Zaslow moved past her to bend to the car and open the back door. She saw him lean in, reaching for the painting and she dashed around the front of the van, reaching for the driver's door, just as she heard him yell, "Bitch!"

A gunshot rang out as she was about to wrench the door open. She ducked instinctively, covering her head with her hands, pressing her face to the cool metallic door.

"You lying, cheating little witch! Did you really think you could—could..." His voice trailed into silence.

Brigit straightened just a little, and she leaned forward to peek around the front of the van. But Zaslow wasn't looking at her anymore. He was staring through the chain-link fence at the baseball diamond. Blinking in confusion, she followed his gaze, only to see a dark, menacing form standing out on the field, right between home plate and the pitcher's mound. Where had he come from? How had he managed to walk out there without either of them noticing? He wore a black coat, with a caped back that swayed in the wind. The collar was turned up, and his face was completely hidden in the shadow of a black felt hat.

"Enough, Zaslow," the form said, only Brigit got the creepy sensation that no part of him moved to issue the command. Not even his lips.

Danger washed over her like a cold breeze. She could smell it, *taste* it in the air, and her heart chilled in her chest.

"Mr. Darque," Zaslow said, and his voice had gone from

shaking with rage, to quivering in fear. "What are you doing here this early? I'm not supposed to meet you for another hour."

"You told me my painting would be here, Zaslow. I came to collect it. Though it doesn't matter now."

"I—I d-don't under—"

"I paid you to steal the painting. Not to have it copied."

"Oh, that. Don't worry about that, Mr. Darque. It's the best way to do these things," Zaslow blustered, but his voice was far from steady. "I thought—"

"I did not employ you to *think*, Zaslow. Nor to make copies. That painting should never have been seen, especially by *that one.*" When he said that last part, he turned toward where Brigit crouched beside the van, afraid to stand up and show herself. "Your *thinking* has ruined my plans, Zaslow."

He cocked his head toward Brigit's car, where Zaslow still stood near an opened rear door. The dark man lifted one hand and pointed a finger. A bolt of blue fire shot from it, blasting through the chain link as if it were butter. The bolt hit Zaslow dead center of his barrel chest and sent him hurtling backward through the air. He landed on the blacktop of the parking lot, rolling over and over before coming to a dead stop. And then he lay still. A thin spiral of smoke rose from his chest.

The scream she'd intended to emit died of fright and never emerged. She swallowed the air she'd sucked in, and looked back toward the dark form in the field. And she saw the blackened hole in the chain link, where that bolt had blasted through.

She had to get away from here. She had to get Raze away from this thing. She straightened from her hunched position on the ground, gripping the van door, ready to tug it open and jump behind the wheel, her eyes never leaving that deadly being.

He looked right at her and she got an awful feeling of

impending doom. That hand rose and pointed in her direction. Her heart slammed against her ribs, and she dove away from the van as the blue fire raced toward her. She hit the ground, somersaulted, tried to breathe. God, what if he missed her and hit Raze?

The fire—or whatever it was—burned into the ground near her head, hitting like a bolt of lightning, and leaving bare, charred earth and wisps of smoke. As she whipped her gaze back to that evil, perhaps inhuman form, its hand took aim again. She scrambled to her feet and ran for cover, heading away from the van, toward the hulking bleachers, thinking she could hide behind or under them. Blasts that rocked the ground with their impact landed at her heels all the way.

"Brigit!"

She twisted her head at the sound of Raze's voice, but her ankle turned, and she went down hard. Pain shot up into her leg. Panting, she looked back to see Raze, levering himself out of the van on the driver's side.

"The pendant," he rasped.

His feet hit the ground, and he gripped the door for support, only to fall to his knees all the same. God, what had Zaslow done to him to make him this weak?

"Use the pendant!"

Raze sagged forward, landing softly on the ground, eyes closed.

Automatically, Brigit reached up to clasp her pewter fairy, but she found nothing there, and belatedly remembered leaving it on Adam's pillow. An act of love.

"If she was wearing her pendant, old man, I wouldn't be foolish enough to take aim at her."

That deep, calm voice floated through the night, and chills raced up Brigit's spine. She looked up, saw that thing lifting his hand toward her again, and knew he had her this time. That fiery spear would run her through, and there was nothing she could do.

~

Adam saw it. He didn't believe it, but he saw it. Some black enshrouded wizard or something, hurling lightning bolts at Brigit as she ran for her life. And he didn't know why, or what this was all about. He only knew he had to protect her, if it meant his life.

He ran over the blacktopped parking lot to the grass at the edge of the diamond. Brigit struggled to her feet, faced her attacker. He saw her stand a little straighter as she realized she was trapped. Nowhere to hide.

He ran faster, harder, his lungs burning. And then, just as that thing lifted its deadly hand toward her again, Adam launched himself. He growled with physical effort as he pushed off with his feet, and his body arrowed into the space between Brigit and the dark thing. Like a diver, only there would be no water to cushion the landing. And maybe it wouldn't matter anyway, because by the time he landed, he didn't think he'd be feeling much of anything. He saw the fire leave the dark man's fingertips as if in slow motion, as he sailed through the air. And he had a second to wonder at it, just before the blue lightning hit him in the chest, hot and hard and sizzling. Like a shotgun. Like a sledge hammer. He felt his ribs crack under the impact, felt his body driven backward. Its voltage had his nerves screaming and the burn! God, the burn was like a brand in the center of his chest. He hit the ground so hard he couldn't draw a breath. But he saw what happened. He saw that blue fire double over itself, as if ricocheting off his chest, and he saw it shoot back to its source.

Adam's eyes followed. The blue bolt smashed into the man on the mound, and he vanished. Just like that. Gone.

Adam felt himself slipping away too. But he knew Brigit was okay, just by the way she whispered his name as she fell to the ground beside him. And he didn't regret what he'd done for a second.

God, that burning. Gritting his teeth, he lifted one hand and grasped his sternum. His palm closed on something so hot it was searing his skin. He tore it from his chest and dropped it into the grass. Blackness descended, and he found his only regret in leaving this world was that he was leaving her. He loved her, and he'd never even told her so.

Brigit stared, blinking in disbelief. The shape burned into the center of Adam's chest was a familiar one. She searched the grass and found it. Her pewter fairy. He'd been wearing it. He'd found it there on his pillow, and he'd put it around his own neck.

She reached out to retrieve her pendant from the grass, only to draw away fast when it burned her fingertips. Frowning, she looked closer. The once-clear quartz point held lovingly in the pewter fairy's embrace was blackened now, charred as if something had burned it. And she realized that somehow, the bolt of fire had hit the crystal. She'd seen it rebound back to annihilate its owner. Had her pendant somehow been responsible? But how? Was that why Raze had been yelling at her to use...

Raze!

She twisted her head to see him lying on the ground beside the van. So still. And again, she leaned over Adam, shaking him gently, torn in two.

Tires skidded on pavement and a door slammed. Footfalls pounded toward her, and she heard a man swearing out loud. Then he was kneeling beside her, and she frowned in confusion.

She knew him. The man Adam had hired to check up on

her, the private investigator. Mac Cordair. It didn't matter why he was here. "Help him," she whispered. "Please, help him."

His fingers pressed to Adam's neck, and then his head lowered to Adam's chest. His lips thin, he grabbed his phone from a pocket and shoved it at her. "Call nine-one-one. Have them send an ambulance. Hurry."

She staggered to her feet, saw him bending over Adam's body, positioning his hands over Adam's chest again as she made the call.

Brigit paced the emergency room. She couldn't stop crying. Adam's friend Mac stood in a corner, looking a little shell-shocked and staring into a cup of coffee he hadn't yet tasted. Brigit didn't suppose her story about a man in black hurling lightning bolts at them had made much sense to Mac as he'd driven her to the hospital, behind the ambulance with its flashing lights and screaming siren.

It still made no sense to her.

She only knew what she'd seen. And what she'd seen had been Adam, throwing himself in front of her, saving her life.

She had held herself together until they'd bundled him and Raze into an ambulance. Another had arrived a few seconds later. They'd taken Zaslow away in a black vinyl bag.

Despite his confusion, Mac had convinced Brigit to tell the police she'd arrived after the fact. That she'd seen nothing, and had no idea what had happened.

They were busy right now at the field, with a team of electricians, trying to find the source of the high-voltage charge that had killed one man and put another in the hospital. When they found nothing, they'd probably attribute it to summer lightning, blasting down from a clear sky.

Brigit jumped to attention when a doctor came into the waiting room, and quickly went to her. "How is he?"

"Alive, but still unconscious," she said softly, and she placed a gentle hand on Brigit's shoulder. "He took a powerful jolt, Miss..."

"Malone. Brigit."

"Brigit," she repeated. "His heart rate is normal now, steady, and he's breathing on his own, but he might be unconscious for quite some time."

"But is he going to be all right? When he wakes up, will he—"

The hand on her shoulder tightened. "*If* he wakes up, Brigit. I have to be honest with you. Right now, we can't even be certain he will. He could slip into a coma. And if he does come around, there could be brain damage."

"My God," she whispered. "My God."

"Then again, he might be just fine. There's no way to be sure of the extent of the damage, right now. We'll know more in a day or so. I'm sorry the news isn't better."

Brigit tried to keep her knees steady. Tried not to sink to the floor

"As for the man who was brought in with him, Mr. uh..." She flipped a chart open, scanned it. "That's right. Malone, same as you. He's sleeping off the effects of a pretty potent tranquilizer. Other than that, he's just fine."

Brigit's head came up. "He's not sick?"

"No. Just sleepy."

So Zaslow had been lying to her about that. Torturing her. And probably enjoying it. He'd deserved that blue bolt to the chest. Her knees gave, caught again. She swayed just a little, and steadied herself.

She hadn't realized Mac stood just behind her until she felt his arm settle around her shoulders.

"I want to see Adam," Brigit managed to whisper.

The doctor—Dr. Evans, she recalled belatedly—nodded. "You can go in, sit with him for a few minutes."

She turned to glance up at Mac.

"Go on," he urged. "He'd want you there. I'll see him later."

Dr. Evans stepped aside, held the door open for her, and Brigit, drawing a deep breath, walked through.

Adam lay still on the bed, eyes closed, but he didn't look ill or weak. He looked wonderful, like he was only sleeping.

She moved slowly toward him, blinking back her tears, and she sat right on the edge of the mattress, her hand running over his face, tracing his cheekbones, and the line of his jaw. She bent lower, retracing that path with her lips. "I'm so sorry. God, I never meant for this to happen. I never wanted you to be hurt."

Her fingers sifted his hair. Stroked it. "I love you, Adam. I never said it out loud, but you knew, didn't you? You know it's true, even now. I love you. I want you to come back to me, so I can tell you. I want to be able to look into your eyes when I say it. Okay?"

Her tears dampened the skin of his face. She brushed her lips over his and tasted them. "Please, Adam," she whispered. "Please..."

The soft, steady beeping sound jumped and quickened. The pace of the sounds picked up, and a second later, Dr. Evans was leaning over her, gently tugging her away. "Come on, Brigit. That's enough for now. We have to be careful with him right now."

She sniffed, knuckling her eyes dry. "Yes. Okay, whatever's best for him."

She didn't want to leave him, but she did, going back down the hall to the waiting room. She sank into a chair, feeling apart from herself. As if all this was happening to someone else, and she was just a bystander, looking on.

But it wasn't happening to someone else. It was happening to Adam. If he died... God, if he died, how could she possibly live with herself? This was all her fault. She should have found another way. Some other way to end it all.

One thing was certain. Right or wrong, it was over now. Zaslow was gone. Raze was going to be all right. She hadn't gone through with her plan to betray Adam.

The only question was, would he survive? And if he did, would he ever want to look at her again?

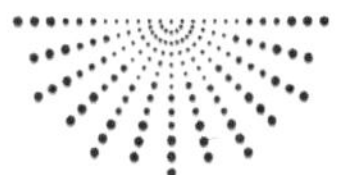

CHAPTER 22

"All right," Mac said, and he gave Brigit's hand a squeeze. "All right, I'll go for now. But only to the nearest motel. I'll call in to check on things."

"And I'll call you if there's any change," Brigit promised.

"Or if you need me. For anything. And I mean it, Brigit," he said, stepping into the elevator, turning to face her. "I love that oaf in there like a brother. And *he* loves..." He stopped speaking all of a sudden, frowning as his gaze shifted to something behind her. His eyes changed, altered, took on an entranced quality.

Brigit turned to see what had captured his attention so thoroughly. A woman stood there in the all but deserted hallway, looking around uneasily.

The elevator doors slid closed. The line of his vision was broken. Mac was gone. And the woman's green eyes found Brigit, and then she blinked, and narrowed them.

She was beautiful. Golden blond hair framed her delicate face and spilled down over her shoulders. She was slight, short, and fragile looking, like Brigit, but with an inner strength that showed in her sparkling emerald eyes.

She took a step closer, lifting a hand as if reaching out. "Brigit?"

Brigit blinked hard and rapidly. It couldn't be. It couldn't possibly be... but something inside her was saying that it was. "Bridin?"

"Is it really you, Brigit?"

Brigit stepped toward her, shaking her head in wonder. "My sister," she whispered in blatant disbelief. And then she saw the pewter fairy pendant twined around a quartz point, resting against her skin. "Bridin..." Brigit's voice failed her. But she moved faster, and her sister did likewise, until they were hugging in the center of the waiting room.

Brigit's arms held tightly to her sister's body, and she felt her frailty. The petite build, the apparent fragility, the hospital gown and wrist band. But she felt the strength underlying all that, too. She held her hard, trembling all over, and when she finally backed away, her tears made it hard for her to see clearly.

"I can't believe this," Brigit said, sniffing, and brushing at her cheeks. "Bridin, what...how...? Are you a patient here? Are you all right?"

Bridin's almost-smile was perfectly sane, and more...it was knowing. Her eyes were filled with emotion, but no tears. They also held wisdom, "I made myself sick so they'd bring me here. I knew you were coming, Brigit. I had to find you. It's time to fulfill our destiny."

A little chill ran up Brigit's spine, and she licked her lips. "How could you have known I would be here tonight?"

But Bridin was scanning the waiting room. "Where's Raze? I thought he'd be with you."

"Raze? How do you know Raze?"

The green eyes widened. "He's not sick, is he? I never thought of that! Is he all right?" She swung her head, looking around frantically.

"He's fine," Brigit said, touching her shoulders to calm her. "Raze is fine. He's just sleeping off a tranquilizer."

"Then why are you here?" Bridin asked, her body relaxing, her face returning to its placid, calm mask as she faced Brigit once again.

"It's...it's a long story."

Bridin lifted her hand and pressed her chilly palm to Brigit's cheek. Then she tilted her head and closed her eyes, as if she was *feeling* something there.

Eyes closed, Bridin said, "Oh, Brigit... you could have been killed. It was so dangerous, to go there and face him alone. And that man... the man who tried to destroy you when he realized who you were. He's the Dark Prince. His family murdered ours, Brigit. They were the reason we had to flee Rush. And he's kept me his prisoner all my life. He'll do anything to stop me from going back."

Her arms closed again around Brigit, and she held on with surprising strength. "He wanted the painting because he knew it was my message to you."

"The painting?" Brigit felt her blood run cold.

"Yes. I painted it for you, Brigit. I gave it to Raze to deliver to the gallery the night I sent him back to save you from the fire."

Brigit's head was spinning. "You sent Raze to save me?"

She nodded. "I...know things. See things sometimes."

Brigit tried to digest what all of this meant. And eventually, Bridin's grip eased, and she backed away. "You think it's true, that I'm insane, don't you, Brigit?"

Brigit shook her head. "No. It's obvious you're not insane. This whole situation is insane, a dark prince who hurls lightning bolts is insane, an enchanted painting is insane, but not you. I'm just having trouble accepting that all this is real. Everything I thought I knew about reality and what's possible has been turned on its head tonight."

"I'm just glad he didn't kill you."

"He tried, but Adam jumped in the way and something happened. The dark one is dead, I think."

"Adam was wearing your pendant. The Dark Prince's blast was reflected right back onto him. But he isn't dead. I'd sense it if he was. The blast wasn't a killing one. Seems our enemy balks at the outright murder of fay princesses. Lucky for him, he intended to show mercy, not to obliterate you, or it would have certainly destroyed him. As it is, I believe he's gone back to Rush. The blast put him in nearly as bad shape as it did Adam. I sense..." Her brows knit together. "I sense he's weak, and in pain. And that he knows I've escaped him once and for all. But he's not dead. Not that one."

Brigit blinked, slowly letting her mind absorb the truth, reeling, because she could no longer deny or doubt it.

"It's all so simple," Bridin told her. "The fairy tail is real. You don't know about Rush because you don't need to. I remember everything because I must. I have to fight Tristan for the throne, and I have to restore our kingdom. Brigit, it's time for me to go back."

Brigit lifted a hand to stroke her sister's hair. "I've only just found you again, Bridin. I don't want you to leave me now. Not yet."

Bridin smiled gently. "I won't leave you. I can't. The only way either of us can pass through the doorway to the other side, is the same way we exited. Together. Unless you come with me, Brigit, our kingdom is lost."

Brigit backed away, shaking her head. "But...I can't. I can't go back with you, Bridin. I'm sorry, but—"

Bridin's head jerked up, and for the first time, real emotion became apparent in her expression. Anger colored her eyes a shade darker, and her lips thinned, jaw clenched. "It's our destiny to return to Rush! We must go back. Our people are depending on us."

"Your people, you mean. God, Bridin, I don't even remember this place. There has to be a way you can go back without me."

"There isn't." Bridin inhaled nasally, so deep her chest expanded. Her chin came up. "So I have to find a way to convince you. My own sister."

"You don't have to convince me of anything, Bri—"

"This Adam. The one who saved you. He's in there?" She jerked her head toward Adam's room.

Brigit nodded.

"And you fear he's dying?"

"No..." Brigit sighed, lowering her chin to her chest. "I don't know. Maybe."

"Come on, then."

Bridin struck out across the waiting room, her steps fast and purposeful. Brigit ran after her when she realized her intent, but before she caught up, Bridin had burst into Adam's room and was at his bedside. She leaned over him, touching his face, just the way she'd touched Brigit's earlier.

Bridin pressed her palms to either side of Adam's face, as Brigit rushed over to her side, scared half to death. Then Bridin went still and her mouth fell open.

"What is it," Brigit asked, searching her sister's face.

"It's him," Bridin whispered. "He's the one I'm supposed to find."

"What?"

"He's the one who knows where to find the doorway," she said softly. "This man knows the way back to Rush. He's been there, Brigit. I saw him in a dream. He's the one who's going to show us the doorway back home."

"Bridin, you don't understand. He's the reason I can't go back with you. I love this man."

"We can't let him die," Bridin whispered.

"No, we can't let him die," Brigit said softly. Then she narrowed her eyes and looked up at her sister.

"I thought you said it wasn't a killing blast?"

"For a fairy, it wouldn't have been. For a mortal..." She shook her head sadly.

"Is there a way we can...help him?"

Bridin stared into Brigit's eyes. "I can help him. But if I do, you have to promise to come back with me. I want your word. Give it to me, and I'll save your Adam's life."

Brigit's heart twisted into a hard little knot. But she looked down at Adam, so still in that bed, and she knew she had no choice. She couldn't let him die. Brushing a tear from her cheek, she nodded. "Yes. I promise. If you help him, I'll go with you. Maybe… maybe he can come with us."

Bridin shook her head slowly. "If he does, he'll die. I foresaw that, too. I cannot lie to you, my sister. Your Adam must show us the way back, but he has to stay in the mortal world. In Rush, his fate is death."

"Oh, God."

"Promise you'll come with me," Bridin said. "And I'll help you save him now."

Brigit felt her heart breaking, but she nodded. Bridin seemed to sag a bit in relief. Then she bent over Adam, laying her palms on his temples, closing her eyes. Seconds ticked by, and Brigit waited, watching, praying.

And right before her eyes, the crystal point dangling from Bridin's neck, hovering just above Adam's face, began to glow very softly. A gentle white gleam suffused the quartz. And it beamed downward, touching Adam's face, bathing it.

Brigit blinked and rubbed her eyes, but the apparition didn't go away. Not until Bridin shook her head, and stood straight again. "I'm not strong enough. Not by myself. There are still too many of their chemicals floating around in my bloodstream, diluting my magic. You'll have to help me, Brigit."

"M-me?"

Bridin looked at Brigit's neck, frowned. "Where is your pendant?"

"I..." She gave her head a shake, and thrust a hand into the pocket of her jeans, pulling out the pewter fairy, with its broken chain and blackened crystal.

"Well, it's no good like *that*," Bridin said. "Cleanse it. And hurry up. We don't have much time."

Brigit frowned, just staring at her.

Bridin's eyes softened. Her tone gentled. "I'm sorry, little sister. It's so vital to me to get back. I've been waiting so long for this day. I...I'm being impatient and short-tempered with you, forgetting you don't understand the ways..."

She stepped closer to Brigit, took her hand, and laid it across her own upturned palm. "But you know you have magic in you, don't you, Brigit?"

Brigit nodded. "Yes. I know. I think a part of me has always known."

"Close your hand around the pendant, little sister." And as she said it, she closed her own, delicate hand around Brigit's, so the pendant was trapped in their fists. "Close your eyes, and work up your energy. Get mad. Think about the Dark Prince and the way he hurt Adam."

Still unsure she could control her own abilities, Brigit complied. She closed her hand tighter and squeezed her eyes simultaneously. As if summoned against her will, that scene at the ball park came rushing back to her. And she did feel angry, despite the distractions at hand.

"That's it. Now, focus all that anger on the evil caught in your crystal. It's his evil, Brigit. Aim your anger at it and fire, just the way he did when he hurled his evil at you. Use your anger as a weapon, and your goodness to blast that evil out of the crystal."

That odd state of focus that always came over her when she was painting began to steal over Brigit again, right then. Only instead of fixating on an image she wanted to reproduce, it was all directed toward that evil creature who'd hurt Adam.

"Send it back where it came from, Brigit."

From the tips of her toes, a wave of *something* rose, up through her body, filling her, rushing upward tingling every nerve ending like an electrical charge. Her lips parted and it escaped, bursting from her in the form of a shout. "Get out!"

And then the feeling was gone, and she felt weak, as if she'd just run a mile.

Bridin's hand over her fisted one eased, and with her free hand, she gently pried Brigit's fingers open. When Brigit looked down at the necklace resting in her palm, the quartz point was as clear and as sparkling as a flawless diamond. She blinked down at it, then up at her sister.

"Magic," she whispered. "You'll get used to it. Now, you have to do it again. For Adam."

Her gaze went to Adam, lying so near death in that bed, and her heart tripped over itself with the force of what she felt for him.

"Come on, Brigit. Help me bring him back. We have to hurry. As soon as the Dark Prince recovers his strength, he'll be back here. And his henchmen will be looking for me soon as well." Bridin took the pendant out of her hand and put it around Brigit's neck, tying a knot in the chain because the clasp was broken. "Now, go stand over there."

Brigit moved to the opposite side of the bed. She felt as if she was in a dream. Everything was out of focus and surreal. Dazed, she watched her sister, imitating her every move. When Bridin leaned over Adam and placed her hand against his left temple, Brigit leaned over and pressed her palm to his right one. Her cheek touched her sister's, and their pendants met, the chains twisting together right over Adam's face.

"Now," Bridin whispered, "Make him live."

~

Strength surged through Adam's body, shooting out into his limbs and zinging through his veins more powerfully than that electrical charge had done.

"Live!"

That command, spoken more fiercely than any drill sergeant's meanest bark, rang in his ears. And it took him a full minute to recognize that beloved voice.

"Live, Adam! Be all right! Dammit, *live!*"

Soft, warm hands were pressed to either side of his head, and Brigit was shouting in his face. He thought he'd better respond soon, before she slapped him or something.

"Adam, wake up!"

"All right, all right," he rasped, forcing his eyes open. "Give a guy a break, would you?"

"Adam?" she croaked.

She leaned over him, and her beautiful eyes brimmed with tears. Her lips trembled into a half-smile as she searched his face. "Adam?"

Lifting one hand to the back of her head, he pulled her closer, kissed her mouth, tasted her tears. And when he let her go, and she straightened away from him, his vision was a little clearer, his body a little stronger, as if he'd drawn sustenance from that kiss. Damned if he didn't believe he had.

And then he saw the other woman standing nervously near the door, peering out on occasion.

She was beautiful, the other one. Not a nurse. A patient, by the way she was dressed, and...

Ah, but what did it matter?

He met Brigit's eyes again, and all that had happened came rushing back to him. He shivered a little, shook his head. "Brigit, what in hell has been going on here?"

The door opened and another woman came in, this one, a doctor.

"Brigit, I know you want to be near him," she began, "but he needs to rest and—" She broke off, looking at Adam as if seeing a ghost. And then she said a word that Adam was pretty sure she hadn't learned in med school.

"Brigit?" Adam prompted.

"I... I'm not sure."

The doctor finally snapped out of her state of shock, and came further inside, gripping Adam's wrist, flicking a pen-light into his eyes, muttering under her breath.

Glancing around at Brigit, the doctor said, "You two are going to have to step out while I examine him."

"No, Dr. Evans," the strange, golden, rail-thin woman in the hospital gown said softly. "I'm afraid we can't do that. Adam's leaving. Right now, and so are we."

Every eye in that room turned to the woman who spoke with such quiet authority. And for some reason Adam couldn't figure out, he agreed with her.

"Who are you?" Dr. Evans asked. "Are you a patient here, or—"

"No," Brigit said quickly. Maybe a little *too* quickly for Adam's peace of mind. "She's my sister,"

Her sister! He sat up straighter in the bed.

"She wanted to take a nap and a nurse gave her that hospital gown to wear."

As Brigit spoke, her sister surreptitiously moved one hand behind her back, but not before Adam had seen the ID bracelet on her wrist. He also saw the pendant she wore, and realized at least part of what Brigit had said was true. She was her sister. The mysterious, elusive Bridin had somehow materialized in his hospital room. And that meant—his heart began to crumble into tiny bits of dust. That meant that his time with Brigit was just about over. She'd found her sister, or her sister had found her.

And it was time for them to fulfill their destiny, and for him to fulfill his, if he could.

Maybe he was still unconscious. Maybe this was all a dream. A nightmare.

Brigit looked at him with an unmistakable plea in her eyes. And he responded, doing what he knew she wanted, just as he always seemed to.

He took the doctor's attention away from Brigit's sister. "I'm all for getting out of here."

Adam distracted them all by getting out of the bed. Brigit looked relieved. She pushed past the flustered doctor to yank open a closet and produce his jeans and running shoes.

"Mr. Reid," Dr. Evans said, "a few hours ago you were clinically dead. We had to electrocute your heart three times to get a rhythm. We weren't even sure you were going to pull through. There is no way you can simply walk out of this hospital and—"

"Look, doc, no offense, but I'd really rather see my own M.D. It's a short drive, really." He pulled on his jeans, snapped them, tugged up the zipper, and stuffed his feet into his shoes.

Bridin closed her eyes, seemingly intent on something. Then Adam heard that universally cloned, hushed voice come over the P.A.: "Dr. Evans to E.R., STAT. Dr. Evans to E.R., STAT."

Dr. Evans blew a sigh. "Nobody leaves," she said. "I'll be back shortly and we'll discuss this."

She waited until Adam shrugged and sat down on the bed. "All right, if you insist."

"I mean it," she said. And then she left.

Adam got up. "I'm assuming there's a reason for the hurry."

The P.A. fired up again. "Security to the sixth floor. Security to the sixth floor. Code green."

"That would be the reason," Bridin said. "One missing patient, who might be a little bit off in the head." She made the universal sign for crazy with a forefinger.

Adam paused, staring from one to the other.

"It's all right, Adam. She's right. We really do need to get out of here."

"Of course you do," Bridin said. "The man you met earlier knows exactly where we are. If he's not too weak from that blow of his own power, he'll come for us, make us both his prisoners, and probably kill you, Adam."

Adam met Brigit's eyes. God, there was so much he wanted to say to her, to tell her and to ask her. But he saw the urgency there. He'd find time to tell her... to tell her everything, before she left him for good.

And then he'd spend the rest of his life aching for her.

The three of them slipped out of the room, moving fast toward the elevators.

"We have to get Raze," Brigit whispered as they hit the elevator button.

"I already did that," her sister said softly.

"What do you mean? You've been with me the whole time." Brigit went silent when the elevator doors opened to reveal a skinny, white-haired, stubble-faced man, grinning sleepily.

"My girls," he said, arms opened wide. When they both hugged him, Adam knew he had to be the legendary Razor-Face Malone.

Brigit insisted they couldn't go back to Adam's place. Or to her own.

They wound up renting suites at a hotel in a nearby town, and they sat around in one of them until the wee hours became dawn.

Raze and Bridin filled Adam and Brigit in on everything. How they knew each other. Why Bridin had painted *Rush* in the first place, and how she'd put an enchantment on the painting before sending it out to find her long-lost sister. Which was why the Dark Prince couldn't just destroy it himself, and why he'd hired Zaslow to do it for him. But Bridin's magic had been strong, and the painting had done its job. It had brought the sisters together again.

"The fairy tale is true," she told Adam. "And now Brigit must return with me to Rush."

Brigit looked right into his eyes, and he saw the tears pooling in hers. He wouldn't make this harder on her. "I know," he said softly. "I've known all along she had to go back." He reached across the table, took Brigit's hands in his. "It's okay," he told her, because he knew she was hurting as much as he, and he wanted to make it easier for her to leave him. "It's okay. I'll be all right."

Raze cleared his throat, and sent Bridin a silent message. She nodded, and they both rose and went to their own rooms. Brigit got to her feet, and stumbled into the bathroom, closing the door behind her, and Adam knew she'd gone in there so he wouldn't see her crying. She wanted to spare him from knowing how much this was hurting her, the same way he'd been trying to spare her from seeing his pain.

Damn, if this didn't kill him, he didn't think anything ever would. After a while he heard the shower running. He sat on the bed, telling himself he could get through this, knowing it was a lie.

Brigit came out of the bathroom, wearing one of the complimentary hotel robes, and all of a sudden, it didn't matter. He'd fall apart. He knew damned good and well he would. But not until after she'd gone.

She stood there, right beside the bed, and she stared down at him, and her heartache was in her eyes. He held up his hand, and she took it.

"Come here," he told her.

She crawled onto the bed beside him. Snuggled into the crook of his arms, pressing close. Her damp, dark hair was cool against his chest, and he didn't care.

"Adam, I don't want to leave you. But I promised her. She said she'd help me save your life if I did, so I promised."

"It's all right, angel," he whispered. "You have to go back. I know that. I've always known."

"How?" She lifted her head, searching his eyes.

"Maire told me. She told me not to fall in love with you, that you had to leave me in the end. That my job was simply to show you and your sister the way back."

"I'm so sorry, Adam."

"I tried to listen to her," he whispered. "God knows I tried. But I couldn't do it, Brigit. I started falling in love with you the second I laid eyes on you, all those years ago, in that vision your mother showed me. And I never stopped."

He drew her closer, kissed her lips. "And I never will."

"I'll never stop loving you, either, Adam. Maybe...maybe someday—"

"I'll live for that someday." He ran his hands through her satin hair.

"I still can't get used to it. I'm..."

"A fairy princess," he finished for her. "An enchantress who stole my heart."

Her smile was tremulous and sad. "The pendants glowed, Adam. When we leaned over you and they dangled close to each other, they glowed."

He rubbed her shoulders, held her closer, so that she lay down again. "Will you do something for me, angel?"

He felt her lashes brush his chest when her eyes closed, felt the heat of her breath when she whispered, "Anything."

He swallowed hard, his heart swelling. "Will you put it all out of your mind for just a little while? We don't have much time left together. Right now... all I want to do is be with you. I want to hold you and love you. I want this night...because it's going to have to last us awhile."

"Yes." She turned her face to his chest, and pressed her lips there. "But first I need to tell you... what I was, in the past. What I did."

"The forgeries. I know already. We all make mistakes, Brigit."

"You knew?" She stared at him, her eyes wider and rounder than he'd ever seen them. "You knew what I'd been. . . that I'd forged paintings for Zaslow?"

"Yes."

"Adam, I had to do it. Raze was so old and frail and sick. We were living in a condemned building, stealing or begging just to eat. He would have died—"

He held her tighter. "I know you wouldn't have done it unless you felt you had no other choice. But it doesn't matter now. I don't care what you've done in the past, you understand that?"

"But..."

"When you left last night, why didn't you take the painting? I told you it didn't matter to me." He continued stroking her hair as he asked the question.

She sat up again, and stared so deeply into his eyes he thought she could see his soul. "I couldn't. You've been betrayed so often, Adam. By your father, and then your wife. I couldn't hurt you that way. I wanted you to know that you could trust someone and not have it blow up in your face. I wanted to give you that, if nothing else, so that you could find someone worthy of you, someone who deserves a man like you. Someone to love."

His throat swelled, because her words were so dead on. She hit his sore spots with speeding bullets. But they were shots that healed. Warmed him through and through. Made him know that he was all right. He could think about the past, about his father and his wife, and he could deal with it. Because of her. All because of her.

"Well, you succeeded, then. I learned to trust someone. I trusted you, angel, and you didn't let me down."

She closed her eyes. "I'm glad."

"But I'll never be able to find some other woman to love." He shook his head slowly as he looked into her eyes. "Because I love you. And there's never going to be anyone who can make me feel the way you do. Not ever. You're magic." He closed his eyes because he felt tears threatening, and he didn't want her to see them.

"I feel the same," she told him. "There will never be anyone else for me, Adam. I'll live forever on the love you and I have between us."

He cupped her head at the base of her neck. "I want to make sweet love to you, angel. I want this night to be the one you remember when you think of me."

Her answer was a single teardrop, which he promptly kissed away.

CHAPTER 23

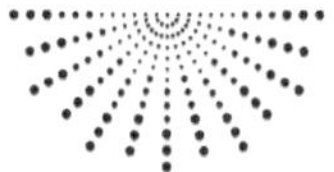

As she rode with Adam in his car on the drive back to Mystic Lake, Brigit couldn't stop thinking about the future. It loomed before her like a gaping black hole, devoid of life. Devoid of happiness. Devoid of anything good at all.

Because it would be devoid of Adam.

She would find a way to get back to him. She would, someday. Though her sister had said the battle to regain control of Rush might take years, Brigit was determined.

And afraid. Terrified that the time when she could find her way back to Adam would never come. Or that by the time she finally was free of her promise to her sister, it would be too late. He would have found someone else.

He held her close to his side, driving one-handed. His arm tight around her as if he didn't want to let her go.

At Bridin's gentle insistence, she and Raze followed in the other car, Brigit's car. Bridin had known Brigit wanted to be with Adam. Known she'd *needed* to be close to him, especially now, when she was so very close to losing him forever.

And Bridin had known other things, too.

Early this morning, while Adam had been sleeping after

making love to her all night long, Brigit had been unable to rest. She'd left the hotel, slipping through the lobby and going outside to put her bare feet in the cool grass. To feel the morning dew on her toes and the morning air in her lungs and the morning sun on her face. To be sure everything hadn't turned black and withered and died.

And her sister found her there. She'd come up softly, so Brigit hadn't heard her approach. And she'd settled herself down in the wet grass beside her.

Brigit tipped her head to the side, resting it on her sister's shoulder. "I love you, you know."

"I know," Bridin said, and rested one hand in Brigit's hair. "And I love you, too, little sister. I wish...I wish I could go back without you. I wish I didn't have to hurt you this way. If there was another way—"

"I know." Brigit closed her eyes to prevent her tears. "I don't deserve him. That's why this is the way things are turning out. I haven't been a good person."

Bridin's hand clasped Brigit's. "You are good, Brigit. You are. Don't doubt that anymore. You've risked everything you cherish, even your own life, to be sure the people you love most are cared for and safe. There's nothing bad about that."

"But the paintings—"

"You have a gift," Bridin told her, echoing the words of Sister Mary Agnes so long ago. "So do I. Our mother had it, too, Brigit. She painted all the illustrations in those books she made for us."

Brigit hadn't thought about that before, but realized now it went right along with the rest of the story. Their mother had painted those vellum pages. So naturally she had inherited the talent from her. From Maire.

"You don't have to copy other people's work, you know," Bridin went on. "If you just imagine the image you want to paint, just fix it in your mind... Whatever it is you want to create, create it in your mind first, and keep it there. Focus on it the way you do on another painting. And paint. It will work. You'll see."

It did sound as if it would work. That Brigit had never had the confidence or the desire to try it before, surprised her. Why hadn't she seen what was so obvious to her sister?

"You're going to paint a storybook for your own little one. Carry on the family tradition."

"My own...?"

Bridin ran one hand over Brigit's belly, and for the first time she smiled fully.

Brigit choked. "You mean I'm—"

"You mustn't tell Adam. He'll never let you go back to Rush if you do."

Brigit's joy in her sister's revelation died a slow, painful death. Her first thought had been of sharing this with Adam. But she knew her sister was right. Telling him would only give him more reason for grief in the coming months and years.

And yet keeping the truth from him was just as wrong.

"Adam is waking, Brigit. He'll be worried about you if he finds you gone. Go on. Go to him."

Brigit swallowed hard. Her eyes were watering as she gave her sister a ferocious hug, and then hurried back to her room.

Now, in the car beside Adam, she told herself again and again that she might be able to survive without him, after all. Because she was carrying Adam's child, and so she'd have a part of him with her always.

It was a solemn group that marched through the woods to the spot Adam had visited as a child. He wasn't certain he could find the way back there, and part of him, most of him, actually, hoped he wouldn't be able to. Hoped it simply wasn't there anymore.

But he had a sick feeling in the pit of his stomach that it would be there. Just the way he remembered it. And he was about to lose the woman he loved forever.

Yet he stoically forced himself to do what he knew he must. He loved Brigit too much to deprive her of returning to Rush. To her own world, her own people. He knew she had never felt like she fit in here, in the mortal world.

He'd already asked Bridin about going with them, and he'd known the answer before she'd explained. Maire had told him long ago that his fate in Rush would be death. That her daughter had foreseen the same future for him left no room for doubt. This was the end.

He led the way, as the four of them hiked up the hill behind his house, and into the woods. His muscles seemed lumbering and slow, and his chest felt heavy. His feet barely dragged over the uneven ground, and with every step, his throat tightened more and made it harder to breathe. His eyes burned like fire every time he looked at Brigit.

God, she was beautiful. The sun slanted through the trees, setting her ebony hair on fire. Her eyes glimmered when she glanced his way, and she was battling tears, too, though they brimmed more deeply each time their eyes met.

"I love you," he said, for no other reason than that he had to.

"I love you," she replied in a tortured whisper, and she squeezed his hand.

God, how the hell was he going to live without her?

"Are we close?" Bridin called from behind.

Adam shook his head, looking back over his shoulder at her. Her green eyes glittered with anticipation, but he saw the sympathy there, too. She didn't like doing this to her sister. Even old Razor-Face seemed to be battling tears.

"Bridin, I have to warn you," Adam said, though he had to clear his throat several times in order to make his words audible. "I came out here not too long ago, trying to find the spot, but I couldn't do it."

"Of course you couldn't. You came here a bitter, untrusting, cynical man. Your heart was older than Raze's whiskers."

"My whiskers and I resent that remark, Bridey." Though Raze's tone was light, Adam could hear the sadness in his voice.

"Today," Bridin went on, "you come with the heart of a child, Adam. Today, you'll be able to see the path as clearly as a four-lane highway. For though you're crying inside, your heart is filled with love and goodness."

He looked down, shaking his head. And then he stopped, because he *did* see it. A wavering trail, and it was so much more vivid than any other animal path in the woods, so different. "Dammit," he muttered.

"Adam?" Brigit seemed worried.

Bridin stepped forward. "You see it, don't you?"

He nodded, but his eyes were on Brigit, not her sister. And he saw his own heartbreak reflected there as her tears began spilling over.

"Lead on, Adam," Bridin said.

He did. Gently, he pushed Brigit behind him, and crouched down when they came to the berry briars. None of those fragrant white blossoms, this time. Instead the branches were heavy with fat blackberries.

"We have to crawl from here," he told them.

"So, crawl then," Bridin said.

As the three of them stood watching, Adam self-consciously dropped down on all fours. He crawled along into the arched tunnel of berry briars, and he wished he'd never emerge. He wished he could grab Brigit and run off into these woods and never be seen or heard from again.

But that wouldn't be fair to her, would it? He'd be denying her the chance to fulfill her destiny. He kept going, peering behind him to see Brigit crawling in the same way he was. And he knew the others followed as well. The ground swelled, and he crept over the rise.

Finally, he emerged from the briar patch. And he blinked, because he was on the far side of the same grassy hill he remembered. Despondency thickened his blood until it crawled through his veins like molasses. He walked halfway down the miniature hillside. And then he stopped and just stood, staring into the dark mouth of the cave.

Shaking his head in wonder, he turned and watched the others emerge from the briars, one by one. Brigit hurried to his side, and slid her arms around his waist, burying her head against his chest as a loud sob escaped against her will. He held her close.

Bridin came next, and then Raze. There was a long moment of silence, while they all stood staring.

"Well," Bridin said at last. "This is it, then."

Raze moved toward her, put his hand on her shoulder. "I'm going with you, Bridey."

She shook her head. "It will be dangerous."

"Bridey, girl," Raze said, and then he turned to Brigit. "You girls need to know something. Your father, Jon, he asked me to watch out for you. Way back when you were just babies. I was no more than a bum. Hell, what did I know about caring for little girls? I was the one who left you at St. Mary's, and delivered your father's note, because I knew they'd care for you there. And when you got separated, I went with you, Bridey, because I sensed you were the one who needed me most. I lost myself for a short time, when that Dark Prince got me under his spell, but I came around soon enough. I'd sworn to be guardian to both of you, for as long as I could. This doorway will open for me, Bridey. Your father promised me it would."

Brigit clung to Adam as Bridin hugged the old man hard.

"Aside from you girls, I got no ties. And there's nothing in this world I'll miss." He touched Bridin's shoulder. "I want to go there, Bridey. I want to see it."

Smiling gently, Bridin nodded.

"It's just a cave," Adam whispered, closing his eyes as he held

Brigit still harder. "Maybe there's nothing on the other side. We don't even know—"

"You know," Bridin told him. "It shows in your eyes, Adam. Come along, and walk us to the gateway. It's time."

Brigit clung harder for a second. But then she slipped out of Adam's embrace. Bridin bent over and crawled into the cave. Raze behind her. Grating his teeth, Adam followed with Brigit close to him, all the way. Inside, they found the larger, room-like area where he'd played as a child, and he ran his hands over the stone to feel the spot where he'd carved his name such a long time ago.

"Come," Bridin said. She led them once around the room, and then back to the entrance. And then she was scuttling back through the passage, toward the gleaming yellow light at its end.

Adam crawled behind her, his stomach knotting, his pulse pounding. He kept telling himself it wouldn't be there. It wouldn't. It couldn't.

And he emerged, and stood just in front of the cave's entrance. Before him there was a wall of dense vapors—a wavery film of something that looked the way heat waves look when they rise from hot pavement. And he put his hand on it, but couldn't push it through.

"Rush," Brigit whispered, as she emerged from the cave and straightened. She turned in a slow circle, looking all around her, and Adam knew she didn't see the barrier. For her, it wasn't there. Just as it hadn't been there for him when he was a child. She could pass through...but he'd be unable to.

His heart contracted painfully.

Brigit threw herself into his arms, sobbing aloud now, clinging to him with surprising strength.

"It's going to kill me, Adam. God, I don't want to leave you. I love you. I love you!"

"I know." His tears flowed freely now, and he stroked her

hair, kissed her face. "I know, baby. I love you, too. This is the hardest thing I've ever done."

"Look there," Raze said, pointing, and everyone followed his gaze.

Castle spires stood beyond the trees in the distance. Softly gray and silver, mingling with the clouds.

"The Kingdom of Rush," Bridin whispered.

She turned then, touched Brigit's shoulder, drawing her away from Adam just a little, and pointing. And Brigit looked toward those towers, and her eyes widened a little in wonder.

Bridin's eyes filled with tears as she stared at those spires, and Brigit reached out with a shaking hand, to brush them away.

"Leave them," Bridin told her. "I haven't been able to cry since I left here."

"Bridin..."

"I have to go, Brigit. It's my destiny. You know that."

"I know. I'm coming." She turned back to Adam, and he held her once more, knowing the time had come to let her go. He loved her, God, how he loved her.

He dipped his head, and kissed her long and deep. And then he straightened away from her. "Just know I love you," he told her. "Never forget that, Brigit. Now go, go on."

Covering her face with her hands, Brigit turned and ran away from him, sobbing out loud, as she passed through that shimmering veil, and disappeared into the forest beyond it.

"You'll be rewarded, Adam Reid."

"I'll be in hell, Bridin. Please don't let anything happen to her." He turned slowly, and ducked back into the cave. Into blackness and emptiness. And he knew he'd never emerge from the dark again. He'd never feel the sunlight. He'd never smile. He'd never be happy. Not without Brigit.

He made his way to the large room inside, before his strength gave out. His legs wouldn't hold him any longer, so he sank to the floor with his back braced against the cold stone wall, and he broke down. Grief pounded his body like a hurricane, and he wondered if he'd ever find the strength to get up again.

~

Brigit sank to the ground beneath an odd-looking tree, with pictures in the swirls of its bark, and she sobbed.

"My sister."

She sniffed, shook her head, refusing to look up. "No. It's no good, Bridin, can't you see that? I'm no good to you here. I'll never be any good without Adam. I need him."

"This is Rush, Brigit. This is your home. It's where you were born."

"But my heart isn't here. It's back there, on the other side, with Adam."

She cried softly, and in a second, her sister whispered, "I know."

The serenity in Bridin's voice reached her. She finally lifted her head, met her sister's gaze.

"I'm sorry," Bridin told her, and she lowered herself down to the moss-covered ground, and put her arms around Brigit. "I'm so sorry. But you're right. You'll be no good here. I can see that. And I believe his love is true, because he loved you enough to let you go. And I believe yours is true as well, because you gave him up in order to save his life." She shrugged. "I had to be sure."

"What difference does it make?" Brigit bit her lip, but her tears continued flowing all the same. "I've left him back there. And you said yourself we can't pass through the damned doorway unless we do it together."

"It's true. I needed you to get back. But I do not need you in order to remain. My place is here." She stroked Brigit's hair, leaned close and kissed her cheek. "I thought yours was, too. I thought once you set foot here, once you breathed the air of Rush, you'd..." Her voice trailed off and she shook her head. "But no. Your place is back there, in the mortal realm, with Adam."

Brigit stopped crying. She met her sister's eyes. "But how..."

"There's only one way, Brigit." Bridin reached up to the back of her own neck, unclasped her pendant. "If one of us has possession of both the pendants... either of us may pass through the doorway alone."

Brigit frowned, shaking her head slowly. "I don't understand. Why didn't you say so in the first place, Bridin? I'd have given you the pendant if that's—"

"Giving up your pendant is only symbolic. It stands for a far greater sacrifice. It means giving up your magic."

Brigit blinked in surprise. Giving up the magic? But she'd only just found it.

"I love you, my darling little sister." Bridin bowed her head, "But it is the only way."

Brigit took the chain from around her neck, brought the beautiful fairy to her lips and kissed it softly. Then she pressed it into her sister's hand. "I give my magic to you, and my pendant. I won't need it where I'm going."

Bridin bit her lip, closed her palm. "Thank you," she whispered.

"I love you, Bridin."

"We'll see each other again," Bridin insisted, nodding hard as if to insure it would be true. "When the kingdom is safe Brigit, I'll come through again."

Brigit hugged her sister hard. "Thank you. Thank you, Bridin."

"Go on. Go back to your Adam."

Brigit straightened away from her and turned. Raze had been standing nearby, watching with damp eyes and an occasional sniffle. But then he went rigid, and waved a hand to hush them, and Brigit listened, hearing the sound of hoof beats in the distance. "Someone's coming."

"Go!" Bridin gripped Brigit's arm, pushing her back toward the cave. "Go on, now before something happens to you."

"You go," Brigit whispered back. "Go, hide in the forest. Hurry."

Bridin nodded, turned away. But she whirled around, once again, to hug Brigit with all her might.

And then Raze grabbed Brigit and kissed her cheek. "I'll watch out for her, my girl. Don't you worry."

"Goodbye, Raze. I love you!"

Raze turned away as the hoof beats drew nearer. He gripped Bridin's arm and ran off into the trees, and they were soon invisible within the embrace of that mystical forest. The forest that had once been Brigit's home. She stared at it, and at those castle spires beyond, for only an instant.

And then Brigit turned and ran to the doorway without a backward glance. She ducked her head and crouched low as she crept back inside the cave.

She found Adam there. He sat on the floor and his face was wet with tears that shimmered in the darkness. He seemed lost in agony, and he only blinked in confusion when he saw her.

Then he blinked again, and slowly got to his feet. "Brigit?"

"It's all right, Adam," she told him, hurrying to him, pressing herself close as he enfolded her in his strong, trembling arms.

"God, is this real? If it is, Brigit, I'm sorry, but I can't let you go back. I can't let you go. It's impossible, and it can't be right. Not when it feels so damned wrong. Not when—"

"Shhsh." She tipped her head up, and planted a kiss on his mouth. "I told you, it's all right. I'm staying."

He just stared in disbelief, shaking his head slowly. "Staying?"

"Yes. Yes, Adam."

Gradually, his lips pulled into a smile, and his eyes widened.

"Staying?" he asked again. A wobbly smile lit his face. "Say it again."

"I'm staying, Adam. Right here with you, forever if you think you can stand me that long."

His arms tightened around her waist, and he lifted her right off her feet, turning her in a circle. Then he let her slide down the front of him until her feet touched the ground, and he bent his head to kiss her, and kiss her, and kiss her.

And when he came up for a breath of air, he held her hard, burying his face in her hair and inhaling. "I love you, Brigit. More than anything in the world. I want to marry you." He drew away so he could look down into her eyes. "Say you'll be my wife."

"I think that would be for the best," she told him, and she gripped his hands and brought them down until his palms rested on her abdomen. "Since my sister tells me I'm carrying your child."

He closed his eyes. Bit his lower lip. And she marveled at the tear that rolled down his cheek a second later. "You're not a fairy," he whispered. "You're an angel, Brigit. You're the angel sent from heaven to save my life. To give me *back* my life. And I'm going to cherish you..." His hands rubbed her belly gently. "...And our baby, for as long as I live. I promise."

"I'm not magic anymore," she told him.

"Oh, yes you are, angel." He dropped to his knees, and pressed a kiss to the part of her that sheltered his child. "Cause if this isn't magic, I don't know what is."

Then he rose and kissed her. It was an endless kiss filled with promises, and dreams....and magic.

PART III
HAPPILY EVER AFTER

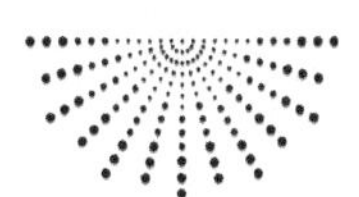

EPILOGUE

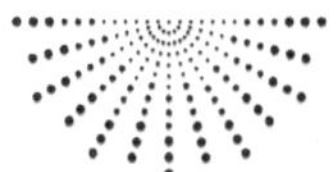

There were tears of joy in Adam's eyes when he leaned over his wife and gently placed their newborn son into her arms. "His name is Jonathon, after your father," he told her, kissing her face, tasting her tears. He couldn't take his eyes from the wriggling bundle nestled in the downy white blanket. He had his mother's curling, jet-black hair and sapphire eyes, his father's nose and chin and cheeks. To Adam there was no one in the room other than the three of them. No doctors or nurses milling around, cleaning up, removing latex gloves, commenting on his healthy son. Just him and his wife and little Jonathon.

"And Adam, after you," Brigit said. Her son had a grip on her finger, and it seemed she couldn't look away.

"Jonathon Adam Reid." And he kissed his baby boy, and then he kissed Brigit.

"He chose a good day to be born, didn't he?"

"A perfect day," she replied. "The day the first copies of his own personal fairy tale—the one his parents had created just for him—hit the shelves. I think he knew."

"Speaking of which," said one of the nurses, interrupting them. "I brought my own copy. Will you autograph it for me?"

She picked up the huge storybook from where she'd dropped it when she'd rushed in here, hours ago. It was bound in a lovely leather cover. Each and every page had a beautiful, whimsical painting illustrating it. Paintings created by Brigit, with the remnants of magic she seemed to have retained despite the loss of her pendant.

Adam hoped, for Brigit's sake, that the pewter pendant had helped her sister. She hadn't heard from Bridin since she'd left her in Rush, and Adam knew she worried about her. But there was a certainty nestled deep in Brigit's heart, that no matter what might happen to Bridin, she'd be all right in the end. She talked about that feeling often. She'd told him that she believed in it with all her heart.

She turned her attention again to the storybook. Within the book's pages was a tale of adventure every child would cherish. All fiction, of course. Or...pretty much so. Unlike her sister, Brigit had assured Adam as she'd offered advice on the plot he'd constructed, she had not inherited the ability to predict the future.

"My kids are going to love it," the nurse said softly. "I can't wait for the next book in the series."

Fairytale, the cover said, in elegant golden calligraphy lettering that glittered magically in the overhead lights. *Book I. Written by Adam Reid. Illustrations by Brigit Malone Reid.*

"I especially love that opening page."

The baby in Brigit's arms made a startled sound, and Adam could have sworn he reached for the book.

"Darling," Brigit whispered. "He wants you to read him his story."

The nurse chuckled and handed the book to Adam. Then she discreetly slipped away. Adam sat on the edge of Brigit's bed, and she held little Jonathon up as if he needed a better view of the pictures.

"Once upon a time," Adam began, and if his voice was choked, it was because of his tears, and because of the swelling in his heart, and because he was wondering again, as he often did these days, how he had gotten so lucky. "There was a little boy. His name was Jonathon, and he was the most precious thing in his parents' lives." Adam reached out one hand to stroke his son's glistening black hair. "They gave him all the love in their hearts, because they knew how very much every child in the world deserves to be loved."

Adam paused, leaned down to kiss his wife, and then his son, and then he turned the page. "One day, Jonathon went on a great adventure, and this is the story of that adventure. It happened on *the other side,* in the enchanted land of the fairy folk, the land known as Rush...

The End...
Or is it?

**Continue reading for an excerpt from
book 2 of the By Magic series**
By Magic Enchanted

EXCERPT: BY MAGIC ENCHANTED

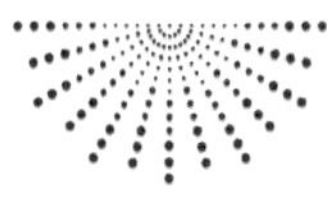

CHAPTER 1

Tristan of Shara, master of all he surveyed, drew his mount to a halt and watched the one woman who could take it all away from him, fighting for her life.

The three men who'd cornered her in the forest were common garbage. Criminals who didn't give a damn who ruled the realm, so long as they could roam free. He knew their type. This trio happened to be Albinon, but their kind existed in every race. They were the selfish ones who lived without a conscience or a single moral fiber. They took what they wanted without remorse. And he had a fair idea what they wanted from Bridin, could guess it by the gleam in their pink eyes.

Bridin stood with her back against a sparkling stone wall, all embedded with crystals, while the three closed in around her. She held her chin high, meeting their eyes with a defiant stare and a toss of her honey blond tresses. The pendant she wore caught the moonlight and glinted. The pendant would protect her from Tristan. It would do her little good against those three. Its fairy spell was meant for him, and his kin, and any he sent to do his bidding. And only for them.

She was Tristan's sworn enemy. She was the one obstacle to

his dream of a peaceful reign, a kingdom no longer divided, a faithful following. The one thing he'd wanted all his life. The thing he now held in his hands, though his grasp, he knew, was tentative. Because of her.

He should turn the black stallion around and let them have her. They'd kill her when they'd finished with her. There was no doubt of that.

Moonshadow stomped a forefoot and tossed his head, shaking his wild mane in excitement.

Tristan dug his heels into the animal's sides and drew his sword. It hissed against its sheath as he pulled it free, and the men froze where they stood. Bridin's gaze lifted, met his, held it. Moonlight bathed her face and shone its reflection in her eyes, transforming them into green flames.

He couldn't look away. This was the first time he'd seen her since she'd escaped him many months ago. His heart leapt in his chest at the sight of her, as if he was glad to see her again. Foolish, of course. He shook the odd notion away and broke eye contact with an effort. Looking into the eyes of a fairy princess was too dangerous, and he wasn't foolish enough to linger in the fiery wells of her eyes. It was not the first time she'd tried to enchant him that way. Pity she still hadn't realized his will was far too strong.

Instead of proving it by holding her fairy eyes with his, he leveled his gaze as well as his sword on the nearest ruffian, easing Moonshadow forward until the tip of the blade touched the man's chest.

"We seen 'er first," the Albinon blustered, backing up a step and scanning Tristan head to toe as if taking his measure.

"Do you know," Tristan asked slowly, "to whom you speak?"

The man's pink eyes narrowed in his pale-skinned, hairless face. "Don't know, don't care," he said, and then he spat on the ground. "Only know there's three of us, against one of you. You'd best be on your way."

Moonshadow was well trained, and took another step forward at the merest nudge of Tristan's knees; just enough to keep Tristan's blade in contact with the man's chest.

"You ought to kneel," Tristan said, twisting the blade against the man's ragged shirt, "when approached by your prince."

The man blinked and stared up at Tristan, eyes widening. Tristan slanted a glance at Bridin, but she only glared at him, her eyes sparkling with defiance.

From the corner of his eyes, Tristan saw the man's two companions fall to their knees at once, groveling in the rich black soil. Very slowly their apparent leader, genuflected as well.

But Tristan's gaze never left Bridin's. "Well?" he asked her.

She stepped forward, her jaw tight. No flowing gowns for the former heir to the throne of Rush, he noted. No, she wore garments more suited to life in the forest where she hid out with her band of rebels. Tight-fitting leggings and a tunic of leafy green, with a belt at her small waist and a scabbard at her side. An empty scabbard. Her knee-high boots were of soft brown suede. She moved forward to stand at his horse's side. A warm breeze lifted her golden hair and sent a strand blowing across her face. Fists anchored on her hips, feet set apart, she gazed up at him like a warrior goddess.

"I'll never kneel to you," she seethed, eyes flashing. Then she turned to the closest of the bowing criminals, planted a booted foot against his backside, and gave him a shove. He landed on his face in the dirt. "Nor should you! Fools! Don't you know me? I'm Bridin of the Fay, daughter of Queen Maire, and your rightful ruler!"

"Gods of Rush have mercy," the toppled man muttered as he slowly pushed himself up off the ground and back-handed dirt from his mouth. He got to his feet, looking from Bridin to Tristan and back again as he retreated. "We're no part of this fight," he said, his voice dropping to a fear-filled whisper. "Have at it, kill each other if you will, but leave us out of it!" Whirling, he raced away into the sheltering trees, his cohorts on his heels.

Tristan sat silently upon Moonshadow, his gaze riveted to Bridin's. He didn't try to stop them. He didn't care where they went or what they did. They represented no challenge. Killing them would have been like picking off songbirds with a slingshot. Too easy to be sporting.

Bridin, on the other hand, was a worthy opponent. So much so, it was going to be almost sad to see her conquered in the end.

"So," he said softly, caught in the trap of her emerald eyes like a fly in a spider's web, and hating his own inability to look away. "You made it back to Rush."

"No thanks to you."

He didn't dismount. It would have done little good anyway. As long as she wore the pendant, he couldn't touch her. Couldn't harm her. And she knew it.

All the same, she edged sideways and bent to retrieve her gleaming sword from the ground where it lay. She didn't sheathe it, he noticed. And then he frowned, because as she bent, her pewter fairy pendant swung free, and he saw that she wore two of them now.

But the other had belonged to her twin.

"Your sister?" he asked automatically.

"Very good, Tristan." Straightening, she wiped the gleaming blade free of dirt with the edge of her tunic. "That note of concern in your voice sounds almost genuine." She smoothed her long hair away from her face, holding the sword in one hand, studying its sheen. "Brigit is fine. Living a mortal life with her mortal husband and their baby son on the other side."

"Loyalty, it seems, is not one of her strengths." He'd fully expected both twins here plotting against him. But there was only one. Only Bridin.

Her eyes snapped up to meet his once more.

"This is not her battle, Tristan. It's yours. And mine."

"As it's always been." Tristan dismounted slowly and saw the wariness in her eyes. When his feet touched down, she backed up a step, lifting her sword.

"No closer," she said.

A warrior goddess, yes. A fierce fighting woman, the sort from which legends were made. Standing there with that sword at the ready, her slender hands curved around its hilt, long fingers almost caressing the gilding there. That rough stone wall behind her, glittering with the crystals embedded in its granite face. Like her. Rugged beauty. Unattainable treasure. Gemstones embedded in rock. If he were a painter, he'd capture her just this way. Standing there armed and defiant. Beautiful and deadly. She took another step backwards as he advanced.

Tristan frowned and shook his head. "Don't tell me you're afraid of me now. You never were before, Bridin. Nor did I ever give you reason to be."

Her sparkling blue eyes narrowed on him. "You brainwashed my uncle," she said in a voice low and trembling with anger. "You convinced him I was insane and in need of constant care. Made me a prisoner in my own home from the time I was a little girl, Tristan, and set your own people to guarding me there in the mortal world. All to prevent me from returning to Rush and taking my kingdom away from you." She tossed her head in the same agitated manner his stallion did when he smelled battle. The wind took a few more strands of spun gold and whipped them into motion. "And you say I've nothing to fear."

He shrugged and stepped closer. She held her ground this time, bending a little more at the knees, and lifting her sword a bit higher. "It was a cruel step to take," he said. "I admit that. But my choices were limited, Bridin. I was barely grown, a boy of seventeen with the responsibilities of an entire kingdom. My brother advised me to have you murdered and be done with it.

Surely, given the choice, you'd have preferred your gilded cage to death?"

"Given the choice," she whispered, "I'd prefer to see you beheaded."

He lifted his brows. "You know that's a lie."

She averted her gaze abruptly. And Tristan was glad. There was nothing more disturbing to him than staring into those mesmerizing eyes of hers. Many a man, mortal and otherwise, had lost his soul in such a way. And while Tristan had long since become convinced he was not susceptible to her fairy allure, looking into her eyes still had an unsettling effect on him. Like staring too long at the sun.

"I took care of you, Bridin. Saw to it you had every comfort. Surrounded you with mortals who adored you. The nurse, Kate. And the old man. Razor-Face, wasn't it? Whatever became of him?"

He saw the defensiveness that clouded her eyes and the sudden tensing of her fine jaw. She'd loved the old man dearly, and now had the look of a she-wolf protecting her cub. "Raze is nothing to you. Your battle is with me, Tristan, and me alone." She met his eyes again. "I will have my throne back," she said. "And I'll see you and your followers driven from Rush once and for all. My kingdom—"

"My kingdom," he said, "is no longer called Rush, but Shara. As it was a thousand years ago when your family drove mine out and took it from us by force. For ten centuries, Bridin, my people were condemned to live in the darkest part of the land, where even the sunlight fears to venture. A prison too cruel for the most vile criminal. One that doesn't even compare with your own as a child under my care."

"Your care?" She tossed her head. "Your care was nonexistent. You were my captor."

It was a lie. He had cared for her. Always. But he would not stoop so low as to admit that.

"The blood of my ancestors cries out to me for justice, woman, and I will not ignore their pleas. I cannot. Ruling the kingdom is the reason I was born, and my father reminded me of that sad fact often enough so that I will not forget. The kingdom is Shara, its rulers are Sharans, and will be forevermore. And if you try to take it from me..."

He let his voice trail off, unable to complete the sentence. She knew it; he could see that in the glint of victory in her eyes.

Boldly Bridin stepped forward. She slid her sword smoothly, slowly, into its sheath, and stood so close to him that her chest nearly touched his. She tilted her head back and looked into his eyes. "If I try to take it?" she asked him. "Go on, Tristan of Shara. Tell me what will happen if I try. You'll kill me? Is that what you were about to say?"

He parted his lips, but no words escaped. Her eyes...gods, the power in her eyes! He wanted to grip her slender shoulders and shake her until she understood that fighting him would be useless. He wanted to toss her over Moonshadow's saddle and carry her back to his castle to fling her into the dungeons where she could no longer torment him this way. But he could not. So long as she wore the pendants, he could not lift a hand to her.

But she could touch him if it pleased her. And she did. She lifted her hands to either side of his face and slipped her fingers into his hair. "You can't hurt me, Tristan. Because for all those years you kept me prisoner, you were feeling the allure of the fay, though you'll deny it with your dying breath. You felt it. You know you did. You tried to get inside my mind, the way you did the mortals. So you could alter my thoughts as you did theirs. But instead, it was I who touched your mind, Dark Prince. And you can't get me out of it now."

"You're wrong," he said, but his words were harsh and coarse.

"When I pretended to be sick, you took me to a hospital," she went on. "Even knowing it was likely a trick on my part, you took me. You couldn't do otherwise. You couldn't stand to see me suffer and think I might die. And even now, even should I take these pendants from around my neck at this very moment, you couldn't harm me. I told you I'd own your soul, Tristan. And I do."

"You own nothing!" he said, but he felt her words sinking into his flesh like blades, before melting into pools of molten steel that burned him inside. And her scent, the scent of the forest where she lived, and something else, drifted up into his nostrils and made him dizzy. Dammit, she was using the most powerful weapon of the fay against him, and he was succumbing when he'd deemed himself immune to it.

"No?" she asked. And she lifted her head, pulling his down to her, and touched her lips to his. He stood rigid, fighting her magic with everything in him. But she moved her lips, sucking at his as if they were moist plums.

He couldn't touch her. He couldn't... he mustn't...

His back bowed over her, and he dropped his sword to the ground. His arms slid around her waist, and he pulled her body tight to his. His lips parted and he kissed her. For the first time in all the years he'd known her, he kissed her the way he'd always fantasized, dipping inside to taste the honeyed recesses of her mouth, feeling her heart pound against his chest and her hips arching against him, and her hands clawing at the richly woven fabric of his tunic where it lay upon his shoulders. As if she'd like to rip it from him. She shuddered in his arms, her taut body going soft, molding to his. She opened her mouth to him, and her fingers tangled and tugged his hair. And he wanted her then. Be it by fairy magic or...or something else. He wanted her more than he wanted to breathe again.

Then suddenly she pulled her mouth from his, turned her head away, and whispered, "Enough."

And as soon as she said it, some invisible force pushed him backward. His arms fell to his sides, and his heart thundered like the hooves of a thousand stampeding horses. "Gods," he muttered, still struggling to catch his breath. In all his imaginings...it had never been...like that. And then he frowned, because he'd bypassed the enchantment of those pendants, somehow. "I touched you," he said, lifting his brows in question.

"Only because I allowed it." She was breathing hard and fast, and her face was flushed. She didn't meet his eyes.

It dawned on him slowly, gradually, but when it finally did, he knew he was right. As maddening as the kiss had been for him, it had been equally so for her. At least equally. She looked as if she was having trouble standing, as if her knees would buckle at any moment.

"You wanted it, too," he whispered in disbelief, stating his thoughts aloud to see her reaction. A pretty reaction, it was. Pretty and pink and suffusing her face with denial and fury. He smiled very softly, stepping around her, better to see the effect of his words on her averted face.

"And now perhaps you know what I've always known, Bridin." It was only a small lie; he hadn't always known. But he should have. "That in attempting to invade my soul, in attempting to charm me with those magical fairy's eyes, you inadvertently gave me access to yours. This power you have over me...it's two-pronged. It runs both ways, my fay princess. And you could no more allow harm to come to me than I could to you. You let me into your soul, Bridin. And I'm not leaving."

She shook her head, her gaze averted. A trembling hand rose, and her fingers pressed to her lips as if in wonder. "No."

"Yes."

"You're wrong. I care nothing for you! I'll fight you, Tristan, and I'll win. Rush will never be yours."

"It's mine now."

"That's a lie! There are constant uprisings, constant skirmishes in the outlying villages. My people will never bow to your rule."

Tristan lowered his head. It was true. There hadn't been true peace in Rush—in Shara—since his father's armies had retaken it more than twenty years ago. But Tristan knew his duty, he knew why his father had begot him. Tristan of Shara had been bred and born to be king, and to hold the land his father had taken. If he couldn't manage it, then he might as well not be alive. His father had made sure he understood that. So he would do it. Fulfill his destiny, live up to the part he'd been born to play. Serve his people by seeing to it they never had to return to that land of darkness to which they'd been banished so long ago.

His mission in life was all there was, all there would ever be for Tristan. He'd had this lesson drummed into his head from the time he was old enough to talk and listen. He'd been denied everything else. Love. Affection. Recreation. Friends. None of that mattered. His indoctrination and training were all he'd needed, according to his father, and they had served him well.

Until now.

Well, he had a plan. He'd always had a plan. And that was why he'd taken Bridin prisoner and kept her all those years. Not to prevent her return. But to put it off... until he could convince her to return with him, at his side. At the point of his sword, if need be, but at his side nonetheless.

"There will be peace and harmony in Shara again," he told her. "Your people will bow to my rule and cease their senseless rebellions... just as soon as they see their beloved princess kneeling before me. Calling me king."

She jerked her head around to face him. "I'll die first."

"I'll see to it you're given that option. When the time comes." He retrieved his sword from the ground, lifted it, aimed its tip at her throat.

She jumped out of reach before he could slice those pretty chains and leave her unprotected and at his mercy. He sighed in disappointment. If he hadn't been such a fool, he'd have ripped the pendants free when she'd kissed him, instead of dropping his weapon and groping her like a buck in rut. Physical desire meant nothing, dammit. Securing his hold on the throne was all that mattered, and all that should be on his mind.

He wasn't even certain he could break the chains and free her of those pendants, given the power of enchantment in them. But it might have worked.

As long as she wore them, though, she was safe.

Tristan turned away from her and easily swung into the saddle. He was disgusted with himself for forgetting his mission, even for a moment, and disgusted with her for being the cause of his error.

"When you attempt this foolish coup you're planning, and fail, Bridin—when you're utterly defeated—come to me, and I'll dictate the terms of your public surrender."

He kicked the stallion's flanks and pulled on the reins. Moonshadow whirled and galloped away, leaving the beautiful fay princess shouting obscenities after them.

Bridin stomped into one of the many caves that lined the forested hillsides of Rush. She swore as she entered, drawing the gazes of everyone present. But she only looked back at them, and in a very loud, very firm voice announced, "We attack the city at dawn."

She saw Raze's reaction. He lowered his head and shook it slowly back and forth, rubbing the ever-present gray stubble on his chin with one hand. The others remained still and silent, watching her, awaiting an explanation.

It was her cousin Pog who slowly rose from the stone slab where he'd been resting. He paced toward the small fire that danced and snapped in the center of the floor, providing the hideaway with warmth and light, and he studied its flames, and then her face for a long time. She knew all too well what he was doing, and avoided his eyes. Not that it helped.

"You've seen him. The Dark Prince."

The fay male's powers of discernment were incredible. Pog was gifted, far more than most. And as a third cousin or some such, he'd been leading the forest dwellers in her absence. It had been he who'd brought them to these natural catacombs, and then converted the place into a virtual fortress city. It had been he who'd kept them busy, inciting villagers to revolt against Tristan's rule in order to keep the interlopers off balance and preoccupied. And it was he who'd kept her followers loyal to her. All had been ready for her return. Many had been waiting for a very long time.

She owed Pog a great deal. But right now she felt nothing but irritation with him. "What difference does it make whether or not I've seen Tristan of Shara," she snapped.

There was a gasp, and all eyes turned on her.

"My lady," Pog said softly. "You break the laws of your ancestors by speaking the Dark One's name. It's been outlawed for centuries. Since the banishment of his people to the Dark Side. You know that."

"And a stupid law, it is," she replied, tossing her head, and refusing to apologize. "What harm can speaking the man's name possibly do?"

No one spoke. They only stared. Drawing a deep breath, Pog turned to the few others who had gathered here. "Go. The princess Bridin and I would speak alone."

One by one they shuffled out. All manner of beings, from the hairless, pink-eyed Albinons, to the pint-sized wood nymphs, to the fay folk, until only Raze and Pog remained in the room with her.

"All right, Bridey-girl," Raze said. "Tell us what happened." He sat in a stoop-shouldered pose on a stone, and didn't bother getting up.

She pursed her lips, staring into the flames. "Nothing. I met him in the forest and we quarreled. Nothing more than that."

"You seem awfully angry over a mere quarrel," Pog observed, tilting his head as he paced a circle around the fire. He was lean and graceful, long-limbed and light. He could move through the forest without making a sound, nor was he likely to be seen with his leaf-colored garments and bark-colored curls.

His fragile appearance might be misleading to some, but not to Bridin. She'd come to know him well since her return, and she knew he was powerful, both in physical and magical strength. Slow to anger, but impossible to sway once his mind was made up.

So she'd best make her arguments and make them well. "I'm not angry at all," she said softly. "I simply believe the time is right. Our archers have been honing their skills. We've made enough arrows to fill every quiver. We have weapons enough to fight six wars. We've gone over our plans again and again. I see no need to put this off any longer. We attack at dawn, while those Sharans sleep off their ale."

Pog frowned and tilted his head. "What makes you think they'll imbibe on this eve more than any other?"

"Today is Tristan's birthday, Pog." She averted her eyes. "I was reminded only when I met him in the forest."

"His birthday?" Pog seemed amazed. "How in the world did you know—"

"I was his prisoner for most of my life," she explained, still not meeting Pog's gaze. "One comes to know a person fairly well in that amount of time. I know Tristan as well as he knows himself. He is three and thirty today."

Pog looked at her, a cloud of concern darkening his brown eyes. "Too old to remain a prince. He ought to be king at his age."

Raze frowned hard. "But he can't be king until he marries. That's the way the law here works, isn't it?"

"Yes," Pog told him. "That's been the custom for as long as anyone can remember. The question is, why hasn't he married?

What is he waiting for?" He looked at Bridin. "You say you know him better than anyone, my lady. What say you?"

She shook her head. Bridin had her suspicions, topmost being that the man had a heart of stone and no woman in her right mind would wish to be his wife. His only care was for the kingdom.

They had much in common in that regard. For taking the kingdom back from him was the only thing in the world she cared about.

"I don't know why Tristan hasn't married, nor do I care. The point I'm trying to make is that the prince's birthday celebrations will last long into the night, and at dawn his men will likely be inebriated and unconscious. Even those who might wake will be too ill to fight. You know soldiers and their love of any excuse to indulge in drunken revelry."

"Yes." Pog nodded hard. "Yes, I do believe you're right," he said at last. "I'll call a council meeting and inform our forces to make ready."

"Good," she said. She turned to go, wishing only to curl up in a warm blanket and try to sleep, but then she paused, looking back at Pog once more. "Just one thing," she said.

He lifted soft brown eyebrows and waited.

"Tristan is not to be harmed."

"My lady?" Pog's eyes were round with confusion.

She hated the way he was looking at her. As if she was insane. She knew that look too well, had seen it throughout her childhood. She searched her mind for all the logical explanations she had thought of for this command. But they seemed weak now. "Sparing his life will ease the minds of those who've been loyal to him. They'll be grateful to us, and more willing to bow to my rule. Besides, if we keep him in our dungeons, then others of his family—that black hearted younger brother of his, for example—will not dare attempt to retake our city for fear we'd harm him at the first sign of trouble."

Pog tilted his head, and she knew by the narrowness of his brown eyes that he was trying to read her thoughts.

"If those reasons are not good enough, Pog, then this one should be. I am your princess and it is my command."

He bent his head. "Yes, my lady. It shall be done."

"Make sure of it," she said, and then she turned to go. She left the main room by one of the many tunnels that opened off it, and headed through the smoky torchlight into her chamber. She paused once on the way, when she heard echoing footfalls scooting off down another passage. Small footfalls. Light ones, like those of a child. Snatching a torch from the wall, she followed the sound, but saw no one.

She sighed hard and shook her head, telling herself she was only nervous. And then she went on to bed. But she didn't sleep.

Each time she closed her eyes, Tristan's voice came back to haunt her, or his touch or the feel of his mouth on hers and the shock of her intense response. His kiss had left her weak and longing...

She swallowed hard. He'd been right. She couldn't see him harmed any more than he could lift a hand to her. And it made no sense. She hated him. *Hated* him. He'd kept her prisoner in the mortal world until she'd become old enough and smart enough to escape him. He was ruling the city that rightfully belonged to her. His father's troops had murdered her mother in the battle to retake that city.

And yet... and yet she couldn't see him harmed. The very thought made her heart feel heavy and tight.

Damn him. Damn him.

Read more of By Magic Enchanted

Don't miss the rest of the books in the By Magic Series:

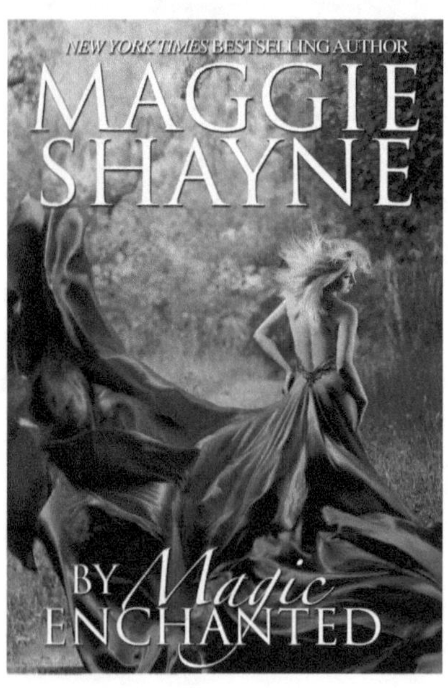

NEW YORK TIMES BESTSELLING AUTHOR
MAGGIE
SHAYNE
BY Magic
BORN

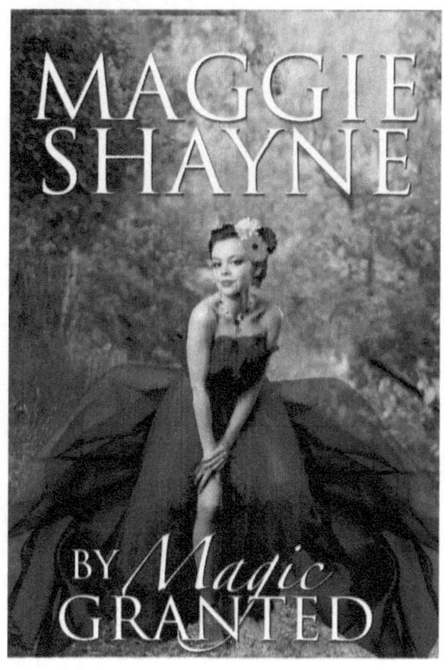
MAGGIE
SHAYNE
BY Magic
GRANTED

ALSO BY MAGGIE SHAYNE

SMALL-TOWN CONTEMPORARY SERIES

The Texas Brand

The Oklahoma Brands

The McIntyre Men

The Texas Brand: Generations

THRILLERS & ROMANTIC SUSPENSE SERIES

Brown and de Luca Return

The Fatal series

Shattered Sisters

Danger After Dawn

PARANORMAL ROMANCE

The Portal

Wings in the Night

The Immortals

By Magic

ABOUT THE AUTHOR

New York Times bestselling author Maggie Shayne has published more than 60 novels and 23 novellas. She has written for 7 publishers and 2 soap operas, and is a 15-time RITA® Award nominee and a RITA® winner.

Maggie lives in a beautiful, century-old, happily haunted farmhouse named "Serenity" in the wildest wilds of Cortland County, NY, with her husband and soul mate, Lance. Maggie is a Wiccan high priestess, legal clergy, and an avid follower and coach of the Law of Attraction

www.ingramcontent.com/pod-product-compliance
Lightning Source LLC
Chambersburg PA
CBHW031138160726
47991CB00004B/1472